The Revelations

Alex Preston was born in 1979 and lives with his family in London. His first novel, *This Bleeding City*, was an international bestseller, won the Spear's and Edinburgh first book awards and was selected as one of Waterstone's New Voices 2010. It has been translated into twelve languages. Preston reviews books for a number of national publications and is a regular panellist on BBC2's *The Review Show*.

Further praise for *The Revelations*:

'Preston writes with black-edged wit about the kind of spoilt, confused young adults bred during the boom years . . . [a] mature, tightly written exploration of the way spiritual yearning can become indistinguishable from the more destructive aspects of capitalism.' Amanda Craig, *Prospect Magazine*

'Compelling . . . a smooth moral tale about the machinations of ambition.' Stephanie Bishop, *Times Literary Supplement*

'A devastating critique of how a fictional evangelical movement fails the young who have turned to it in order to find meaning in their dog-eat-dog lives. Instead they end up in a maelstrom of illicit sex and lies.' Katie Law, *Evening Standard*

'Preston succeeds in capturing this fundamentalist creepiness, poised to turn sinister . . . strikingly well-written and intriguing throughout.' Peter Carty, *Independent*

'A provocative and daring novel with a powerful emotional core.' *Easy Living*

'Fluent and engaging . . . throws light on the secretive organisations that continue to thrive within some of our most powerful communties.' Tom Williams, *Literary Review*

'A cleverly  mmercial and literary. It's atic

in its intentions and execution . . . Preston's characters may be preachy (although they have serious misgivings about whether they believe in what they're saying) but the novelist himself is not. He lets us form our own conclusions about who is to blame for what. This book is very intelligently questioning and analytical about religion generally and Christianity specifically.'
Viv Groskop, *Observer*

'The charismatic priest, David, is manipulative without being cartoonishly menacing – a skilful bit of work on Preston's part . . . a sensitive, thoughtful writer.' Carrie O'Grady, *Guardian*

'A very gripping story . . . A strange and compulsively readable tale of City slickers seduced by a promise of spiritual awakening . . . I was electrified by the oddity of all the characters. At times – especially when they are all together on the retreat – I thought of Iris Murdoch's 1958 novel *The Bell*, about a collection of religious weirdos, and wondered whether Preston would do for evangelicals of 2012 what Murdoch had done for the tormented high church homosexuals.' A N Wilson, *Financial Times*

'Preston's writing is fresh and original . . . he can certainly tackle an issue in a way that will resonate with readers.'
Erikka Askeland, *Scotsman*

'Insightful, thoughtful and subtle, *The Revelations* engages with the subject of religion without ranting or preaching and without easy conclusions.' Graeme Alister, *Word Magazine*

'Cool, intelligent, smoothly plotted novel with believable characters whose spiritual yearnings are taken seriously.' Suzi Feay, *The Tablet*

'A dark, enticing story with echoes of Donna Tartt's *The Secret History* . . . gripping.' Julie Fisher, *bookmunch.co.uk*

'A hugely intelligent and entertaining novel.' Ben Peel, *We Love This Book*

By the Same Author
This Bleeding City

The Revelations

ALEX PRESTON

faber and faber

First published in this edition in 2012
by Faber and Faber Limited
Bloomsbury House
74–77 Great Russell Street
London WC1B 3DA

This paperback edition first published in 2012
Typeset by Faber and Faber Limited
Printed and bound by CPI Group (UK) Ltd, Croydon, CR0 4YY

The right of Alex Preston to be identified as author
of this work has been asserted in accordance with Section 77
of the Copyright, Designs and Patents Act 1988

The Revelations is a work of fiction. Characters, events and
place names are products of the author's imagination, or, if real,
are not portrayed with geographical and historical accuracy.

A CIP record for this book
is available from the British Library

ISBN 978-0-571-2775-9-9

For Ary

Part One

The Revelations

One

The train clattered through the darkness. It was an old train and the carriages bucked and wheezed, struggling against the buffers that stopped them flying off into the night. The sea lay in shadows to the left; to the right was a thin strip of pale blue horizon, trees, and a mountain range that rose and fell, visible only by the sudden absence of light. On the left side now a refinery on the shore. Gas flares lit the water red and gold, gold and red. Mouse pressed his nose against the window and watched the flames dance upon the water.

He slid open the window and lit a cigarette; it burnt down quickly in the blast of rich, warm air that swept into the carriage. When the cigarette was finished he sent it spinning out into the night, following the small red spark as it was whipped away by the wind. It was now entirely dark outside the hurtling train. He stared into the blackness, past the chubby ghost of his reflection, thinking ahead to London, the Course and Lee. He reached into his bag, drew out his battered mobile phone and sent her a text, grinning as he typed.

He walked from Euston, dragging his suitcase behind him. It took him over an hour, but he liked walking in London at night when there were few people around. Taxis, lights extinguished, carried tired drivers home to the suburbs. A young couple walked ahead of him, elbows linked, perhaps drunk. Their bodies swayed together and apart like fronds of seaweed. The girl tripped and the boy placed a protective arm around her shoulders. Mouse hurried past them, wheezing.

He made his way into the echoing darkness under the Westway and stepped carefully along the pavement that clung to the edge of the underpass.

Little Venice dozed in the warm September night, slabs of light thrown onto the water from a handful of lit windows. A moorhen hooted somewhere out of sight. Mouse quickened his pace, his feet scuffing the stones of the towpath. Rubbish floated in the lagoon, drifting between the thin fingers of a willow tree that stirred the water absent-mindedly, picking through beer cans and polystyrene cups and plastic bags. In the shadow of Trellick Tower, he stopped to smoke a cigarette, sitting on his suitcase in the long grass that bordered the path. The vegetation was thick and dry. He plucked a stalk of grass and ran the feathery end under his round chin. He needed a shave. He wanted to look good for the Course. Flicking his cigarette into the water, he grabbed the handle of his bag and continued along the canal.

Finally, he came to the boat. It sat moored between two barges, uglier and higher than its neighbours. *Gentle Ben* – the name in ornate serif lettering on the stern – was an old Dawncraft Dandy, once the white weekend plaything of a pinstriped yuppie. It was now a dirty cream colour, the curtains were brown and raggy, the toilet gurgled foul smells. But the boat allowed Mouse to live in London, to exist among his friends; he loved the flap of the water against the hull at night, the dawn song of birds in Kensal Green Cemetery, the gasometers that sighed as they sank, moaned as they rose. A Jolly Roger fluttered gaily from the stern of the boat, the white skull just visible in the dim light. Mouse let himself into the cabin, turned on the generator and threw himself down on the narrow bed.

*

4

Lee Elek sat on her balcony, looking out over the lights of London. A book lay open on her lap, but it was too dark to read. The petals of the heavy-headed rose that climbed the trellis behind her had faded to grey in the dusk. Her hair was twisted into a bun and held in place with a pencil; a single blonde strand dropped down her cheek and she drew it into her mouth, feeling the sharp ends of the hairs, prodding at them with her tongue. Darwin was asleep beside her bare feet. The dachshund was dreaming: his short back legs galloped the air, his wet black nose twitched. Lee lit a cigarette. Music played on the stereo inside, quietly enough that single notes only emerged occasionally, hesitantly, wrenched from among the sounds of the city: taxis rushing up Kensington Church Street, aeroplanes queuing to land at Heathrow, shouts from the bars on the High Street. She drew smoke into her mouth and blew it out of her nose.

She had stumbled out of the library earlier, her breaths coming in quick gasps. It was one of her moodswung days. She couldn't focus on the self-righteous saints and strung-out mystics she was supposed to be writing about. She skipped lunch and spent the afternoon walking purposeful diagonal paths across Holland Park. Darwin whipped along on his leash behind her like a crashed kite. An hour before the gates of the park closed, she sat down heavily on a bench in front of the Orangery. She took deep breaths, stilled her mind, and ran her hand through Darwin's soft brown coat. She usually knew how to drag herself up from these depths, but this time she couldn't shake the feeling of doom that smudged her vision and quickened her breath.

She walked home along the High Street, stopping to buy herself sushi from the Japanese takeout on the corner, teriyaki beef for Darwin. Up the winding staircase to her flat under the eaves of the old Kensington house. They ate dinner together on the tiny veranda and then music and wine and cigarettes and a book and slowly the warm day faded around her. At seven thirty she watched the parakeets make their way squawking overhead, flying along the faded milky rails of vapour trails. She imagined them towing the night behind them as they arrowed westwards towards Holland Park, a dark cover attached to the feathers of their tails. She had bestowed upon the birds great symbolism, looked for them desperately if they failed to appear, straining her thin frame over the balcony rail to see around the spire of St Mary Abbots. As if they were the only thing left of hope.

Darwin woke with a start, glanced up at Lee through long dark lashes, then stretched with a creaking yawn. With a last look out over the flickering city, Lee went inside, Darwin trotting behind her. Brushing her teeth in the small oval mirror, she thought ahead to the Course: tomorrow would be their first session as leaders. She shivered. Looking deep into the mirror, past the freckled remains of the summer that sat upon her nose, she imagined standing up on the stage the next day and fainting, falling face-first into the crowd of new members. She blinked and spat into the sink.

A high single bed was perched beneath the skylight in Lee's small, untidy bedroom. An upright piano stood against one wall. Photograph albums were spread out on the floor, half-filled with black-and-white pictures. Books rose in rickety piles either side of the bed, several more sat face-down next to her pillow. She swept them to the ground. Lee peeled back the white duvet cover, took off her clothes and let them lie where they fell. She lifted Darwin onto the foot of the bed, slid under the duvet, and sat up very straight, her eyes wide open, watching the rise and fall of the sausage dog's sleeping body. It would all be fine once Mouse was here. She pictured his face: the darting, protuberant eyes, the chubby cheeks flushed red, the shriek of blond hair. Her phone beeped. She read the text and smiled, sank back onto her pillows and stared up at the ceiling, the mobile still gripped in her small, hot hand.

*

Marcus Glass lay on his back looking up at his wife. Abby's eyes were tightly closed. Her bottom lip, was leached of colour as large teeth bit down upon it. Her hands were pressed to her chest, flattening white breasts. She let out a series of high-pitched moans. He never felt further from her than when they were having sex. He didn't know whether her groans were indicative of pleasure or annoyance, couldn't tell if her pinched face meant that she was lost in the moment or boiling with frustration. He placed his hands on her large thighs and she, irritated, opening her eyes for a moment, lifted them off and resumed her grinding rhythm.

'Don't move.' Her voice came thick and sharp. 'Now, move a little bit. Just there. No. No, not there. Now come out and go back in again.'

Marcus was fairly sure that she was already pregnant. He kept a record of her periods on his calendar at work and watched for tampons in the bathroom bin. As he looked up he saw a slight heaviness around her jaw, a swelling of her nipples. But they continued to have sex as if it were a religious ritual, with the same unthinking repetition. He knew it was partly for the relief of orgasm, for those white seconds in which she could spit herself out of the world. But she didn't enjoy any of the build-up. He saw her struggling above him.

He blamed the Course. It never used to be this bad. When they were first together it had been wonderful. Occasionally difficult but ultimately magnificent. Now it was like watching someone labouring up a hill, leaning into the wind and trudging desperately towards the top. He could see her nails digging into her chest and knew that there would be ten crescents of blood by the time they finished.

'That's it. You've almost got it. A bit faster. That's it.'

Marcus thought about death to stop himself coming. Abby insisted that she was more likely to conceive if she came and so she pushed herself towards orgasm after increasingly joyless orgasm. As Marcus began to move more quickly beneath her, as he became aware of the friction and the warmth and the first whispers of pleasure, he thought of clay-cold death. But he had to work hard to stop himself panicking. Once, he had thrown Abby backwards, staggered to the bathroom and plunged his head into a basin of cold water until the frantic beating in his chest stopped. But now, two years into their marriage, he was able to control the rush of terror.

'Oh, come on, Marcus. Sorry, I mean, please. Keep going. No, not that fast. Relax. Don't come just yet.'

He pictured his father on the tennis court. It was high summer and their shadows danced beneath them. Marcus was hitting the ball well; the heavy air hummed with the whump of his ground strokes, the quiver of the strings, the skidding of quick-stopped trainers. He sent his father running from one tramline to the other, cut drop shots skimming wickedly low over the net. The day heated up around them. As Abby's moans rose in pitch, Marcus remembered the moment he saw his father's racquet drop to the ground; the ball he was about to hit thumped into the fence at the back of the court. His father sank to his knees. Marcus leapt the net and fell to his own knees to face his father. Through the white T-shirt, translucent with sweat, Marcus could see a dark triangle forming just below his father's throat. He remembered thinking it looked like a vagina. A purple vagina creating itself beneath the damp cotton. Slowly, his father fell backwards. Marcus pressed at his chest, panted stale air into his lungs, screamed and shrieked until his mother came sprinting down from the house, wringing her hands and already sobbing. Marcus's sister arrived a few moments later, by which time it was clear that their father was dead. As his sister sat down, deflated, against the cross-hatch fence of the tennis court, Marcus watched something change in her face, something irrevocable that would colour everything that followed. He recognised it because he felt the same thing himself. He was nineteen.

Bellowing, Abby came. Marcus, with a little exhausted sigh, followed. He felt himself grow limp quickly afterwards, suddenly lost within her. Abby scrunched her eyes shut, milking the last shudders. When it was over she seemed smaller, slightly ashamed. She rocked backwards and lay with her pelvis tilted upwards, a pillow thrust beneath her buttocks. Marcus got up and walked to the window. Outside there was nothing but dark sky and, in the distance, the black coffin of Trellick Tower. He pressed his hands on the cold glass, carefully arranging his left hand so that it covered the reflection of Abby's face. After a few minutes she turned the light off, pulled the covers up over her bare shoulders and curled her knees to her chest.

*

David Nightingale sat in his study, with the stillness of the rectory at night wrapped tightly around him. The high sweep of his forehead was bathed in green light from the lamp on his desk. Behind him on the wall was a wood-framed poster. Almost a decade younger in the photograph, his hair still sandy-blond then, he smiled above that year's advertising slogan: *Come and Have a Deep and Meaningful*. It had been a good Course as he remembered it. The first year they had expanded outside London. Now a map on the opposite wall showed hundreds of red flags dotted around the country: churches where the Course was taught. He shuffled the papers he had been working on, leaned back and stretched, looking up into the pleasing shadows of the high ceiling, the delicacy of the cornice-work. Occasionally he heard the distant howl of a police siren on the King's Road. Otherwise there was nothing but the ticking of the clock on the mantelpiece and the creaking of his wife preparing for bed in the room above.

He looked over the Course accounts. He had long stopped trying to follow the sophisticated investment vehicles that the Earl had set up. Money was funnelled through Cayman Island trusts, distributed among the various charities and not-for-profit organisations that came under the Course umbrella, managed by banker members who waived their fees and saved their best opportunities for the Course's monthly investment meetings. David whistled to himself when he saw how much had been set aside for developing the Course internationally. The US remained the primary target. He and the Earl had just returned from a trip to New York, where there was standing room only for David's speech in the ballroom of the Plaza. Eager priests had rushed to press his hands afterwards, snapping up copies of *The Way of the Pilgrim* and the Course DVD. It was good to be back at St Botolph's, though. This was where it all began. This was the Course's home.

Only on the nights before the start of a new Course did he regret giving up smoking. He picked up a pencil from his desk, gripped it between his fingers, drew it to his lips and inhaled, breathing in the sweet tang of the wood, the sharpness of the lead. He realised how ridiculous this was and chuckled quietly to himself. He hadn't smoked since university. And this was the tenth year he had been leading the Course. Strange that he still felt the nerves, still worried that he would bound onto the

10

stage in front of the young upturned faces to find that he was stuck for words, floundering in the glare of the bright lights and wide eyes. There would be new Course leaders tomorrow. He let his mind settle upon each of them in turn: Marcus, Abby, Mouse and Lee. He knew they would be anxious, perhaps unable to sleep, and he allowed their imagined nervousness to merge with his own. Lee's face dwelt the longest in his mind. She was troubled – he realised this – but the air of quiet panic that hung around her was one of the reasons she'd be so good as a Course leader. Nothing pushes people away like piety. A certain fragility of faith, if kept in check, could be comforting. He would need to watch her, though.

Lying in bed later, he listened to his wife snoring. His arms were behind his head and he flexed his biceps in a nervous, monotonous rhythm. He was proud of his body. He had not developed the middle-aged dough of his peers; he jogged along the King's Road every morning, played tennis at the houses of wealthy Course members on Saturday afternoons. Propped on his pillow, he looked down at his wife, watched the tremor that passed along her upper lip with each exhalation. She no longer dyed her hair; mousy-grey strands fell down her face and trembled in her breath. He ran over his speech one final time, frowning and smiling as he would on the stage, pausing for a ripple of laughter, glancing down for a moment and then fixing the room with the intensity of his pale blue eyes. When he had finished, he pressed his palms together, muttered a prayer, placed a hand gently upon his wife's sleeping face and with a quiet 'Amen', he turned onto his side and fell asleep.

Two

It was five o'clock and the church was luminous in the late afternoon light. A gardener moved around the flower beds that lined the churchyard, carefully sinking down onto his knee pads to tend the immaculate bright borders, tempting blooms into the year's last warmth. The banners were up on the King's Road, tied to the black railings of the square. The wind caught them and they fluttered, compressing and expanding the C of 'Course' like a mouth. Aeroplanes queued to land overhead, following the path of the river, barely moving in the pale, clear air.

The spire was of tawny Portland stone, surmounted by a capstone and cross. Octagonal, the skin of the spire tapered towards the wrist-thin point, supported by dark iron bands. The four columns over which the spire was raised had settled or bent over the years, meaning that it had slipped from its true perpendicular. When completing his renovations, David Nightingale had considered rectifying the spire's minor but noticeable misalignment. After consulting with the Course members who had raised the funds, however, it was decided that the slight wonkiness was part of St Botolph's charm.

Inside, the glory of light that exploded through stained-glass windows illuminated a fine gold altar cloth, burnished chasubles and a coracle-sized collection plate. Everything gleamed. Someone was practising the organ: a toccata with fumbled trills. The organ pipes cascaded down the wall at the back of the nave, silver and bronze bars protruding like fangs from a rose-window mouth. Where once a rood screen would have hung, there was now a television monitor bookended by black speakers. Ten years earlier the shabby church had struggled to fill half of its dusty pews with an ancient congregation; now chairs were packed tightly along the side aisles, smaller television screens were arranged in the transept. The music stopped. Footsteps down wooden stairs, the echo of a slammed door. Then silence in the light-filled church.

*

As they walked down the gravel pathway towards the church, Lee tugged at the sleeve of Mouse's jacket and hung back, her heels kicking up dust. She was slightly taller than him, and looked very slender next to his stout frame. Taking her hand in his and squeezing, he gave her a hopeful smile. Lee looked away. In her ears she wore stones of different colours: one lapis blue, one turquoise. Mouse dropped her hand and followed her eyes to the church's bright spire. He decided that he liked September. It was a wistful month, a month to curse not having made more of the summer, a month when thoughts turned to night-living winter. Yet on evenings like this, when the sun slanted across the sky, picking out the wrought-iron balconies that hung like birdcages on the facades of the houses surrounding the square, September was magnificent.

'Are you OK, Lee?'

'I'm fine.'

'A wee bit nervous?'

'Oh, I suppose a bit. I've been working too hard. Not sleeping enough. Not sure that I'm up to being a leader.'

'You'll be brilliant, you know you will. The Course is going to pull you out of all this.'

'I know. I'm hopeful, I really am.'

She squinted her blue-green eyes at him. Her legs, emerging from a frayed denim skirt, straddled the path. She was as thin and white as a wishbone. Mouse took her arm and led her past the gravestones of the ancient cemetery that encircled the church. Vines climbed over cracked graves, lichen dappled chipped stones, creeping into the cavities of letters no longer legible. They made their way into the shadow of the portico, through heavy oak doors that sighed in greeting, and into the cool church.

*

Abby was the only one who worked for the Course full-time, and she had been at the church since early that morning. She spent the first few hours of the day bustling around after Sally Nightingale, laying out copies of *The Way of the Pilgrim* on the chairs in the church, arranging candles in the tall brass holders that led down the aisle. When all of this was done, she made her way down into the crypt, found the room with its circle of wooden chairs and drew out her books. She made notes, read and reread the passages from *The Way of the Pilgrim* that would form the core of the discussion, but still she felt a jolt of nerves when she thought of herself actually teaching the Course. She rose from her seat and stood very still in the cave-like room, breathing the musty air.

She wore a tartan shirt with its sleeves rolled to the elbow and a grey vest underneath. When she stood, her black leggings seemed to cup her buttocks, holding them disdainfully away from the thighs beneath them. She knew from her mother, who told her often, that her large body would lose its bouncing firmness. That she would begin to sag and become doughy like her sisters. But for the moment, she wore her leggings with pleasure.

14

'I thought you might be down here.'

She jumped and turned around. Marcus was standing in the doorway, the gloom of the crypt behind him. His black hair disappeared into shadows at the edges, his handsome face jutted out into the light cast from the spots in the ceiling. He stepped towards her and wrapped his arms around her shoulders. Warmth rose from her stomach to her chest and sat there until Marcus peeled himself away. His voice was quiet.

'We should go upstairs. David wants to speak to us.'

She looked at him, frowning.

'I'm sorry about last night. It was bad again, wasn't it?'

'No, it wasn't bad. It's too complicated to be bad. Some of it was fine.'

'Did you think about your dad again?'

'I wish I hadn't told you. Not if you're going to use it against me . . .' Marcus turned and strode across the room. She followed.

'I wasn't using it. Why do you think I was using it?'

Marcus looked at her. 'I'm sorry. I'm just nervous about tonight. Have you seen Mouse and Lee?'

Ignoring his question, she took both of his hands in hers until his eyes softened. She leaned forward and kissed him, her lips moist and warm.

'I love you. You know that, don't you? I just want to have it all go right this time.'

'I know. I do too.'

Marcus had reluctantly left work early that afternoon. He found breaks in the routine of the week difficult. He was used to building a protective shell around himself in the office, and had to peel this shell off in layers, slowly shaping his mind for a less combative atmosphere. He hated his job at the law firm, where he helped to restructure hedge funds that had gone bust in the Crash. Abby kept urging him to quit, taking his hand in hers in the shadows of 6 a.m. and begging him to stay in bed, phone in his resignation. But they needed the money, and although Marcus had inherited a small amount upon his father's death, it wasn't enough to pay for the mortgage, for their booze and dinner parties. So he stayed at the law firm, and every day that he was there he imagined another little spark of his youth fizzling out. He edged his phone out of his pocket and checked to see if he had reception.

'Have you heard from work?' Abby asked.

'No. I don't think we expect a judgement until tomorrow, perhaps Thursday. If we're lucky they'll settle next week.'

They could hear Mouse's voice in the church upstairs. Abby placed her hand on one of the wooden chairs, took a deep breath, and then followed Marcus out and into the dark corridor. They made their way past the gift shop, whose illuminated windows were full of Course T-shirts and copies of David's book, *The Way of the Pilgrim*, with its bright green cover. They walked past the room in which Mouse and Lee would host their own discussion group later, up the narrow stone stairs, and into the echoing church.

*

A line of chairs had been arranged in the space between nave and chancel, at the foot of the steps leading up to the sanctuary. Marcus and Abby hurried down the aisle. David Nightingale was sitting on the steps, facing the chairs. A jug of squash sat at his feet. He filled two plastic glasses.

'Mr and Mrs Glass! Here, have something to drink. We've been waiting for you guys. Come and take a seat.'

Marcus took a glass of squash, passed one to Abby, and sat on a chair next to Mouse. The priest leaned forward on the steps, elbows on knees, and Marcus shivered as the full force of David's smile was turned upon him. He made himself meet the very pale eyes for a moment, and he felt lost. The priest beckoned for them to pull their chairs closer towards him. When he leaned forward his chinos rose up from his ankles, revealing pale, hairless calves above black socks. He rubbed his hands together and began to speak.

'It's so wonderful to have you guys here. With just over an hour to go, I imagine you must be nervous. I can understand that – it's a huge responsibility for you. But I've a very good feeling about tonight. About tonight and the next few months. You lot have been crucial to the growth of the Course thus far and it's absolutely right that you should become leaders.'

He paused and frowned.

'We need to make sure that nothing stalls the growth of the Course. Momentum is everything; keeping Course member-ship growing is all-important. Even those who try to do us down can't argue with the fact that the Course is attracting people back to Christianity. Every lost member is a tragedy – a personal tragedy for the one that leaves, but also a serious loss to the Course. It's up to you, my representatives at ground level, to make sure that we keep our new members. It's not always easy; some of your group will stop coming, either be-cause they can't be bothered or because the intensity is too much. Keep these departures to a minimum. You should re-member that often the most vehement atheists, the most dogged agnostics, end up being the most committed Course members. If they have thought hard enough about faith to have strong feelings in the opposite direction, then they have opened a small gap which will let God in.

'Try to think back to when you first joined the Course. Re-member how cautious you were, how uncertain about the size of the commitment needed. I want you to be very gentle with the new members. You must treat them as I treated you – as

17

children. By the end of the six weeks, you'll be firm friends with the new members, but there'll be ups and downs in the mean time. Keep your own emotions in check, keep your guard up at all times. You're all passionate young people, but don't let those passions distract you from doing God's work. Now let's tune up. May the Lord bless you all. I'm relying on you.'

He rose, turned, and strode up onto the stage. The four friends, fizzing with excitement, followed. Abby checked her microphone, 'Bah, bah, one-two, one-two,' then sat at the front of the stage, swinging her legs. Lee played an E chord as Marcus and David tuned their guitars. Mouse thumped the drums, adjusting the height of the snare and shifting his foot pedal slightly. Marcus put down his bass and sat on the stage next to Abby. David came and crouched behind them. The church was dim and vast. Mouse stopped drumming. Lee sat very straight at the piano, her right hand quietly picking out the melody from *Pictures at an Exhibition*. Chattering voices rose from the courtyard outside the church. People would be arriving soon. The Course was about to begin.

Three

David threw a switch and the main church lights came on, golden chandeliers that hummed when they were illuminated. Course members began to drift in from outside. Lee was lighting candles at the front of the church. The click of her lighter made Marcus want a cigarette. Abby stood behind a row of trestle tables at the back of the nave, a smudge of red pasta sauce on her cheek. She waved to him. Marcus walked towards the row of pews where his and Abby's names were printed on a whiteboard, nodded at the altar, sat down and put his head in his hands as if he was praying.

Marcus had started coming to the Course because of Abby. She had made it clear that it was the only way she'd stay with him, and he attended at first in the same way that he'd gone to piano lessons as a child: resolved to perform everything asked of him as badly as possible in the hope of being swiftly excused. Only slowly did he realise that the church might offer a means of negotiating the fear that shot its bright splinters across his mind whenever he thought of death. In the quiet ritual, the music and, above all, the promise of an existence beyond the grave, Marcus found peace.

It was something to do with the high windows. He could only see sky through the windows, nothing of the grubby world outside. It enhanced the sacred feel of the place, the sense of safety. His father hadn't believed in God, or rather he gave the impression of a man whose diary was too busy to consider something so putative, so far in the future, as an afterlife. Marcus didn't want to die with that kind of uncertainty. And since his own death existed in a kind of eternal present for him, he needed to make sure that he was always prepared; the time he spent in church was a totem he held up against the fear. He would live on afterwards; unlike his father, whose cold, blue skin as he was heaved into the ambulance spoke of nothing but rotting and decay.

At university Marcus had attended chapel almost shamefully, happy to use Abby's involvement in the college choir as an excuse to spend winter nights in the quivering candlelight of evensong. Still, back then, he wouldn't have considered himself a believer. But things filter through. And slowly patterns revealed themselves until, on the first Course Retreat he had attended, he found himself more or less converted. Or, if not entirely converted, then at least able to hold in his mind at the same time the sane, rational view that belief in God was akin to belief in magic, an atavism that had no place in the bright, scientific now, and a quiet recognition that, somehow, irrationally, God was there. And the friends from his old life seemed to drop away as the Course increasingly filled his spare time with prayer weekends and charity days, and the problems and questions that his cynical rational mind raised were silenced by the sheer business of it all.

The buzz of voices in the church rose in pitch, pulling him back to the present. Marcus began to pray, the same prayer that, if he was not too tired or drunk, he repeated every night before sleeping: *Lord, protect me. Give me good health. Look after my heart, my lungs, my bowels. Look after my Abby, too. Grant her the baby she wants. Don't let me die just yet, God.*

He opened his eyes to see that the room had begun to fill up. More candles had been lit and the spotlights at the back of the hall shone forward onto the stage with the altar glowing behind it. He rose and made his way to the back of the church. Abby was holding a clipboard now, directing people to different queues depending upon whether they had attended the Course before, whether they had been identified in her initial screening process as useful or prominent. Mouse and Lee were taking details of new members. Marcus thought how happy Mouse looked: his plump cheeks blushing with pleasure, his eyes goggling at the girls. He greeted each member with a broad smile, nodding and chatting as he noted down their email addresses, mobile numbers, jobs. The Course prided itself on the amount of information it had about its members.

'Marcus, can you do something for me? Just stand in the aisle and stop old members sitting too near the front. They've had their time in the sun. Thanks, darling.' Abby pushed him gently in the back and he stood and watched people stream past him, in awe of the Course's ability to attract a constant supply of the young and wealthy.

When everyone was inside the church – perhaps seventy in total, of whom twenty were new members – the doors were shut with a deliberate bang. The lights dimmed and the candles fluttered as David stepped onto the stage. He grinned, blinking in the spotlight that leapt from the back of the church. He looked enthusiastic, friendly, youthful despite his grey hair; his eyes turned upon the congregation and there was a murmur, then total silence.

'Welcome to the Course. If your experience of tonight is anything like that of the many hundreds of others who have attended over the years, then Tuesday nights will become an oasis for you, a way of escaping the grind and the grime of London and entering a place of peace, a sanctuary where you can explore some of the most fundamental issues, where you will be welcome, make friends, and get a free meal, if nothing else.'

21

He smiled and again there was a rustle of whispering followed by silence.

'This is a community where all questions are welcome, where thought and exploration are encouraged, and hopefully where you'll find people capable of answering your questions. My wife Sally and I are always happy to speak with you personally; you can email us; I even do a podcast thanks to my team here who are dragging me into the twenty-first century. You should also look out for our Course leaders, who will be guiding your discussions later. They are guys just like you, who a few years ago were sitting exactly where you are now, feeling and thinking exactly the same things. Although I had fewer grey hairs back then.

'Tonight I'm going to tell you about a student at Durham University who was a committed atheist, a big fan of Pink Floyd, and the yard of ale champion of St John's College bar. That student was me . . .'

Marcus listened to the priest's voice. David was a great performer: not only the dazzling charisma, but also the softer moments, the wry humour, the dancing hands, the quick shift between puckish and earnest. Every so often a laugh to relieve the pressure, and then gravity. And always the world of the Course held up against terrifying London. In the priest's own story, in the anecdotes and tangents that spun off it, everything returned to the promise of repose and release offered by the Course.

'So I came to London when I left Durham. I suppose because all of my friends did, and because all of my friends were going into the City, I thought I should too. I imagine many of you had a similar experience. I became a merchant banker, and I found it a really dark and unforgiving existence. I remember getting terribly drunk in pubs on Saturday, just drinking for the hell of it, because the week had been so tough that we felt we owed it to ourselves. And so Sunday was a day of hangovers. We'd limp down to the boozer around lunchtime just to take the edge off with a pint or two. It was really a miserable life. I even thought about suicide once or twice, during the darkest days.'

He paused for a moment and took a sip of water. He looked down at his hands which were splayed out on the lectern, inhaled deeply and continued.

'But, partly because I had the wonderful Sally at my side, I lived through it. I survived. And why I want you to know this is because you need to be clear that I am not here to judge you, or to pry into your private lives, but only to show you one path, a path that has been very fruitful for me. We are here to talk about the meaning of life . . .'

*

Lee was reciting poetry in her head. It was lines from a poem that she had studied at university and had become for her a mantra, a way of stilling her mind and dragging herself up from her slumps. She kept a notebook beside her as she worked in the library, jotting down things that seemed to carry some special meaning, that felt as if they might help. Now she wasn't listening to David; instead she turned inwards, letting the cascade of words cleanse her mind as they passed through it. *O Thou, that art the way, pity the blind, /And teach me how I may Thy dwelling find.* She watched Marcus, saw the fine strong lines of his jaw, and how he glanced across at Abby, smiling, every so often. She drew in a deep breath and let it out with a sigh, looking around in surprise at the noise of it. She could feel Mouse's leg jittering against hers. She tried to ignore it, then attempted to find something soothing in the friction of her friend's thigh. David's voice kept intruding on her

23

thoughts, though, and she bent her head forward and shut her eyes, laying a soft hand on Mouse's knee.

Lee missed her dad. She spoke to him two or three times a week on the telephone, but sometimes it wasn't enough. She felt exposed without him close by. The previous night he had rung off abruptly, and she thought she had sensed reproach in his voice. She knew he didn't approve of her faith. She turned the conversation over in her mind, trying to work out if she had invented his coldness. She did that sometimes when she was down: saw hostility everywhere, imagined rifts with friends, heard criticism from her tutors when none was meant. She called the line of poetry back to her mind, and behind it layered the melody from one of her dad's pieces of music. She smiled, eyes still tightly shut.

Her dad, Lazlo Elek, was a composer, the child of Hungarian dissidents who had died in jail in Budapest. He was sent to live with relatives in Suffolk at the age of nine when his parents were implicated in the 1956 uprisings. He found early fame with a cello concerto dedicated to his parents, began to be spoken of as the next Bartók. He married a girl from Ipswich and wrote prodigiously, although he never quite lived up to the promise of that early concerto. As he aged, his work became more abstract, more mathematical; he became prone to fits of depression and repeatedly burned near-finished scores. When Lee played the piano, she imagined her dad's fingers placed over hers, guiding not only the correct note and tone, but also the feeling of the music, the touch that took a piece from a work of human creation to something divine. Only when she was playing with him did she truly live the music. She sometimes wished she had never come to London.

'We are all looking for meaning,' David continued. 'Life can feel very empty sometimes. With all the rush and bustle, we can get lost, become rudderless. It's why you'll find yourself asking certain fundamental questions as you lie awake at four in the morning. Why am I here? Wasn't I meant to do something more than just get up, go to work, get drunk, go to sleep, and then repeat it until death? I feel, many of us here feel, that there's something wrong with the modern world. That our age is one of greed and grasping and selfishness. We need a new way of living, a new way of negotiating life. The Course will give you a road map, it'll show you guys a clear and fulfilling way to make sense of life in this mad, bad world.'

*

Mouse was moving his leg frantically, bouncing on the heel of his brown loafer. He looked eagerly up and down the rows around him, noting with appreciation the delicate girls with blonde hair. A good crop of new members. He imagined what it would be like to press his tongue against the damp parts of their bodies: the nooks and declivities, the creased skin at the joints of their long limbs. Whilst his love for Lee existed as a dull but constant ache, he made sure that there were always other girls. Girls of a certain type – blonde, tall, distant. Always unavailable, they'd already have boyfriends or husbands and would treat Mouse with a kind of little-brotherly fondness that he both played up to and loathed. He'd spend long night hours on the boat fantasising about these girls, knitting their faces into surprised masks of pleasure or pain, knowing that they'd always be out of his league.

Mouse watched Lee, taking advantage of the fact that her eyes were tightly closed. Her chest rose and fell very slowly, quivering as her lungs emptied. He looked at the threads that snaked down her thighs from her frayed skirt. When she was drunk and let him stay over in her tiny flat with its air of girlish chastity, he would creep into her room in the darkness of 3 a.m. She always slept with the duvet tucked between her legs, and Mouse would stand in the pale orange light of the London night and look at whichever leg was visible. He would strain his eyes against the dimness, trying to see into the shadows where her thighs disappeared inside the frilled shorts she wore to sleep. He kicked her chair with one particularly forceful jerk of his leg. She very deliberately laid her hand on his thigh and squeezed. He smiled a broad and hopeful smile.

*

'I always worry about doing this so early on the first evening . . .' Abby watched the priest with wide eyes as he spoke. 'I'd like to ask everyone to be quiet for a moment. Just think about what you have heard so far. If you'd like to pray, then I encourage you to do so. But if not, just enjoy the silence here. Enjoy a bit of time away from that constant noise outside.'

Abby thought back to when she first attended the Course. She didn't go just because Lee was a member, although she saw the change it worked on her friend: a greater seriousness, a sense of commitment. Nor did she go because she felt any profound spiritual need. It was because she had been standing in the rain on Battersea Bridge after an argument with Marcus. The rain was falling so hard it was as if the river was trying to reach up to the clouds. It was a terrible argument: they had screamed at each other until she ran from the flat, out of the front door and down to the river. She stood on Battersea Bridge and thought about jumping. Not in the way that someone seriously considering doing so would think about it, but in a way that tried to shape her mind into that of someone who might. To Abby, this was as good as doing it. She stood there, imagining the rush of the air, the downward plunge, the shock of the water. At that moment a bus had rumbled past, throwing up the contents of a large puddle, soaking her. Part of her thought that she must have jumped, she must have lost her mind and jumped. But she looked up, saw the bus, and on its back was an advert for the Course. The cool, smiling eyes of David Nightingale. *Shouldn't there be more to life than this?* in bright red letters. She signed up the next day.

Abby prayed that the evening would pass well. She prayed for Marcus. She prayed that she might be pregnant. That the butterflies in her stomach might signal that something was being created. And she prayed that if she was, she might keep it this time. That in nine months she'd lie listening to a baby's moth-flutter breath. She would make David godfather. She opened her eyes for a moment, saw him with his head bowed and closed her eyes again.

She remembered the night she had lost the first baby. Very early on. Not even a baby. A clot, a smudge of cells. She had been working late with Sally Nightingale on a proposal for exporting the Course to other Christian denominations. It had felt just like the return of her period, a pain which built from nothing into a sharp twisting of her gut. Sally had taken her into the rectory and waited outside the door of the bathroom, asking in a reedy voice what she could do. When she saw the blood Abby had known immediately. She was businesslike and brave about the whole thing, biting her lip and wincing to stop herself crying out. She found painkillers in the bathroom cabinet, bundled up tissues to stanch the flow and mopped up the bluish drops that were falling onto the tiled floor.

When she came out of the bathroom it was the priest and not his wife who was standing there. The light from the bathroom falling into the darkened hallway cut a bar across him, illuminating the whiteness of his teeth and his hair. She realised that he already knew everything and slumped into his outstretched arms. It was such a relief that nothing more needed to be said. They had descended the stairs, David's arms still around her, and he drove her to the hospital. They sat in silence in the white light of the waiting room until the doctor had called her into the curtained cubicle, checked her over with brusque, efficient hands, and sent her home.

The priest's tenderness had reminded her of the first time she went on the Retreat. It had been held that year at a down-at-heel hotel in the West Country whose burly proprietor was a Course member. There were chickens in the courtyard outside the rooms. Abby had heard the fox in her sleep, had dreamed the terrified shrieks of the hens, the sound of jaws snapping shut. She woke early and went out to the henhouse, which was a silent mortuary, blood and feathers. David was sitting in the dust cradling a chicken. It was still just alive, its bare neck white and raw, blood darkening its breast. David spoke to the chicken in a quiet voice, stroking the bird's broken wings, murmuring into its feathers. He was like that with her when she miscarried; after the hospital, he drove her home. He waited until Marcus had let her in, sitting in his purring car and watching them embrace in the doorway.

*

The lights in the church brightened suddenly, and David raised his head and opened his eyes.

'Music is the closest of the art forms to God – when you lose yourself in a piece of music, it's a truly spiritual experience. The music here at St Botolph's is justly famous. So sit back and enjoy. Let me introduce: The Revelations.'

Spotlights swept the stage, focusing on the band's name which was spelled out in blue letters on the skin of Mouse's bass drum. David stooped to pick up his guitar, nodding to one of the helpers who sat at the side of the stage adjusting the settings on his amp. The four friends rose from their seats and walked together down the aisle. The air around them hummed as they climbed the steps and took up their instruments. Mouse spun his drumsticks several times before beginning a thrusting, military beat. Then Marcus came in with a bass line that roared through the church. Lee sat at the piano, her visible cheek stained with a vivid pink blush at being so observed. The priest strummed power chords and then Abby sidled up to the front of the stage, her hips moving slightly. She hunched her large shoulders forward, brought her hands up either side of the microphone and began to sing.

The music was not spectacular in itself: choruses cribbed from stadium rock anthems, verses that strained against the weight of the meaning they attempted to impart. But there, in the warm light of the church, with some of the older members joining in at the back for the choruses, arms held out, eyes closed, it was hard not to be moved. The four young people were earnest and beautiful, still retaining enough of their youth to touch the audience. The priest played a brief and nimble guitar solo, one leg raised on his amplifier, his eyes staring up into the shadows that clustered in the roof of the church. Abby looked extraordinary on the stage. As if she was made to be seen among such expansive scenery. She didn't seem awkward or heavy or masculine there. Marcus watched the young men in the audience stare up at his wife as she sang and tried to see her reflection in their eyes.

The second song was much softer than the first. The lights on stage were dimmed so that only Abby was clearly visible, with Marcus and David shadowy figures either side of her. Mouse and Lee were both lost in the darkness. Lee started to play a series of arpeggios, the music rising out of the silence. Mouse tapped out a gentle rhythm, the drumstick struck

29

against the rim of the snare. Then Marcus and David came in, and Abby began to sing.

> 'You are a deep sea,
> You are an abyss.
> The more I lose, the more I find,
> So I'll lose myself in your kiss.
>
> You are a fire that burns
> Without being consumed
> That takes away the cold
> And guides me safely home.'

Abby rocked sensuously on her hips as she sang, one arm twirling up towards the roof. Marcus wondered if Abby was thinking about him as she sang, or about David, or Jesus. It was a strangely ambiguous song, just a love song which, because of the setting, was interpreted by the audience as something holy, a hymn. He imagined Abby as the central pillar of a cross, with David and himself as the arms.

After the music, they ate. Sally Nightingale stood at the back of the room with other Course volunteers doling out food. Marcus was always struck by how attractive the volunteers were. The young men wore aprons over their smart-casual work clothes, smiling with large teeth that were extraordinarily white. The girls were thin and pretty and blonde, dressed in immaculate suits from the office or the expensive bohemian smocks of the stay-at-home mothers. It wasn't only that the Course attracted its members from the wealthy roads that surrounded the church; some travelled from the other side of London to attend. The Course had links with the top universities, with major public schools, with law firms and investment banks. It was marketed to these institutions as a philosophical way into religion, as a path that encouraged the aggressive questioning of faith. So the people who attended were bright, successful, inquisitive.

A group of politicians stood at the back of the church talking to their banker friends. They would eat later, after the Course, piling into restaurants on Beauchamp Place or Walton Street. Having recently won power by a thin margin, the politicians wore about them an air of restrained celebration. They were all very young, Eton-educated, near-identical in sober suits and blue ties. They slapped the wide backs of the financiers who were laughing over-loudly at their jokes. Their haughty, exhausted wives, brandishing babies in their arms, chatted to one another in the shadows of the side aisles, discussing schools and nanny troubles. The politicians had been members of the Course since its early days and would now be instrumental in helping David and the Earl to further embed it in the nation's consciousness.

Next to the bankers and politicians, hoping to pick up some tradable news, Marcus recognised a number of hedge-fund managers whom he had worked with over the past few years. They always looked slightly ashamed to see him: he was a reminder of the potential for failure in lives that usually never contemplated it. He sat on the Course investment committee with some of them and they shouted over one another to convince him of the brilliance of their ideas. The Earl, who chaired these investment meetings, came and stood beside Marcus as he queued for dinner.

'See the markets today, Marcus?'

'Yes, although I wasn't around for the close. I had to be here. I'm a Course leader this year.'

'So you are. David told me about it the other night in New York.'

The Earl leaned heavily on the table, looking at Marcus

through narrow eyes under a low brow. He was a big man, ex-army, who wore his sleeves rolled to the elbow, revealing large forearms covered in wiry black hair. His crew cut was shot through with silver, a giant watch sat on his wrist, and a pair of large Oxfords were shined to mirrors on his feet. He edged his hands down the table towards the steaming pans of pasta. Marcus took the food he knew he was too nervous to eat, and went back to the circle of seats. The Earl walked with him.

'I'm concerned that some of the funds aren't positioning themselves correctly for a further slowdown. Seems like they think we're through the worst of it. I'm not so sure. And with the expenditure required for our US expansion, I'm feeling very nervous, Marcus. David seems so focused on driving new membership that he forgets how much all this costs.'

Marcus sat down beside the Earl.

'I could have a word with a few of the members if you think it'd help. Perhaps we should raise a bit of cash now while people are feeling bullish.'

'I don't want to ask until we have an idea of how well America goes. I think people might start to resent the ten per cent. I don't want to ask them for more if we can help it.'

'The people who pay their ten per cent already earn enough not to worry about it. And it helps them feel better about their jobs. About the moral compromises they have to make at work. Knowing that some of the cash will go to helping the Course.'

'That's always been the plan. I have meetings in the City all day tomorrow. I might see whether I can't persuade a few of the bigger donors to reach into their pockets again. If we're targeting America then we have to do it properly, and that takes obscene amounts of money. The pay-off, though, if we do get it right, will be immense. It'll take the Course to a whole new level.'

When they had finished dinner, the new members were led downstairs into the crypt where the discussions would take place. David and his wife moved between the two groups, entering silently and perching like owls as the conversations developed. The first evening was spent on introductions, an overview of the six weeks ahead, the planting of seeds. The crypt was still very cool, and some of the girls wrapped scarves around long necks, the young men pulled on blazers and jumpers. In the church upstairs the chatter of the old Course members slowly faded as they filed out into the night.

In Marcus and Abby's group there were five girls: pretty but not strikingly so, just down from university, young and nervous. Four young men sat talking in whispered voices to the girls, staring down at their loafers, ties loosened. Banker boyfriends, Marcus guessed. One of the girls suddenly looked up at Marcus, drawing back her blonde hair with one hand, passing the back of her arm across thin, pale lips. Her eyes were wide and bright and Marcus could see that she was already falling, that she was one of the ones who arrived convinced, and only needed the merest nudge to accept the Course wholeheartedly. An older man in a grey suit sat slightly withdrawn from the rest of the group; Marcus couldn't tell whether he had moved his chair back, or chosen it because it was set apart from the others. Abby introduced herself, and the discussion began.

*

In the other room, Lee was feeling detached. Her head ached and she missed Darwin. The sense of unease that had fallen upon her in Holland Park the day before hadn't faded. It was insane that these young, bright people should turn to her for advice, should seek her help with their existential issues. Mouse leapt to his feet, nodded to the room and smiled broadly.

'Hi! I wanted firstly to thank you for coming. My name is Mouse and this is Lee, a very dear friend of mine. We'll be your guides over the next six weeks. It's going to be a brilliant time for you. And I just want to encourage you to open yourselves up. Leave all your cynicism and scepticism at the door and give this a chance. We're doing this for the first time, too, and while that may mean we don't know the answers to all of your questions, it does mean that we are very keen to learn, and we'll do everything we can to make this as transformational an experience for you as it was for us. Isn't that right, Lee?'

Lee felt as if the room was turning, as if her chair had been moved into the centre of the circle. The faces rotated around her, their grins and frowns distorting grotesquely with the beating of her heart.

'Yes,' she said, 'Mouse and I will do our best to make this somewhere you feel terribly safe. Make this a place of refuge.' She gulped air and tried to smile.

She looked at their group. Twins, girls with white-blonde hair and pointed features, their wide eyes over-made-up and blinking too quickly at the strangeness of it all. Next to them was a tall, pale boy with long hair falling down over dark eyes, lips that were very large and red, a black leather jacket buttoned to the neck. Two rather lost girls, mousy, hesitant, stared at their shoes and flicked through *The Way of the Pilgrim*. Then, next to Mouse, a Japanese girl who had bob-cut hair and wore a dark grey dress leading down to tiny trainered feet.

*

Next door, Marcus was already floundering. Everyone had been introduced. Each in turn spoke a few words about their lives, what they hoped to get from the Course. It was time for Marcus to address them. David stood in the shadows at the entrance to the room, watching. Abby's mind had gone blank. She sat berating herself for her silence, biting down on her lower lip. Finally, knowing that David was depending on him, Marcus began to speak.

'I encourage you not to look at *The Way of the Pilgrim* quite yet. Just keep it at home and spend your time between now and next week's session thinking about the emotions that you have experienced tonight.' Marcus was always worried that the overtly religious nature of David's book would put some people off. He found it disconcerting that the Course insisted on marketing itself as a forum for philosophical enquiry when it was so clearly focused on pushing a fairly narrow form of evangelical Christianity. He found it stranger still that no one seemed to mind. The religious nature of the Course accelerated swiftly after the initial session, but very few members stopped coming. Perhaps David was right, that people just needed an excuse to embrace it all. The Course provided that excuse.

'I think I should make one thing clear from the start, though,' Marcus continued. 'The Course has been the most positive force in my life over the years I've been a member. Abby and I have had some difficult times and I really don't know what we would have done without the Course to support us. I mean, I look at young people struggling to carve out an existence in London and I just wish I could persuade them all to come along. You don't just come here to talk about the big questions. You also find yourself at the centre of a really vibrant social scene. We have dinner at each other's houses, we go to each other's weddings, we are godparents to each other's children. I really haven't kept in touch with that many of my friends from before the Course. I haven't needed to. The people you will meet here will be your friends for life.'

Marcus saw the priest smile at him before ducking further into the shadows. He bridled against the group that had been chosen for him and Abby. He knew that they were seen as a safe pair of hands, comfortingly conforming to the priest's vision of a Course couple. He was certain that Mouse and Lee would get a more interesting group and he felt suddenly exhausted, astonished that life had moved so swiftly, so certainly to this point, where he was sitting in a damp room trying to convince people to accept a God the certainty of whose existence only flickered at the edge of his vision, disappearing if he stared at it straight on. The older man – whose name was Neil – moved his chair forward with a scraping sound that made everyone stop and turn to look at him.

'Could I ask a question? About the sermon tonight . . . if one calls it a sermon?' He was perhaps fifty and what hair he had left clung perilously to his scalp above his ears; the top of his head was entirely bald. His skin was tight and tanned and seemed to constrain his jutting cheekbones with difficulty. He spoke in a sharp voice; a voice of boardrooms and corporate retreats. Marcus could see the silk lining of his suit shimmering. 'I wondered if anyone else prayed when David asked us to be silent? I wasn't expecting to, but I found myself praying, and it was an extraordinary experience. I haven't prayed since school.'

There was a pause and then one of the blonde girls hesitantly raised her hand. 'I did. I remember my mother used to pray with me when I was a child. She is very religious and I remembered one of the prayers and I said it, and I was mainly saying it for her.'

Slowly the scales of shyness began to drop away, and Abby

and Marcus answered questions in voices that echoed the quiet humility of the blonde girl. Calm descended upon the room.

*

Lee found the twins extraordinary. They didn't finish each other's sentences so much as perform a canon, with one talking over the other, slightly ahead or behind. They blinked their large eyes at the room and reminded her of stage-school children with their bouncing enthusiasm and lisps. Lee could see that even Mouse was rather taken aback. She smiled in encouragement as they held forth.

'And Daddy used to take us to church on Sundays when Mummy was ill . . .'

'When Mummy was ill the whole house was silent, like a church. We used to pray for Mummy to get better . . .'

'And when Mummy didn't get better, in fact when she died, we made a pact, didn't we, Alice . . .'

'Yes, a pact, Ele.'

'That we wouldn't believe in God. We'd stop praying and we'd live raucous lives. And we did . . .'

'We lived astonishing lives.'

'But we feel it is time to come back to the church now.'

Lee cleared her throat and the group turned to face her.

'I think that's very important,' she said, leaning forward, her thin shoulders hunched, her face very serious. 'The idea that you can come back to the church. I know I've done some bad things in the past; I was a tearaway as a teenager and I disappointed a lot of the people around me. But what you learn is that this church is very forgiving. It doesn't matter how far you've gone, you can be saved. I find that idea incredibly comforting. It reminds me of that line in Catherine of Siena that

37

says "God's forgiveness to all, to any thought or act, is more certain than our own being". It's a religion that recognises that we are fallible, a religion founded on forgiveness.'

Mouse smiled at her.

'Lee is the brains of this operation. Go to her if you have any deep questions. Come to me if you want to know where the nearest drink is. Now, maybe I should say a few words about next week's session . . .'

The clock, which reminded Lee of the clock that she had watched as she sat her finals at university, a clock whose hands moved in mysterious leaps, jumped on towards nine and then David came in and thanked them and they were all out in the balmy night. The church's lights were still on and they threw out a soft glow into the courtyard where the new members stood with their Course leaders, suddenly unwilling to leave the place and each other.

'Does anyone want to come to the pub?' Mouse lit a cigarette and took a long drag, blowing the smoke up so that it was caught in the light thrown from the church, a blue haze dissolving slowly into the night.

Four

Abby stared into her lemonade. The glass was old and chipped; fissures that would one day destroy it ran like veins under the surface. When Mouse banged his hand on the table to emphasise a point, the bubbles in her lemonade shuddered, some were dislodged from the side of the glass and went shooting upwards. She watched the tiny explosions as they leapt free of the liquid. She centred the glass on the beer mat, squared the beer mat to the table.

Abby's stomach hurt. She kept telling herself it was her stomach. As fear fluttered through her mind she tried to convince herself that the pain was higher up, further back, tried to make herself burp as if that would somehow prove something. She thought back to the meal in the church, the pools of grease that shone iridescent in the spaghetti sauce, the starchy stickiness of the pasta.

Neil – the only one from her discussion group who had come to the pub – sat opposite her. They were both quiet, listening to the chatter further down the table. Neil was drinking a glass of white wine. She could hear an edge in Marcus's voice that told her that he had passed from merriment into drunkenness. The twins had bought shots of tequila. She had handed hers to Marcus. She watched the lights of a fruit machine dance up and down Marcus's white shirt, saw his hands move as he spoke. He threw himself back laughing, almost toppled from his stool. Now all she wanted was to lie in bed with a hot-water bottle on her stomach and Marcus, sober, asleep beside her.

She realised that Neil was speaking to her. She smiled distantly at him.

'My daughter died last year,' he said, placing his hands flat on the table in front of him.

'I'm so sorry, that's terrible,' Abby said. She looked at his downcast eyes. 'How did she die?'

'She'd been ill for a long time. It was only obvious right at the very end that it was anorexia. That it was killing her.'

'Oh, God,' said Abby, leaning towards him.

'You don't expect these things, do you? Not if you're a normal happy family. You don't look out for them. I just thought she was thin. I keep turning over her life in my mind, looking for clues. We gave her everything: holidays, a fantastic education, a bloody pony. And her brother – completely normal. Although heartbroken about his sister, of course.'

'Of course, I can imagine.'

'A chap at work put me in touch with David. I suppose everyone thought that I'd gotten over it too easily. I was back on the trading floor two weeks later. It did me good to lose myself in my work like that. But quite a few of my colleagues have been to the Course over the years. And to be with young people like you, talking about very serious subjects – it's wonderful. A bit like going back to university.'

Abby reached over and laid her hands on his, gently collecting his fingers in her own. They sat in silence for a while and then she lowered her hands back into her lap.

*

Marcus was sitting at the other end of the table talking to the twins. He had a meeting at eight o'clock the next morning with one of the senior partners. Initially, he had told himself that he would have one drink and then take Abby – who was looking tired and ill – home to bed. But Mouse's manic conversation, and the promise of another drink, and another chaser, had kept him at the table. He had edged himself away from Abby, whose disapproving glances had only a very minor effect when he was feeling like this. He tried not to look at her and concentrated instead on the twins, whom he couldn't tell apart, and who were talking so quickly that he only had a vague sense of what they were saying, and so instead looked into their long-lashed eyes.

*

Lee stood outside with the tall, dark-haired young man from her group. His name was Philip. He still wore his leather jacket buttoned up to the throat, even though the night was mild. They smoked in the darkness, and Lee felt tired, but peaceful. She peered inside the cars that passed down the King's Road, saw young people heading out for the evening, tired City workers coming home, old ladies perched over their steering wheels straining their eyes into the shimmering street lights.

'I really don't know why I'm here,' Philip said.

'What? Here with me?'

'No, at the Course. It's not like it'll do any good.'

'What do you mean?'

'I thought this might be a way of making myself believe, of convincing myself that it all means something. I can see it won't do any good. You're all lovely people, but I don't think I'll be coming back next week.' He was drinking vodka and tonic. He drained his glass and laid it gently on the window ledge. Lee turned to face him, taking his elbow firmly in her hand.

'Give it time,' she said, her voice suddenly sharp. 'You've

only been to one session.' Her voice softened and she loosened her grip from his elbow, letting her fingers trail down his arm to take his hand. 'You'd be surprised how it works on you. I've seen people who swore they were atheists at the first session speaking in tongues by the time the Retreat comes around.'

'Oh, no, I couldn't do that.'

'That's what they said, too.'

Philip smiled shyly at her.

'I was a choirboy when I was a kid. I used to go to these wonderful cathedrals and sing. It was awesome to hear your voice rising to fill all that space. But I got so bored during the services. I couldn't really follow the words, or at least I didn't see how they were relevant to me. Whenever I've been back to church since, I still get that feeling. As if the priest is speaking a language that I don't understand, as if the service is designed to bore you into submission.'

Lee dropped his hand and lowered her eyebrows, her cigarette held between her fingers like a baton conducting her words.

'We're not supposed to listen to it all. Remember it was once in Latin, all of the service sung in a language that much of the congregation wouldn't have understood. I use it as a time to relax, to still my mind, focus on my breathing. Don't think that you can reduce it to something easily comprehensible. The beauty of the service lies in its mysteriousness.'

Lee's cigarette had burned down and she turned to go back inside. Philip reached out to stop her.

'And the stuff you hear? The stuff about sex? How we'll all go to hell if we fuck before marriage? That's not part of the Course really, is it?'

She looked up at him, a cool indifferent smile on her lips.

'We have to take the Bible as the basis of what we believe. It's what the Course is founded upon. And it says sex should

42

only be between people who are married. That homosexuality is evil. So yes, it is part of the Course. It has to be. But I think, more than anything, the Course teaches that whatever you do, you're not beyond hope.'

She reached up, placed a kiss on his pale cheek, and then walked back inside.

*

Mouse sat talking to the Japanese girl, whose name was Maki. He laid his hand heavily on hers whenever he wished to emphasise a point.

'And the wonderful thing about his work is that it is so bloody honest. You sit there reading him and you think . . . you just think Christ this is brilliant, you know?' He had forgotten which author they were discussing. 'So, do you live in England? Are you over studying?'

'Actually I work for a fashion designer on Bond Street.' She had a slight American accent.

'Oh, what's that like?'

'Shallow, depressing. It's why I came to the Course. I heard about it from a girl at work. She's an ex-model who now helps design the swimwear collection.'

'Oh, yes, Pippa Walsh.'

'That's right. Anyway I told her I was feeling lost in London, lonely and so on, and she told me about the Course. I'm not really any religion, you see. My parents were nominally Shinto, but they got married in a Christian ceremony and when my dad died he was buried by Buddhist monks. I like the ritual of Christianity. I like the hymns.'

Mouse went to the bar to get another drink. He was looking forward to going to work the next day. He had taken the job at the library to be close to Lee, but, over time, had found himself warming to a life caught somewhere between student and academic. He had wanted to join Lee on the MA, but couldn't afford the fees and so instead applied for a position as assistant librarian in the art deco monolith of Senate House. He saw Lee most days: she chose to study in the Special Collections Reading Room where he worked. They had lunch together. Lee regarded him as a talisman, a charm that had helped her to a distinction in the MA and would now see her through her PhD. Mouse was happy. He was able to spend much of the day fetching Lee books, watching the sun move across her or the way she frowned and sucked her pencil as she read.

On the days that Lee stayed at home, or when she had to walk to Gordon Square for lectures, Mouse would climb up to the library's upper floors, where readers were forbidden to enter and the hundreds of rooms were used to store books. He walked along long corridors of identical wooden doors, negotiating dog-legs and corners that seemed to defy the logic of the building's external architecture. There were certain spots that drew him to them – his favourite was the hall on the fourteenth floor that reached up to the lofty ceiling three floors above and was entirely empty. The wind always moaned there, no matter what the weather at ground level. Otherwise it was a room of absolute stillness.

The library had originally been designed to be much larger, with a second tower rising up towards the Euston Road to give the impression of a vast modernist steamship cruising through Bloomsbury. The project had run into financial problems and the building was cut off parallel with the northern edge of Russell Square. Because of the untimely foreshortening of the architect's vision, there were corridors that led nowhere, warrens of narrow passages that culminated in brick walls, rooms with no purpose whose air was never disturbed by human breath. These orphaned spaces were Mouse's realm: it was here that he spent his days, here that he felt at home.

He had discovered hidden rooms where collections of children's literature of the 1920s and 30s were stored. He would sit for hours staring at copies of *The Arabian Nights* and the fairy tales of Hans Christian Andersen illustrated by Arthur Rackham and Edmund Dulac. He would take the staff lift to the fourteenth floor and search out Rackham's *Wind in the Willows* and Dulac's *The Little Mermaid* and then, with a cup of tea held carefully away from the friable pages, he'd allow himself to be taken into other worlds.

His life at the library complemented his existence at the Course. Not only because he was able to watch over Lee, but also because the librarian who was nominally his boss was working on a seemingly endless piece of Marxist criticism, attempting to unpick the economic coding that linked the Bible and the Bhagavad Gita and the Declaration of Independence, and was irritably shut in his office for most of the day. This meant that Mouse was able to work the hours he wanted, was able to take days off to attend Course events. He had no defined holidays but managed to get up to Scotland to see his mum regularly. He felt that his life had a fine degree of symmetry to it: of course he wanted Lee to love him, but until that time arrived, he was able to stay close to her, monitor her, stop her from doing anything drastic. He saw her come back into the pub, followed by Philip. Mouse bought himself a beer and returned to the table. Marcus was sitting with his arm around Abby, who was leaning on his shoulder, her eyes tightly closed.

'Listen, Mouse, Abby's knackered. Shall we finish up with a couple at ours? Abby can go to bed. I've got some good bottles of wine in the rack.'

'Of course, sport. Have you got the car? Is Abby chauffeur tonight?'

It was ten o'clock. Neil went home. Mouse and Maki rode in the back of Marcus's Audi while the others followed in a taxi. Abby, almost crying with tiredness and worry, drove. Mouse and Marcus played a ridiculous word game, with Marcus shouting answers over his shoulder as Maki laughed and Mouse bellowed. Abby began to sweat. There was a party being held at the Natural History Museum. Paparazzi gathered on their mopeds, shot long lenses out of car windows. The boys pressed themselves to the glass to see who was there. They continued their game, Marcus screaming now.

'You repeated. You can't repeat. You forfeit. Shame! Shame!'

'I bloody didn't. You lie! Prove it. Did I, Maki? Did I repeat, Abby?'

Abby felt as if she were floating. She gripped the steering wheel but was rising up above it, vertiginous. She leaned hard on the accelerator and sent the car rocketing along Queen's Gate, up Kensington Church Street and on to Notting Hill Gate. When she had parked, and Marcus and Mouse had steered Maki to the front of the ugly block of flats, she rested her head on the steering wheel and allowed herself one deep sob. A growling taxi pulled up beside her and she saw the twins get out, watched Lee stagger towards the door on the arm of the tall young man with dark hair she had been talking to all night. Mouse would be jealous. Abby rose wearily from the car. Lee held the door for her and they took the lift up together.

Marcus had opened a bottle of wine and passed glasses around. Already there was music playing from the laptop on the table. He heard Abby slam the bedroom door; he turned the music down a little and told Mouse to blow his smoke out of the window. Mouse drew himself up onto the wide windowsill and looked down on the empty street below. The flat was on the seventh floor of a brutal square block that was notably unsightly among the cool white mansions of Notting Hill.

Marcus went to the kitchen to get some olives and saw Abby standing in the hallway, her toothbrush raised to her mouth. She reached her head into the bathroom, spat into the sink and then spoke to Marcus.

'I thought you had a meeting tomorrow.'

'I do. I'm fine.'

'I'm sorry, I'm just very tired.'

'I know you are. I won't be much longer.'

'Will you sleep in the spare room? And try to keep the music down?'

'Of course I will. 'Night. Sleep well.'

''Night, Abby,' Mouse yelled from the sitting room.

She shut the bedroom door softly this time, and Marcus turned the music down until it was barely audible, opened more windows and moved Mouse's ashtray to the windowsill.

The night began to dissolve around them. Maki left after the second bottle of wine was finished. She seemed to be quite sober, even though she had drunk as much as the others. Marcus walked her to the lift, whistling as they waited for the creaking machinery to ascend. He stood looking at her in the lift; as the doors closed, she bowed very formally. He mirrored her and held the bow until the doors met.

When Marcus came back into the sitting room Mouse had opened a bottle of whisky and was pouring it into tumblers, thrusting the glasses urgently into the girls' hands, bellowing at Lee and Philip who were sitting in the corner, talking earnestly. Mouse turned the music back up and began to dance in a strange, rhythmic shuffle, his arms twitching at his sides, his stomach wobbling, his bulging eyes rolling. Marcus took his arm and steered him over towards the window. The twins danced together, expending little energy, occasionally leaning towards each other to whisper something and laugh.

Marcus and Mouse sat along the windowsill smoking, swirling the ice in their glasses, and watching the twins dance. Lee was sitting on Philip's lap in the corner. He moved his lips very close to her neck, whispering to her. Time passed. They saw people coming back from bars, stumbling along the middle of the street, arms around shoulders in the false bonhomie of midnight drunkenness.

*

Marcus had put a film in the DVD player – something of Abby's in black and white that was bleak and Scandinavian. The twins were half-asleep, slumped across the sofa. He was still sitting in the window with Mouse, cold but not wishing to move or recognise the stiffness of his joints and the iciness that was creeping through the glass. Philip and Lee continued to talk in soft, serious voices in the corner. Marcus tried to follow the film. The camera swooped low over a lake, a man looked out to a range of mountains, a girl cried in her room, the film ended. Marcus stood up.

'I've got to get to bed. It's two. I can sleep for four hours. Five if I don't go for a swim. Feel free to stay. Or go. I mean, do whatever.'

Mouse looked up at him, stretched out his short legs and lit a cigarette. The twins woke at the same time and yawned, rubbing their eyes and smiling as colour crept back into their cheeks.

'We have to leave now,' said Lee suddenly. Her eyes were watery, red lines clustered in the milky corners. She groped on the floor for her bag, stumbled as she slipped on her heels and leaned over to place a wet kiss on Mouse's lips. She stood back, grinning.

'I'm shitfaced,' she said proudly.

Marcus felt very tired. 'Bye, Lee. G'night, Mouse. Hang around as long as you like. There's more booze in the kitchen.'

He undressed in the spare room and walked down the hall in his boxer shorts to brush his teeth. Philip and Lee were already on their way out, his arm around her thin shoulders. Marcus realised that Philip hadn't taken off the leather jacket all night. Lee turned and waved unsteadily as they left. Marcus looked into the sitting room, where Mouse and the twins were playing some sort of drinking game involving the last of the whisky and a pack of cards. Marcus nodded at them and turned back down the hall.

Drunk, unthinking, he walked past the spare room towards his own bedroom. He opened the door and saw Abby sitting on the end of the bed, her shadow thrown across the room by the bedside lamp behind her. She was naked with her knees drawn up to her chest. She didn't move when he came in. She was looking at herself in the ancient free-standing mirror that she had inherited from her grandmother. It was liver-spotted with age and misty in the corners. The white sheet beneath her was stained a deep red. She had stripped off the duvet and the blood had slowly spread out, soaking through to the mattress, and was now dripping where she sat at the foot of the bed, a single drop every few seconds that landed in a pool on the cream carpet with a noise like a ticking clock. She let out a sob.

'Oh, Abby.' He was suddenly sober.

He went to the bathroom and found a towel. Very gently he lifted her to sit upon it. Then he climbed up behind Abby and placed his arms around her, looking at their reflection in

49

the mirror. He saw a thin mist over her face; long-dried tear-tracks led down from her eyes. Neither of them moved for a long while. Then, very slowly, he helped her to stand, holding the towel in place. She watched as he stripped off the sheet and used the unstained corners to soak up the blood on the mattress. Holding the towel between her legs, Abby waddled to the other side of the bed. She lay down on the clean stretch of mattress and Marcus lifted the duvet over her, tucking it in tightly as his mother had done for him as a child. He found some painkillers in a bedside drawer and held the water glass as she swallowed them. Finally, he left the room to fill a hot-water bottle in the kitchen. By the time he returned she was already asleep. He pulled a chair beside the bed and sat watching her gentle breaths which hardly stirred the thick duvet cocoon. He placed the hot-water bottle at her feet. He heard Mouse and the twins leave, heard the girls' high young voices in the street below.

Marcus sat until the first fingers of light crept into the sky outside the window. A star shivered above the rooftops of the houses opposite, then faded into the dawn. Abby occasionally drew in the sharp yelped breaths of one who had recently been crying. Marcus smoothed his hand over her brow and mumbled soft words to her. He was still in his boxer shorts and he realised that he was very cold, his feet numb and clammy. Abby's blood stained his fingers and was turning brown under his nails.

Marcus had known Abby for so long that when he looked at her face it was not like looking at a real person. Her face had the ridiculous familiarity of his own reflection, such that when he did try to consider her objectively, he found it both fascinating and frightening. Her skin was tanned, her dark hair unravelled on the pillow. She was striking-looking, but her size and the sharp intelligence of her manner meant that boys had avoided her during her teens. It had left her lacking confidence, nervous and suspicious when Marcus first started paying attention to her. But slowly she had fallen for him, and, despite the rows, he loved her. He felt a sudden rush of pleasure. He was proud to have her. He knew the child would arrive, and when he did – it was always a he in Marcus's mind – they would raise him with boundless love.

He jumped as his alarm went off. Abby opened her eyes as he slammed down his hand on the trilling clock. He watched as she remembered, wishing that he could keep her trapped in the fog of waking, draw her back from the revelation that caused her lip to quiver, her eyes to widen as she peeled the duvet from around her and saw the umber towel knotted between her pale thighs.

'I'm so sorry, Abby.'

She smiled weakly. He couldn't find anything else to say. He crawled into the bed and drew her against him. He held her for twenty minutes until, regretfully, he lifted himself up and went to the bathroom to shower. He stepped into the glass cubicle and turned on the jet of water, feeling the hot needles stinging his skin. After a few minutes Abby joined him. The shower wasn't really large enough for both of them, but they pressed closely together, slick with soap and shampoo. They helped each other clean away the traces of blood. Marcus rubbed at the back of her legs with a flannel and saw the skin redden under his touch. When they came out of the bathroom, the sun was coming into the flat and Marcus didn't mind the wreckage of the sitting room and the kitchen, found he could ignore the brown stains on the mattress in their bedroom. He made them both tea and they sat and watched planes cut across the fragile morning sky.

'Do you want me to stay? I don't want you to be alone. Do you need to go to the hospital?'

'No, I'm fine. This is just what happens. I'll take the day off. I'm OK now, really I am. You've got that meeting. You should be going.'

He left her sitting on the sofa, the tea growing cold in her mug, the shadows of birds flashing across her as they passed on the way to the seed feeder that Abby hung outside the kitchen window. In the lift on the way down he adjusted his tie, picked at a spot and smoothed down the hair of his sideburns. Out on the street he looked up and saw Abby was watching him, the mug held out in front of her like a chalice. He turned and, walking backwards, raised his arm. She smiled as he tripped, regained his balance and finally disappeared around the corner.

Five

There were no curtains in Lee's flat. She always woke early, with the first whitening of the sky outside her window. Philip was still sleeping. She reached for a glass of water and pinched her fingers to the bridge of her nose, frowning. Darwin regarded her with lazy dark eyes. The dog had climbed onto the bed soon after the noise and the movement stopped, and Philip had drawn his knees up to his chest to avoid kicking him. Now Philip's legs half-hung over the edge of the bed. He gripped one corner of the duvet in his fingers and pressed it against his cheek. Otherwise he was naked. He groaned in his sleep.

She knew that she should fight the distaste that she felt whenever she brought a boy home. Or rather whenever she woke next to a boy. She wished she could persuade them to leave while she was still drunk. They violated the beauty of mornings in her flat, the privacy and serenity of feeling that she was the only person awake in the whole of Kensington. Their foul breath, stubble, demands for tea or – far worse – more sex left her feeling shot through with guilt, disgusted with herself, lonely.

Once, sex was all she thought about. In her last two years of school she had a string of boyfriends, all unsuitable, all much older than her. Her boyfriends would drive her to house parties around town where she'd sleep with them on badly stuffed sofas, cheat on them with their friends in dark spare rooms, dance with them on tables wearing only her pants. She was always drunker and louder than any other girl there, but she got away with it because she was also the youngest and prettiest. At the end of the parties, she would sit and rearrange her underwear beneath her jeans as the sun rose from the sea and the milk floats and fishermen and other early-morning movers made their way through the streets of the little town on the Suffolk coast.

She'd given up boys when she started the Course. Four years of near-celibacy. The occasional kiss, certainly. A few hands slipping under the waistband of her pants, but nothing more. Then, around the time she began her PhD, she'd started fucking again. Looking for the rush she'd felt as a teenager, the illicit coital glow. But now she couldn't look at them when they came: she squeezed her eyes tightly shut when their breath quickened to a pant, terrified of the masks their faces became at the point of orgasm, unrestrained and beastly. She knew that she didn't have a bad reputation at the Course yet. Her delicacy, the austere beauty of her features protected her against that, for the moment. But David was aware. She could feel him watching her, could sense the silent hum of his antennae tuned towards her.

Lee eased herself slowly out of bed and stood naked in the soft blue glow of the morning. She was still wearing her earrings: lapis in the left ear, turquoise in the right. The hair between her legs was the colour of damp sand. The floorboards were ancient beneath her bare feet; she could feel the circling grain of the wood through her soles. She lifted Darwin to the floor and stepped quietly over to her desk in the corner of the room. It was 5 a.m. She was careful not to knock the pile of books that sat on the desk: reading for her PhD that she had been putting off for weeks. A new life of Julian of Norwich and a collection of essays on Anglo-Saxon literature that she had ordered from a Midwestern university press. She picked up her camera and checked the lens, adjusting the settings for the dim light. Then, moving silently, she approached the bed, lifted the duvet, and took photographs of Philip.

His cock looked like a baby mouse. Not that it was small. It was not large but she had seen smaller. It was the colour that did it, the vulnerability, the sense of something not yet ready to see the world. It was curled back on itself, hiding beneath the tightly wound coils of hair that tapered in a line up to his belly button. His toenails were too long. She remembered that he had scratched her legs with them when they first went to bed. He had a tattoo on one shoulder – a Chinese symbol that looked like an insect. She could see how the ridged pigment protruded from the skin; she had to fight to stop herself touching it. Checking the pictures on her camera's monitor, she judged that she had taken enough, and replaced the camera on the cluttered desk. She picked up her clothes from the floor and, followed by Darwin, made her way through to the sitting room to dress.

Only one boy had surprised her in the act of photographing him, six months earlier. He was a softly spoken black boy from her critical theory seminar group called Paul. She had dropped the camera when he opened his eyes, those dark brown eyes that reminded her of Darwin. His nipples were the most extraordinary violet colour. It was the nipples that had made her linger too long over him, trying to get a shot that did them justice. Even in her morning-after guilt she recognised that Paul was very beautiful. They had stared at each other for several moments before Lee backed away, picking up the camera and holding it in front of her as if it might hide her nakedness and shame.

'Why are you doing that?' He had still been half-asleep. She thought later that she might have been able to pretend that he was dreaming, but she liked Paul, and had tried to explain.

'I'm sorry. You scared me. It's . . . It's just that it helps me try to understand why I'm doing it, when I can see it in the third person.' She looked down at the camera and saw that her hands were trembling. Paul lifted himself up and rested his head on his palm, his elbow pressing into the pillow.

'Was I that bad?'

'No, it isn't that. But I'm a Christian. I'm supposed to believe in not having sex before marriage. But I keep doing this.' She went over to the desk and drew out a large red photograph album. She held it out to Paul and he spent some minutes flicking through it. Twenty-five men in all. Each of them had his own page with his name and the date inscribed in Lee's neat, looping handwriting. The first was her supervisor at university, an older man, thickset with wispy grey hair, the date just over two years earlier. Paul handed it back to her with a raised eyebrow.

'So you want to remember the boys you fuck? I can understand that. I'd like a photograph of you, too. Something to carry around and look at when I'm down. Remind me I'd done it with a girl like you.'

'No, that's not it. I mean, maybe a little bit. I just feel like I need to keep a record of this, that's all. This time in my life. I tried to stop it when I first went to church. Had this bizarre period of celibacy. But it didn't work. I just couldn't do it.'

What she didn't admit to Paul, barely even expressed to herself, was that she needed the guilt. She had been the first of them to attend the Course. She went with friends from school one Wednesday night in the summer holidays before she started university. An unassuming church sat on a hill above the harbour in her home town. One of her childhood friends was the daughter of the vicar and Lee and a few others had gone that evening out of solidarity. She sat in the hall of the church and listened to the gentle words of the priest. When they were asked to pray Lee could hear the sea in the distance booming against the breakwaters along the front. She thought of all the boys, all the ugly drunken writhing, all the cheating and the guilt and suddenly she found herself sobbing.

In the discussion group afterwards, Lee sat and listened to her friends talking about how they prayed in secret, how they felt that they needed to believe in something, how the modern world disappointed them. She realised that she had given them little credit for their intelligence. Her friends would sit and listen as she played the piano, stare down at their plates while she and her parents indulged in long and spirited dinner-table conversations; she shone so brightly that they never got the chance. She felt ashamed as she looked into their kind, open faces and saw a huge amount of love for her. The priest sat and smiled as Lee spoke. She told them everything. Every sin and slip and all of the shame that stained her. All of the boys – too many to count – but never any love. The boys who she knew were in love with other girls, the boys whom other girls loved deeply. Her friends waited for her to finish and then they all hugged her. Finally, the priest put his hand down on the soft pile of her golden hair and blessed her.

She had walked from the church glowing. She felt new-made, humble. Her wickedness seemed a thing of adolescence, meaningless in the light of her new-found faith. But slowly it came back. And she got drunk and fucked more boys and she needed to be cleansed again. So she went back to see the priest and slowly she began to believe very deeply, grew to feel that she had a personal and precious relationship with God. The priest gave her the details of a Course session that took place in the chapel of one of the neighbouring colleges when she went up to university. For several years she followed the rules of the Course with great seriousness. But then the slumps set in, and she found her bad old ways returning. And this was why Philip, long and bony, was lying in her bed, snoring gently.

Lee dressed, fed Darwin and sat on the balcony drinking coffee until Philip stumbled out in his boxer shorts, his skin very pale in the first rays of the sun.

'Hi,' he said, looking past Lee and out over the city, hands clasped to his shoulders in the fresh morning air.

'Hi.' She left a pause. 'Do you want coffee?' Her voice was cold and there was only one chair out on the balcony, expressly to discourage any early-morning company.

'No, I'd better . . . I should just go. I'll see you at the Course next week. It was good to meet you.'

'Yes. Can you show yourself out? Mind Darwin doesn't follow you.'

*

She knew that it would be awkward during their next discussion session, and it was. The following Tuesday night, when a warm rain wrapped the church in a swirling veil, she saw him watching her as she walked down the aisle to take her place for David's speech. She was wearing a black jumper over a white T-shirt, black jeans and trainers. She could feel Philip's gaze across her back, in the nerves of her neck, in her hair. She thumbed through *The Way of the Pilgrim*. Mouse came to sit beside her and she hugged him gratefully, then turned to the pulpit, still vaguely aware of Philip's gaze. David looked down at her and smiled, then out to the rest of the room, his grin widening as he took in the rows of eager, upward-looking faces.

'Good evening, my children,' he said, holding his arms out and stepping forward to the microphone. 'You are now part of our family. And as you attend the Course over the next few weeks and, I hope, over the years to come, you will find yourself feeling increasingly that your family is here. Some of you may have come to the service on Sunday. Doesn't matter if you didn't, but those who were here will have got a measure of the intensity of the bond between us, the strength of this community. It feels sometimes like intensity isn't approved of in the outside world, as if it somehow isn't cool. Well here at St Botolph's, intensity is very cool. We encourage it.' He smiled and took a sip of water. The lights dimmed slightly. Lee rested her head on Mouse's shoulder.

'I hope that, over the past week, you might have noticed some changes in yourself. Maybe you haven't. Often we're too caught up in the business of our lives and we don't have time to think about how we're feeling. Sometimes it's hard to make space for God. But if you have felt something different, if you have found yourself praying, and maybe you've read some pages of the Bible, well, that's all great.' His smile faded and Lee noticed a subtle shift in the atmosphere. The light around the priest grew colder, wind whistled in the roof. She shivered. David clasped his hands together.

'Now I mentioned that this is a family. And families work best with rules. So today I'm going to talk about some of these rules and about why we have them. I used to leave this part until the end of the Course. No one likes hearing about rules. We are always being told what to do: *mind the gap, don't walk on the grass, get to work on time*. So I'm only going to talk about the really major ones. There are signs all along Beachy Head which say *stay away from the cliff edge*. Well, the rules I'm going to talk about tonight are like that – life-savers.'

Lee found herself zoning out as David spoke about the need to attend church on a regular basis, the necessity of nightly prayer, the fact that they were now missionaries for the Course and had to think about how others would view them. She was due to go up to her parents' house the weekend after the Retreat. She would sit and play the piano all day Saturday in her dad's music room at the top of the house. You could see the sea through the window if you leaned out a little as you played. A grand piano sat in the centre of the room, sheet music was piled in corners, there was a desk at the back beside which stood a wire basket full of crumpled paper. She would often kneel by the basket with her dad looking for melodies that he had abandoned during his fits of frustrated rage. A mobile made of piano keys hung in the window, black and yellow-white keys that clunked together like bones when they were stirred by a breeze.

She was worried that her dad might commit suicide. It had started as a passing fancy and then grew in her mind until she couldn't drive from her head the picture of him slumped at his desk, an empty bottle of pills clutched in his delicate hand, his long white hair flowing out across the wood. He was terribly fragile, Lee knew this. Disappointed in the gradual diminuendo of his career. He had never been close to Lee's mother, a quiet and efficient woman who worked in an administrative role at a teacher training college in Ipswich. Her parents hadn't shared beds since Lee was a child. Now Lee wasn't there to look after him, and her trips home were less frequent than before she'd moved to London. She recognised that her own demons were handed down from him and she hated the thought of him battling them alone.

She and her dad would take a long walk by the sea on the Saturday evening while her mum watched telly. He always asked her to tell him about her university work. He loved to hear her stories about mystics and visionaries, martyred virgins and ancient anchoresses. Lee enjoyed reciting the Old English poems most of all. On stormy days, her dad would rise from his chair and pull on his coat, helping her into her Barbour as she slipped a scarf around her throat. They'd march along the tideline, eyelashes pearled by the salty spray from breakers, the sky so low that the highest waves seemed to grab handfuls of the dark grey clouds. Lee would quote poetry at her dad in a lilting voice, occasionally tripping as she forced the words into her mind, but always full of drama and tragedy: *The Seafarer*, *The Wanderer*, *Deor*. Her dad would repeat verses that struck him as particularly moving, his voice still heavily accented as he stumbled to shape his mouth around the unfamiliar sound of the ancient language. They'd hold hands as all brightness leached from the day and return, cheeks red, to the warmly glowing house.

The night before, her dad had emailed her a piece of music that they had worked on together during her last visit home. Drawing on her translation of the Old English love poem *Wulf and Eadwacer*, it was a desolate, minimalist piece, built around a series of distant notes that developed tentatively into the refrain, sung by a soprano: *A difference exists between us*. Her dad had tried to convey the loneliness of the original poem, the sexual longing, the betrayal. She had sat at her computer and played the piece time after time. With Darwin curled at her feet, she listened to the haunting, austere music and cried: for herself, for the nameless author of the poem, for her dad.

Lee realised that David was looking at her. Mouse had his hand upon her knee and was tapping out a jittery rhythm with his fingers. David blinked as she met his eyes. The church was utterly silent.

'Now for the reason I decided to talk about our rules tonight. One of the things I hope that you guys have discovered about the Course is that we aren't exclusive. All who come here are welcome. All those who join our family, who respect that family by acknowledging and abiding by the rules that keep us together, are welcome. You may have heard things about the Course – there have been newspaper articles, disaffected former members, rival priests who envy our crowded pews.' He smiled sadly.

'The Course isn't for everyone, and I'm afraid some of you will leave. Some of you will feel that we ask too much of you, that you can't cope with the pressure of living up to Christ's ideal. What I say to you is this: embrace that pressure, strive for the perfection that Christ achieved and when you slip, the Course will be there to help you up. And you will find that all the other pressures in your life, the things we were discussing last week, fall away when you start abiding by the rules of the Course. We have been described as being outmoded and old-fashioned. I disagree firmly with the idea that our teachings don't have any relevance to the modern world. Quite the opposite. But when I hear that people think us old-fashioned, I say yes, that's probably true.

'We believe that the best family, the most stable and endur-ing family, is one where a man and a woman come together in love. And when that love is recognised in the eyes of God. Sally and I weren't blessed with children – in many ways our children are you lot – but, back when we were planning for a family, we felt very strongly that a mother and a father, living together as man and wife, was by far the best way to raise kids. And I know this isn't a cool or a politically correct viewpoint, I know it is very old-fashioned. But look at the statistics, think about it logically. It's what nature intended, it's what God in-tended.' The light softened now and David smiled out at the congregation.

'Weddings are wonderful. It's still the happiest day of my life, the day when I turned to watch Sally walk down the aisle. And weddings have become as important a part of the Course as our Tuesday-night sessions. They're a place we can all get together and celebrate the wonder of love, the joyous pact between a man and a woman. And all I'm saying here is that this is our ideal. If you don't want to get married, fine. If you're gay, that's OK too. You're still welcome here, although you might find that you don't always feel entirely comfortable. Because we believe that it is when sex is twinned with married love that it's at its most intense and holy, it's only then that it's truly a gift from God. I have many unmarried friends who say that their partnership is every bit as strong as a proper marriage; I have many gay friends who believe that their love is blessed by God. I can only say what I truly believe, what I'd tell my own son. Marry a woman who will love and cherish you. Save sex until after you're married. It's the path to happiness, to fulfilment. Some of the most depressed, disappointed people I know are those who chose to be gay in their younger years and realised, too late, that it is a dead-end lifestyle. Now they are old and full of regret. Sex is a gift of God serving two purposes: it represents the joy of love between a man and a woman, and it brings forth new life. Don't lose sight of these things. Struggle against temptation. Often the most difficult battles end in the most magnificent victories.' He shuffled some papers on the lectern and stepped down from the pulpit. The applause built slowly from the back of the room. Lee clapped very gently, and her palms were damp with sweat.

She emptied her mind during the music, trying not to think of David or Philip. It was why she loved the piano. The mathematical precision of the notes, the complex feats of dexterity needed to execute the pieces perfectly; all of this helped her to step away from herself. But then they were sitting in the discussion group, and Mouse was beginning to talk about chastity and purity and guilt. David was standing in the shadows of the doorway, and she could again feel his eyes upon her.

'We all get urges.' Mouse's voice was clipped and firm and

droplets of spittle flew from his mouth as he spoke. 'But we control them. Or we hold them in as best we can until our love is blessed. I've lost girlfriends because of this. Of course I have. But I know I'm right. Saving something so precious for the right girl seems only sensible. And when I do find her, when we're married and one in the eyes of God, well, then it will all be worthwhile. It will be something incredibly special and powerful.' The twins sat forward, their heads bobbing; every so often one of them would giggle. Lee could see that Mouse hadn't shaved for a few days. A light dusting of blond hairs, not thick enough to be called stubble, fuzzed beneath his round cheeks.

'Don't you think that some of the people who need the Course most might be put off by all this?' Philip asked, chewing the end of his pencil. 'I mean, the Course is targeted at young people, and young people struggle with their sexuality, they struggle to keep their emotions in check. It just feels like it's a very negative way of putting it. Very unforgiving when you compare it to the rest of the Course.' Lee realised that Philip was looking at her.

'The Course will welcome anyone,' she said, quietly. 'And particularly if they're struggling with these kinds of issues. But David's right: promiscuity leads to a very lonely existence.'

A silence descended. Philip continued to look at Lee. She stared at the ground and then desperately towards David in the doorway. The priest moved forward into the light and was about to address the room when Mouse, his cheeks very red, began to speak.

'It's like so much of modern life,' he said. 'Always looking for the next fix, constantly jumping from one cheap thrill to the next. A stable marriage between a man and a woman may seem unglamorous, but it's the key to a happy life. It's why the Course insists upon this above all else. It's for our own good.' Mouse was standing now, pacing within the circle of chairs, one tightly balled fist smacking into the other palm. Lee thought he looked unhinged, but then she saw the twins leaning forward and blinking their long-lashed eyes and she realised that Mouse was just copying David. Even his voice was growing to sound like David's. A voice that had been so different when Lee first discovered him, tubby and awkward, hiding in his tiny room high above the college quadrangle.

Lee talked very little during the discussion; her eyes were blank and distant. Philip smiled at her, nodded when she did speak, tried to make his own comments enthusiastic and endearing. When the session was finished, he stood at the door, looking over at Lee as she gathered up her Bible and her papers. Mouse had already left for the pub with the twins and Maki. Lee pretended to read a passage in *The Way of the Pilgrim*, hoping that Philip would go on without her. David coughed quietly in the shadows behind Philip.

'Hi, Philip, would you mind if I had a quick word with Lee? Just some administrative stuff we need to go through.'

Lee looked up, smiling coolly.

'Oh, Philip, were you waiting for me? I'm so sorry. I'll catch you up.'

Philip nodded and waved, backing out of the room. David stepped in and sat on the chair beside Lee. Lee was still tracing her finger across the lines of the green book, not seeing the words, a feeling of dread building in her stomach.

'I wanted to speak to you after the discussion tonight. I saw the way Philip was looking at you.' David's voice was very gentle. 'I don't want you to think I'm prying, or judging you. But you're a Course leader now, and that carries with it certain responsibilities. I don't want to lose you, or him.'

Lee closed the book and folded her hands on top of it, staring down at her nails. She felt blood rising to her cheeks.

'When Sally and I were first together,' David continued, 'it wasn't the done thing to be exclusive in relationships. It was our first year at Durham, and it was that part of the seventies that still wanted very much to be the sixties. So whilst it was very clear to me from the start that Sally was the one I wanted to be with, we slept around. Or rather I did. I used to get drunk and when I woke up next to the girls, I'd barely recognise them. I always hoped that when the bare back I was squashed up against turned over, it'd be Sally. But Sally was the only one who wouldn't sleep with me. I can't tell you how empty it all made me feel. Walking home in the early mornings after those one-night stands, I really hated myself.

'It was a bit like religion. That same era, it was trendy to get involved in all sorts of different religions. Buddhism, Jainism, Sufism – anything Eastern and enlightened worked. And even though we were all brought up Christian, and we went to sing carols at Christmas, it felt like Christianity was the one religion you really weren't allowed to go in for. I remember these ridiculous meditation parties – some people would be smoking marijuana, and others would be chanting nonsense. I always felt very awkward, but wasn't sure enough of myself to follow my own path.'

David reached over and placed his hand on Lee's. She looked up at him, shyly, strands of blonde hair falling in front of her eyes.

'I proposed to Sally after finals. I took her for a picnic by Prebend's Bridge, on the Wear. I produced the ring with a bottle of champagne. It was perfect. We were married the following spring. And perhaps a year later, with Sally's help, I became a Christian. I still feel that the two were very much linked. Both were like coming home for me. The joy of sharing my bed with the one woman I loved above all others was so much like finally accepting the one true God. I hope this makes sense to you.'

She looked at him, frowning.

'Yes. Yes, it does make sense.'

'Take Marcus and Abby. You should use them as a model. I know that they have had their troubles, but there is something indestructible at the heart of that marriage. They'll be able to face anything together, because that union is so extraordinarily strong. I see Marcus looking at Abby sometimes and the love in his eyes is frightening.'

He lifted his hand from her lap and took her chin between his thumb and forefinger.

'You are such a beautiful, intelligent girl, Lee. You don't need to be doing this, to be giving yourself away so easily. You will make somebody a wonderful wife one day. In the meantime you must just try to control yourself. You know that I think wine is a wonderful thing, one of God's great gifts. But all of you drink too much, and it's much harder to keep your passions in check when you're drunk.'

He drew his hand up, across her cheek, brushing the strands of hair away from her mouth and tucking them behind her ear.

'I will try, David, I really will. I want you to be proud of me. Sometimes, though, it feels like it takes everything I have just to get through the day. Like I'm leaning against a door, trying to keep it shut, trying to stop something terribly frightening from coming out. It's why I'm always so tired.'

'And what's behind this door?'

'I don't know. I just know that it's dark and horrible and scares me. I start to panic just thinking about it.'

'You must fight against it. The Course will be there for you when you come out the other side of this phase you're going through. But if you backslide too far, if you let the Devil come too close to you, it may be that you are too distant for even the Course to reach you. If you become known as a slut, Lee, I might have to ask you to leave. For the good of the Course.' These last words were like glass pressed into her skin, each word pearled blood on her pale skin. Tears began to run down her cheeks and David's voice became softer.

'I understand what you've been going through. And I don't want to turn away from you – you're a key member of our community. I'm just trying to warn you. You know I see myself as a father to you lot. The four of you need to stick together. There's something about you guys that is quite astonishing. On stage, obviously, but also when you move around the church, when you speak to Course members. I don't want to lose that. It's why I wanted to speak to you now, before things get any worse. Have a think about what I've said. Come and see me any time if you'd like to chat.'

He rose and placed his hand on her hair. Lee bowed her head, feeling the joyful shiver of forgiveness. When the echoes of his footsteps had disappeared from the church above, she made her way upstairs, put on her coat, pulled her hat down so that it nearly covered her eyes, and walked out into the damp night.

Mouse had saved her a seat next to him in the pub. Philip was watching from the corner as Lee moved her chair closer towards Mouse, linked her arm through his, and whispered in his ear that she loved him. He blushed and smiled. When they had finished their drinks, they made their way out into the damp night. Philip grabbed her shoulder as Mouse scampered ahead to hail a taxi.

'I wanted to talk to you,' he said. 'I had a really good time with you the other night. But I got the feeling you were ignoring me this evening. Please tell me you aren't upset with me.'

'I'm so sorry.' Lee looked genuinely distraught. 'I can be a bitch sometimes, I know I can. I really didn't mean to hurt you.'

'You didn't hurt me, or rather you haven't yet.' Philip tried to laugh, his lips peeling back from his teeth. 'Listen, could I get your number? I'd really like to see you again, just the two of us.'

She looked at him and narrowed her eyes. Her hat sat on the line of her brow and the rain collected in droplets on the cotton. Her lips were bloodless lines, unkissable.

'No, Philip. I'm so sorry. You understand, don't you? It's just a really difficult time for me. I have to go. It's wet and Mouse is waiting for me. I'm sorry, I really am.'

She ran, leaping over puddles, to where Mouse was standing, holding the door of a taxi. Looking out of the fogged back window, she saw Philip watching the cab move out of sight, the rain swirling around his tall frame. She took hold of Mouse's hot, plump hand and squeezed it tightly.

Six

It rained every day for a week as the heat of September gave way to a bleak and wintry October. It was cold rain, the kind of rain that slants under umbrellas, soaks through the soles of shoes and explodes off paving stones. Marcus and Abby turned in on themselves, giving way to stillness and reflection. Two of the boys in their discussion group had left after the first week, though their girlfriends remained. Marcus had phoned the boys, emailed them, talked to their girlfriends, but to no avail. In the shadow of these departures, their second session had been a downbeat affair. Neil had spoken about his daughter, tears streaming down his face.

'One of the reasons I find the idea of God so attractive, one of the reasons that I hope beyond hope that it's all true, is so that I know that Phoebe isn't just rotting there in her grave, that she's somewhere she'll be looked after by someone who really understands her. I listened to David's speech tonight about sex and I thought – I didn't even know if Phoebe was still a virgin, if she'd been hurt in love, if that was maybe why she became ill.'

Abby had crossed the room to embrace him. They'd only briefly touched on the topic of the evening's talk. Marcus could tell that there was little risk of the prim girls in their group giving way to their baser passions. He could hear Mouse holding forth next door and envied his friend his fluency and his conviction.

They hadn't stayed long at the pub afterwards, and when

they got home Marcus made them Horlicks which they drank in bed, chatting with the duvet pulled up to their chins. They both guessed what had happened between Lee and Philip, and wondered whether they should mention it to David. If Philip left because of Lee, it would mean that they were three members down after the first two weeks. They didn't blame her, though. They could see how fragile she was, how lost. Marcus reached over and stroked Abby's soft, wide cheek. Since the miscarriage, Abby had insisted they sleep in the spare room and Marcus liked the change. There were no pictures on the walls; it was like a hotel room, quiet and anonymous. During the week they telephoned each other regularly, softened their voices and murmured until Marcus had to hang up because his boss was standing over him, or Abby saw Sally struggling with a pile of hymnals and rang off.

They made a nest of the apartment during the weekend. Marcus scuttled out to buy newspapers and small luxuries: croissants and wine. They held hands at church on Sunday morning. Abby sang more quietly than usual, leaning on the pew in front of her. She stayed at the altar rail for a few seconds after taking communion and Marcus waited beside her, watching her lips move silently. When they came back to their seats, she knelt again and prayed until the final hymn was sung. They left as soon as the service was over and spent the afternoon lying on the sofa with a duvet over them, watching sentimental old films.

Abby telephoned her mother that Sunday afternoon. She didn't tell her exactly what had happened, and Abby's mother pretended that she had misunderstood, rather than face the embarrassment of talking to her daughter about her feelings. Abby had two older sisters. All three of them had been star performers at the local grammar school, had shone at university. But Abby knew that her mother worried that the girls

71

had inherited her own fatal flaw: they married badly. Abby's parents had divorced when she was eleven. At the time she only read Jilly Cooper novels and found the drama and the heartache of the divorce rather glamorous. But she missed her father, who had subsequently married a small, thin woman in a direct reproach to Abby's increasingly vast mother. Abby's eldest sister had already been married twice, the first time for under a year. Susie, the middle child, was in a spectacularly loveless union with a maths teacher, ghosted by a pair of silent children. Her mother always looked at Marcus through eyes hard with suspicion.

On Sunday night they forced themselves out to a pizza joint on Westbourne Grove. The restaurant was full of couples like themselves: bankers and their wives who wouldn't see each other all week, younger hedge-fund managers with trophy girlfriends who talked too loudly and laughed too easily, one of the partners from Marcus's law firm. But Marcus liked the pizza, and he squeezed Abby's knee under the table and spoke to her about his childhood; she had heard the stories a hundred times before, but Marcus knew they soothed her. He could see her fighting to stay brave, to force the dark thoughts from her mind, and it reminded him of Lee, how she would bite her lip as she struggled against her slumps.

As the day of the third session of the Course dawned, Marcus rose very quietly from the bed and changed in the hallway. He knew Abby had had a bad night. He had woken in blackness to find her clutching her pillow, twisting and grasping it and then forcing it down onto her belly. She screamed silently for a moment before sitting up very straight, her eyes open, her chest rising. Marcus had taken her in his arms and held her until she fell back asleep. He lay beside her, unable to find sleep himself, until he saw the hand of the alarm clock creep round towards six.

The pool in the chrome and frosted-glass gym behind Moorgate was almost empty. The traders from the surrounding banks tended to work out in the evenings; their wives came in for Pilates at lunch. One older man swam a slow, dignified breaststroke, his head squeezed tightly by the swimming cap and goggles. He sank beneath the water with each stroke and then, surfacing, seemed surprised to emerge into the same, still world. Marcus stood on the side of the pool and felt the ridges of the tiles beneath his feet, the rush of blood as he drew in great lungfuls of air, the pinch of his own goggles at the bridge of his nose. Then he plunged into the water, which was always colder than he remembered, and he was all motion, his legs thundering in his wake, his arms grasping the water and pulling him through it, a breath every three strokes on alternate sides. Sometimes he let it go for longer before breathing, waiting until his lungs were screaming, his neck straining. He loved the way sound was deadened beneath the water. He could pretend that he lived in that easy liquid world, where, while he was moving, nothing could touch him, and all the dirt of existence was washed away by the rushing water.

Later that day he sat in his office and thought about Abby. He had turned his chair to face out of the window, hoping to give the impression of one lost in the intricacies of a case. He watched the rain tracing patterns down the glass, drops gathering others in their wake as they slithered downwards, dividing their transparent bodies like amoebae viewed on a microscope slide. He knew that he took Abby for granted, knew that the complexity of their history together, the fact that they had come through so much, made him think they were invincible. But she had moved from sadness into something more forlorn over the past few days, and he felt powerless. He was so used to turning to her when he was strung out, so used to her being the strong one. It disturbed his sense of the order of things for her to be laid so low. Her face, younger, smiling, came to hover in front of his half-closed eyes.

He was doing this with increasing regularity, allowing himself to drift off into nostalgia, layering one memory upon another until his present-day self almost disappeared into the shadows cast by those former Marcuses, who always seemed brighter and more alive, still enchanted by life. His dreams always centred on the others – on Lee before her sadness set in, or Mouse back at university, or Abby in the first days of their love. It was when the memories tumbled on top of each other, interlacing so that he could barely separate them, that he realised how lucky he was to have the three of them. How, perhaps, the Course was just a way of making sure that they were always together, sealing fast the bond of their friendship. He wished sometimes that their four lives could be as ordered and synchronised as when they were on stage. It was only when they were playing music now that they seemed to work well together.

He remembered Abby walking down the aisle at their wedding. A small, sparsely furnished church near her Derbyshire home. She had arrived at the church early and the blast of Mendelssohn had caught him by surprise. He felt his heart leap in his chest and Mouse, standing beside him, had put an arm around his shoulder. Marcus had turned and looked into the white arch of light coming through doors that let the spring afternoon into the church. At first he could see nothing but the glare of the light, which seemed to him somehow linked to the bellowing of the organ. Then, coming out of the light, he saw Abby walking with slow, dainty footsteps down the aisle. Her wedding dress hung cobwebby over her chest, the veil smudged her features. She clasped a posy of wild flowers tightly in her hands. Marcus could see that they were already wilting. Her father seemed to be leaning against her as

74

they made their way down the aisle. Behind her now, almost blocking out the light, came the bridesmaids.

The oldest sister had reacted badly to foundation applied that morning by the make-up artist and her face was a wide, red beacon glowing behind Abby's shoulder. Susie, the middle sister, who was ashamed of her size, drooped down the aisle, shyly looking out for her husband in the crowd and then turning her eyes back to the worn stones of the floor. Lee looked stunning. Bone-thin, but poised and delicate between the two hulking sisters. Marcus watched Abby's father scuttle to stand beside his diminutive wife. He was a history teacher at Matlock College of Further Education, disappointed-looking, cowed by his wives, ex- and present. But he stared at his youngest daughter with eyes that brimmed with love.

Abby's mother, sitting beside Marcus's as if somehow wishing to claim for her solitary state the reflected decency of widowhood, fanned herself with the service sheet. David and Sally Nightingale sat in the aisle behind them. Only a few of the congregation were not Course members. Daffy from university; a couple of Marcus's friends from school – now bankers – who looked terrifyingly old, their stomachs straining against their morning-suit jackets, thin-lipped wives on their arms; Abby's frail-looking aunts and her gruff cousins who wore their suits with the resentful air of petty criminals in court. The rest of the congregation bore the healthy glow of spiritual enlightenment. The Course members always brought their children to weddings and the men took turns to pace up and down at the back of the church with the toddlers, while mothers jogged babies or retreated demurely to the side aisles to breastfeed.

When the organ stopped and the local vicar lisped his welcome, Marcus began to panic. There was a pigeon trapped in the roof of the church. It made circles of the low roof, trying to find a way out; its hysterical wingbeats kept time with Marcus's heart. Marcus looked at Abby and, behind her, the sisters who seemed like a dreadful premonition of her future. Lee smiled wickedly at him. He saw Abby's mother glaring with tiny black eyes at her ex-husband and his wife. Marcus's own mother was already sobbing quietly into a handkerchief, his sister looking over at him with something like pity.

Marcus tried to slow his breathing as he stepped forward to join Abby in front of the altar, but his heart thumped violently in his chest and his palms were coated with cold, sticky sweat. He felt as if he had entirely lost control of his life, as if he had abjured any sense of agency when he joined the Course, and he was now about to marry at the age of twenty-five, to tie himself for life to a girl and a religion he felt that he had stumbled upon by accident. He stammered his way through the service, looking at Abby as if she were a stranger, feeling no sense of the holiness of the occasion, of the joy that he saw in the faces of the Course members looking up at him. When Mouse jokily patted his pockets searching for the ring, Marcus felt the panic rising into his throat. He was convinced that he would pass out, that he would have a heart attack like his father and die, there, in front of his family. The church held none of its usual comfort. He felt terrified and alone standing up in front of people who suddenly seemed very distant; he saw something cold in the clear eyes of the Course members. Then, very quickly, the service was over, and Marcus and Abby walked out into the wide, bright day through a cheering crowd.

Abby took his hand in hers as they sat in the Rolls-Royce outside the church. There was confetti in her hair and her palms were as cold and moist as his own. She looked at him with nervous, hopeful eyes, a smile twitching the corners of her mouth. He reached over and kissed her as the car pulled away and he heard cheering behind them. They sat in silence for the remainder of the journey to the venue. Marcus couldn't shake the butterflies in his stomach, the feeling that he didn't have the final say in his own life any more. He cracked his knuckles and wondered when he would be able to smoke.

The venue was a four-star hotel on the outskirts of Derby, twenty minutes' drive from the church. Marcus looked out of the window of the car as they passed rows of down-at-heel shops, council estates and abandoned factories. His mother had wanted them to get married in Surrey, where there would have been room to hold the reception in the garden. But after a series of negotiations in which he had not been involved, but which had clearly led to some chilliness between their respective mothers, it was decided that the wedding would take place near Abby's home in Derbyshire.

The driveway that led to the hotel wove between the pristine fairways of a nine-hole golf course. The car stopped to allow four pastel-clad golfers to cross. Their silver hair shimmered in the sunlight and one of them turned to give Marcus a thumbs-up. He smiled wanly back. The hotel was an old manor house built of dark stone that seemed to absorb the day's bright light. Attached to the main building was a low modern wing that housed the swimming pool and gym. When they had come to visit the venue with Abby's mother, the hotel manager had insisted on showing them the sports complex, which she assured them was *unrivalled* in the whole of the East Midlands. The manager was now waiting, hands linked in front of her, outside the entrance to welcome them. A marquee had been attached to the hotel and French doors led out from the dining tables to the dance floor. A gentle breeze ruffled the tent's white fabric as they stepped from the car.

Later, as the sun sank slowly over the trees that blocked the grey council high-rises of Derby, Mouse and Marcus stood on the putting green smoking. The hours had raced by, aided by gin-and-tonics and the champagne that Marcus's mother had paid for.

'I can't quite believe you've done it,' said Mouse.

'There were a couple of times when I thought I might not make it. You were an excellent best man. To tell you the truth, today has been one long panic attack for me.'

They stood and watched the sun disappear.

'Abby looked grand.'

'Yes, she did. I was proud to be marrying her.'

'She's not like her family. You know that, don't you, sport?'

'Of course.'

'You know what it made me think of, standing there with you today?'

'What?'

'It reminded me of when we'd go to listen to Abby sing in the choir at university. It occurred to me today how none of her family ever came along. If I had a child who had that kind of talent I'd want to be there for every performance, you know? It's strange that neither of her parents came to hear her, even for Christmas carols.'

'Mmm. I don't think any of them really like her very much. It's funny, we spent a lot of time in church back then. I mean, given that it was before the Course. I suppose I must have gone at least once a week all the way through university.'

Mouse took a drag on his cigarette and turned to Marcus with serious eyes.

'I wonder sometimes if those days laid the foundations of our faith. Even though we were drunk or stoned some of the time – most of the time – and even though I never listened to the words really, it did give us an appreciation for that kind of beauty, set in our minds the idea that there was something better, purer, than the life we were leading.'

They stubbed out their cigarettes and made their way into the marquee. Dinner had finished and it was time for the first dance. Toddlers were strewn like obstacles across the dance floor; blitzed on ice cream and wedding cake, they screamed and stamped and roared. 'Love Cats' began to play, and Marcus bashfully held out his hand to Abby, who took it and allowed herself to be guided to a clear space of dance floor. Marcus was a bad dancer. It didn't help that he and Abby were more or less the same height. Neither of them seemed able to decide who would lead. His feet grew independently shy of the rest of his body, curled themselves up bashfully when called upon, tried to hide under the hem of Abby's dress. She was drunk and threw herself gamely into the dancing, but her enthusiasm merely served to highlight Marcus's own awkwardness. Finally, as the song jittered towards its end, Marcus felt a hand on his waist and Mouse stepped in to dance with Abby.

Even though Mouse was much smaller than Marcus, he seemed to be able to reach above Abby, to harness her energy and turn the two of them into a swirling image of graceful recklessness. Marcus felt a small shot of jealousy as he watched them. Abby let out howls of delight and continued to dance wildly with Mouse as the next song came in and others stepped onto the dance floor to join them. Lee was slow-dancing with Daffy even though it was an upbeat number. Marcus could see Daffy's thigh working itself slowly between her legs. Course dads danced with their children, who, having worked off their sugar rushes, now nuzzled sleepy chocolate-stained faces into their fathers' crisp white collars. David and Sally Nightingale jitterbugged together, eyes locked, revelling in the weight of shared history conferred by the vintage of their perfectly synchronised dancing. Marcus stood holding his glass of champagne until his sister came and dragged him onto the dance floor, her small white face turned up lovingly to his as they danced.

Much later, Mouse and Marcus were again out on the putting green smoking. One of Abby's cousins was sleeping on the first tee behind them. Mouse had grabbed the last two bottles of champagne as they made their way out of the marquee. He passed one to Lee and Abby, who were in drunken conversation at a table in the corner, and opened the other as they strode across the squares of light thrown from the hotel windows onto the wide lawn. Marcus had found a golf ball in the bushes and dribbled it from one side of the putting green to the other, finally punting the ball as far as he could into the distance, hopping and holding his foot in pain as the white ball flew off into the black night.

'Did you see Lee kissing Daffy?' Mouse asked.

'Was it a kiss? I wouldn't really call it a kiss.'

'It was a kiss. Nightingale saw her. I was watching him.'

'Poor Lee. You mustn't think badly of her for it.'

'I thought she was better. She seemed almost like her old self the past few weeks.'

There was the sound of breaking glass from inside the marquee. Marcus saw that Mouse was looking at him intently.

'I thought you did well today. I can tell you now that I was worried beforehand. You've been acting strangely for the past few weeks. And you seemed so nervous in the church.'

'I was nervous. I still am, I suppose.'

'I had taken a few wee precautions.' Smiling, Mouse reached into the pocket of his suit and pulled out a white cylinder. He rolled it between his thumb and forefinger and then brought it up to his nose, inhaling deeply.

'Is that a joint?' Marcus was laughing.

'Just, as I say, a precaution. I thought about smoking it with you before we went into the church. Then I thought you might want it to get you through the reception. But you didn't need it. Seems a bit of a waste now.' He looked at the joint and then up at Marcus.

'Oh, come on, let's smoke it. For old times' sake.' Marcus reached into his pocket for a lighter and then looked back at the marquee. 'I just can't let Abby see me. I promised her I wouldn't do drugs again once we were married. It would look bad if she caught me the day of our wedding.'

They walked into the shadow of the hotel, skirting flower beds and balconies. Mouse led the way while Marcus followed, stopping occasionally to sip from the champagne bottle. They came to the low square bulk of the sports complex. A door stood open, emitting a faint blue light, the smell of chlorine. The swimming pool was lit from beneath, white lights shining upwards through the water, the gently rippling surface dappling the roof. Marcus imagined that they were in a cave, that the fake rubber trees in the corner were ferns, the pipes hanging from the ceiling stalactites. In one corner of the hall there was a sauna, pale wood bleached almost white. Mouse stepped inside.

'There won't be a fire alarm in here. Close the door.'

Marcus stepped into the small room that smelt of pencil wood and sweat. It was warmer than the rest of the hall. He pulled the glass door shut behind him and looked through it to the pool, whose surface was now quite still. He sat down on the lower of the two benches that lined the back wall. Mouse was perched above him and reached down for the cigarette lighter. It was almost entirely dark inside the sauna and the sudden flaming of the lighter hurt Marcus's eyes. Soon the small room was filled with the warm, woody smell of dope.

After a while, Marcus stood up to clear his head. A smile was strung out across his face. Mouse was leaning back against the wooden wall, his eyes closed, the last of the joint burning down between his fingers. Marcus retrieved the stub, took a long drag and then extinguished it in the dregs of the champagne bottle.

'I'm going to miss that,' he said, his words coming out very slowly.

'I'm going to miss you.' Mouse's voice was suddenly very serious and Marcus felt the smile fade from his lips. He could only just make out his friend in the darkness and sat clumsily down beside him. He put an arm around Mouse's shoulders and tried to find words suitable for the moment.

'You're a good friend. The best I've got.'

There was a noise in the pool outside. Marcus lifted his arm from around Mouse and crossed to the glass door of the sauna. In the dim blue glow of the pool, he could see someone swimming. The long white body barely ruffled the water as it moved through it. A length underwater, then a length of graceful breaststroke, then a fluid and powerful crawl.

'Mouse, come and look.'

Mouse rose and pressed himself alongside his friend.

'It's Lee,' he said.

The swimmer moved to the steps at the edge of the pool and rose slowly from the water. It was the dimmest corner of the pool, but Marcus could see that Mouse was right. Water fell from Lee's skinny naked body as she walked along the tiles beside the pool. Standing for a moment, her arms raised up, stretching her skin tightly over accordion ribs, nipples flattening across high breasts, she took a deep breath and dived back in. In a strange way, Marcus thought she seemed to know that she was being watched. She deliberately swam over the underwater lights so that her body was a dark silhouette, barely bulging at the buttocks, moving quickly as her legs began to froth the water. She was pushing herself faster and faster, as if racing against herself or attempting to work out some hidden rage. Finally, she stopped in the shallow end, standing up in the corner nearest to where Marcus and Mouse were watching her. The water lapped just below her waist; the dip of each wave revealed the small damp tangle of her pussy. She stretched her arms up again and then lay back in the water, her hips pushed upwards, her legs and arms gently paddling to keep her afloat.

Marcus had been so focused on Lee, on trying to sear the image of her onto his mind, that he hadn't noticed Mouse. Half-turned away from him, his face pressed to the glass, Mouse's body trembled every so often. One of Mouse's hands had disappeared into the front of his grey trousers. Marcus was about to say something, but then Lee began to swim again, this time backstroke. She swam slowly, her white body held high, the water cascading over her stomach and chest. Marcus, ignoring his embarrassment, unzipped his flies and drew out his cock. He saw Mouse look over at him, and could just make out an encouraging smile on his friend's lips. With their faces close together, looking out through the glass and breathing heavily, they lost themselves in the image of the girl cutting through the water. Marcus came first, shooting out a white gobbet that landed with a splut on the glass door. Mouse followed almost immediately afterwards, letting out a half-sigh as he pulled himself off. Marcus watched his friend's face twist and then relax in the dim light. They were both panting, their breath steaming the glass. Marcus reached down to zip his flies.

As if she knew exactly what was going on inside the sauna, Lee swam to the edge of the pool and lifted herself out. She took a towel from a pile lying on a deckchair, dried herself slowly and then pulled on the bridesmaid's dress that was hanging over the arm of the chair. Marcus and Mouse smoked a cigarette together, wanting to allow some time before leaving the building. When the cigarette had burned down to a stub, they made their way quietly back to the marquee.

Marcus kept the image of Lee in his mind throughout his honeymoon. She must have gone to bed immediately after her swim, because he didn't see her again before he and Abby were whisked off to the bridal suite and then, early the next morning, to Gatwick. And when they made love on the starched white sheets of their Corsican chalet, when they swam naked together in the hidden coves around Propriano, when Abby lay back for him in a hollow on a wooded headland outside Bonifacio, Marcus felt that they were somehow paying homage to Lee. As if they were pursuing an ideal that she had created during her midnight swim.

*

Marcus jumped. Someone had come into his office. He had an erection and he realised that he had fallen asleep. It was still raining; the drops were racing down the glass. Whoever was behind him cleared his throat again. Marcus swung his chair around. Michael Faraday, one of the senior partners, was standing with his eyebrows raised and his hands in his pockets.

'Michael, good to see you,' Marcus babbled. 'I was just thinking about the Crystal Capital situation. Well, actually that's a lie. I had been thinking about Crystal Capital but then I started thinking about rain, and why we don't hear about acid rain any more. Whether it's because it isn't a problem any more, or if it's because we have much bigger ecological things to worry about now.'

Marcus shimmered his most winning smile at the grey-haired partner.

'No idea. Don't give a fuck either. I want you to drop Crystal and come with me. I've a case I think will really grab you. Fascinating business and needs your brain on it. A Chinese bank is trying to sue Plantagenet Partners. It's going to be a massive job. Hope you're not busy over the next few weeks. I'm going to need you to run through walls on this one. Most complicated buggeration of a case I've seen.'

Marcus tried to adjust his cock under the desk, stood awkwardly, and followed the partner out. They walked down the corridor together.

'The first thing you should know is that the Chinese have a bloody strong case. You're going to need to be pretty tricksy on this one. I've already made sure that the boys at Plantagenet have got rid of all the records relating to the transaction that they don't absolutely have to keep. You might want to encourage them to lose a few more. Software issues, or something. This case will teach you that being a good lawyer means always being one step ahead of the law. Hope I'm making myself clear . . .'

Marcus was late for the Course that night. He had slipped away as soon as Faraday went to buy his dinner, but the Tube chuntered slowly, pausing ominously with flickering lights between stations. When he finally arrived at Sloane Square, he ran flat out down the middle of the King's Road. He came to the familiar black railings and sprinted up the gravel driveway and into the church. David's voice was very low, very intense, and stopped Marcus as he slipped inside the heavy wooden door.

'Hopefully some of you will have felt something when we prayed at the end of the last session. If you didn't feel anything, then don't worry. It happens at different speeds and with different intensities for different people. But just keep on praying, keep on asking God to come into your life. And he will come. I remember a Course member several years back who approached me on the final day of the Course. He said that he had been asking God to come in and was beginning to despair when he sat in the church silently after one Tuesday-night session. And what he realised, he told me, was that God had been there all along, that he simply needed to open his mind a little more to see that.'

Here he put his hand on the Bible that sat on his lectern, closed his eyes and nodded. From his vantage point at the back of the church, Marcus could see Leo, the lighting and sound engineer, slowly increasing the intensity of the white light until it looked as though the priest had a halo. David opened his eyes suddenly and fixed the room with a fierce gaze.

'What happens when it gets difficult? When the doubts that we – quite naturally – feel grow into something more fundamental, more painful? What happens when we lose our ability to speak to God? For me, it was to do with suffering. You may know that the Course runs a charity out in South Africa that buys a Bible for every schoolchild in Soweto when they reach the age of twelve. I went out there seven years ago and it was quite wonderful to see the joy on the faces of those young people as they were handed their Bibles and given a blessing. But I also saw some very painful things. I went with a group of the children to visit their parents in an AIDS clinic. I took two of the kids to get tested there themselves. One of them had the disease. I spent time talking with this wide-eyed, happy little girl, and I knew that, because her mother was sick and she had no other family, she wouldn't be able to get hold of drugs to treat her condition and would very likely die young and alone.'

David looked up, his pale eyes moist.

'I found myself assaulted by some very serious doubts. What were we doing giving these children Bibles, I asked myself, when there were things they needed so much more? And how could my God, the God I'd given my life to serve, allow this to happen? These doubts caught me quite by surprise. I think that many of us feel that once we have filled that God-shaped hole that we all feel inside us, that we're there, that we've done all of the hard work. But faith requires constant attention. It took me a lot of prayer, a lot of late-night discussions with Sally, and the Bishop and other Course members, before I found my faith again. The problem of suffering is one of the great struggles for the believer, and it's one you must continue to fight. Now let us pray.'

Marcus made his way tiptoeing down the aisle and took up his seat beside Abby, who was bent over in prayer, her hair hanging down in fronds that were caught in the candlelight. After a few moments he was standing again as they made their way to the stage. He hadn't been able to attend the last band practice and knew that he was going to struggle to keep up. His fingers felt fat and lethargic, he was still thinking about the case Michael Faraday had brought him in on, was still mentally outside the church, unprepared for the shift away from the everyday world.

As the weeks passed, Course regulars were allowed to move further forward in the church, so that the new members grew used to the sense of being part of a revelation, a happening. Marcus looked at the congregation as his guitar stumbled its way through the first song. Three blonde girls stood with their faces turned upwards, broad smiles unleashed at the stage. They sang along with Abby, swaying as they sang. They were the wives of three of the Course's largest donors – a trio of hedge-fund entrepreneurs who were millionaires by twenty-seven. One of the girls was enormously pregnant. Her belly rocked from side to side as she moved. Marcus could see the outline of her belly button pressing against her black T-shirt.

Abby had sung the first song standing very still, her hands

pressed together in prayer, her eyes closed, her face turned up-wards. The next song was faster and Marcus had to lean over his bass and watch his fingers, looking up every so often to try to work out which chords David was playing. Marcus felt that the band was only a small step away from catastrophe. He was certain he was about to lose track of the music altogether. Lee was slumped at the piano, dejection hovering in a cloud over her, her chords thin and without feeling. Mouse was spinning his sticks in the air, half an eye on the three girls in the front row. Only David held them together, his rhythm guitar accel-erating as the song moved towards the chorus.

It was then that Abby started to dance. David approved of dancing. He believed that it helped the congregation draw closer to a state of ecstasy. But Abby was really moving, lifting the microphone stand off the ground and slamming it back down, kicking her legs up in the air and whooping between the lines of the chorus. Slowly, the audience picked up on her energy, and the three girls in the front row raised their hands above their heads. Neil, Maki and Philip, standing in the pew behind the girls, began to shuffle awkwardly. Some of the younger members off to the side stood on their chairs, people moved to the open spaces of the aisle and the Lady Chapel and danced wildly, shaking their heads and holding their hands up to the stage, which was now flooded with bright white light. The twins spun in a tight circle in the centre of the aisle, gripping each other by the elbows. The stained-glass window behind the band was luminous, the altar cloth glowed gold. When the final chorus arrived everyone was singing, the music pounded with the rhythm of their hearts, the dancing reached a frenzy and the three girls at the front were shriek-ing, thumping their chests and then screaming out. Then the final chord and the last echoes swirled up into the high silence of the roof.

Abby bent double, her arms hanging down at her sides. Marcus was breathing heavily. His fingers were numb from playing, small blood blisters grew in the channels that ran across his fingertips. The cheering started. Throughout the church they applauded, calling out and laughing and shouting their approval. Even Lee was smiling. Mouse was juggling his drumsticks and then played a quick roll on the snare. When the cheering stopped, they left the stage and made their way downstairs for the discussions.

Marcus and Abby were still flushed, their cheeks red and their chests rising. Marcus knew that it was in music that he came closest to God, came nearest to the appreciation of the divine that Abby seemed to find so easy. It allowed him to escape himself and the cynicism that questioned religion in a mocking voice, that laughed at Abby's credulousness. There was another round of applause from their group when they walked into the small room in the crypt. Marcus took Abby's hand and they bowed together.

'Thanks, guys,' Marcus said, sitting down. 'I enjoyed that. Now tonight I'd like to talk to you about the issue of suffering. Because, as David said earlier, it's one of the biggest questions we face. I almost ended up leaving the first time I did the Course, just because I couldn't get my head around it. And I still have trouble with it. I still have doubts. So I'm going to ask my lovely wife to help out if I go slightly off-message.' He looked at Abby and smiled. She still seemed wired: she was sitting on her hands and rocking forward on the balls of her feet, leaning into the centre of the circle.

'You heard David refer to it in his speech, the fact that there are much easier ways of explaining away suffering. Either that God isn't able to stop children getting leukaemia or whatever, or that He can't be everywhere at once and helps some but not all, or that He doesn't want to end their suffering. And when you watch the news at night it makes it very difficult to believe that an omniscient, omnipotent and omnibenevolent God exists.'

Marcus saw David in the doorway watching him. He paused for a moment, looked at the faces all turned towards him, saw that Abby was still sitting on her hands, although she was now rocking her chair backwards, coming perilously close to falling. Marcus rose and stood behind his wife, his hands upon her shoulders. He knew he was mimicking David's tone, his modulation.

'When Eve ate the fruit in the Garden she took a decision that would affect everything that came after. She acted with her own will rather than being a slave. And thus the moment of Original Sin was also the moment when we gained freedom. And every small victory, every freely willed act, is a celebration of that first rebellion. God punishes us through the suffering in the world. He punishes us because that is the natural balance of things: we had the chance to stay in Eden, to live a life of comfortable slavery, but we chose freedom. And how much richer even the most tragic life, even a life cut short, knowing that we have the freedom to make our own choices, to carve our own way through that life . . .'

Marcus felt like he was growing, inflating to fill the room. It was not a feeling that he enjoyed. He stared down at the faces of the members of the group, the young blonde girls and their boyfriends, Neil, Abby; he looked over to David, who was smiling broadly in the doorway. He continued to speak and there were no questions, no interruptions, just the purity of thought expressed in clear, calm words. But all the time there was humming at the back of his mind the static of hypocrisy. He knew he sounded slick, knew they were all hanging on his words, that Abby would be proud of him. But he felt fraudulent and spivvy.

When the session was over he tried to slip away from the group. He wanted to sit in the car in darkness until Abby had finished helping Sally clear up the dinner pans, then drive them back to the flat to continue their reclusive life. As he climbed the pale stone stairs into the church he felt an arm around his shoulders. It was David.

'That was wonderful, tonight. You seemed inspired. Did you feel like the Spirit was moving in you?'

Marcus paused. David began to rub his thumb gently down the line of Marcus's collarbone. Marcus shivered.

'I don't know. It felt very fluent and easy, but I don't know if it was spiritual. You know that I had a problem with this part of the Course, and so I've worked really hard to make sure that I'm on top of it, that I know all of the arguments and can regurgitate them almost without thinking.'

They were now walking down the aisle together. Their voices were distorted by the height above them. Marcus watched Abby collecting forks in a bowl; Sally followed after her throwing paper plates into a black plastic bag. The priest dropped his hand from Marcus's shoulder. They sat down together facing the altar. Marcus tried to explain himself, but he felt his words were now muddled and fumbling.

'When I was speaking earlier it felt a lot like it does when I'm arguing a case at work. You know it's very rare that anyone I'm defending is innocent. We're expensive, so we usually get the guilty guys. I don't ever get to do anything as glamorous as speaking in court. But I always get sent in to speak to the other side's legal team. And it's because I can speak like that, with that fluency, giving the impression of being totally in charge, totally on top of things. When, in fact, I'm peddling half-truths and relying on intimidation and legal sleight of hand. It was like that tonight. All that stuff about Original Sin and Free Will – it's not enough. It's not enough of an excuse for the bad stuff that happens in the world. And I know it's bullshit, but I spout it anyway.'

The priest was silent for a moment, then stood up slowly. He hovered over Marcus. Marcus could see the muscles in David's jaw working. He watched the priest's hands. The right hand seized the fingers of the left and squeezed until they were white, corpselike.

'I've built something astonishing here, something that will outlast all of us.' David's voice was icy. 'I've been watching you very carefully. I'm worried that I made the wrong choice when I decided to bring you into the inner circle of this church. Look around you. You could be someone here, really make something of yourself. The Course is exploding. It's going global.' He focused his eyes on Marcus's and extended his cold, thin hand to Marcus's shoulder again. He pressed his thumb on the collarbone.

'I'm trying. I just thought that I should tell you if I was having these doubts, rather than keep them to myself.'

David continued as if he hadn't heard, increasing the pressure on Marcus's collarbone.

'Have you stopped to think about why two of your members left after the first week? Because it certainly wasn't Abby's fault. People can sense the contradictions in you, how you struggle against yourself. You drink too much, you smoke too much. I watch you; I can see all that excess. I see the flames of hell lapping at your feet. Remember that the Devil is always there. He is desperate for me to fail, for the Course to fail. So I have to look for him at every turn. Don't let the Devil work through you, Marcus. Don't let it be you that he uses to bring this all down. I am watching you.' The priest dropped his hand from Marcus's shoulder and began to walk away from him. Course members scuttled in the shadows of the north and south aisles. David turned back towards him, his hand held in the air, fingers still in pincer grip.

'I'll see you on Sunday. Remember what I said.' David's voice had returned to its public register. Marcus watched the priest make his way to the door and out into the night.

Marcus sat for a while longer, feeling flat and confused, his collarbone throbbing. Then the lights began to go out, and he was sitting in darkness. He knew the layout of the church and found his way in blindness to the door and out into the damp autumn night. He sat in the Audi and listened to the radio until Abby's outline appeared against the warm yellow of the open rectory door. She bounded towards the car, climbed into the passenger seat, and let out a long, contented sigh.

'That was just marvellous. I'm still buzzing.' She fiddled with the radio as they pulled out onto the King's Road. Marcus stared ahead into the dark.

'It's the first time I've felt really properly alive since the baby,' she continued, speaking over a stuttering procession of different radio stations. 'It's amazing how music can lift you out of yourself. It's what David always says, isn't it? That we're nearest to God in music and silence.'

Marcus accelerated through an amber light, clenching the steering wheel hard. Abby found a channel that played buoyant dance music and sang along happily as they made their way through thick traffic homewards.

*

Marcus reached for a bottle of red wine as soon as they walked in the door, slumped on the sofa and opened a copy of the *New Statesman*. Abby knew he had read it weeks before. She watched his eyes, which didn't move with the text but instead seemed to stare through the paper into the distance. He slurped the wine as he drank it, rolling it in his mouth and sucking air over it on his tongue. It sounded disgusting but Abby sat at the table watching him and didn't say anything. She felt suddenly terribly far from him, unable to bridge the distance between them. When they brushed their teeth she saw him spit purple into the sink and noticed that his lips were still stained black from the wine.

Later in bed she tried to talk to him. She knew he had drunk enough to make him irritable, but she needed to connect with him. She needed to let him know how proud she was of his preaching – because that was what it was, he had preached and it sounded just like David. She pressed herself against him, felt the familiar boniness of his body, the muscles under his armpits and along his neck, the hard curve of his arse.

'You were amazing tonight, darling. I know you must be exhausted, but I want you to know how proud I am of you.'

Marcus stopped himself speaking for a moment. He knew he was irrationally angry. He hadn't eaten dinner and had drunk just enough to pull a black veil over his mind. He always regretted these rages in the morning, even though in the moment he felt such enormous clarity, felt as though the world was transparent and he could finally see the workings of the machine. But he loved Abby, and he struggled to keep his thoughts inside.

'I'm so tired. Please, let's just go to sleep.'

'But I can't. I want to talk about it with you. Did you feel my energy? I mean, the way I danced in that song it was like I was full of something burning. I think we're going to do an amazing job this year. It's sad that we've lost a couple already, but I really think the rest of them will stick it out. Wouldn't that be marvellous?'

'Yes, that'd be great. 'Night.'

She was quiet for a moment. Then, slipping her hand slowly

inside the tracksuit bottoms he wore to bed, she took hold of his cock.

'Let's have sex, darling. I really want you. And I think what happened tonight might have been a message. I think it's maybe a sign that if we do it tonight it'll all work out.'

She felt Marcus growing hard, wrestled her nightie over her head and switched on the bedside light. When she turned back to him she saw Marcus lying staring up at the ceiling. He was cracking his knuckles.

'What is it?' She placed her hand on his stomach.

'I don't want to have sex. Not after tonight.'

'Come on, darling. You were just like David in that discussion group, magnetic.' She took his cock in her hand again and found it small and limp.

'I'm sorry. I just don't find things as easy as you do.'

She began to tug gently at his penis, taking his hand and placing it over her pussy.

'I don't find it easy, darling. But it gets easier the more you do it.' She began to move herself back and forward, pressing herself against his fingers.

'But I get the impression that with you it's instinctual, something that comes naturally. It's a real struggle for me.'

Abby was panting slightly. Marcus's cock was still small and shrewlike in her hand.

'Why do you always have to make everything so difficult, darling? Just relax and go with the flow. Good things will happen, I promise.'

Marcus pulled his hand away from her and sat up in bed.

'What is it? What's wrong?'

'Jesus, I don't know if I can handle this.' He wouldn't look at her as he spoke.

'What do you mean, this?'

'I mean us, a baby, the life you have chosen for us. I'm beginning to wonder how we got old so quickly.'

She stood up, clasping her nightie in a ball at her chest. Her voice came out very clear and controlled.

'It's not my fault. Your life is not my fault.'

'What does that mean?'

Her voice when it came was still soft, but cold and spiked.

'It means I think sometimes that I'm making the same mistake my sisters made. Marrying weak men. My mother always said that we would never be happy together. I think she might have been right.'

She was breathing heavily, twisting the soft cotton nightie into a ball. Marcus still wouldn't look at her. She tried to take his hand, but he drew it away.

'I'm sorry, darling. I didn't mean it. I love you. That's my problem, I just love you so much. And I need for us to be together, for us to have a child. I'll try very hard to make things better for you.'

But Marcus was already gone. Whenever they argued like this he would retreat into himself, draw up his defences and become as still and silent as a monk, lost to Abby.

'Don't do this, please don't do this. Speak to me. What are you thinking?' He sat immobile as she stroked his hair. Abby began to cry, large hot tears rolling down her cheeks.

'Why are you crying?' he asked, his voice very cold.

She looked down at him as she stood, her nightie clutched to her chest. 'Because you're not,' she said, and ran from the room. She slammed the door as she left.

Marcus sat on the bed and watched the windows of the high Edwardian houses opposite. Scattered yellow squares of light glowed against the dim white walls like the doors of an advent calendar. A train rattled somewhere. When he went to look for Abby he found her sitting very still on the sofa, her nightie on, the main lights in the room casting her shadow on the wall behind her. Marcus sat down next to her and placed a kiss on her wrinkled brow.

'I'm sorry,' he said.

'I'm sorry, too.' She turned to him and draped her arms around his shoulders. He felt her hot breath on the skin of his neck.

'All I want is for you to be happy. I know I haven't always been there for you, but this time I am. We're going to make a baby, and you'll be an amazing mother. And I'll love the baby all the more because half of it is you.'

'Oh, darling,' she said, and pressed her wet face into the hollow of his neck.

They made their way back to the bed in the spare room. A bird was singing somewhere in the darkness outside the window. They slept tightly curled together that night as they had done when they shared his single bed at university, and he fell asleep with the beating of her heart thumping against his cheek, the words of a prayer circling his mind. *Don't let me die just yet, Lord. I don't want to die.*

Seven

This girl was very good. Mouse liked her expressionless face, the clinical air she had about her. Once he had walked out without speaking to the masseuse. There had been a lasciviousness in the way she greeted him, something sluttish in her clothing and smile, something that suggested she was open to going further than a massage. But this one clearly understood what he was looking for. When her fingers rested on his perineum, he allowed himself a brief sigh of contentment, encouraging her to stay there. She was naked. There was a long mirror down one wall of the room and he watched her breasts move as she ran her hands up the inside of his thighs. Dark nipples. She sucked her lip in concentration. She looked a little like Lee. Brown hair but the same sense of seriousness. He thought she was Swedish, but didn't want to ask.

Mouse had slipped out of work early and made his way to the large Georgian house on Gloucester Place. He was always staggered by the economics of it, that a place of such grandeur could be maintained by six or seven masseuses and their balding, unthreatening male receptionist. He paid one hundred pounds for his forty-five-minute session. Something soothing and Eastern played on a hidden stereo. A gamelan, a sitar. She sat astride one of his thighs as she massaged his arse and he could feel the soft slick hair of her pussy on his skin. It amused him that these girls – some of whom were English and well-spoken, a step above the sex-trafficked skag addicts in the brothel next door – fooled themselves into thinking that what they did was somehow better than prostitution. Eastern mysticism was in high vogue, and they must have felt that it lent dignity to their compromised lives. He had found the place through a website that promised 'enhanced consciousness' and 'a way to rebalance the chakras'. Of course it was nothing more than a posh handjob. But the pretence suited Mouse, who didn't want to have sex with these girls, just needed an hour of being touched, an hour when he could lose himself in physical pleasure without feeling that he was breaking the rules of the Course.

He had argued with Lee earlier that day. It was not a serious disagreement, just one of the small moments of friction that invigorated their relationship. He knew he had been staring at her too much in the library earlier. Perched behind his desk, he had been conjuring a daydream of exquisite beauty starring Lee against a deserted rocky beach and pine trees growing down to the sea. He stared at her and imagined her naked back pressed to the rough bark of the pine, her feet in the water and her arms stretched above her, her breasts falling forward as she dived in. She smiled at him the first few times she caught his eye, but then her expression grew increasingly irritated. A tall and aristocratic-looking student sitting next to Lee kept glancing at Mouse, whispering in her ear and then looking back at him with a frown. By this time Mouse was imagining Lee in the empty hall high above them in the tower of Senate House, her clothes scattered on the parquet floor, her hair falling down over her shoulders like Dulac's Little Mermaid.

Lee had refused to have lunch with him and had disappeared towards the Brunswick Centre on the arm of her newly appointed protector. She didn't come back that afternoon. After a sad sandwich in the staff cafeteria, Mouse went back to the library, found where the tall boy had been working and removed three pages of notes from his desk, folding them and placing them at the bottom of the bin as he made his way to the lift. He called ahead and booked his massage and then set out along the Euston Road.

As he lay on the bed with its sheet that was bobbled from too many washes, too many attempts to rinse out the oil and come and sweat, he felt the heaviness that had dogged his day lifting. He had been to a dinner party at the house of an older girl from the Course the night before. A girl who had once seemed to offer an escape from his obsession with Lee. Three years ago, he had taken her to the theatre, and then on to a bar, spending money he didn't have getting her drunk. He had tried to kiss her in the taxi back west, and she laughed at him, told him that he was a dear pal, but she had a boyfriend, didn't he know? Now the boyfriend had become a husband, the girl's stomach strained against the material of her maternity dress, and her cheeks glowed every time she looked at her wealthy, successful mate. Mouse had played his part during dinner – the doting, unthreatening friend, laughing at her jokes and reaching out to touch the taut skin of her stomach to feel – there! – a kick. But he raged as he walked home, shouted prayers into the night sky, screamed at the desperate unfairness of it all.

The masseuse asked him to turn onto his back and he did so. He could see her looking at him, at the large belly that sat above his short, skinny legs, giving his body the appearance of a toffee apple abandoned on the bed. His cock stood straining, pulsing against the bulge of his stomach. She began to massage his feet, rubbing warm oil onto the hard pads of his soles.

He was worried about his friends. Lee was a constant concern, but now Marcus and Abby seemed argumentative, strung out. They rarely came to the pub after the Course. Dark pouches hung beneath Marcus's eyes. The Retreat was like a beacon ahead. Only three more days and then they'd be together for the weekend, and all things would be well again. David had told him that the Retreat would be held at the Earl's country house on the edge of the Cotswolds, Lancing Manor. Each year it was somewhere different, the exact location never revealed to the new members until the night before. Mouse thought back to the Retreats he had been on so far: some of the best days of his life. He didn't know what he'd do without the Course.

The girl began to move her way up his body. First his calves; resting her arse on his foot, she ran her oiled fingers up one leg and then the next, kneading the muscle, moving her thumbs in circles around his knees. Then his thighs, which she pulled and stretched, making her way slowly up to the join of leg and groin, the fold of skin where his pubic hair started. She brushed his cock by accident and he felt it thrill.

*

Lee had discovered him. Three weeks into term and he had only left his room in college for lectures and meals. Sitting on his own in the wood-panelled dining hall under badly painted pictures of morally upright fellows, he would shovel the food into his mouth as quickly as he could, reading a novel to discourage any of the other outcasts from claiming him as one of their own. He watched the surrounding tables with bored scorn. Marcus's voice was always the loudest, his laugh audible from the quadrangle below. Everyone knew Marcus. And Abby at his side, striking and statuesque, but Mouse could see her in fifteen years' time when she'd be hulking and matronly. Daffy and all of the other laddish types who followed Marcus around were not the sort of people Mouse had come to university to meet. So he sat reading the novels of André Gide, with his blond hair flopping in front of his eyes, and left when his plate was clean.

One evening, scurrying across the quad after dinner, he saw a girl watching him from a window high in the wide blank wall of the college's main building. He recognised her vaguely. She was friends with Marcus and his crowd. Her face looked young and lost as she peered out into the misty air. The face disappeared into darkness and Mouse climbed the spiral staircase to his own room, the smallest room in college. His clothes were still in his suitcase, perched at the foot of his bed. Books were everywhere, reaching in perilous piles towards the ceiling, three deep on the windowsill, filling the drawers of his dresser. He opened the window and stared out across the college lawn towards the parks. Only a small desk lamp lit the room behind him and he felt somehow powerful up there in his cupboard of a room, looking down over the world.

He watched people walking back to their rooms after dinner, heard brief snatches of conversation. Then there was a knock on his door. Mouse panicked for a moment, stared around his room and thrust handfuls of dirty socks and boxer shorts into drawers, stuffing them between tightly packed books. When he opened the door he saw the girl who had been watching him from the high window earlier. He stepped forward and tried to pull the door closed behind him to block her view inside. She placed one hand on the door frame. She wore a hooded sweatshirt and tracksuit bottoms, scuffed trainers on her feet.

'Can I come in? You're Alastair, right?' Her voice was deep and cool.

Mouse looked behind him and sucked his stomach in as she squeezed past him.

'Wow, this room is tiny. Bad luck. My name is Lee, by the way.'

She took off her shoes and sat down on his bed, lifting his suitcase onto the floor. He saw her eyes scanning the piles of books. She reached over and picked up a tattered copy of *The Wind in the Willows*.

'Oh, I love this. I had forgotten how much I did, but then I read it over the summer. It's magic.'

Mouse's eyes bulged even more. He sat down in his desk chair, knocking a pile of books over as he swung round to face her. They were only a foot apart and Mouse could smell her shampoo.

'Do you really like it? I think it's a serious work. I mean really very spiritual. It's my favourite. I read it when I can't sleep.'

Lee looked around the room. *Treasure Island* lay open on top of a copy of *Eugénie Grandet*, *The Famous Five* rubbed shoulders with *La Vie mode d'emploi*, *Struwwelpeter* with *Les Fleurs du mal*.

'What are you studying?' she asked.

'French.'

'So why all the kids' books?'

Mouse blew his fringe upwards and spun a pencil on his desk.

'I've always taken them with me. My dad is in the army and we travelled around a lot when I was young. I just got used to having my books around me. All I have to do is read the beginning of *The Lion, the Witch and the Wardrobe* and I feel . . . I don't know, safe. It's a wee bit sad, I suppose, but no worse than television.'

She set down *The Wind in the Willows* on top of the Bible that lay beside his bed. She took off her jumper; her singlet rode up as she lifted it, revealing a flat white stomach. Mouse tried not to look at the softness of her breasts under the vest, the black bra straps on her shoulders. She leaned over suddenly and, very close, breathed a question at him. He felt a flutter of panic, felt time slowing, making the air around them heavy.

'What's your accent? Where are you from?'

She stroked his flushed, fleshy cheek with cold fingers. He spoke quickly, stumbling on his words.

'I'm from Scotland. Well, I grew up in Germany and then came back over here when I was thirteen. We were in Shropshire for a wee while and then my dad was posted to Barry, outside of Dundee. It's where his family are from. I don't really know what my accent is. I try to make it as ordinary as possible. It's just how I speak, you know?'

With the light cutting along her cheek, he thought she was very beautiful. He could see fading summer freckles across her forehead, lying like stars along her arms. He noticed that she wore different-coloured earrings in her ears. He wondered if she knew that they didn't match. Her tracksuit bottoms were frayed around the heel. He felt suddenly ashamed of his body, the way his stomach pushed out beneath his T-shirt, his goggling eyes.

'What are you doing here? I mean, I'm glad you came over, but I didn't think people like you mixed with people like me. Why aren't you out with Abby and Marcus?'

She drew back a little and smiled at him.

'I saw you at dinner the other night and I thought you looked nice. I don't want to hang out with just those people. I want to meet people like you. I think we could be friends.'

'Well I don't. I didn't ask you to come over. I just want to get on with my work. All of the other students in my tutorials have spent every holiday since they were kids in France. They worked in Paris on their gap years, have pretentious parents who insist on French at the dinner table once a week, you know? I'm at a disadvantage from the start and so I am going to need to work really hard to keep up. I think you're grand, Lee, and I'm pleased to have met you, but maybe you should go. I can't really deal with this now.'

She looked at him with a frown, knitting her eyebrows together, then pulled back the duvet and slipped into his bed. He watched her wriggle like a fish for a moment and then saw the tracksuit trousers slither slowly to the floor.

'Will you read me a story, Alastair?'

'Um . . . OK. Call me Mouse. People call me Mouse.'

So he opened *The Wind in the Willows*, took a deep breath, and began to read.

'The Willow-Wren was twittering his thin little song, hidden himself in the dark selvedge of the river bank. Though it was past ten o'clock at night, the sky still clung to and retained some lingering skirts of light . . .'

Lee slept in his bed that night. She wore one of his T-shirts and they lay in the close darkness hugging, talking in whispered voices. He massaged her thin back with his thumbs, feeling the closeness of the bones under her skin. She let him kiss her lips, but kept them tightly closed when he tried to move his tongue inside. He was also allowed to feel her breasts and her arse through her clothes, but she pushed him away when he tried to slip his hands under the waistband of her pants. Neither of them slept, and when the sun rose he sat on the windowsill reading aloud from *The Wind in the Willows* again. She lay back with her eyes closed, smiling.

*

It was the closest he had come to something sexual with Lee. And it was why he went for these massages. He had enough self-knowledge to realise that it was in pursuit of those early nights with Lee that he went to the tall Georgian house in

Marylebone. He slid back to the present, away from memory, as the girl massaging him started to apply oil to her naked body. Her breasts shimmered, her stomach glistened. She began to chant.

'Om, shanti, om . . .'

Pressing her breasts together, she slid over his body, rubbing herself against him, all of the slippery warmth of her vibrating with her chanting. He began to intone the mantra and allowed his mind to empty entirely, felt the world centre on his groin. She moved faster, flinging her body over his; she was panting. Mouse's voice rose to a wail as he came hot shots over his own belly, over hers. She mopped at herself with a towel and then handed him some tissues. In the aftermath he felt empty. His breath came tightly into his chest, escaping with a high wheeze. The girl dressed in the mirror and then left the room. Mouse made his way out into the afternoon. He was carrying his drumsticks.

He decided to walk down to the church. He wasn't due there for another few hours and the massages always filled him with a strange energy. He couldn't go more than once a month, though. The emotional and financial expense precluded it. He always felt a heady sense of guilt afterwards. He nurtured it, enjoyed it as one can enjoy any pain that is rare and self-inflicted. It helped to give shape to his time at the Course knowing what it was like to sin.

He dived through the underpass at Marble Arch and came out into the north-eastern corner of Hyde Park. It had been a cut-glass autumn day, the leaves threw a multicoloured net over damp grass. Now with the light fading over them, two boys flew a kite which was silhouetted against the rich blue of the western sky. He watched the kite shudder for a moment in the high air, whip in the wind and then crash to earth. He walked along the avenue of trees down towards Knightsbridge, imagining those who once rode alongside him, Victorian ladies with their bodies hot under stiff-collared clothes perching side-saddle as gentlemen with enormous sculpted moustaches raised their hats and bowed. Mouse ran up the hillock upon which Achilles was perched and placed his hand on the cold bronze of the statue's calf. Then along the south side of the park, past the rose gardens and the last dying games of football, until he came out by the lake.

*

Those first few weeks with Lee were bright in his mind. When it had all seemed ahead of him, when it had promised so much. He wasn't to know that he wouldn't get any further, that her coldness was something more than the initial prudishness of a sensitive teenage girl. They spent all of their time together during that wonderful autumn, and it felt to Mouse that he lived under two skies: the natural sky above and the artificial sky that Lee cast over him. Mouse carried her books to the English faculty and left her with a lip-kiss at the door before running to his own lectures. They'd walk to dinner together and then sit and smoke cigarettes until it was time to go to the pub, or to Marcus's room to hang out with Abby and the others. Marcus had the biggest room in college and there was always booze and often drugs on offer. Mouse didn't mind that Lee described him as her discovery, presented him to the others with a note of possession in her voice. He wanted to be owned by her.

They were generous with him. For his nineteenth birthday Marcus and Abby bought him an early edition of *The Lion, the Witch and the Wardrobe* inscribed to him with their love. Lee gave him a golden signet ring and had an invented coat of arms engraved upon it. She placed it upon Mouse's finger as they lay in bed the night of his birthday. He held it to the light, looked at the engraving of a turret with what he thought was a mouse rampant atop it. He laid his hand down on the bulge of his bare stomach and saw the ring shimmer, then placed it gently over Lee's left breast. They slept in the same bed for the first term. She said she was lonely in her room alone. She would let him take his clothes off and press himself against her, sighing with pleasure as he ran his hands over her flannel pyjamas, circled her nipples through the soft cloth, ground his groin against her thighs. But still she wouldn't let him go any further; she kept her pants on under her pyjamas, and threatened to leave when he insisted too vehemently.

Lee had asked Mouse along to the Course one night in December. A freezing wind nudged them along the wide high street as they walked out after supper. Lee wore a coat with a sandy fur collar and clung hard to Mouse's arm as they reached the dark quadrangle of the graduate college. They had made their way into the dimly lit chapel where candles flickered above carved wooden choir stalls and chairs were set out in a circle on the ornate mosaic floor. Mouse sat and watched Lee, contributing little to the conversation. When they sang he mouthed the words silently, preferring to listen to Lee's rich, low voice rising to fill the small chapel. When they came out into a night made suddenly bright with snow, breathlessly cold, she had turned to him, eyes streaming.

'So what did you think?'

'I thought it was brilliant,' he replied. 'Really moving.'

'Do you think you'd like to come again? I'd love it if you would.'

He thought for a moment. 'I'll give it a try. I've been thinking for a wee while that I needed something new, some way of negotiating life. Life just seems . . . it seems unfair at a very deep level. Not just the inequalities in society, but the way that the most successful people also seem to be the most awful. Something isn't right with the world and I need a way of dealing with it. I'm not sure that this is it, but if you believe in it, I'll come with you.'

'I saw a Bible in your room.'

'I've been trying to read it a little bit every night. It's a cultural document, you know? It all makes a bit more sense now.'

At the next service, a guest speaker had stood in the centre of the circle of chairs and fixed each of them in turn with his pale eyes. His sandy hair was flecked with grey and he wore a white shirt, chinos and a blue blazer. Mouse thought he looked like a banker. But when he spoke, the small chapel came alive. He had talked about the emptiness of modern life, the way that everything had lost meaning in a world cheapened by consumerism and sex. He marched up and down the room as he spoke, slamming his fist into his hand for emphasis, and Mouse, who hadn't been to church since his mum took him to Christmas services as a child, was hooked. He and Lee had gone to the pub with the speaker afterwards. His name was David Nightingale.

*

A bicycle screeched to a halt behind Mouse. He dropped his drumsticks and scrabbled in the gutter to retrieve them.

'Watch where the fuck you're going!'

Mouse had stepped into the road without looking. He had crossed the park and was walking down Queen's Gate. The sun had sunk from the sky and now it was almost dark. The yellow taxi lights that flashed past seemed like the warmest lights he had ever seen. Finally, he was on the King's Road and he could see St Botolph's spire black against the dusk sky. Mouse rapped out a tattoo with his drumsticks on a wheelie bin. He was looking forward to playing later.

He made his way past the vicarage, keeping to the shadows. He could see Abby and Sally Nightingale in the rectory's kitchen. Abby was talking and helping to roll out sheets of pastry, while Sally nodded and smiled every so often. The church was empty when he went into it. A flickering lamp glowed in the Lady Chapel, and the ceiling was lit by the spotlights that illuminated the church from the outside. He relished being in the church on his own. He reached down and pulled out a prayer cushion, knelt upon it and rested his head in his hands.

'O, God, protect my mum. I'm sorry that I'm not always there for my friends. I'm sorry that I sometimes think and do things that I know disappoint you.' He spoke the words out loud in a small, soft voice, more Scottish than his everyday accent. 'Please, Lord, I pray that I might achieve all the things that David asks of me. I pray that the Course might grow and flourish. O, Lord, let all be well.'

He bent forward until he was almost lying flat and pressed his hands to the cold stone floor. He felt safe in the darkness of the old church. He understood the age of the place, recognised the terms for its distinguishing features, knew the faces of the saints in the main altar window as he knew those of his friends. He had a photograph of the inside of the church pinned to a cork board on the wall of the boat. Lee had taken the picture just before the start of a Course evening, looking up through the candles towards the spotlit altar. He liked to line up his eyes with the shot when he came into the church. He laid his cheek against the stone floor, shut one eye, made a soft clicking noise and then slowly rose to his feet.

He felt islanded that evening: very distant from the other members of the Course; not scornful, or resentful of their privilege, but as if they were from a reality so profoundly different from his own that they might as well have been characters from a novel. He sat slightly apart from Lee as David stood to introduce the guest speaker – a well-known artist who had been a heroin addict until he was persuaded to attend the Course. Mouse half-listened to him, keen to get on with the music and the discussion session when they would talk about the Retreat.

It was Lee who had suggested they form a band. She used to take Mouse to the college music rooms late at night when neither of them could sleep that first cold winter at university. She'd play the 'Promenade' from *Pictures at an Exhibition* in the dark, and Mouse would sit very still as Lee rocked backwards and forwards, humming softly behind the music. Marcus was a decent guitarist and played after dinner parties when everyone would smoke and sing, Abby's voice standing out above the others, high and clear. Mouse had learned to play the drums. He was co-ordinated and had a good sense of rhythm, and Lee was endlessly patient playing alongside him as he bashed away on the college's kit until one of the serious musicians came and told them to stop. For Christmas that year Lee gave him a snare and a high-hat which he carried up to Scotland on the train and practised as the snow built up outside his window.

They played gigs in bars and clubs throughout university, had a regular slot in a pub on Sunday afternoons, did friends' birthdays, the wedding receptions of their friends' older siblings. It was another way to spend time together. It was only when Lee introduced Mouse to the Course, and they met David, that they realised that music was a way to God. When they moved to London, and Abby and Marcus joined the Course, David persuaded Marcus to take up the bass, implementing a stricter regime of band practices. It was David who chose the name of the band and had *The Revelations* printed across Mouse's drum kit. David and Lee had regular songwriting sessions, where Lee would adapt lyrics from the religious texts she studied at university and David would set them to music.

That evening at the Course they played one of these songs. The older Course members knew the words and stood with their arms wide and their faces towards the roof, singing. Staring out over the candlelight, Mouse found himself mouthing along as he drummed. Lee had taken the lyrics from Julian of Norwich's *Revelations of Divine Love*; he remembered her scribbling them in an old exercise book one afternoon at her flat, thumbing through a tattered copy of the mystical text as she wrote. Now the ancient words were new-made, sung over driving rock music.

> 'In falling and rising again,
> We're always kept in that same precious love.
> Between God and the soul there is no in between,
> So we pray and our prayers fill our hearts
>   with your endless love.'

He thumped his foot down on the bass drum, smashed the cymbal and tapped away at the high-hat: it was the perfect instrument for him. Only when he was playing the drums did he lose the feeling of jittery energy that had once sent him running in mad bursts around the quads at university, that caused him to fiddle and jiggle and jerk his way through life.

In the discussion group they talked about the Retreat. Mouse stood up immediately as the group settled in the room in the crypt.

'It's the most brilliant experience. It should really be viewed as the pinnacle of your time here. Although there are sessions afterwards, they draw heavily upon what you learn at the

Retreat. It's a time for us to bond, for us to really talk – not in the way we do here, but with real depth. There'll be a few wee services to go to, but the rest of the time is yours to speak with David, speak with us. I have to say I'm jealous of you. I'd love to have my first Retreat all over again.'

'My first Retreat', said Lee, 'made me feel like a child.' Her voice took on a dreamy note. 'It was all so simple, and so perfect. Beautiful autumn weather and time to spend with friends. And they've all been like that, ever since. The Retreat is an oasis.' She was wearing a short denim skirt over dark tights and her hair was tied with an elastic band in an untidy pile on her head. Mouse could smell something rich and un-washed when he moved close to her. He noticed that her tights were laddered.

'Do you ever get anyone who freaks out? I've heard it can be pretty intense.' Philip was looking at Lee, but Mouse answered him.

'It's such a friendly atmosphere. We'll all be there, you know. It's like a massive, brilliant sleep-over.' He smiled.

'But someone told me you have to speak in tongues. I don't know if I want to do that. It sounds a bit weird.' Maki looked at Mouse with her eyebrows raised, but he just smiled and nodded. David had prepared them for this.

'Don't worry too much about what you hear. The whole speaking in tongues thing is just a small part of the Retreat. It's . . . it's a bit like those Magic Eye books. Some people find it really easy, some people just don't get it. If you let yourself go with the flow, you'll get there. Just don't fight it.'

Lee nodded.

'You know David is always going on about how empty the world feels?' she said. 'How our lives are so fragmented and superficial? When you hear the tongues, this beautiful, eerie music, and everyone is chanting together, it makes all of that go away for a while. It's this most extraordinary feeling of release, as if everything suddenly makes sense. And the silence afterwards, it just blows you away . . .'

When the discussion groups were finished, Marcus and Abby said goodbye. Mouse watched them walk off towards the car, Marcus's arm around Abby's broad shoulders. A police siren wailed down by the river and Mouse shivered. Lee came up behind him and slipped her arm through his. Huddled together, giving the impression of one body, so closely were they linked, they made their way to the pub under misty cones of light that hung down from the street lamps.

Mouse kept her clasped closely to him as they sat in a dimly lit corner. At first, they were quiet, and he felt her breaths rise and fall under thin ribs, let her pale, drawn face rest on his shoulder as they watched people go to the bar and play fruit machines and walk out to smoke cigarettes. Lee sighed.

'You know that image from Bede?' she said.

'Hmm?' He had been enjoying the silence and now brought her into focus with difficulty.

'The one that says our lives are like the flight of a sparrow through the night into a bright mead hall? We fly from darkness into light and laughter and then out again into darkness. Sometimes I feel like I've already come out the other side. That my teenage years were my real life, when I lived everything so intensely, when I was completely carefree and wild. And these days I'm just in darkness, flying along without any idea of where I'm going.'

Mouse took a sip of her drink and lifted his arm from around her shoulders. He turned to face her, frowning.

'Honestly, cheer up, will you? The Retreat's almost here. Things can't be as bad as all that now, surely?'

'I'm afraid they are.' Her voice was very low.

'Jesus, Lee, will you get a grip? This self-pity, this constant

114

misery, it's just exhausting. I could strangle you sometimes.' His voice rose in pitch and Lee winced. 'You're young, you're very beautiful, you're scarily clever. A lot of girls would die to have what you have. You need to pull yourself together. This can't go on.'

'Please don't do this. I'm really tightroping at the moment. I need you to keep me steady.' Lee was knitting her hands in her lap.

Mouse could see that Philip and Maki, who were standing at the bar, had stopped talking and were watching them. He lowered his voice.

'Your problem, you know, is that you have forged this identity for yourself around religion. Lee the sexy little party girl has been replaced by Lee the pious saint. But it's not a good religion, not a real one. It's based upon those hysterical women you are such an expert on.'

'I'm going to go . . . I'm leaving now.'

Mouse gripped her wrist and spoke in a violent whisper.

'No you're not, you're going to sit here and listen to me. What you believe is a heavily mediated, crackpot version of religion. Two hours, two short hours is all we have of Jesus, if you read out everything that he actually says in the Bible. Our entire religion is founded on those two hours. Your problem is that you concentrate too little on Christ's words and too much on the hysterical writings of a bunch of madwomen.'

'Some of their stuff is amazing. You've said so yourself.' His hand still gripped her wrist painfully.

'Some of it is beautiful poetry. I can see how it's helpful alongside the real thing. But not as a replacement. I've met some girls in the Course over the years who seem to have based their belief on St Francis, St Augustine. Both heavily mediated versions of real faith. But at least those saints were adepts, at least they were fully schooled in the doctrine, and could serve as reasonable proxies for Christ. Your women are just early incarnations of Christina Rossetti, wringing their hands and moaning and pretending it's a religious experience rather than just frustrated sexuality and thwarted ambition. Hildegard, Catherine of Siena, Margery Kempe – hysteria and weeping were to them what sex was to the Wife of Bath. They won't help you.'

'But they do help me. They make a huge difference to me. And you didn't mention Julian of Norwich. She's no hysteric.'

'Julian spent all her days locked in a cell meditating on Christ's suffering on the cross, fixated on his wounds. This is exactly why you're such a mess. You've put suffering and guilt at the very centre of your conception of faith. These women were writing about their religious feelings, but they were also conveying the very painful truth of what it was like to be a woman in fifteenth-century England. Don't confuse the two. They're leading you in completely the wrong direction. Faith should be a comfort, not an ordeal.'

'They're my role models, and I won't have you talk about them like this. It's fucking hard to say how I feel. When I'm right down in my slumps, I can't find my own words to express it. And not only do the women mystics help me say how I feel, they rephrase my unhappiness as something positive. They make me feel that there might be something good the other side of all this pain.' Her eyes were bright with angry tears.

Mouse let go of her wrist, a little ashamed.

'Do you remember when those boys slapped me?' Lee said, looking at him sharply.

Mouse did remember. They had been walking down the King's Road on the way to the Course the previous summer when two gym-inflated bankers stumbled out of a pub and stood blocking the pavement ahead of them. The bankers had taken their suit jackets off and their ties hung loosely around thick necks. They were sweating and Mouse could see their muscular chests pressing wetly against shirt fabric. As Mouse and Lee passed, he heard one whisper to the other and then, so quickly that he could hardly register it, the banker had turned and slapped Lee hard on the arse. The two men stood, laughing, as Mouse and Lee continued up the road.

'Just keep walking,' Mouse had said, clutching Lee's arm. 'It's not worth it.' Shame and fear sent blood to his round cheeks and goggled his eyes. Lee's mouth hung open and he could see her mind whirring. The bankers' laughter still reached them through the warm summer air. Suddenly, her mouth set in a hard line, Lee had ripped her arm from Mouse's grip, turned, and started running back down the road towards the bankers, rummaging through her handbag as she went. The one who had slapped her, his thinning hair gleaming in the early evening sunshine, looked bemused at the sight of the madly rushing girl, her blonde hair flying out behind her like smoke from the fire of her rage.

As she reached the banker, her pace unchecked, he half-raised his arms to fend her off, an uncertain smile on his lips. At the last minute before impact, Lee leapt into the air, at the same time drawing something out of her handbag with her right hand and plunging it into the banker's neck. Mouse started running towards them, his heart thumping. The banker sat down heavily as Lee rolled away from him, picked herself up, and turned to look at Mouse, a triumphant grin stretched across her face. The second banker was bent over his friend, slowly drawing what Mouse could now see was a black and yellow Staedtler pencil out of the knot of muscle that ran between the banker's neck and his shoulder. A thin plume of blood darkened his white collar. The two men, one crouching, twirling the pencil in his fingers, the other leaning back and breathing heavily, looked at Lee as she walked away from them, awe in their eyes.

'Of course I remember,' Mouse said, taking his signet ring off and spinning it on the table. 'How could I forget?'

'Well, when I was running towards them, all I could think of was Judith slaying Holofernes. How none of the men around her would protect her, and so she had to become a hero herself.' She looked at him pointedly, and he felt again the shame of that evening when she had expected him to protect her and he had only felt how plump and childlike his body was next to those brawny bankers. 'And while not all of the women I study are as physically heroic as Judith, they do show you how to act in the world. That enduring can be a heroic act in itself.'

'I'm sorry,' Mouse said. Lee hugged him towards her, her voice softer now.

'I've got my demons at the moment. I need you to help me fight them. If the Retreat goes well, I'm sure it'll pull me out of this slump. It has to. Otherwise, I don't know what I'll do.'

They finished their drinks, waved to Philip and Maki who were still talking at the bar, and walked out into the cold night. Mouse escorted her to her bicycle and then strolled home, up through Holland Park and past the tree-hushed squares of Notting Hill.

The boat rocked him slowly to sleep that night as he lay with the Retreat bright in his mind. He pictured Lee running laughing ahead of him, saw David standing above him and looking down with pride. There was a sudden stab of guilt as he recalled the massage earlier, but then he remembered standing in the church at the last Retreat and hearing the heavenly chanting of the Course members, the tongues and the tears and the happy loss of control. Mouse slept as the moon passed through the sky, its reflection crossing the water of the canal. The boat sighed as a breeze whipped up early in the morning and then dropped again, leaving the water very clear and still in the first brightness of dawn.

Part Two

The Retreat

One

Marcus parked on the crest of the bridge and looked down the canal. To the right the horse chestnuts of Kensal Green Cemetery trembled in the breeze. The graveyard's wall was crumbling and Marcus could see through a gap to the rising ground which stretched up from the shrunken tombstones of the children's garden to the vast mausoleums of colonial grandees. Marcus occasionally came up to visit Mouse on Sundays in summer, when they would sit and drink cans of cider on the roof of the boat and then wander through the cemetery inventing stories for the dead. Foxes would leap surprised from undergrowth as they passed, woodpeckers sweeping in bouncing flight over their heads. Now Marcus could see Mouse making his way up the towpath pulling his old suitcase with one hand, holding his snare drum and high-hat over his shoulder with the other.

Abby was trying to get the car's radio to work. A long blare of static came from the speakers. Lee sat in the back pressing her temples with her fingers, taking controlled breaths. She had cut her hair very short the previous night. She told Marcus and Abby how she had been suddenly infuriated by the long blonde hair and had cut it herself in the bathroom sink. Jagged edges stuck up on top of her head; Marcus thought she looked like an adolescent boy. The shortness of her hair made her blue-green eyes and angular cheekbones seem unearthly and disturbing, shorn of the softening frame of her long hair.

Lee's neck, where she had cut the hair in a severe line at the back, was as slick and white as a scar.

Marcus was impatient to be on the road, to head westwards and shake free of the grim city. He leapt from the car when Mouse appeared on the pavement and squeezed the suitcase and drum into the boot. Mouse climbed in beside Lee, lifting Marcus's guitar onto his lap.

'Blimey,' he said as he caught sight of Lee's hair. 'Auditioning for the Sex Pistols?'

'I wanted a new look. Now be nice about it.' She leaned over and placed a breathy kiss on his cheek.

Abby switched off the radio and suddenly they could hear the ducks on the canal, the birds singing in the cemetery. Then Marcus started the engine and they pulled out onto Harrow Road and were away. The skies were heavy unbroken grey above them. Marcus drove haltingly along the A40, braking for speed cameras, nosing from lane to lane, trying to cut a clear path through the traffic. Just before the widening of the road at Hillingdon, a traffic jam snaked back from the charred carcass of a burnt-out car. A lane was closed, and people edged past the scene, noses glued to their windows, looking for bodies.

'So who's not going to make it through the Retreat?' Mouse asked. 'I know you've all been thinking about it. There are always drop-outs at the Retreat.'

There was a silence. Marcus looked into his wing mirror and waved as the car behind let him through.

'Of course we've been thinking about it.' Marcus looked across at Abby. 'The twins will be fine. Neil's a good bet. I think most of our group are in for the long haul. What do you think, Mouse?'

Mouse lit a cigarette and opened the window.

'Maki's hard to read. She seems spiritual, to understand the need for faith, but we should keep an eye on her.'

'What about Philip?' Marcus asked. 'Do you think he'll stay?'

Mouse paused, drew on his cigarette, and spoke.

'Yes, I do,' he said. 'Partly because I think he's thought more than anyone else about it. He's laid the foundations of the revelation. But also, he's nervous, and those nerves can be helpful, they bring you to that fine point where you just have to let yourself go.'

Marcus saw Lee take a drag on Mouse's cigarette. Her voice was low and tired.

'I'm not so sure. I think we might lose him,' she said.

'Really?'

'It seems to me that Philip wants everything that goes with being a Course member, but I don't know that he wants God. He's just a bit too eager. And thinking about faith doesn't do any good without feeling it first.'

Marcus frowned in the rear-view mirror.

'I'll have a word with him. We have to make sure we don't lose anyone else. David is depending on us. If you feel like anyone's wavering you have to leap on it. It's not just keeping them here, but making sure they're fully converted. We need to deliver, to prove to David that we can do this.'

The clouds had begun to break up as they drove through the cut in the Chilterns and the world unravelled itself beneath them. They came off the motorway at Banbury and then they were almost at Lancing Manor, and Marcus felt a surge of pleasure in his stomach.

The Earl had been at school with David and was reported to have financed the Course's initial sessions, supported the priest as he wrote *The Way of the Pilgrim* and took his orders. He was on the boards of a host of City corporations, had links to shady business ventures in offshore tax havens, hedge funds that had benefited from the Credit Crisis. He attended most Course sessions and played the organ at St Botolph's on Sunday mornings. His house was said to be astonishingly grand.

They got lost around Chipping Norton. Abby had been reading the directions but, during the discussion about the new members, she had let the map fall to the floor. After they had negotiated the sandstone wiggle of the town for the third time, Marcus stopped the car outside a truckers' cafe and looked at the map. Heading back on the main road towards Banbury, they came upon David's silver Mercedes plodding slowly northwards. Marcus could see the priest leaning forward over his steering wheel as his wife stared out at the passing countryside. Marcus honked and the priest looked in his rear-view mirror and raised his hand. Marcus followed David as he took a right turn and drove along a ridge between two valleys. Marcus watched the priest's eyes, which whipped back to the pursuing car in the mirror every so often. They made their way through a number of windswept hamlets; a wood appeared on the left. Nightingale slowed, began to indicate, and Abby let out a cheer.

Nightingale's Mercedes turned into a shadowy driveway through black iron gates. Marcus followed down the gravel track above which trees clasped a thick canopy. The track ended in a turning circle in front of a high, dark house. Lancing Manor had two large wings that shot off from the main building, further outbuildings and laundry rooms that were linked by covered cloisters. The rickety gables and turrets seemed to be climbing the body of the house, clambering over one another, reaching up to the low clouds. Rooks perched monkish on the gabled roof, their beaks the colour of bones. The ivy that grew up the front of the house seemed to be gathering itself for some great effort, balling itself into a fist in an attempt to pull the building into the ground, sending out single vines as scouts snaking along the brown Hornton stone. The house was perched on the brow of a hill looking down over thickly planted pine trees and, halfway down the hillside, where the ground flattened out before plunging down into the misty valley, a lake that was bright with weed in the midday sunlight. A boathouse stood in the shadow of over-hanging trees at one end. The Earl came out of the oak doors, rubbing his large hands.

'Welcome to Lancing Manor. You found the place without trouble? Good, good.'

He was wearing a thick brown jumper and corduroys, his heavy body somehow more at home in front of the vast, dark house than it was in London. David embraced him and turned to help Sally with their luggage and his guitar case. Marcus and Mouse hefted their own belongings into the entrance hall. Marcus watched as Abby and Lee looked upwards, slowly real-ising the size of the great room they had entered, a room whose shadows were punctuated by etiolated stems of green-white light that fell down from stained-glass windows set high above. A staircase reared in front of them from the black-and-white chessboard marble of the floor. Embers dimly glowed in the fireplace, along whose mantel carved stone vines exten-ded themselves between armless caryatids. Doors led off the hall, interrupting bookcases filled with dusty works of philo-sophy, Latin and German texts whose names Lee revealed with a sweep of her thumb down leather spines. A thin woman with short grey hair came through a swing door and nodded severely in their direction.

'This is Mrs Millman,' said the Earl. 'She'll show you to your rooms. I'll walk with you, David. I thought we'd put the young-sters in the east wing. Keep all the trouble in one place.' Mrs

Millman made her way up the staircase with the delicate steps of a wading bird. The four friends followed her.

The dust increased as they climbed the staircase to the gallery that encircled the hall. The fan-vaulted ceiling was hung with giant pendants. Shards of sunlight fell into the dusty air, shimmering with the colours of the stained glass. Marcus could make out the pictures depicted in the glass of the high windows, scenes of martyrdom and religious heroism: Sebastian pierced by arrows, Moses on the Mount, Daniel among the lions. On the walls hung portraits of what Marcus assumed were the Earl's family. He saw a young girl with a bright parrot perched on her thin hand, a dog sleeping at her feet. He thought she looked like Lee. Further along there was a stern Roundhead, a jovial Victorian slumped behind an enormous belly, a pale woman with an Elizabethan ruff dandling a baby. Then the Earl, perhaps twenty years younger, his hair – longer then – a dark flame atop his head. Behind him Lancing Manor, presented against a fantastical background of mountains and ravines, rose dark and gloomy. The artist had ignored any sense of perspective and so the painting looked primitive, wild, the Earl the master of a dismal kingdom, rooks circling above him.

They passed through white doors and then in single file down a long corridor whose windows looked out over a courtyard on the right-hand side that reminded Marcus of the quadrangles at university. But the courtyard was empty and the fountain that bubbled in the centre served only to highlight the stillness of everything around it. The wallpaper of the corridor was pale yellow and the walls here were hung with photographs of stiff Edwardians in formalwear. There was something ghostly in the stare of those long-dead people, their faces trapped in forced joyless smiles or stern Imperial frowns. The photographs had faded in the evening sunlight that had fallen through the windows over the decades. Some of the lost-looking women holding pudgy babies seemed almost to have disappeared into the walls behind them. Marcus tried to work out which of the mewling infants was the Earl. Finally, they came out to a landing at the top of what looked like a maid's staircase. Three white doors opened to light-filled bedrooms. Mrs Millman turned and stood in front of one of them and smiled. Her face was transformed; pinched disapproval was replaced by something warm and welcoming. Colour rose to her grey cheeks.

'I thought you'd like to be up here. The rest of the members will be in the servants' quarters on the lower floors, but these rooms are so nice and light. Bit of a climb, but worth it, especially in the mornings. Now you four get settled in and then do come down to the kitchen for some tea.' She picked her way carefully downstairs.

Marcus and Abby took the room in the centre. Mouse carried his bag into the smaller bedroom on the right, while Lee stood reading a tapestry on the wall before entering the room on the left. Marcus looked again at her short hair and saw how dark roots now made up the bulk of it; just the tips were still blonde. Her hair was returning to the colour it had been when he first knew her. He turned and walked into his room. Abby flopped onto the large bed as Marcus closed the door and crossed to the window. The light outside had begun to fade. The room looked eastwards and Marcus saw darkness gathering on the horizon. Below he could make out an ancient chapel whose dormer windows gave it the air of an enormous dovecote. Beside it he could see the roof of the dining hall which stretched out from the main house like an arm. The hall's roof had been turfed over, a black iron railing around the perimeter and spiral stairways leading down into the garden. The ground dropped away swiftly after the hall, down to the lake that was now almost hidden in the gloom of the valley. It was five o'clock.

Lee and Mouse were already in the kitchen when Marcus and Abby came down. They sat beside one another at the long table in the centre of the room. A fire burned in one corner. Mrs Millman stood by the wide black Aga buttering toast while Mouse held forth on the frieze of mermaids he had seen carved into the wall of a room he entered by accident on the way down to the kitchen.

'. . . and they seemed to be swimming towards you, beckoning you somehow . . .' He waved his teacup as he spoke, the dark liquid slopping close to the rim of the cup with each frantic movement. Then the Earl and the Nightingales arrived and a sense of seriousness descended. Mrs Millman retired to a chair by the window to polish a box of silverware. David sat at the head of the table and placed his fingers around his mug, fixing each of them in turn with his pale eyes.

'This Retreat is going to be an entirely new experience for each of you guys. Not only because you are Course leaders this time. There's something special about this place, something holy. When I decided to leave my job as a banker, to devote myself to God on a full-time basis, I came up here for a week to think about it. You can feel the history here, a history of strongly held faith. So spend time with the new members, help them on their path to conversion, but also spend time with yourselves, take this time to push your own spiritual development a little further along.'

The priest leaned forward over the table and lowered his voice.

'The Retreat is the decisive moment in any Course. It's where we find out how we've done, whether the seeds we've planted will sprout or not. This is where we get our new members to commit to the Course, where we lay foundations that will last a lifetime. Any drop-outs from here on hit us very hard. If new members leave after the first few sessions, it's unlikely they would have seen it through to the end in any case. If they come away with us here, then we should be able to complete the conversion. Don't let up, don't allow yourselves to relax. Make sure that you look back on your first Retreat as Course leaders as a successful one. We won't tolerate failure. We can't.'

Marcus had been aware of something nagging at him for a while, something dimly perceived, at the verge of his consciousness. Only when David paused in his speech to sip his tea did Marcus realise that he could hear traffic. Not the road they had come in on, but the relentless drone of a motorway: articulated lorries and caravans, car transporters and pantechnicons. Dusk had fallen outside and, looking out of the kitchen window, he could see a thin belt of yellow light above the trees fading into the night sky. David continued to talk for the next twenty minutes, reminiscing about previous Retreats. Then it was time to go out and greet the new members who had come up from London in a coach that barely squeezed its way through the gates and under the canopy of trees.

The front of the house was illuminated by the coach's headlights as the new members stepped blinking from the vehicle's dark interior. Neil was first, followed by Maki and the twins. Philip was the last to make his way down to join the cluster of twenty or so who stood close together in front of the large doors. Marcus could see their breath caught in the lights that blazed from the coach. He walked out and picked up the twins' suitcases as David bounded out to welcome the new arrivals. The priest swept his pale eyes over the Course members.

'Hi guys. This is where it begins for you. For many this weekend will be one of the most important experiences of your lives. Savour it all. Prepare yourselves for miraculous things. Approach the weekend with an open mind and you'll find yourselves changed beyond recognition.

'Now come on inside, make yourself at home. We'll have a brief service of thanksgiving before dinner. The Course leaders have been getting to know the layout of this extraordinary place, so do ask if you get lost.' The Earl stood bearlike behind him, nodding every so often.

*

The chapel was very cold. Candles had been lit along the aisle; otherwise the small church was dark. Marcus's hands felt stiff and unresponsive on the frets of his guitar. Only he and Lee were performing that evening. The whole band would play together for the main ceremony on Saturday night. They had tuned up, and now they were waiting for the members to come down from the house. Lee was fidgeting notes from the piano with her right hand.

'How are you doing?' he asked, resting his bass on the ground in front of him and going to sit next to her at the piano. She shuffled thin buttocks up the bench and he began to play along with her, watching her fingers and trying to copy the melody. He realised that she was playing *Pictures at an Exhibition*.

'I'm OK,' she said.

Marcus felt her swaying slightly as she played. Without missing a note, she placed her left hand on his and helped him to find the melody. Her hands were colder than his, the frosty pressure of her fingers made him shiver slightly.

'You love this piece of music, don't you?'

She stopped playing for a moment and looked over at him.

'Yes. My dad taught it to me when I was very young. It makes me think of him.'

132

She started to play again, now extemporising a harmony over his refrain. She closed her eyes.

'It reminds me of what my dad's music used to be like, before he got depressed. His new composition is so bleak, so empty. The stuff he doesn't burn, I mean. It seems to me that all of his new music aspires to silence. When I speak to him on the phone, he's often silent for a long time. We sit and listen to each other breathe. Sometimes he'll hang up without saying anything.'

Marcus stopped playing. He sat back and watched Lee nod her head in time to the music.

'It's like he has used up all of the ways of saying what he needs to say through music and language, and silence is the only voice left to him.'

'Do you think that you inherit your slumps from your dad?'

Lee stopped playing and turned towards him, her hands folded in her lap.

'Of course. But he's further along than me. I'm certain that my dad will kill himself soon. It's something that I have known for a long time. And I miss him already. Because this silence – that's what it is. It's a kind of suicide. He's backing away from the world and finally he will make his move complete.'

She was chewing on the inside of her cheek. Marcus could see blood on her teeth when she opened her mouth. He took her hand, feeling horrified and helpless.

'You talk about my slumps, but none of you know what it's like. When I'm in one of them it's like being in a dark cell with one other creature, and then you find out that dark creature is yourself. It's a bond between me and my dad – that we both go there – but it doesn't make it better. It doesn't make you want to go on surviving.'

Marcus saw that people were beginning to come into the chapel. He stopped playing and looked down into the shadowy nave. Mouse and Abby sat in the front row, huddled together for warmth. He smiled at them and then turned back to Lee. Leaning towards her, he spoke in a low voice.

'I'm so worried about you.'

'Don't be.' Her voice was suddenly hard. 'Please stop worrying about me. And stop telling me that you're worried. Sometimes if you think about something all the time, and harp on about it, it can make it real. I'm fine, really I am. I'm finding ways of coping.'

Marcus saw David come into the chapel, followed by Sally and the Earl.

'Now let's just play some music,' Lee said. 'Worry about yourself, about Abby. I can look after myself.'

Marcus lifted up his bass and began to pick out a series of notes, following Lee, who was playing a rousing tune that marked David's passage down the aisle. The priest turned and stood in front of the low altar, his white shirt and chinos bright in candlelight. The new members looked nervous and excited. The atmosphere was constructed to be as fertile for revelation as possible; nothing should feel forced. Each of the new members had been given a candle to hold as they entered the small chapel. Marcus watched the careful way each of them held the flames, trying not to allow the wax to spill from the white cardboard collar that formed the handle.

David read a passage from St Luke – 'He was praying in a certain place, and when he ceased, one of his disciples said to him, "Lord, teach us to pray".' The cold dark room echoed with the sound of his long vowels, the stentorian manner in which he declaimed the Lord's Prayer. Marcus laid his guitar across his knee and sat on his hands to keep them warm. While the priest talked, Marcus thought back to his first Retreat. He had travelled down with Abby to a tatty hotel near Exeter where chickens pecked in the yard outside their window. Those days in the balmy air of an Indian summer had changed Marcus. They had brought him closer to Abby, but also made him face up to the creeping realisation that someone – God, perhaps – was trying to win him over.

The coincidences had been occurring with disturbing regularity in the days leading up to that first Retreat. Phrases from the book he was reading on David's orders – C. S. Lewis's *The Screwtape Letters* – had been appearing on billboards, in graffiti on the sides of buildings, were spoken in meetings when he was half-listening, leaping from the surrounding drone. The number sixty-two cropped up everywhere: receipts, payslips and telephone numbers, page numbers in books that seemed full of hidden meaning, whispered significance. He would find a song repeating in his head on the way into the office; on the way home he'd sit next to a tramp singing the very same song in a voice far too beautiful for his grizzled face. But the biggest coincidence, the moment that had shocked him into belief, had occurred on the Saturday morning of that first Retreat.

Marcus and Abby had been arguing in her room. Because they were not yet married they had separate bedrooms and Abby didn't think they should sleep together during their time at the Retreat, should obey the laws of the Course at least here. Marcus had shouted at her and stomped from the room. Outside it was warm enough for him to take off his jacket and sling it over his arm. An estuary swept across the horizon and he strode purposefully down towards the sea. He was twenty-three and he walked with the bouncing steps of an athlete. The sea was further than he thought but he pressed on, past low cottages and cows watching him with stupid curiosity. Down a narrow lane with flint walls overgrown with ivy he came upon a small church. Norman, with a leper gate and crumbling roof. The door bore a heavy padlock; looking in, with his hand cupped to the grubby window, Marcus saw that the inside was empty, the church disused. The graveyard had been overtaken by nature. Nettles grew in thick clumps above red-veined dock leaves, brambles were knotted around teetering gravestones and rabbits scuttled under apple trees as he made his way further into the cemetery.

Marcus liked to look at dates. When he went to art galleries he spent as much time calculating the ages of the artists when they died as he did looking at their paintings. Picasso filled him with hope, Toulouse-Lautrec terrified him; Dalí was a beacon, Jackson Pollock a tocsin. It was the same in cemeteries. Whenever he walked around Kensal Green with Mouse he looked hungrily for signs of extreme longevity, but was often brought up short by the graves of teenagers, people dead in their twenties and thirties. He watched particularly for family tombs where parents had outlived their children. So in the little churchyard in Devon, Marcus tore back brambles and scraped away lichen, bringing his face down close to the dappled gravestones. Most were very ancient, almost unreadable, telling of plague-deaths and children snatched by smallpox and dropsy. Then, as he was about to leave, he saw a newer stone in the corner of the graveyard, the sandy earth seemingly fresh-dug. A bunch of tulips lay upon the earth below the stone. The engraving upon it made Marcus's throat close up in fear.

'Marcus Glass. Taken from us aged 23. Grant him rest, O Lord.'

He staggered backwards, the few wispy clouds in the blue sky above him circling wildly for a moment. He had a sudden and vivid picture of his mother and sister at his father's funeral, their faces pinched with sadness. He found his finger returning to trace the path of his own name, his own age. He knew that it was a sign. After the series of coincidences that had marked the last few days, this was the heavy-handed proof. When he returned to the hotel he went to find David and told him everything, told him that he was ready to really believe. David embraced him and he felt a shadow lift from his mind.

*

Lee nudged Marcus. He jumped. Lost in memories of his early days in the Course, he had missed the end of the reading. He began to strum a succession of quiet deep notes as Lee played slow descending chords. Abby sang a solo first, then the congregation joined with her. The plainness of the song suited the dark little chapel. Marcus could see the faces of the twins as they sang, twin mouths beaming, twin cheeks shining. It was a simple refrain, a prayer repeated over the same chord sequence.

> 'I must become God,
> And God must become me,
> So that we can share
> The same "I" eternally.'

Abby swayed from side to side as she sang, her eyes closed. There was something hypnotic in the music. Just as it felt that the hymn was fading into monotony, David began to improvise in the spaces between words, singing a descant in a high, fragile voice.

'Yalullialla. Yaweahalalla. Hanna, hanna . . .'

It was the sound of the desert, the sound of ancient civilisations, and Marcus took a deep breath, trying to inhale its extraordinary purity. David was standing with his arms held out, his face turned up to the roof, a wide smile showing his bright teeth. Almost before it had begun, it was over. David muttered a final blessing and then led them up the aisle and back up to the main house. Marcus could see the dazed expressions of the new members. There were glasses of white wine on the round table in the centre of the entrance hall. Maki came over to Marcus and handed him a drink.

'That was amazing. Was that . . . ? I mean, is that what speaking in tongues sounds like?'

'That was it. Or at least how David speaks. I guess everyone has their own way of doing it. It's beautiful, isn't it?'

Maki just looked at him with wide dark eyes.

After the wine, they made their way down to the dining hall, where Mrs Millman was standing in the corner stirring pots of stew and vats of rice. The Course members sat down at the long tables in the candlelight. They seemed lost in the vast dining hall. The hall had mullioned windows and dark tapestries of hunting scenes. A mahogany armoire stood along one side of the room, its front inlaid with elaborate carvings of Greek myths. Wooden doors at the far end gave onto the garden. Marcus sat next to Abby and Maki and they talked and drank and he felt a sense of optimism sweep over him. Abby looked happier than she had for weeks and even Lee was smiling, laughing along with the twins and Mouse, while Sally Nightingale spoke to Neil and Philip at the other end of the table. The Earl sat down opposite Marcus and ate in silent concentration, spearing pieces of beef aggressively. When he had finished, he leaned forward towards Marcus and Abby.

'How do you like the old place?'

'It's extraordinary,' said Abby. 'I've never been anywhere quite like it.'

'It's perfect for the Retreat. Don't know why we haven't had it here before. David was always a little nervous about it. This was where he underwent his own epiphany, you see. He wrote

The Way of the Pilgrim here, so Lancing Manor has always held a special place in his heart. I think it's a huge compliment to you lot that he agreed this year.'

'I think it's a good bunch. The new members, I mean. And I suppose he has seen us grow up with the Course. I like to think that this group of Course leaders is quite special to him.'

Marcus put his hand on his wife's arm.

'I have been working a great deal on the US expansion,' the Earl said, his heavy eyebrows lowering as he spoke. 'Over there, of course, it's even more important that people shouldn't worry about their wealth. It's a society that is shaped by money and we have to recognise that. Particularly in the areas we're targeting: the North-East and California. Greed has temporarily replaced faith for these people, but they remain believers. You can see it in their eyes. We need to let them know they can have both.'

Neil had come to sit beside Marcus. He leaned forward to listen to the Earl, his mouth hanging slightly open.

'People don't grasp the meaning of the story about the camel and the eye of the needle,' the Earl continued. 'They think it means that it is impossible for a rich man to enter heaven; it doesn't. What Jesus is saying is that we will be held to higher standards. If we have gained wealth and power during our days on Earth, then we need to make sure that we behave impeccably. To those who have, more will be given. But only if we use our gifts correctly. Fitting a camel through the eye of a needle is child's play for God. Indeed it may be that the verse is just a mistranslation, that the "needle" referred to a gate in the walls of Jerusalem through which it was perfectly possible to drive a camel. Whichever, there's nothing to stop you being a good Christian and rich.'

Neil was nodding. David came to stand behind the Earl.

'The Course has been so successful in the City because it

doesn't seek to judge people on how they behave in the office. It would be ridiculous to expect people to live like saints in a world that is as dog-eat-dog as ours. Christians would quickly be wiped off the map. So we ask people to come to the Course and ask God's forgiveness when they have done wrong, and to use their money where they can to help further the Course's good work.'

David looked hard at Neil.

'You know,' David said, raising his voice so the other members would hear, 'the Bible is clever enough to know that the pursuit of wealth presents major problems for Christians. You should use it to guide you. There are twice as many verses in the Bible about money as there are about how to pray. Did you know that? Almost half of Jesus's parables deal with cash. It isn't easy to be rich and godly, but look to the Bible and you won't go far wrong. And then, when you're spectacularly rich, remember to give a good lot of it back to the church. Christians can't afford to be squeamish about wealth – it is, as the Earl says, a horribly competitive world.'

After dinner, the Earl and the Nightingales left the Course members to drink and talk in the dinner hall. Some of the girls from Marcus and Abby's group made their excuses and went up to bed at the same time. Marcus waved at them as they said goodnight and opened more bottles of wine, passing along the tables and filling empty glasses, smiling and chatting to the Course members. Someone found an ancient stereo with a pile of old CDs and the twins pulled Neil and Philip up to dance, singing misremembered lyrics in raucous voices. It grew darker in the hall as the boys blew out candles while moving tables to the side of the room to clear space for the dancers. Only the fire illuminated the dancing figures. Abby and Lee swung each other around energetically; Abby's hands seemed huge on Lee's frail body. Mouse and Marcus walked out into the garden for a cigarette, closing the heavy wooden doors behind them.

The night was clear and cold, the noise of the motorway loud in the still air. Marcus followed Mouse up a winding spiral stair whose steps were carved into the stone of the wall. At the top they made their way through an archway and onto the grassy roof of the dining hall. Mouse's face was surprised by the flame of the lighter; seemingly about to speak, he drew back from Marcus, his eyebrows raised, the cigarette slack in the corner of his mouth. He then moved towards the flame. Marcus lit his own cigarette, and two red coals glowed in the darkness. They leaned on the metal rail that ran around the edge of the lawn and looked over towards the shimmer of the motorway that sat above the pines.

'He was good tonight,' said Mouse.

'Pretty good. It's a wonderful song. It's the best song for the tongues.' Marcus exhaled a long stream of smoke. He had been smoking too much recently. His lungs felt like old plastic bags. Abby was always complaining about his smoking, asking how one who was so scared of death could smoke. He had tried to explain to her once. How smoking was something he did because he was young. As soon as he gave up smoking, it would be a recognition of the fact that he was ageing, that he had left behind the eternity of adolescence. She had rolled her eyes the way she always did when he tried to explain the way he rationalised things she didn't agree with.

'I need to quit these things.' He also liked to talk about quitting and had done for as long as he could remember. He coughed and spat into the bushes below. A sad moon rose over the trees, slowly ripping itself free from the motorway lights.

'Imagine how he must have felt when they built the road. Imagine how peaceful it would have been before. I suppose motorways have to go somewhere, but it seems strange that they'd put it here, among all this.' Marcus swung his cigarette hand out over the invisible view. The flashing ember left traces across his retinas.

'The Earl hasn't been here that long,' said Mouse. 'I did some research on Lancing Manor in the library. He bought it in, I don't know, 1992 or something. He made an awful lot of money in one of the privatisations. Electricity, perhaps. It was when he bought his title. I looked it all up.'

'Really? But what about the pictures, the photographs? It felt like his family had been living here for generations. It seems a bit fraudulent.'

Mouse paused. 'I don't think it's fraudulent. Or no more fraudulent than the building itself, you know? The Earl just wanted to get the whole thing right. Because his family couldn't have lived here for that many generations. Lancing Manor was only built in 1890. None of it is older than that. It's why it manages to feel so authentic. It's new enough to be convincing.'

'I always find him a bit sinister. I know he does amazing things for the Course, but I can't shake the feeling that he's only in it for the money, that all the talk of building the Course into a global franchise is just so that he can somehow make more cash out of it. I'm sure he gets backhanders from the hedge funds we use for the Course's investments. I can never understand why we stick with some of the funds that are clearly going down. Except that the managers are Course members.'

'But that's it, isn't it? The Earl is sending out a message that he'll stick with people as long as they keep attending the Course. I think he wants to make it so that you can't get anywhere in the City unless you're a Course member. You've seen how the bankers all get together after services. They look after each other. Anyway, the Earl doesn't need money.'

'What do you mean?'

'I heard him talking to Neil earlier. He's just made twenty million pounds on his Chinese stamp collection.'

'What?'

'When everyone else was buying up the Chinese stock market, the Earl sat down and tried to work out what else would rise in value when the economy took off there. He settled on stamps. Stamp collecting is a very middle-class hobby there, as it was here, I suppose. The Earl realised that as the middle class grew, stamps would rise in value. He bought up some major private stamp collections in the late nineties. Sold them at Sotheby's in Hong Kong last week.'

'That's amazing.'

They smoked in silence for a while. Mouse put his arm around Marcus's shoulder and spoke softly in his ear.

'Will you speak to Lee? I'm so worried about her at the moment. She's worse than ever. I can barely look at her.'

'I've tried. It's hard to get through to her. She seems so distant.'

'It's not just her promiscuity. Although have you noticed how that side of things always flares up when she's in one of her slumps? Sometimes when I see her face the sadness just swamps me. The poor thing needs help.'

'Should we tell David?'

'I think he's already spoken to her. He knows everything.'

'Of course he does, he's David.'

'Will you try again? We all look up to you. You know that, don't you, sport?'

'That's . . . that's really sweet. Thanks.'

Mouse squeezed Marcus's shoulder and then let his hand fall to his side. Someone coughed in the darkness.

'Marcus? Mouse? Are you up there?'

It was Maki. She walked across the grass and leaned

between Marcus and Mouse on the metal rail. Drawing out a packet of thin menthol cigarettes, she lit one as Mouse sent his own spinning down into the shrubbery.

'My friends told me that the Course would be a good way to meet real English people.'

Marcus liked the softness of her voice, the kindness in her dark eyes.

'But I hadn't realised quite what a small world it would be. I feel very foreign among so many girls who look alike.'

'It's not surprising though, is it? Given where the church is, where it draws its followers from?' Marcus tried to read her face in the dim light as he spoke. 'The church is supposed to represent its local community, and even though people come from all over London to join the Course, to worship at St Botolph's, the place necessarily attracts a type of person who feels comfortable in that square among those high, disapproving houses.'

'Or wants to feel comfortable there,' Mouse said, fiddling with his signet ring. 'When I first joined the Course, I found it very intimidating. It was like being at university again, all of these rituals that everyone else seemed to know inside out. But I wanted to be part of that world. It was glamorous and the people were so grand-looking.'

'Don't you find it a bit claustrophobic, though?' said Maki. 'I do wonder how effective the Course can be when it draws from such a narrow group of people.'

'St Botolph's is just the beginning,' said Mouse, lighting another cigarette. 'It's the base for our global expansion. And at the moment we do need people who are able to finance this evangelism, who can work for free or very little while we get the thing established. Remember that St Botolph was the patron saint of travellers and missionaries. We won't be stuck in

Chelsea for ever – we're getting out into the world and spreading the word.'

'I suppose so . . .' She stared out into the darkness.

'You're part of our family now,' Mouse said quietly. He put his arm around her shoulders. 'We're incredibly fond of you. I really don't know what we'd do if you left.'

'I didn't say I was leaving. Just that I don't feel totally comfortable yet.'

'You will, though. Because we love you, and we want you always to be one of us.'

'That's really sweet. Thank you.'

Marcus and Mouse waited for Maki to finish her cigarette and then the three of them made their way back down the spiral stairway and into the dining hall. Abby and Lee were standing in front of the open doors of the armoire. The twins were only visible from the waist downwards as they burrowed among the dark shapes hanging in the cupboard. Marcus saw Abby running her hands over one of the shapes and realised that it was a long fur jacket. Maki walked over to join the girls and the twins emerged, fox stoles wrapped around their throats.

'Let's put them on,' said Mouse, running over to the cupboard. 'Why don't we get dressed up and go and find the motorway?' His words tumbled out as he pulled down a rabbit-skin jacket and wrapped it around himself, seized a bottle of red wine and threw open the doors of the hall, turning around with a laugh. He dragged a chair over to the cupboard and rummaged along the top shelf until he found a blue three-pointed hat.

'I'm going to be Napoleon,' he said, pulling it down over his head. It was far too big for him and covered his ears. His eyes bulged from the shadow cast by the brim.

Invigorated by Mouse's enthusiasm, the other Course members jostled to find coats that fitted them. Only Abby hung back for a moment.

'Should we really be taking these? It seems rude, without asking.'

'We won't damage them. Come on, Abby, no one will know.' Mouse was shouting now, already down the steps and pointing towards the haze of synthetic light that hung over the pine trees.

There were enough jackets for all of the members, although Philip's was too short and meant that he held out his arms like a zombie as he walked. The twins had to hitch up the long tails of their own jackets, making their way daintily down the steps of the dining hall and onto a path that ran between thickly planted pine trees downhill to the lake. Mouse used his lighter to illuminate the path as he scuttled wheezing ahead, past the lake and the boathouse whose roof was brushed by pine branches. The earth at their feet was red; Marcus drew in a breath, savouring the scent of the soil and the pines and, faintly, woodsmoke. Or the woodsmoke might have been a scent-memory, a smell that had at some previous time existed strongly for him alongside the smell of the earth and the pines and was therefore repeated here.

The hill steepened as they descended. Ferns trembled in damp clumps above clusters of mossy rocks. Marcus slowed to help Abby climb over the knotted roots that spread from the bases of the trees. Then down into a gully where the ferns grew very thickly, and without the light of the bright moon that fell between the trees they would have surely had to turn back. Mouse roared ahead with the twins following closely in his wake, fur coats flying like capes behind them. Mouse had one hand pressed down on his head to keep the hat in place. Marcus felt Abby slip her arm inside his jacket and about his waist. Lee had her camera around her neck and was taking photographs of the group, the flash pausing time for a moment, freezing them as they made their way down the hill. Neil brought up the rear with Philip. Looking back, Marcus laughed at Philip's horizontal arms, at the expression of dignified discomfort on his face as Lee took his picture. The roar of the road was now very loud in their ears and seemed to quiver in the needles of the pines.

Without warning they came out of the wood and were standing at the top of an escarpment that led down to the motorway. The road was cut deep into the hillside, so that they looked down onto the bright street lights. Marcus could see that Mouse was already heading towards a footbridge that crossed the road half a mile to the south. His stout frame was outlined against the ridge of the hill, purposefully striding, his cap like a ship atop his head. The twins still followed behind him, although they were finding it hard to keep up with his bounding steps. The motorway below them was six lanes across, busy despite the late hour with articulated lorries thundering freight through the night. He turned and followed Mouse along the escarpment, Abby still clutched close against him.

The bridge was suspended a hundred feet above the motorway. It seemed very flimsy to Marcus as he led Abby along it. There was no wind from above, although the machines rushing beneath them seemed to create their own strange currents, sucking the air from around the Course members and then a sudden rush as the lorries surged past. Mouse was standing at the centre of the bridge, leaning far forward over the handrail, waving his hat to the vehicles below, a cigarette pointing downwards from his wildly grinning mouth. Marcus caught some of his friend's exhilaration. He slipped out of Abby's embrace, danced forward, then turned back and took his wife's hand before leading her out to the middle of the bridge.

The noise from the traffic below made speech impossible. The roar whipped thoughts from their minds and the breath from their chests. The bridge shuddered when the largest lorries passed beneath, hummed and trembled the rest of the time. Marcus saw Philip come up behind Lee and place his strange zombie arms around her shoulders. He gripped Abby's hand tightly in his own. He could see that Mouse was shouting, screaming down into the roar of traffic below. It felt as if they were linked by something, as if a chain of feeling hung between them like bunting out there in the high and dangerous sky, as they stared down on the man-made sublime.

A convoy of military vehicles passed beneath them: Land Rovers and tarpaulin-covered trucks followed by transporters carrying tanks and amphibious vehicles. Through the open backs of the trucks, Marcus could make out soldiers leaning against the shuddering material, some of them trying to sleep, some talking over the roar of the engines. One of them looked up and Marcus imagined that the soldier might carry the image of the young people silhouetted on a bridge away to battle, that it might rest in his mind like a talisman, a reminder of home. Looking down on the military vehicles, Marcus thought of toys he had collected as a child and arranged in careful formation to show his father when he arrived home from work, battlefronts drawn out on the kitchen floor. When the convoy had passed something in the air changed, and Marcus was aware that Abby was shivering beside him; he saw Lee slip gracefully out from under Philip's arms. Only Mouse was still standing braced against the roar below, his chubby cheeks livid in the glare of the street lights, the hat now back on his head giving him the air of a mad general leading his troops on a final suicidal mission. Lee knelt at the entrance to the bridge and took Mouse's photograph. Finally, Mouse joined them, his large eyes wet, his mouth hanging stupidly open.

Making their way back up the hill towards the house, there was a sense of deflation, but also of a communal recognition of this deflation, a feeling that they were together in feeling rather disappointed by the natural world, by the inconsistencies of the sloping ground when compared to the tarmac and metal perfection that they had just witnessed. Marcus drew his rabbit-skin jacket closer around his shoulders and pressed his lips down into the worn fur of the shoulder. He breathed in the greasy softness of the pelt. Abby looked dazed and had to lean on him every so often to catch her breath. They skirted the edge of the lake, whose waters were an oily reflection of the night sky. Philip came to walk beside Marcus and Abby.

'I'm nervous about tomorrow,' he said. Marcus looked over at him. His face was very pale in the moonlight.

'Why's that?' Marcus felt Abby squeeze his hand in his pocket.

'It feels like it's going to be a test of everything that has gone before. That if we can't embrace it all, we'll somehow have failed. I'm worried I'll be standing there in the service and I'll feel as uninspired as I always did, back when I was a choirboy and I used to see church services as a kind of endurance event, used to long for the sermon because it meant we were entering the home straight.'

They were walking through the darkest part of the wood now, and Marcus could barely see Philip beside him. Abby stumbled on a root and then spoke, leaning across Marcus to address Philip's shadowy outline.

'When I spoke in tongues for the first time, all of the rest of the service suddenly made sense. We become a community when we pray, or sing together. In that comfortable, familiar space it's amazing what you can do.'

'I really hope so.'

'Try to think of it as abstract art. You know the way a painting can be terribly moving, even though it is just a few splashes of paint on a canvas? The way something by Pollock can be more powerful, and beautiful, than a Constable landscape? It's because it entirely bypasses our consciousness. The tongues, the music, the words of the service – you should think of them like that. As something beyond the scope of your rational mind.'

'That's helpful. I'll see if it works in the chapel tomorrow.'

Finally, they broke free of the woods and saw Lancing Manor looming above them, a black shadow against the starlit night behind. A turret rose up like a coil of smoke from the house, a light burning in its narrow window.

Back inside the dining hall, Mouse initiated a half-hearted drinking game, but Marcus could tell that everyone was tired. He made sure the coats were hung back in the cupboard and drank a glass of water. He wanted to leave while there was still a feeling of community hanging between them. It was something he remembered from his first Retreat, when the Course members, who had until then seemed somehow suspicious, distant and self-satisfied, gathered around him and he felt warmth radiating from them.

'I'm going to bed,' he said, looking over at Abby. She smiled at him and they walked down the dining hall holding hands. They made their way through the heavy doors and into the main hallway, where a single lamp stood on the mantelpiece, a solitary point of light in the darkness that reared up above them. Abby shivered as they crept up the stairs and down the long corridor past the ghostly photographs. Their room was warm. Mrs Millman had lit a fire in the grate earlier when she came in to close the curtains. Their duvet was turned back and the bedside light cast a cosy glow across the white sheets.

Marcus helped Abby with her zip. She let the dress fall to the floor and stepped out of it. She wore white pants, a black bra that was fraying under the arms: Marcus could see a safety pin holding one strap together. Her thighs were milk-white as she took down her pants, bending to place them on a chair. She turned towards him, carefully unhooking her bra, and he lost himself in the wide expanse of her face. She undid his belt with a flourish and helped him take down his boxer shorts. They lay down together on the bed, which creaked and sagged reluctantly beneath them.

Abby kept laughing as they fucked; at one point he looked down at her and saw a smile flash across her face, igniting in her eyes and then exploding across her pink lips. Every time they moved, the bed groaned and Abby squealed laughter. Marcus thrust into Abby, stopping when he was entirely inside her, feeling their bodies intersecting at so many distinct points, hot skin against hot skin. They fell asleep and woke still pressed close together. Abby cradled Marcus's head in her arms, hugged his face to her chest. He had no idea what time it was, nor for how long Abby held him. He lay and listened to her heart and the distant moan of the motorway. They slept again and when they woke it was growing light outside. Marcus could hear people moving downstairs. Milky sunlight fell into the room through the gap in the curtains.

Two

Marcus and Abby had breakfast in the kitchen, where Mrs Millman stood over the Aga stirring a pot of porridge. David and Sally sat side by side, very close together. Marcus wondered if they had had sex the night before. He and Abby slouched opposite them feeling somehow seedy, still swimming in the pleasure of their night together. The Earl was wearing a tweed jacket and a dark blue tie. He perched low over his bowl of cornflakes, his narrow eyes surveying the Course members as they came in to eat. David smiled at Marcus.

'Mouse and Lee have already been down. I think they're in the chapel preparing for this evening.'

Marcus couldn't tell if there was reprimand in his voice.

'What's the plan for the day?'

'Some discussion groups this morning, lunch in the dining hall at one o'clock and a walk this afternoon if the weather holds out. Then, of course, the service.'

'The forecast isn't that good, I'm afraid,' Sally said, buttering a slice of toast.

Marcus and Abby ate quickly and in silence, then hurried back upstairs. They took a bath together as they had at university, carefully adjusting their limbs in the ancient iron tub with its rusty lion's-claw feet. Abby ran her fingers slowly down the inside of his thighs as they lay in the hot water, singing softly to herself. Marcus watched as the thousands of tiny bubbles that clung to the nest of his pubes were dislodged by her fingers and rose swiftly through the water like champagne. By the time they had dried and were down in the chapel it was ten o'clock and the Course members sat around chatting.

Marcus still couldn't remember the names of the girls in his discussion group; one was Lizzie and another Sarah, but he didn't know the others and the remaining boyfriends were just flushed cheeks on vague faces. He was glad to see that most of his group were surrounding David and the Earl. David was standing in front of the Stations of the Cross describing the meaning of each scene while the Earl interjected occasionally with stories about the artist he had invited to paint the images directly onto the walls of the chapel. Philip sat with Mouse and Sally in one corner. Mouse was talking very quickly, his hands dancing as he spoke. Lee sat apart from them, her legs stretched out along a pew, her arms around her shoulders. A beam of sunlight fell into her short hair and she lifted a hand to shade her eyes from the brightness. Marcus took Abby's arm and they made their way to the front of the chapel, where Maki and Neil were inspecting engravings on the pillars in front of the altar.

'Morning.'

'Morning, Marcus. Hi, Abby. Have you seen these inscriptions? The lettering is exquisite.' Neil ran his finger over the text, which Marcus recognised as a chapter from Ecclesiastes: 'Rejoice, O young man in thy youth . . .' The letters were like runes, difficult to read at first, but once his eyes had become accustomed to the jagged shapes, Marcus saw how perfectly they expressed the regretful wisdom of the words. Abby stood behind Neil and reached over to run her own fingers over the inscription.

Neil and Maki sat down on the steps leading up to the altar

while Marcus and Abby leaned back against the front pew. Marcus began to say something, but Abby cut him off.

'It's about getting rid of your inhibitions, this weekend. All those things that get in the way when you're in London. It's why we always come out to the countryside. Silence, music, peace. This is what we need to get closer to God.'

'I've been reading the Bible,' said Neil, 'and I keep feeling like I almost get it. As if there's something very obvious that I'm missing. But I'm almost there. I know I am.'

'Let today carry you in its current. Don't try to force it, just let yourself be open to whatever happens.' Abby was glowing; she reached out a hand and laid it on the arm of the older man, who was dressed in stiff smart-casual: chinos and a blue button-down shirt. Maki, who had been hidden in the shadow of one of the pillars, leaned forward.

'What about the tongues? I heard David last night and I just can't imagine a situation where I'd be able to do that.'

'What did you think when you heard it?' Abby tilted towards Maki, mirroring her.

'I suppose it was beautiful. It sounded like just another part of the music. It's the thing I like best about the Course, the music. So it was nice to hear, but I don't know if it meant any more to me than that. I certainly didn't understand it.'

'I don't think you need to understand it. And you certainly don't need to join in. I think the way that it's presented, people expect the Course to change everything. It doesn't need to. It can be the start of a journey; it doesn't always take people all the way to their goal.'

'Hmm . . . I'm just not sure it's for me.'

'Why did you first come to the Course, Maki?' Marcus asked, aware that he should be supporting Abby.

'I suppose it was to make friends, mainly. But also to find somewhere, I don't know, spiritual. I've always felt that I needed to believe in something, I just never discovered exactly what.'

'Well, you have friends here. And the Course is an extraordinarily spiritual experience. It seems to me that you just need to allow yourself to believe. Feel good about the fact that you found exactly what you were looking for. Sometimes we can get so caught up in the search that we don't allow ourselves to accept that we've reached our destination.'

They spoke for another hour; Philip came over to join them after a while. They leaned back against the stone pillars, spread themselves out across the pews, listening carefully to each other as they talked, each awaiting their turn to speak, measuring their words precisely. Sally and the Earl sat down, smiling, as Marcus told the members about C. S. Lewis's conversion.

'He was travelling down to Whipsnade Zoo. He set out on his trip as an agnostic and arrived a believer. You need to realise that the conscious mind is the last thing to change. The more you read and the more you think about God, the more He works behind the scenes. It's why the kind of epiphany that Lewis describes isn't as instantaneous and unreasoning as it first appears. If you lay the groundwork then God will do the rest. And here at the Retreat, we try to do as much as we can to create an environment that allows that change to take place.'

Only Lee still sat apart from the various groups. The beam of light had moved across the room and now she was in the shadows, dust thick in the air around her, her short hair flat on her head. Marcus could see that she was looking at the pines through the high windows, watching them dance in the gentle breeze. She turned and caught his eye for a moment and he shivered and reached out for Abby's hand. When he looked back at Lee her head was tilted back again and she seemed miles away from any of them.

At one o'clock, Mrs Millman arrived at the door of the

chapel and called them for lunch. They made their way through to the dining hall, where they continued to talk as they ate baked potatoes piled high with grated cheese and baked beans. After lunch, Marcus walked over to Lee and laid a hand on her shoulder.

'Are you coming for a walk? Do you remember when we used to walk in the meadows at university? We'd always go on ahead. I used to love just listening to you talk.'

'I was thinking about those walks just the other day. Doesn't it seem like a long time ago?'

'In a way, I suppose.'

'It feels like a lifetime to me. We were so young back then. Everything felt ahead of us.'

The Course members were slowly filing out of the hall, disappearing upstairs to collect coats and boots ready for the walk. Marcus gave Lee's shoulder a final squeeze and they made their way up to their rooms. The Earl and David were waiting at the front of the house when Marcus came back downstairs. Abby, wearing a blue Husky and hiking boots, was handing out thermoses of hot chocolate with Sally. The wind had picked up and the sound of the pines blocked out the noise of the road. Marcus pulled his scarf tightly around his throat. Rooks swirled in the air above him, whipped into hurtling arabesques by the wind.

They set off up the driveway, crossed the road that they had driven in on the day before, and descended into the next valley on a worn footpath. The sky's earlier blue was now a patchwork of clouds at varying altitudes, each level represented by a different colour: dark stratus against lighter cumulus, and far above, a blanket of white cirrus. The Earl and David strode out in front with Sally and Neil following closely behind them. Lee walked a few paces ahead of Mouse, who jogged every few steps to keep up with her. Abby held Marcus tightly by the hand. Soon they climbed to the top of another hill; Chipping Norton lay to the south, the chimney of its abandoned mill standing over the town like an accusing finger. They crossed the Banbury road and made their way alongside an old stone wall and down through high-piled leaves at the feet of ancient horse chestnuts.

The ground was soft beneath their feet as they walked down into the dell ahead of them. Marcus helped Abby to climb over a stile that stood in the shade of a huge old oak. He saw that Philip and Maki were walking together, deep in conversation. There was a village at the bottom of the hill. A church was lost within a protective circle of dark trees, a large gloomy house with shuttered windows blindly overlooked the village. The walls that crossed the fields here were crumbling, nettles swamped the verges of the road. Nothing moved.

The Earl led them down a narrow path between the church and a row of tumbledown cottages and then over another stile and into a small wood. They came out on top of a grassy mound looking down over rolling fields, a stream which wended along the bottom of the valley, silver birches that climbed the opposite hillside. Marcus caught a movement out of the corner of his eye and saw a doe crossing the stream, pearls of water thrown up by its long legs. By the time he had raised his arm to point it out to Abby, it had disappeared. They marched on.

Marcus found himself walking with Lee as they headed down towards a wooden footbridge that hung haphazardly above the swirling waters of the stream. She was wearing a Barbour jacket, pink wellingtons beneath her long skirt. She took his arm.

'You and Abby seem happy. Go on – you can tell me – is she pregnant?'

'Not that I know of.'

'Are you trying? I'd love it if you were trying.'

'Maybe. Maybe we're trying, yes.'

Over the bridge and into the woods they went. In the dubious light under trees that creaked in the wind, Lee gripped his hand.

'I'm really struggling with my thesis at the moment. I was thinking I might chuck in the PhD.'

'Really? I always thought it was perfect for you. I liked to imagine you shut up in the library reading ancient manuscripts written by crazy saints.' The others had disappeared, and Marcus led them along what looked like the path; a circle of rooks blackened the air above the trees, cawing.

'I look around the reading room and I see so many girls like me. It's a way of backing away from the world, I think. To be more comfortable in the past than you are in the present. There's a kind of competition for obscurity between these girls. How arcane a subject can you feasibly write about for eighty thousand words? How little could it possibly relate to the real world? I used to think it was a balance; that the Course and my schoolwork were a balance against the rest of life. But it feels like things have become too heavily weighted in that direction, that real life doesn't stand a chance when measured against all that history, all that abstraction.'

'You'll be fine. You think too much. I can see how much you enjoy it: it's something you're really good at. We all need something like that. And it obviously helps with the Course.'

'I don't know about that. One of the things I realise when I read Margery Kempe or Julian of Norwich is just how conventional the Course's idea of God is. It seems strange that David is so heavily focused on redefining the spiritual side of faith – the way we feel and think and act – but doesn't try to challenge that tired Sunday School image of God. The Course's way of thinking about Him just seems so banal – there's no sense of mystery there.' Lee stooped to look at a clump of small white mushrooms that were growing between a delta of roots that shot out from the foot of an oak. Marcus stooped alongside her, placing his thumb into the feathery fronds that sat beneath the tight caps.

'It does feel like we're still being asked to buy into the idea of an old man with a beard,' Marcus said, as the cap of the mushroom broke from its stem, sending up a puff of white smoke that drifted and dissipated on the breeze.

'Exactly. It's childish,' said Lee.

'But who do you talk to, when you pray, I mean? If you don't picture God like that?'

They continued down the thickly wooded path.

'I don't think of God. I say prayers in the way we were originally intended to: as a way of emptying the mind, readying us for the presence of God. In *The Cloud of Unknowing* there's a line that says "of God Himself no man can think". It's in the stillness when you empty your mind that you get closest to God.'

'And that works for you?'

Lee looked at him through narrow, serious eyes.

'I'm not sure. Sometimes silence makes things better; sometimes it's where I feel most trapped. Because the most awful things can creep into that silence.' Her words faded at the end. They walked a little further; then she continued.

'This voice starts speaking to me. I'm not going mad, don't worry. But this voice is very critical, totally unforgiving. It tells me not to be such a goddamn idiot, that it's all my fault, that I need to pull myself together. And it's not my dad's voice, and it's not my mother's. But it's there and it's making me very unhappy.'

Marcus squeezed her hand and looked over at her. With her thin face and small nose, Lee looked very girlish. He thought that she would always look girlish and, although she wasn't as doomed as she liked to pretend, that there would be a time when that girlishness would grow spinsterly and unbearably sad. She brightened her voice and rested her head playfully on Marcus's shoulder for a moment.

'I'll be all right. Of course I'll be all right. I just feel that I'm in this in-between space, where I'm no longer a girl, but I don't really know how to be a woman yet. Part of me wants to skip straight to old age. I think I'd make a fantastic old lady.'

Marcus smiled ruefully.

'I can see that. You'd have cats.' He could make out David and Abby ahead through a hatch of branches. Philip and Neil were striding behind them. It looked as if they were arguing. Marcus tried to make Lee walk faster, keen to catch up with the others. Her hand was damp in his.

'Margery Kempe went to visit Julian of Norwich for guidance, did you know that?' she asked, turning to look at him.

'No.'

'It's an astonishing thought, that Margery, the great visionary, spent time in the cell of Julian, the first woman to write a book in English, the wisest of all the anchoresses.'

Marcus thought what a good teacher Lee would make. Whenever she talked about her schoolwork her voice came alive, her eyes lit up and she seemed to come out of herself. He thought that this was a possible future for her: if she could make it through to the end of university, get a job at a girls' school somewhere, teach and think and make music. Just as when he saw her on her bike, he sometimes imagined a child seat on the rear mudguard, a nodding blond head, creating for Lee a happy future as a balance against her present sadness. She dropped Marcus's hand and walked a little way in front of him, gesturing as she spoke.

'Margery was amazing. She would have been one of those

ball-breaking City traders if she was alive now. Or a television entrepreneur. She set up a brewery in King's Lynn – it was one of the few jobs that women were allowed to do – she had fourteen children, then, at the age of forty or so, decided she wanted to give herself over to religious life. She struggled to get her husband to take a vow of chastity, describes all his objections in great detail in her book, but finally she succeeded and then set off on pilgrimages all across Europe, having increasingly violent visions at each new shrine.'

Lee continued in a distant, dreamy voice.

'She wrote down her visions, or probably dictated them to someone. Some of them are really trivial, she talks about this great miracle when a vision helped her to find a ring she'd lost, but parts of her text are very moving, particularly her visit to Julian, who must have been at least eighty when Margery came to see her.'

They were moving downhill. Lee took Marcus's hand again. Through the trees, Marcus could see thunderclouds raising their dark hoods on the horizon.

'I like to think that one day I could be like Julian. That people struggling with their faith might come and see me, and I could use all of this bad stuff I've gone through to help them.'

'You will, I'm sure of it. I know what you mean about this being an in-between time, too. I'm sure our parents were grown up by this age. Mine had two kids by the time they were in their mid-twenties. And they were so incredibly happy together, happy in a settled, grown-up way. I still feel like a teenager.'

'It's because we had it so easy,' Lee said, swinging the arm that held Marcus's hand. 'I think one of the reasons my father has these terrible fits of depression is that he can never live up to the memory of his parents. They made it through the war, helped to hide Jews in the lofts of churches in Budapest, then they were these great heroic figures in the resistance against the Soviet occupation. They gave up their lives for an ideal. My father just writes music about it. He gets so frustrated because he wants his music to achieve something impossible: he wants it to match up to the physical heroism of his parents.'

Marcus could hear Mouse's voice somewhere through the trees ahead. Lee continued.

'I don't even have enough of a connection to that history to be able to make music about it. Our generation is so divorced from that time of action, that time of strong idealistic belief. I think it's one of the reasons that the Course has been so successful. It allows us to feel noble, to imagine that we're aspiring to a higher ideal.'

'I'm sure that's right,' Marcus said. 'Humans aren't used to being so comfortable: it goes against our nature. It's maybe why I still feel like an adolescent. Because nothing has happened to make me a man yet.'

Lee smiled shyly at Marcus.

'I've never shown you this.'

She reached into the pocket of her jacket and pulled out her wallet. Opening a flap, she drew out a small photograph. They stopped in a small clearing and looked at the picture. It was a photo of Lee as a child, six or seven, standing on a beach in a red polka-dot swimming costume. Her father stood at her side, the sand sloping steeply away behind them to the sea. One of his hands gripped the young girl's shoulder. Lee was smiling in the photograph, a missing tooth blacking her smile, her nose wrinkling.

'I look at this picture all the time. I just can't believe that I was ever this child, that there is any link between the person I am now and that happy, smiling kid. My problem is that I can't recapture what it felt like to be young like that, I can't draw a thread between now and then. A lot of the time, I'm trying to thrust myself back into the person I was then, or as a teenager. Trying to be anyone else but the me I am now.'

Marcus squeezed her hand and they walked on in silence. The others were waiting for them at the edge of the wood. Abby and the Earl were perched on a tree stump sipping from their thermoses; David and Sally were looking through a book, attempting to identify a toadstool that was growing at the foot of a gnarled elm. Mouse stood further off with Maki. Black clouds blotted the sky behind them.

Marcus didn't see the cows in the next field until they were almost upon them. The ground undulated deceptively, with hillocks hidden by clumps of hawthorn, declivities concealed by brambles. Marcus was walking at the head of the group, Lee and Abby following slightly behind him. The cows seemed to rise out of a dip in the ground and then there they were, almost surrounding Marcus, their large heads turning very slowly to regard the Course members. There was a barbed-wire fence running along one side of the field. A narrow passage led between the fence and the cows. There were perhaps twelve of the beasts. Marcus didn't know what sort of cows they were, but they were enormous: huge, swinging heads on thick necks, massive haunches. There was something prehistoric about them.

'Oh, look at the cows,' he heard Abby say behind him. 'I never know if they're black with white patches or the other way around. What d'you think, Marcus?'

He stared into the cows' bloodshot eyes. He edged towards the channel between the cows and the fence and then gestured for Abby and Mouse to pass behind him. The gate leading out of the field was fifty feet away over rough ground. Abby didn't move. He gestured again and hissed.

'Get moving. Quickly.'

'What? Oh, Marcus, are you scared of the cows?'

Mouse scampered past, cheering, and then stood on the other side of the herd, dancing on the spot. The cows swung their heads from one side to the other, as if weighing their options. Two cows began, with great deliberation, to trot towards Mouse. He backed away, still calling out to the others. The cows increased their pace. It didn't look as if they were moving any faster than a slow trot, but Marcus could see that they were gaining on Mouse. One of the cows nearer Marcus edged towards the fence, looking to close off the passage through which Mouse had passed. Marcus watched as Mouse realised that they were going to catch him. Head down, arms pumping furiously, Mouse plunged towards the gate at the edge of the field. The cows' hoofs pounded the earth, sending up damp clods of turf. Diving, tumbling, Mouse rolled under the bottom of the gate and lay on the ground, panting. Marcus watched the cows come to a disappointed halt and then turn and trot back towards the herd.

David came to stand beside Marcus.

'Bloody stupid animals, aren't they?' The priest was carrying a walking stick with a duck's head carved into the handle. 'Let's clear a way through.'

David stepped towards the nearest cow, raised his stick above his head and brought it down hard on the animal's neck. The cow didn't move, hardly seemed aware of the blow. The priest hit the cow again and began to shout, providing a commentary to the Course members between yells.

'Get on! You need to make it very clear who's boss. Get on with you, I say! Show no fear, don't allow yourself to be intimidated. Yah! Get on now! They're more scared of you than you are of them.'

Marcus doubted this last point. The priest was bringing his stick down with regular, vicious strokes on the forehead of the nearest cow. The animal backed away slowly, drawing into the heart of the herd. Marcus took the opportunity to pass closely along the fence and then, walking very swiftly, he moved towards the gate where Mouse was sucking on a straw. Marcus pulled himself up alongside his friend and called out to the others.

'Just follow me. It's fine. Don't run or panic and you'll be OK.'

He saw Maki and Philip come next, then a group of nervous-looking girls, then Sally and Neil. Lee and Abby hung back with the Earl and David. The cows continued to stare at the priest. He had adopted an aggressive stance, one arm holding the stick poised ready to strike in the air, the other raised in a kind of salute, a universal gesture of *thou shalt not pass*. It was the success of this macho pose that undid them. For as soon as the Earl and the girls had passed, David dropped his arms and turned to follow the others. The cows, as if released from a spell, charged.

'Look out,' yelled Marcus, standing up on the fence.

Abby was at the head of the group, her long legs eating up the ground, bounding over tussocks of grass, leaping blackberry bushes. Next came Lee. Her face was set in frightened concentration. She had gathered up her skirt in her fist and ran with her legs splayed, the pink boots swinging out sideways as she charged forward. The Earl moved very swiftly, his head lowered bullishly. David brought up the rear. Perhaps to save face, he was trying to drive the cows back as he retreated, turning every so often and lashing out with his stick, yelling furiously at these beasts of the field who were conspiring to challenge his authority. Marcus could tell that Sally, who was perched on the gate beside him, was holding her breath.

Abby reached the gate first. Marcus held out an arm and helped her over, taking care that she didn't tear her jeans on the nails sticking out of the wooden gate. When he looked up, David had fallen. Lee and the Earl reached the gate and turned. Lee held her hand to her mouth. Sally let out her breath in a yelp. The cows charged towards the priest, who was struggling to get to his feet.

'His foot's trapped,' said Mouse, a kind of fascinated horror in his voice.

Without pursuing his thoughts far enough to reach a conclusion, Marcus leapt from the gate and ran towards David. The cows had slowed somewhat as they approached him, and reduced their pace further as they saw Marcus's sprinting form heading towards them. But still they moved towards the priest, who was now curled in a ball, unaware of the approach of his putative saviour. Just as they were about to close over him, Marcus arrived, throwing himself down over the priest. With his arms up to cover his own head, Marcus felt David's bony body beneath him, could smell the priest's woody aftershave, feel the coarse wool of his tweed jacket against his cheek. The earth thundered around them, and Marcus found himself praying, mouthing the Lord's Prayer through gritted teeth as mud and grass flew over them. He heard the thump of flesh against flesh as the cows crowded around them. Then silence. Hot, sour breath. A wet muzzle against his ear. Marcus looked up to see the cows trotting away from them. He was suddenly embarrassed to be sprawled over the priest. He rolled away from David and then helped him to prise his boot out of the rabbit hole that had trapped it. They made their way together over to the fence. David smiled bashfully as Sally ran to embrace him. Lee and Abby surrounded Marcus. The others cheered.

'What a hero!'

'That was amazing.'

Marcus batted away their praise and, taking Abby by the hand, set off along the footpath. There was energy in the air, a sense of celebration, of danger averted. David hurried to catch up with Marcus and laid a matey hand on his shoulder, re-phrasing the incident as a moment of shared danger met face-on. The others crowded round as the priest spoke.

'I heard you praying, Marcus. Even with the noise of those animals charging towards us, I could hear your prayers. Did you feel God there? Did you feel Him coming down and pla-cing a barrier around us, something those dumb beasts couldn't break through?'

Marcus shrugged. 'I guess. I wasn't really thinking. I just did it.'

'But you know that is when God is at his most visible, when you're in a moment of emergency. That's when He'll show Himself.'

The path brought them out on the other side of the foot-bridge above the motorway where they had stood the night before. Marcus hung back with Abby. David walked ahead with Mouse to the centre of the bridge, and the two of them leaned far forward over the rail, looking down on the traffic roaring past below. There was a classic car rally taking place at Silverstone, and Marcus could see drivers in open-top vehicles gripping their steering wheels as their cars plunged through the cut in the hillside. Their eyes were narrow slits behind old-fashioned driving goggles. As Marcus and Abby made their way over the bridge, Mouse shouted across to them.

'Look! Look, it's Mr Toad! Poop-poop!'

They followed David up through the wood. Birds called out in the dark shadows around them, unseen creatures scuttled across the red earth, the wind caused the trees to groan. Mar-cus put his arm around Abby's shoulders. Mouse and David had disappeared up the hill, seemingly racing each other to the house. The rest were far behind. They came out into a clear-ing by the lake. Lee caught up with them and the three friends stood by the choppy water and looked up at the large, dark house. The turret pierced the low clouds. At the narrow window halfway up, Marcus saw Mrs Millman's bony face pressed against the glass, sharp eyes looking down at them. She edged away into darkness.

Marcus looked at Lee and there, behind her, was a sight that dried his stare. Above the green cylinder of a pheasant feeder, suspended on a wire from the lowest branches of a tree, hung the rotting body of a rook. Hanging by its claws, the rook's wings still stretched outwards, feathers clinging to the spindly bones. It spun slightly in the breeze. Lee turned and let out a muffled scream.

'Jesus,' Marcus said. Abby gasped.

Lee stumbled back and he caught her. He could see that along the side of the lake there was a line of the grain drums that the gamekeeper used to feed pheasants for the shoot. Above each one hung a dead rook, feathers falling from breasts and wings, eyeless, their bodies slowly growing to resemble the bone grey of their beaks. They all rotated eerily in the gloomy light under the pines, stirred by the fingers of the wind. He could follow the path of each gust in the quivering dead birds. Marcus led the girls hurriedly away from the water.

Back in the house, they took off their boots and made their way up to their rooms. They met Mrs Millman coming down the stairs. She smiled when she saw them.

'Hello, young ones. Did you have a nice walk? You just missed the weather. It gets into my bones when it's like this. I wish it would just break and be done with it. There'll be tea and scones in the hall at four thirty, if you fancy it.'

Marcus and Abby left Lee at the door of her room. The hem of her skirt was black with mud and she looked very tired suddenly.

'Have a sleep, love,' Abby said, hugging her friend.

'I will. I'm done in.' Lee smiled at them and closed the door behind her.

Marcus and Abby lay on their bed reading for an hour as the light faded outside. Recently there had been a number of books published by high-profile academics and journalists attacking Christianity specifically or religious belief in general. Abby had a high pile of these books beside her bed at home and was currently working through one that had a picture of the author in the centre of the back cover, fixing the viewer with his notoriously piercing gaze, the high sweep of his equally famous hair barely contained within the photograph. Marcus put down the novel he was half-reading and nuzzled into the soft skin of Abby's neck.

'Don't you worry about reading those? That you might be persuaded? I can never pick them up.'

Abby laid the book down on her lap and reached over to stroke Marcus's hair, pulling his head onto her chest and running her nails across his scalp.

'No, I don't mind reading them. There are places where I think they're spot on. Some of the rituals around faith are outmoded and ridiculous. Some of the more literal interpretations of the Bible are daft. But they use those examples to reject everything about Christianity. And that's as idiotic as the people they're trying to discredit. What I find most interesting, though, is that sometimes I feel these atheists have a closer relationship with the God they say they hate than a lot of believers. It takes a lot of heart to really hate someone.'

Marcus turned to face her and she placed a long kiss on his lips, slipping her tongue into his mouth. They both kept their eyes open and he could see thoughts moving through her mind like eels at the bottom of a pool. She drew away and smiled down at him.

'It's only recently that the big minds have been on the side of the enemy. You just have to read Milton or Bunyan or C. S. Lewis and they provide everything you need to defend against these books. They're a fad, a way for these vain old men to pay for dental work, ensure that they have beautiful coffins to house them for their disenchanted eternities.'

Marcus liked it when Abby got angry. Her cheeks flushed bullfinch red and she breathed very quickly, her face creasing into a frown of concentration. Her anger always passed swiftly; now her face was once again centred upon her wide smile. Rain began to spot on the windows. Marcus could see it streaming down from the clouds over the woods.

'I feel a bit sick,' Abby said.

'I'm really nervous, too.' He took her hand.

'I just feel like there's so much pressure on us. I really want David to be proud of us. I want him to feel like the Retreat has been a success.'

Marcus was quiet for a moment.

'It's different for you, I think. Because you work for the Course. I worry about some of the ways we keep people attending. Sometimes I think the Course should live and die on its own merits. Poor Maki clearly isn't feeling comfortable, but I think we've almost persuaded her to stick it out.'

'If people stay for long enough, they're converted. You know that. The Course just needs time to do its work, and if we have to be a little disingenuous in order to buy that time, I can live with that. Maki will end up thanking us for it. Sometimes you have to commit a few small sins to achieve something as good and holy as conversion to the Course.'

'You're right. I know you are. But you can see why it makes me uncomfortable.'

Abby smiled distantly at him and rose from the bed. 'We should go downstairs,' she said. 'It's time for tea.'

Marcus knocked on Lee's door on the way down. She

answered it wearing a black blouse that clung tightly to her ribs; the sleeves were fitted around her thin arms and the décolletage dived low, showing a thin strip of mauve bra. She was still in her pants, and turned away from Marcus to pull on a new skirt. While Abby waited in the hallway outside, he watched Lee bend to tug the skirt up over her spindly legs. He imagined stepping behind her, pressing himself against her thin body, feeling the flimsy delicacy of her. She looked quizzically over her shoulder at him, thrust her feet into a pair of white trainers and shut the door behind her.

They ate tea in the hall as the rain roared down around them. Mrs Millman brought out plates of buttered scones. The twins toasted marshmallows by the fire and dropped them into mugs of hot chocolate which they passed around the other Course members. Neil had changed into a blue blazer with nautical gold buttons which he polished absent-mindedly with his handkerchief as he listened to David and the Earl, who were sitting in armchairs by the fire. The Earl was speaking loudly about a mine he had invested in after a tip-off from a priest.

'He's out at the Anglican mission in Baku. Does a service every now and then for BP executives and their wives, but mainly he's quietly lining his own pockets. Tipped me off about this uranium find a couple of years back and it has been quite spectacular ...'

Philip and Maki chatted quietly in a corner. When the scones had disappeared, a comfortable lull fell over the group. Marcus lolled in an armchair in one corner with Abby perched on the arm; Mouse, with his nose pressed against the window, watched the rain fall in the darkness outside; Lee sat at his side, her hand on his back. After a few minutes, David rose from his chair, stood next to the fire and spoke, his white shirt very bright above khaki chinos.

'It's time for me to go down and prepare for this evening's service. This is the centrepiece of the Retreat, the heart of the whole Course, really. You guys should make your way down when you feel ready. It is a good idea to sit down there and prepare yourselves to speak to God before we begin. We'll be playing some gentle music to help get you in the mood before we start the service proper at six. I'll be praying for all of you. Good luck and God bless.'

He strode towards the doors, flung them open and stepped out into the darkness and the rain. The Earl followed him into the deluge and Marcus watched them scurry down to the chapel. He stood up, took Abby by the hand and led her outside. Mouse and Lee followed, with Mouse's velvet jacket tented above them. Inside the chapel it was very dark. Marcus and Abby still held hands. Someone flicked a switch and a spotlight cut along the aisle, exploding onto the backcloth behind the altar. David stepped into the circle of light. Marcus followed the beam to its source and saw the Earl perched behind a lighting desk in the shadows at the back of the chapel, his fingers moving swiftly over the controls. The beam falling on David faded imperceptibly, until there was only a golden aura surrounding him. Then another spotlight shone onto the stage to the left of the altar, and the four friends walked together down the aisle and took up their positions. Marcus picked up his bass guitar, Mouse sat behind the drum kit, Abby sat on the edge of the stage swinging her legs. Lee started to play the 'Promenade' from *Pictures at an Exhibition*, imbuing the music with great sadness. Finally, the priest stepped up to join them, and picked out a series of minor chords on the guitar which he strapped around his neck.

Marcus saw the Course members coming into the chapel in twos and threes, picking their way self-consciously down the aisle. Neil and the twins were first, then Philip and Maki, then

Colchester [colkiosk5]

Please keep your receipt
Renewals/Enquiries: 0345603/628

Borrowed Items 24/04/2017 10:23

XXXXXXXXXXXXXX
XXXXXXXXXXX6742

Item Title	Due Date
30130203472666	15/05/2017
30130210834957	15/05/2017

Thank you for using Essex Libraries
www.essex.gov.uk/libraries
or visit www.essexcc.gov.uk/libraries

a cluster of younger girls from his group, followed by their boyfriends. Finally, Sally and Mrs Millman entered, shaking the water from their umbrellas. The members sat in the pews at the front of the chapel, again holding candles that the Earl had handed to them on the way in.

Abby hummed quietly, her eyes shut, her feet still swinging. Marcus turned his bass down until it was scarcely audible. Mouse circled his brushes over the snare so that the noise from the drum was barely distinguishable from the sound of the rain falling on the chapel roof. The Earl was back behind the lighting desk and he brought the spot up very slowly so that the group on the stage seemed to be at the centre of the room. The music rose gradually and Abby climbed to her feet, stretching her arms upwards as she began to sing.

> 'We can never know You,
> Until we know ourselves,
> And we'll never find ourselves
> Until we find You, Lord.'

Mouse had picked up his drumsticks and began to crash out a driving military beat. Marcus turned up his volume switch and, moving into the middle of the stage, David played a series of explosive power chords. The rest of the Course members joined in with the song's chorus, the mix of voices swirling around the small church.

> 'All shall be well,
> And all shall be well,
> And all manner of things
> Shall be well.'

When the music ended, David put down his guitar and

stepped into the beam of light that fell upon the altar. The four musicians left on the stage – now in darkness – turned to watch him. The priest pressed his hands together and unleashed his vivid smile. The rain was still falling. Marcus saw that one of the twins' candles had gone out. He watched her light it from her sister's flame. The silence continued. Then David's voice, low and full of power:

'Welcome. This is a very special night. Each Course has its own character, its own concerns, its own life. This group has grown to be very special to me. Not only is it the first Course to be looked after by our new Course leaders, but I also feel a great sense of holiness among you, a great urge to be close to God. This service will help some of you make that leap. Let us be quiet for a moment. Let us allow silence to work its magic around us, let us dwell with God in that awesome silence that was everywhere before He said *Let there be light.*'

Marcus worried at the strap of his guitar. Threads were coming loose, the leather buckle was cracked and peeling. He looked out into the bent heads of the congregation, downward-turned faces illuminated by the candles they held in their laps. He watched Maki tuck a black ribbon of hair behind her ear to stop it from catching in the flame. After the prayers, there was another long silence and the wind moaned above the sound of the rain. The priest began to talk again, walking down the aisle and facing the Course members as he spoke. Fixing each of them in turn with his bright, pale eyes.

'Don't be afraid of letting yourself go. We are brought up to believe that losing control of ourselves is wrong; but only by letting go of yourself will you find yourself. Turn towards the child in you, the innocent in you. Jesus said: *I tell you the truth, unless you change and become like little children, you will never enter the kingdom of heaven. Therefore, whoever humbles himself like a child is the greatest in the kingdom of heaven.* Let us

174

remember what it was like to have the hope, the optimism of children. Help us, we who are blind like the beggar in Jericho, gain our sight. Help us Lord to open up our hearts to you, to step aside from the sinful, corrupt people we are and move to- wards the people we wish to be. Let us open our arms to you, Lord.'

David placed his hands on Philip's shoulders and turned him to face the aisle.

'Philip, I see good in you. Open yourself up to the Lord. Will you, Philip?'

Philip looked at Maki beside him, then over towards Lee on the stage. 'I will,' he mumbled.

'Alice, Ele.' He took each of the twins by the hand and raised their arms into the air. They held their candles towards him and the priest's face glowed. 'You are the Lord's children now. He loves you with a great love. Will you follow Him?'

'We will,' the twins replied.

David walked back down the aisle and stood facing the altar for a moment, then turned to face the members again, speak- ing very quickly, his head nodding as he spoke.

'Let the Holy Spirit into your hearts, lose yourself in the love of Jesus, fall into His arms and let Him take the weight of your sins, your heartache.'

Lee, still in darkness, started to play the same series of slowly descending chords as the night before, and Abby, her voice clear and powerful, sang alone.

> 'I must become God,
> And God must become me,
> So that we can share
> The same "I" eternally.'

David stood trapped in the beam of light that fell upon the

altar. His white shirt shone as he held his arms up to the roof, turned his head upwards and opened his mouth to sing. The light around him increased again until Marcus found it hard to look at the priest. David began to shake in the light, his thin body stretched out, his long fingers reaching up to the sky. He started to chant, again inserting his words rhythmically into the interstices of Abby's song.

'Weilala, shanti, shanti, leilala.'

The music grew louder. Marcus and Mouse began to play, the drums and bass picking up the rhythms of the priest's song. The light came up on the stage and Marcus blinked out over the audience. The Course members in the congregation started singing along with Abby. All eyes were trained on the priest. The sound was beautiful, a language that hid its meaning behind the words, that danced and swooped and shone around them.

Sally shuffled past Philip and out into the aisle. She held up her hands towards her husband and began to speak in tongues, her eyes tightly shut, her head shaking violently from side to side as she moved in time to the music. The words – like the priest's – seemed ripped from an ancient world, the chanting of a forgotten race. Marcus watched the Earl behind the lighting desk train the spot down the aisle. Mouse was the next to be seized by the Spirit. He yelped and squealed, called out in a high voice as he crashed his cymbals and rolled the snare. Abby fell down on her knees. She tried to keep singing the words of the song but, possessed, strange phrases fell from her lips. She twitched like a compass needle and held her hands up to the sky, shaking them in trembling ecstasy.

The twins were the first of the new members to let themselves go. The girls blew out their candles and made their way out into the aisle to join Sally. Ele took her sister by the hand, held it upwards and began to scream. Alice lifted her own voice alongside that of her twin. Slowly their words came through, the screaming softened into the beauty of the tongues. Sally wrapped her arms around them and hugged them to her chest as they laughed and chanted.

Marcus had never spoken in tongues. He had not been able to give himself up to the Spirit during the first Retreat, and ever since he had found the whole process rather embarrassing. As he played his guitar he yodelled every so often, trying to copy David's voice as closely as possible. He would have liked to be able to abandon himself the way Abby did, rolling on the floor at his feet, a grin of utter exultation on her face, but he knew he would never be able to embrace this central part of the Course. Marcus was surprised that Lee hadn't joined in yet. She was usually one of the first to go, said that she felt as if she was falling into a warm nothingness when the tongues got hold of her. Marcus looked over at her and saw that she was hitting the chords automatically, her shoulders slumped, none of the usual intensity that surrounded her when she was playing.

Neil moved into the aisle, walking with his head held up as if in challenge to his own shyness. He sank to his knees and lifted his trembling arms, fixing his eyes intently on David, who was still stretching skywards. Neil began to keen gently, his cheek pressed to his shoulder as he cried. The girls from Marcus's group chanted as one, leaning heavily against their braying boyfriends, weak from the Spirit. By the end only Philip, Maki and Mrs Millman stood unaffected in the congregation. Even the Earl let out a brief series of grunts and barks.

With a nod to Marcus and Mouse, Lee stopped playing. The Earl, startled from his reverie, brought the lights down so that the priest was held in a golden glow; the rest were in darkness. Abby continued to call out for a while longer, there was the sound of the voices slowly abating, the occasional yelp from Mouse or Neil. The storm raged outside, but its tone was altered. Marcus thought that the deluge seemed somehow tamed by the power of what he had witnessed in the little chapel. As the lights came slowly up, Neil stood, head bowed, in the centre of the aisle. Marcus reached down to help Abby to her feet. The twins pressed themselves against Sally's chest, shoulders heaving. The priest's wife hugged them closely to her, whispering quietly in their small, pointed ears. Then David spoke, his eyes turned seriously upon the congregation.

'For those of you who have just experienced the tongues for the first time, congratulations. It is an immense feeling, to have the Holy Spirit come down upon you and speak through you. For those who weren't moved by the Spirit this time, don't worry. It's not for everyone; it certainly isn't required. Now please take your seats again and let us pray. God, thank you for moving among us in this place. Thank you for blessing us with the presence of your Holy Spirit. May you not leave us now, but continue to speak to us, and through us. Lord in your mercy, hear our prayer.'

After a long silence, the priest walked down the aisle shaking hands with the congregation, smiling and laying his hands on their heads, blessing them and welcoming them into the church. Marcus saw Philip drift away from the group, pretending to admire the ogees that lined the columns alongside the nave. Marcus tried to move towards him, but David was shepherding people towards the door and Marcus was swept up in the happy babbling surge of Course members. The priest led them out into the night, where the rain had finally stopped and mist was curling up towards the house from the lake. Marcus walked up to the hall with Lee, who looked at him with a strange complicit glance as they left the chapel. She insisted on sitting beside him when they got to the hall, perching on the arm of his chair as Abby had earlier, occasionally smoothing his hair distractedly with her cold, thin fingers.

A sense of exultation fizzed around the new Course members as they waited for dinner. The Earl and David poured wine into glasses on a table that had been laid along one side of the hall. A huge vase of heavily scented lilies sat on the main dining table. Sally kept fidgeting with the arrangement, and each time she touched them, orange pollen stained her fingers. The twins stood at the centre of a circle of members, falling over each other to describe what they had just experienced.

'And it was like everything dropped away . . .'

'And you were falling, but you knew someone was there to catch you . . .'

'It would have been scary but . . .'

'But it wasn't. It felt wonderful. I remember taking Alice's hand and it was like we were one person.'

'Exactly, Ele, like we were one person falling together.'

'It was so beautiful. Not just the sound of the singing, but the feeling of love.'

'It felt like we had spent all our lives until that point searching for something . . .'

'And we didn't know what it was we were searching for until the tongues came along. Then we knew. It was that. It was giving ourselves up to the Holy Spirit.'

Neil stepped forward, his bald head shining, and put his arms around the twins. There was a great deal of hugging that evening. The twins gripped Neil passionately, and Marcus was distressed to see the older man's body shaking with sobs. David stepped towards the group and laid his hands on Neil's shoulders. Neil turned from the twins and embraced the priest. Abby strode over to them and wrapped the pair in her long, strong arms. They stood for a while, breathing deeply. Mouse was talking with great intensity to Sally and a couple of the girls from Marcus's group next to the fire. He scurried over to the table to refill his wine glass every so often. Whenever a bottle was finished, the Earl or Mrs Millman opened another. Abby and Lee were also drinking heavily. Lee would give Marcus's hand a squeeze each time she left him to refill her glass. Marcus realised he hadn't seen Philip for a while.

Dinner found most of the Course members drunk. Even David was flushed and beaming, an extra button open on his shirt revealing a hairless white chest beneath. Sally was sitting next to Mouse and they continued to speak very earnestly. Marcus had only had a couple of glasses of wine, partly because he found it hard to stir himself from the comfortable armchair, and partly because he was tired and full of conflicting emotions after the drama of the service. He noticed that Maki was sitting alone at the head of the table. She picked slowly at her food, making ridges in her mashed potato with the tines of her fork, lifting up a piece of lamb and then allowing it to fall back to her plate. Marcus pulled a chair over to the corner of the table and sat down.

'Don't worry, Maki. It's not everything. Some people never speak in tongues.'

Maki was quiet, made another slow tour of her plate with a fork held like a dagger, sending runner beans writhing in its wake.

'It's not that. I just feel this has been a waste of my time. I should have been doing something useful, should have learned another language, or at least gone out and made some real friends. I sat there, looking at you all, and it just struck me as very funny. And a little bit sad.'

'I guess it's not for everyone.'

'It was so un-English, all that emotion. It seemed bizarre to me.'

'It really works for some people.'

'Not for me. You're too bright for this, Marcus. You know that, don't you?'

She looked at him quizzically. He met her gaze and then stared down at the plate of food. He felt hands gripping his shoulders.

'Hey guys, what are you talking about?' Lee brought her face close to Marcus's ear, her breath hot against his skin, sweet with alcohol. Her fingers kneaded the muscles in his neck.

'Maki wasn't carried away by the service. She didn't speak in tongues.'

Lee laughed. When she spoke, her voice was manic, interrupted by stutters and giggles.

'Oh, don't worry about that, dear. Half of us fake it anyway. It's all just part of the game. I bet you David fakes it sometimes. I always find it a bit fishy that the Holy Spirit can be called up on demand like a genie in a lamp. And each performance so perfectly controlled. I always got the feeling that true revelation needed a bit more work than that. And got a lot messier. Now, who wants another drink? I'm going to get shitfaced.'

'Sorry. I'm going upstairs. Goodnight.'

Maki made her way slowly down the hall towards the steps, her head held up, a melancholy half-smile on her lips. Marcus was about to follow her, but Lee draped herself further over his shoulders, the blinking of her eyelashes flashing across his cheeks, her lips dangerously close to his own. He reached for his glass of wine and drank from it, then held it up for Lee to take a swig. She giggled as red liquid spilled down her chin.

Lee sat down in Maki's place and began to eat her meal, chewing the lamb stew loudly, shovelling fluffy white potato between her wet lips. Abby was further down the table between David and Mouse, and Marcus watched her turning from side to side, joining Mouse's discussion with Sally and then, catching something that David was saying to the twins or to Neil, turning back to the new members. Lee had begun to tell Marcus about her visit to Lindisfarne earlier in the year. She gripped hold of his hand as she spoke and he could feel the bones of her fingers through her skin.

'The church has these amazing buttresses that face out to the North Sea, so worn away by the wind and the rain over the years that they seem to be made out of coral, to grow out of the land. When I was there in March there was a storm blowing up and the waves were crashing over them. It was amazing, it really was.'

Marcus, who had only been half-listening, saw Philip standing in the doorway looking over towards him.

'Sorry, Lee. Give me a second, will you?' he said, and rose from the table. He walked over towards the door where Philip had already backed away into the shadows. He was standing in the entrance hall beside a ragged blue holdall, his leather jacket fastened to his throat. He smiled at Marcus and shook his head.

'Sorry to interrupt your dinner. Do you think you'd drive me to the station? There's a train from Banbury at ten. I'll call a taxi if it's a problem.'

'Have you told David you're leaving?'

'No.'

'Don't you think you should? I mean, he might want to speak with you. I know that it can be frightening to hear the whole tongues thing, and not manage to do it yourself. I almost walked out after the Saturday night service on my first Retreat.'

Philip picked up the holdall and turned to look towards the front doors.

'I'd prefer not to see him, if that's OK. I'd just really like to go.'

Marcus stood leaning against the frame of the door. Philip

watched him through narrow eyes. A few moments passed and then, with a sigh, Marcus spoke. 'Fine. I'll take you. I don't think we should force anyone to stay here that doesn't want to.' They walked out into the night.

The mist was now thick in the air outside, licking itself around the gables and turrets of the house, snaking between the trees and lying out along the gravel of the driveway. The lights that shone at the front of the house caught the mist and sent bright swirling haloes up into the air above them. Dampness dripped down from the trees as they crossed to where the Audi was parked.

The mist fell away behind them when they pulled out of the driveway and the night on the crest of the hill was vast and bright above the little car. They drove along the narrow ridge in silence and then turned onto the Banbury Road.

'I felt awkward in there earlier. Awkward and very lonely,' said Philip, staring away from Marcus into the darkness. The moon was dimmer than the previous night, but its light was enough to discern the outlines of the surrounding valleys, farmsteads, villages.

'Sometimes it can take a few attempts before you manage the tongues.'

'It wasn't that. Or it wasn't only that. It was just that nothing had changed. I felt that I had come all this way, sat through all these sermons and discussions and heard all this high talk and then, when it came down to it, I felt nothing. I was in the same boring service listening to the same meaningless words.'

'You just need to give it more time. I'm not completely there myself yet, and I've been doing this for years. You should try to stick it out.'

'I have. I've spent so much time in St Botolph's. And the time I'm not there, I think about you all. It's very appealing for someone like me, someone who you guys wouldn't even consider as a friend in the real world, to find himself in the middle of such a bright, beautiful gang. Tempting for me to just fake the religion to stay part of it.'

'Oh, come on, Philip, that's not fair.'

'Isn't it? Look at Lee. She's always talking about love and forgiveness, but she used me. She didn't think of my feelings for a moment once she had what she wanted, and you'll all be the same. You'll cast me aside because I won't let myself become some gibbering fool in praise of a God that I don't believe in.'

They continued to drive in silence. As they reached the outskirts of Banbury, Philip spoke again.

'I think Lee's really close to the edge. Please watch her, will you? Some of the things she said that night we were together really frightened me. You need to take care of her, Marcus. If you don't, no one will.'

'There is a whole community of us looking out for her, don't worry.'

'I'm just not sure that everyone has her best interests at heart.'

They turned into the station car park and Marcus switched off the engine. They sat in silence for a while. Marcus watched taxi drivers smoking with gloved fingers beside their cabs, a family pulling luggage towards the station, a bus slowly disgorging its sleepy passengers onto the forecourt. He could smell something sweet and industrial in the air. Philip opened the door and set his holdall on the ground outside. He reached over and shook Marcus's hand.

'Thanks for driving me. I liked you best of all of them. You and Abby are good people. I'm sorry I couldn't see it through. I would've liked to be friends with you.'

'We can still be friends.'

'No. No, we can't. Maybe you don't realise it, but you won't ever really be friends with someone who isn't in the Course. You look down on me now. Perhaps you're right to.'

He stepped out into the night and a blast of cold air came into the car when he shut the door. Marcus watched him walk across the forecourt. Philip turned and half-raised his hand before passing out of sight. Marcus switched on the radio and listened to old soul songs, feeling guilty for having let David down, but also, at a deeper level, that he had done the right thing. The signal faded as he turned off the Banbury Road and he drove along the ridge in melancholy silence, spotting the entrance to the driveway by the plume of mist that reached out into the road.

The sound of raucous voices and loud music blared from the hall when he came back into the house. He stood at the steps leading into the long room and saw people dancing, chairs overturned, bottles and glasses everywhere. The Nightingales, Mrs Millman and the Earl had gone to bed. Neil was passed out in the chair that Marcus had sat in earlier. The wardrobe doors were open and Marcus saw that the twins were inside. One or other of them would poke a head or an arm out, calling to Abby or Lee to come and inspect the treasures they had discovered. Mouse was striding up and down the main dinner table, the Napoleon hat on his head, a white fox stole around his shoulders. He was carrying a bottle of red wine from which he swigged as he recited from *The Wind in the Willows* and *Alice in Wonderland*. Lee sat below him, laughing and clapping. She waved at Marcus, her blue-green eyes flashing wickedly. Marcus heard snatches of Mouse's words as he passed, and he remembered the books from his childhood and felt suddenly nostalgic and full of love for his friends.

'Oh dear! Oh dear! I shall be too late . . . How doth the little crocodile . . . Poop-poop!'

Marcus walked over to Abby, who was sitting at a table on her own. She had taken a lily from the vase on the table and wore the white flower behind one ear.

'The Earl', she said, looking up at him with a grin, 'was so delighted by the service that he gave me the key to his cellar. I've been drinking port. Port makes me feel very silly.' Her lips and her large teeth behind them were stained purple. Marcus shook his head and sat down beside his wife.

'Let's have a glass then,' he said.

Hours passed. Neil made his way groggily up to bed. The twins fell asleep in the wardrobe. Marcus looked in to see them curled up on a nest of fur coats. Only the four friends were still awake. Mouse and Abby were talking in a corner, surrounded by bottles of wine. Mouse waved his hands as he spoke, taking off his hat and brandishing it every so often to emphasise a point. Marcus was in his favourite armchair with Lee perched once again on the arm. She was very drunk, slurring as she spoke. She leaned against him, one arm around his shoulders, her fingers playing with the hair at the nape of his neck. Her earlier melancholy had entirely disappeared, replaced with a kind of manic enthusiasm.

'We should go on a proper retreat. I've been reading about this one in north Wales. You go up into the mountains, stay in tents pitched around an old chapel, spend the days praying and walking and swimming in ice-cold lakes. I think that's maybe the best way to get close to God.'

'It sounds amazing,' Marcus said.

'I don't know if David would get jealous, us going on someone else's retreat.'

Mouse strutted over to them, carrying an armful of lilies, the pollen running orange streaks through the white fur of his stole.

'Abby and I would be delighted if you'd join us for a trip to pay homage to our great lords of the high road, the titans of the tarmac. I want to drop flowers down on the lorries, let the blessing of nature purify their sooty hearts.'

Abby was already gently easing a fur out from beneath one of the sleeping twins. Lee wrapped herself in a rabbit-skin coat that hung down to the ground. She left the front open, revealing her low-cut black top. Marcus pulled a bearskin around his shoulders like a cloak. He thought it was probably supposed to be a rug: it trailed behind him as he walked out into the misty night. Mouse and Abby had already started down the path ahead of them. The mist deadened sound as they made their way down into the valley; Marcus could no longer hear the motorway. Lee stopped to light cigarettes for both of them, struggling to get the flame to catch in the damp air. Marcus helped her and took a long drag, blowing the smoke out to meet the misty air. When he looked up, Mouse and Abby had disappeared. Lee took his hand and scurried along the path, making her way fleet-footed over the red earth, skipping above half-hidden roots and tree stumps. Marcus thrust his cigarette into his mouth and struggled to keep up with her.

There was no definite point at which Marcus realised that they were lost. The mist had an extraordinary disorienting effect, and Lee's scampering flight had been so swift that he hadn't noticed that the path, which had seemed well-worn and familiar in the daylight, had merged into the surrounding earth. He let go of Lee's hand and looked around. She turned back towards him, laughing, gesturing him onwards.

'We're not on the path any more,' he said.

'It doesn't matter,' she replied, 'we just need to carry on down until we reach the motorway embankment. We can make our way along to the bridge from there. Come on, this is fun.'

Marcus stopped. He peered further into the trees around

them. It had grown lighter, and when he looked closely he could see that all of the trees around them were dead. The spindly skeletons of pines stretched skywards, the wizened fingers of branches white in the moonlight, the trunks reaching up from the mist that swirled around their roots. There was no foliage on the branches, nothing but mist to impede the searing white light of the moon. Bark peeled back like diseased skin. Marcus pressed his hand against one of the trees and felt the crêpelike wood dissolve under his touch. The world was only whiteness and shadow and the skeleton fingers of the trees all seemed to point at Marcus. He made out a darker shadow in the distance.

'What's that through there?'

He took her hand, which was damp and hot, and led her across the uneven ground, around the rotting trunk of a fallen tree and over a small ridge into a clearing. They were beside the lake, whose surface was trapped under a thick cushion of mist. The shape that Marcus had seen was the boathouse. One of the grain drums stood next to them, its rook corpse turning slowly in the mist above.

'How did we end up here?' He looked up and could just make out the dark mass of the house above them. 'I thought we were much further down. At least we know that this path leads to the motorway.'

Lee didn't answer. She was standing on the bank of the lake, looking out into the thickly packed mist, which glowed where it was illuminated by moonlight away from the shadows of trees. Marcus came up behind her and put his arms around her, pulling the bearskin rug about them both. She was breathing very quickly, and he saw her breath on the air in front of them. She half-turned her head and leaned back against him. He could feel his own heart beating as it pressed against her back.

'It's like the *Morte d'Arthur*,' she said.

'It's beautiful.'

She pulled away from him, walked over towards the boat-house, hesitated for a moment, and then stepped out into the mist that sat above the lake. Marcus jumped towards her, ready to pull her from the cold water. Only when he was beside the boathouse did he realise that she had stepped out into a rowing boat that was moored to the deck in front of the small wooden building.

'Come in. Let's row out into the lake. I want to look up at the moon through the mist.' She moved up to the prow of the small boat and lay back, her legs folded beneath her.

Marcus stepped unsteadily onto the boat. The misty air was a cold blanket around his shoulders. He sat down upon the central bench and felt on the floor for the oars. He rowed them slowly out into the centre of the lake. The water slapped gently against the sides of the boat. After a while he let them drift and made his way towards Lee. The mist was very thick around them; it was as if it were something solid that re-formed each instant to accommodate the gentle passage of the boat through the water. The moon was a faint silver smudge above them, the surrounding trees were shadows. Marcus lay down on the floor of the boat, his head in Lee's lap. He pulled the bearskin over them. He felt the shifting of the water beneath him, imagined the fish moving among the weeds below. Lee ran her long fingers through his hair.

'We could be anywhere. Anywhere, at any time. Floating through an endless night.'

The boat rocked as Lee shifted and leaned over him. He looked up at the halo of her short, damp hair, then shuffled further into the warm darkness of her lap.

'Do you ever think about that time at university?' Her voice was a whisper. He heard her light a cigarette. After taking a drag she held it in his mouth. With one hand she continued to stroke his hair. He spoke into the coarse hair of the rug.

'Yes. I mean, I try not to think about it. It makes me guilty. But it was only a kiss.'

'Yes, it was only a kiss.'

They lay and felt the air thicken around them. Marcus tried to work out whether she could also feel whatever it was that was building in the mist, grabbing hold of his heart and his groin, making his breaths come in shallow gasps. One of her hands continued to caress his hair, finding new paths to trace across his scalp, exposing new trails of nerve-ends that thrilled as her nails travelled across them. His face was pressed against the softness of her belly. A night bird called somewhere in the trees over the boathouse. She stopped stroking Marcus and pushed him gently away from her, lifting the bearskin and wrapping it about herself. He moved back to sit on the central bench. Lee's voice came at him as if from a great distance, as cold as the mist that surrounded them.

'You fake it, don't you, the speaking in tongues? I can tell. I can tell when I watch you because I fake it, too.'

Marcus drew in a cool, damp breath.

'I don't know, Lee. It's tough. Have you ever done it, you know, properly?'

'Maybe once, at the very beginning. I felt like I was drifting away. It was like I get sometimes when I listen to a really beautiful piece of music, or read a poem that really speaks to me. But recently, I haven't felt anything at all. I so wanted it to be this big revelation. I've been waiting and waiting for it, my Damascus moment, but it has never arrived. I think tonight I might have given up.'

A gust of wind skimmed across the lake, billowing the mist. Marcus shivered.

'It always made me feel close to you,' Lee said, 'that neither

190

of us could do it. That we were both faking it. It was a secret we shared.'

Now the moon had disappeared entirely; its only relic was the silver glow that suffused the air. Everything was mist, so thick that Marcus felt that if he reached his arm out from his shoulder, he might never see it again. He could hardly make out Lee across the boat. He grabbed one of the oars and paddled listlessly at the water, moving them in slow circles. He felt Lee shifting around in the boat, caught a glimpse of movement from the prow when he strained his eyes towards her.

'Come over here.' Her voice a heavy whisper. As he sank to his knees, she began to appear more clearly through the gauze of mist. The first thing he noticed was her eyes. They sparkled dangerously and fixed upon him, drawing him towards them. He kneeled on the floor of the boat between her legs. Lee was lying back on the warm pile of furs, bare from the waist down. Her skirt was rolled beneath her head as a pillow. Her black blouse served only to accentuate the pale legs that stretched out from the shadowy mound between them.

'I've always wanted you to go down on me.' She leaned forward and knitted her hand into the hair at the back of his head. He eased himself down until all was blackness and the slick saltiness of her against his tongue. Goose pimples on her thighs. He closed his eyes. The boat rocked as he flicked his tongue over her; she twisted his hair between her fingers as he moved faster. She began to arch her back, pressing herself against him, grinding his head down into her lap. He tried to stretch up and cup one of her breasts. She gently batted the hand away. He buried his face further into the bulge of her pubic hair. He remembered when, as a child, he had built himself a den in the middle of a clump of ferns in the woods at the back of his house, tramping down a circle at the centre and then pulling the encircling green fronds over himself. It

191

was damp and the ferns tickled his skin, but he had felt very safe there. He thought of the den as he whipped his tongue over the soft tufty dampness of her pussy. Lee let out a sighing squeal like air released from a bicycle tyre. Marcus rose back up to kneel at her feet; leaning over, he tried to place a kiss on her lips but she turned away, presenting him with a cold hard cheek. Her teeth were chattering. She pulled on her pants and unrolled her skirt, snaking her way into it on the floor of the boat.

Marcus rowed them back to the shore and tied the boat to the deck in front of the boathouse. He reached out an arm and helped her to step onto the bank. They walked in silence down the path towards the motorway. Marcus lit two cigarettes and passed one to Lee. She took it without thanks. Finally, they heard the noise of the surging traffic in the distance. She quickened her pace, walking a few feet ahead of him as the slope steepened. The mist still wove its fingers between the trees, and Marcus kept thinking he saw shapes forming in the corners of his eyes, figures watching him from behind the adumbrated trunks of the pines. He scurried to catch up with Lee.

'Is it true Philip left earlier?' she asked.

'Yes. I drove him to the station.'

'Did you tell David?'

'No.'

'He'll be cross.'

'I know. I think he has the impression that all he has to do is get people as far as the Retreat and then any reservations will be blown away by the beauty of the voices, by the sense of community and friendship and safety. But Philip was just, I don't know, disappointed.'

Lee sighed and flicked her cigarette into the misty foliage that surrounded them.

They rounded a bend in the path and saw Mouse and Abby coming up the hill hand in hand. Mouse was carrying a bottle of wine. Each time he took a swig he would pass it to Abby, who gulped in turn. They were both laughing and Mouse raised the bottle in the air when he saw Marcus and Lee on the crest of the hill above them.

'Hey you two! Where did you get to? You missed an inspiring ceremony. Abby and I scattered lily petals onto the roofs of the lorries. We allowed nature to cover over the abomination of the motorway-beast.'

He stood before them, panting, and held out the bottle. Lee took it and swigged greedily. Marcus, whose head was beginning to pound, smiled and looked at Abby. Her cheeks were flushed and she had turned up the collar of her coat so that her wide face nestled in a frame of fur. Her eyes were soft and kind and she reached out her arms to him. Marcus stepped into her embrace and tried to return the love that he felt flowing from her, but all he could think about was the boat's hard floor against his knees, the taste of Lee that still flooded his mouth and his nostrils, the sin he had committed. The four made their way back up the hill towards the house, Mouse still chattering wildly.

Lee and Abby went up the stairs together while Mouse and Marcus struggled to impose some sort of order on the chaos of the dining hall. Marcus woke the twins, who stretched and yawned like cats, smiling up at him as he attempted to eject them from their wardrobe lair. Mouse collected glasses and bottles, stacked chairs and straightened the tables. They worked quietly, the house heavy and silent around them. When they had finished, Mouse clapped Marcus on the back and they made their way upstairs together.

'I'm just having the most brilliant time. I live for this, you know?'

Abby was already asleep when Marcus came into their room. The curtains were open and a banner of moonlight fell down across the bed, illuminating Abby's pale skin, her white pyjama bottoms. He crossed to the window and looked out into the night. The mist had receded and now hung only over the lake, which was a silver cloud in the valley below. He pressed his hands against the cold glass of the window. Abby turned over in bed and sighed. Marcus took off his clothes until he was standing naked in the bright whiteness of the moon. There was something purifying about the light, and it was with a sense of regret that he pulled the curtains closed, the darkness covering Abby. He crossed to the sink and brushed his teeth in a thin needle of water, keen not to wake her. He slipped into bed next to his wife, who groaned in her sleep and turned over again, gathering the duvet between her legs. Marcus lay on his back, not minding the cold, and fell into a deep, dark sleep.

He woke twice in the night from nightmares where the decomposing rooks, oscillating in the misty air above the pheasant feeders, came suddenly alive, screeching and flapping their bone-wings, trying to escape the wire that held their feet. Each time he woke, his heart racing, his face hot despite the coldness of his uncovered body, he felt that someone had been in the room until just a moment before he opened his eyes. His mouth was dry but he couldn't move from the bed, frozen by a creeping horror that unfurled in his mind when the night's events came back to him. He heard noises echoing around the dark house, thumps and creaks and, once, the faint sound of someone crying out. He slept fitfully until the sky lightened outside his window. When the hands of his watch moved around to seven o'clock, he rose and dressed silently. He needed to speak to Lee.

Three

The curtains of Lee's room were open, revealing a grey world where the pine trees huddled in conspiratorial conference above the still waters of the lake. The abandoned nests of rooks and jackdaws hung in the trees' tallest branches like lookout posts on ships' masts. Marcus saw Lee's clothes strewn across the carpet and thought that she too, on returning to her room the night before, had crossed to look down upon the lake. Her bed had been slept in. The sheets were crumpled and the duvet kicked to the floor. He could see streaks of the orange pollen from the lilies scattered across her pillow. He wondered if she had taken one of the flowers up to bed with her.

He walked along the corridor and looked down on the empty courtyard below. The photographs of the Earl's ancestors seemed to pass judgement upon him as he crossed in front of them. He stepped down the main stairway and the silence and the gilt-framed portraits and the cool light coming down from the atrium roof made him feel like he was in a museum that had been closed to the public for many years, a repository of dead memories. When he came into the kitchen the lights were off but Mouse was sitting at the table with a mug of steaming coffee, staring out into the bleak morning. His hair was a wild shriek above his head, his shoulders slumped as he sipped at the coffee.

'Hi, Mouse. Are you OK?' said Marcus.

Mouse jumped and turned to look at Marcus.

'Hello, sport. What are you doing up?'

'I couldn't sleep.'

'Me neither. It was a big day yesterday. I feel a bit sad that it's over.' He spoke very quickly, and Marcus noticed that his hands were shaking enough for coffee to spill from the mug.

Marcus sat down next to Mouse and felt his friend's leg jittering beneath the table. He gently put his hand on Mouse's knee. Marcus could smell body odour, vegetation, coffee. The bags under Mouse's bulging eyes reached down his cheeks.

'You know Philip went home?'

Mouse took a sip of coffee.

'Did he?' He shrugged. 'It's a shame, but there's always a few who get freaked out. We shouldn't beat ourselves up too much. I always thought he was a bit flaky.'

They sat together in silence as the house slowly woke around them. They heard doors banging and voices and then Mrs Millman came bustling into the room.

'Well then you two, sitting here in the dark. Let's have some lights on and I'll make bacon and eggs for you both.'

The light surprised Mouse and he turned quickly away from Marcus. The smell of the rashers sizzling on the stove brought down most of the Course members. Abby was wearing one of Marcus's jumpers over her pyjamas and helped Mrs Millman to serve breakfast. She sat down next to Marcus.

'I wonder where the old folks are?' she whispered to him. 'I can understand Lee having a lie-in, but David and Sally went to bed really early.'

Marcus was about to speak but took a mouthful of bacon instead. After a while the Earl and David came into the room together. David hadn't shaved and the stubble made his face look grey and drawn. Marcus wondered if they had carried on drinking after leaving the younger members the night before.

'Morning, guys.' David clapped his hands together as he sat

down. 'Doesn't this look splendid? Thanks so much, Mrs Mill-man.'

After breakfast the Course members went up to their rooms to change for the morning service. Marcus shaved in the small sink, trying not to look too hard into the age-spotted mirror. Abby sang under her breath as she dressed. He watched her move around the room. She stood in a white bra and passed a deodorant stick under her arms, reached across him to wet her toothbrush under the tap and stood looking out of the win-dow as she brushed her teeth. Finally, she pulled on a shirt and a red pullover and came up behind Marcus as he finished shaving. She hugged him from behind, reaching around to stroke his smooth damp cheek with one hand.

'I should go and wake Lee. It isn't like her to sleep in: she's usually the first one up.'

He waited and listened as Abby went out of the room. He heard Lee's door squeak as it opened and he realised that he had heard the same sound repeatedly in the night – it brought back the dry-mouth panic of his nightmares. Abby came back in.

'She's not there. Maybe she went down to the chapel early. I tried her phone but it went straight to voicemail.'

They walked down the stairs together. The Earl and Mouse were talking in the centre of the entrance hall. Mouse watched them descend with a thin smile on his lips. The Earl turned to-wards them.

'Young Mouse and I were discussing the paintings here. I bought them on Cork Street over the years. No idea who they are or who painted them. Unless it says on the frame, of course. They come, I suppose, from country-house clear-outs; I like to think of them as my family. Who knows, some of them might be.'

They made their way out into the damp morning air and

down to the chapel. The Earl walked beside Marcus, leaning towards him conspiratorially.

'I don't know if you heard me last night telling Neil about this uranium mine in Azerbaijan. Astonishing money to be made out there. And some useful tax loopholes to exploit. Let me know if you'd like to put a bit of cash in. Wouldn't have to be a lot. I like to throw a bone the way of you youngsters every so often . . . '

Marcus hardly heard him, mumbled something, and then let the Earl's long strides carry him on ahead. Marcus stopped at the entrance to the church and looked back up at the huge house. Smoke drifted from the high chimneys, rooks squabbled on the roof. He made out the window to Lee's room. The glass reflected the grey streaks of the sky. Abby called his name and he walked through the dark archway and into the chapel.

Lee wasn't inside. Marcus and Abby walked to the stage where Mouse was already sitting behind his drum kit, spinning his sticks and making rat-a-tat noises with his mouth. David and Sally Nightingale were sitting in the front pew, both of their heads bowed in prayer. The Earl made his way in to sit beside them. Abby and Marcus sat on the edge of the stage. She took his hand and whispered to him.

'Where's Lee? We can't play some of the songs without her. It's really very bad of her not to turn up.'

The remaining Course members filed into the church and David walked slowly up to the stage. Marcus thought he detected a slight limp as the priest climbed up behind the lectern.

'Welcome, all of you. I hope there aren't too many sore heads. The Retreat will be formally over after this service, but we'll all be around to chat, to answer questions, to have a cup of coffee afterwards. Now let us pray.'

The service dragged by. Marcus felt as if he was watching

it from a great distance, that time was being spooled out terribly slowly. Each time he looked at his watch he couldn't believe that only three or four minutes had passed since his last surreptitious glance. David insisted on the Sunday service being a formal Holy Communion, and the Earl and Sally acted as sacristans, preparing the bread and wine. Marcus knew how different the words of the service would sound to the new members now that they were fully initiated: charged with extraordinary meaning and significance, no longer the repetition of stale prayers but rich with the promise of greater revelation. He looked over at Abby, whose mouth hung eagerly open, as if inhaling the words, preparing for the joy of Communion. The twins sat in the front row, beaming, barely able to keep their heads lowered during the prayers. Only Maki looked bored. Marcus saw her flicking through the pages of the hymnal, a sad smile on her lips. The band played songs that they knew well enough to cover Lee's absence and then the service was over and the Course members filed out into the grey morning.

Mouse offered Marcus a cigarette and they walked over to the edge of the woods, looking down through the trees to the lake. Abby, continuing up the hill towards the house, called down to them.

'I'm going to find Lee. What time are you thinking of heading home? We should probably offer to stick around and help clear up. We might even get a bite to eat.'

Marcus drew on his cigarette.

'I think I'd like to get back. Let's head off as soon as we can without being rude. You OK with that, Mouse?'

'Sure, grand. I'm going to sleep all the way home.'

They stood and smoked. Mouse had picked up a stick and was tracing patterns in the ground with it. Marcus tried to read something in the runes that Mouse left in the red earth at his feet, but lost himself in the snaking furrows. He found a stone and threw it as hard as he could towards the lake. It landed well short, plunging down through the canopy of trees, sending a pair of jackdaws up squawking into the sky. He saw Abby standing at the back door as he came up towards the house. She scurried down towards them.

'I think she's gone. I think Lee has left like Philip did. Her handbag is gone. Some of her clothes, too. We should tell David. Will you come with me?'

Marcus, feeling suddenly sick, ground his cigarette out in the damp grass.

'Sure, I'll come.'

The Nightingales were packing in their room when the three friends knocked on the door.

'Come in!' David's voice was husky. He was standing over the bed folding a pair of identical white shirts. 'Hi, guys. How can I help?'

Abby stepped forward. Marcus could see that Sally Nightingale was packing her underwear and was attempting to manoeuvre the black lace pile into a suitcase and out of sight.

'It's Lee. We can't find her anywhere. She was, well you know how she gets sometimes . . . She was on the edge of one of her slumps last night. I worry that she might have gone home.'

David stood up straight and looked directly at Marcus.

'I know about Philip. You should have told me before taking him away from here. Sometimes the people who have the strongest reaction against the Retreat are those who are closest to letting God into their hearts. I should have spoken to him before he went. I would have made him stay. We can't afford to lose people. You know that.'

Marcus, feeling his hangover throbbing behind his eyes, stared back at the priest.

'I just don't agree with keeping people here against their

will. He would have taken a taxi if I hadn't driven him. At least the car journey gave me some time to work on him. He may come back, and at least then it'll be his choice.'

David narrowed his eyes.

'If it's anyone's fault, it's Lee's. I could wring her neck. But let's find her first. Didn't she do something like this a few years back? Someone found her curled up with a book out of sight somewhere, as I remember it. Has anyone tried calling her mobile? She's probably still drunk from last night.'

'It's turned off,' Mouse said. 'I've tried a few times.'

They made their way back downstairs together. The Earl and Mrs Millman were waiting in the gloomy hallway. David went to stand beside them and turned to face the three friends.

'You take the top floor, Marcus. Mouse and Abby, why don't you have a look in the woods? She might have gone for a walk. We'll search the ground floor.'

Marcus took the steps up two by two, reached the landing and turned right, away from the east wing where they had been staying. He walked along another long corridor whose doors opened into empty, silent rooms. A rocking horse stood against the wall halfway along the corridor. He stood and placed his hand on its cool, mottled haunches. A child's hand had ripped clumps from the mane, the tail was now just a few white hairs. The saddle was worn slick, the bridle broken and hanging down from between the horse's square white teeth in two ragged strands. Marcus gave the horse a gentle push and it lurched forward, a painful shriek of protest coming from the rust-sealed joints. He walked on, and the eerie screeching of the horse pursued him as he went.

A spiral staircase led up to the tower he had seen from the lake. He ran up the steps and into a dust-filled study. Books lined the walls and a cluttered desk stood against the far wall. In the centre of the desk there was a half-drunk bottle of brandy next to four crystal glasses. One of the glasses was still full. Marcus went over to the desk, sniffed the brandy in the glass and downed it. He cleared the burn from his throat and went back down the steps.

Through a pair of white swing doors, and around a corner, he found himself in a corridor identical to the one that led to their rooms. He looked out of the window onto the court-yard below and realised that he must be in the west wing. The rooms here were largely unused, full of crates and piles of books and furniture covered in dust sheets. Paintings in chipped frames were stacked facing the wall. He came upon the room with a frieze of mermaids that Mouse had spoken about. The frieze was set in the wall above a huge four-poster bed that sagged when Marcus knelt upon it. The fish-tailed women were very beautiful, breasts jutting out from the tresses of hair that fell around them, stomachs flat and swimming-toned. Marcus ran his hand slowly over the bas-relief carvings. Sea horses and dolphins frolicked behind the women, and in the background whales lurked in the depths. Marcus eased himself off the bed and crossed to the gabled window, opened it and leaned out. From his lofty vantage point he looked down on the gravel driveway below. The day had all the grey hopelessness of late October.

Nightingale's silver Mercedes saloon was parked next to the Earl's Bentley. The bus that was due to take the Course members back down to London was sitting with its engine idling on the other side of the turning circle. But his car, which he had parked under the branches of a pine tree when he had come back from dropping Philip at the station, was gone. He ran back down the blank, cold corridors, past the staircase lead-ing up to the tower, and along to his room. He looked on the dresser for his car keys. Then, flinging aside Abby's neatly fol-ded clothes, he searched for the jeans he had worn the previous day. The pockets were empty. He walked down to the entrance hall where David and the Earl were standing drinking mugs of tea.

'She's gone,' he said.

'What do you mean?' David looked at him with raised eyebrows.

'She's gone. She has taken my car. Let me try her phone again.'

He reached into his pocket and dialled her number. Lee's voice asked him to leave a message. Mouse and Abby came into the hall.

'Lee has taken the car.'

'Really? She's a terrible driver. I mean, not to worry you or anything, but she honestly doesn't know one end of a car from the other. She drove me back from the pub once when I went to stay with her. Terrifying.' Mouse smiled at Marcus and started climbing the staircase. 'I'm sure she'll be full of contrition when we get back to London. Now I'm going to finish packing.'

'I would offer you three a ride home with us, but I'm afraid we've got my guitar and our suitcases. There's plenty of space in the bus.' David patted Marcus on the shoulder. 'I know it's a pain, but I'm afraid it's just the price we pay for knowing someone as unique as Lee. She gets these mad spells. But Mouse is right, she'll be fine back in London. She was probably just missing Darwin.'

*

Marcus pressed his cheek to the cold window as the bus edged through shuffling traffic along the Banbury Road to the motorway. Abby had made them ham sandwiches. He gnawed listlessly at a corner, his mouth dry. He slept for a while. When

203

he awoke they were at Hillingdon, creeping along in the slow lane. Maki was staring out at the traffic crawling along the grey motorway, headphones on. She tapped her nails on the glass. The twins were chattering at the front, trying to catch the driver's attention, laughing wildly at private jokes. It had started to rain and the rhythmic swooshing of the wipers lulled Marcus back to sleep. When he woke again they were back at the church.

He lifted his suitcase from the rack above the seats and made his way down the aisle. As he stepped from the coach into the cold rain, Maki took his elbow.

'I'm not coming back,' she said. 'I thought I should tell you. You've been very good to me. Goodbye, Marcus.' She smiled at him, turned, and walked down the path, lifting a small black umbrella over her head.

Marcus and Abby took a taxi home. Abby went to bed as soon as they were in the door, kissing him and trying to drag him with her. He pulled away, called Lee's mobile again and then decided to walk down Kensington Church Street to her flat. Sunday sadness enveloped Notting Hill Gate. Tramps huddled in the entrance of the Tube as he passed, their breath steaming, hand-rolled cigarettes held up to emphasise their words as they shouted at each other. Italian tourists stood with their hands stretched out, bewildered by the rain: they had heard that the English weather was bad, but this? Marcus held his law-firm umbrella over his head, imagining himself inside a protective bubble. The rain pattered down on the stretched fabric. The sound seemed to move in time with his footsteps, rippling through the patterns of his thoughts until everything was dominated by the syncopated rattle of the rain. Marcus started to look for his car where the road described a dramatic chicane and began its descent to Kensington High Street.

When he came to Lee's door, he rang the bell, stood back, and waited.

Her flat was at the top of a tall building whose ground floor housed an antique bookshop. Marcus could make out a first edition of *Surprised by Joy* in the window, alongside a series of framed etchings of famous composers. Higher up, the building was striped with red and white bricks. It was a feature of many of the houses in the area and always put Marcus in mind of a series of lighthouses standing sentry over the sweep of Kensington and Chelsea below them. Marcus rang the bell again. A face peered out from a window on the second floor, then disappeared. Marcus was about to leave when the door opened a crack.

'Are you a friend of Lee Elek?' The voice was that of an old woman. She was lost in the shadows of the hallway and Marcus couldn't see her face. He walked up as close as he could to the door and peered inside.

'Yes, I am.'

The door opened for an instant and the woman dropped something into Marcus's arms. It was Darwin. The dog, recognising a friend, gave a contented yelp and reached up to lick Marcus's face.

'I looked after the dog all weekend. She said she'd be back by lunchtime. I'm going to my book club tonight and I simply can't have the thing yipping around my heels. Goodbye.'

The door shut firmly in Marcus's face. He carried Darwin under the shelter of the umbrella as he walked back home, letting the small brown dog nuzzle against his cheek. His fur was sleek and soft. Marcus let Darwin tumble onto the floor of the flat as he came inside. Abby was still asleep and so Marcus placed some slices of salami and smoked salmon on a plate for the dog in the kitchen and stretched out along the sofa, his head and joints aching. He dialled Lee's mobile again.

He listened to her message, was about to hang up, and then stopped. He spoke in a whisper, covering the mouthpiece with his hand.

'It's Marcus. If you get this, please give me a call. I'm sorry for what happened, I really am. Please come back.'

Abby walked into the room and he hung up quickly.

'What's Darwin doing here?'

'I went down to Lee's. The batty old woman who looks after the dog when Lee isn't there literally threw him at me.'

'So she isn't back yet?'

'No.'

'Are you worried?'

Marcus paused.

'I'm always worried about Lee. But you know somehow that she'll always be OK. She has a weird resiliency. She'll turn up and be charmingly repentant and we'll all have to forgive her.'

Abby made dinner and they went to bed early, Darwin slumped across their feet. In the middle of the night the dog woke and scratched at the door. Marcus realised that there was nowhere for the animal to crap and so, wrapping a dressing gown around himself and slipping a pair of trainers on his feet, he carried the dog downstairs. In the emptiness of the early hours of Monday morning he stood watching the quivering buttocks of the sausage dog as he forced out a stringy shit. The first planes were queuing to land at Heathrow. He thought about how he used to sit with Lee on her tiny terrace and watch them cruise across the sky. He could tell that Darwin missed Lee. He scooped the dog under his arm and made his way back to bed.

Part Three

Exodus

One

The next day Marcus sat in his office and made telephone calls. It was raining again and he was waiting to receive documents from the shady portfolio manager at Plantagenet Partners. He sat with his feet against the glass of the window, his chair reclined and the phone in his lap. Abby had taken Darwin to the church with her and he could hear the dog barking in the background when he called her. There was still no news of Lee and Marcus continued to dial her mobile, his fingers skipping over the numbers on his phone, tracing the pattern that meant *Lee* to him. He spoke to Mouse, who was somewhere high in Senate House: the howling wind made conversation almost impossible, but they arranged to meet for a drink that evening.

Finally, Marcus looked through his address book until he found Lee's parents' number. He dialled it and waited. An old man answered, his heavily accented voice high and impatient.

'Yes?'

'Um, hi. Is that Mr Elek?'

'Yes. This is Lazlo Elek. Who is this?'

'It's Marcus Glass. I'm a friend of your daughter.'

'Yes?'

'Listen, she's not with you by any chance? I mean, I was hoping to get in touch with her and she doesn't seem to be answering her phone. I wondered if she might be with you.'

'No, she's not here. And you're the second person to call for her. That priest of hers was on the phone earlier. Perhaps she doesn't want to see you. Did you think of that? Poor girl might want to be left alone.'

'I'm worried about her, Mr Elek.'

The old man's voice suddenly softened.

'Don't worry about Lee. What did you say your name was? Marcus? Ah yes, you came up to visit, didn't you? Lee will be just fine. We're stronger than people think, the Eleks. I'll let you know when I hear from her. Goodbye.'

Marcus sat staring out of the window at the rain until darkness fell and the City was a smear of office lights seen through the downpour. He lit a cigarette on his way to the Tube and smoked it in four drags before plunging down into Moorgate Station.

Mouse was waiting for him at Euston. He had turned up the collar of his faded velvet jacket and was standing in the centre of the station, entirely still as commuters rushed around him. He had his head turned upwards, surveying the rarely observed heights of the station, taking note of the sooty concrete crevices above him.

'Hello, sport,' he said.

Marcus embraced Mouse and dragged him by the arm through the hassled rush of workers. Mouse seemed reluctant to emerge from his reverie; his eyes remained misty as they made their way down Gordon Street to the Union bar where they used to come and drink with Lee.

They sat down in a shadowy corner of the bar. A football game was being shown on a large screen at the other end of the room. Marcus had bought them both a pint and they sat in melancholy silence, half-watching the game. Finally, Mouse turned to Marcus and spoke, twisting his signet ring on his finger as he talked.

'I'm worried that it was my fault. That I said the wrong words to Lee this weekend.'

Marcus looked up at his friend.

'Don't beat yourself up. There probably wasn't a right thing to say. It's hard to know how to help someone who's that far gone.'

'But if I'd really spoken to her, really broken through . . . She trusted me.'

Marcus sighed and shook his head.

'We're all to blame in one way or another.'

They left the bar and walked back to the train station. Marcus rode with Mouse to Kensal Green, left him at the bridge over the canal and strode down Ladbroke Grove until he came to the bus stop. When he got home, Abby was watching television with Darwin curled up in her lap. Marcus poured himself a glass of wine and ran a bath. Abby looked up at him as he passed, but since he said nothing she went back to staring at the TV, her hand thoughtlessly playing with the dog's long, silky hair.

Marcus ran the bath full and hot, lowering himself down gently into the water, which turned his skin bright pink. He lay back and balanced an ashtray on the dry island of one knee. He lit a cigarette and blew the smoke upwards. Abby didn't like him smoking in the bath. He had filled the glass of wine right to the rim and sat with an empty mind until the bath was tepid and the glass empty. He pulled himself regretfully from the water, tipped the ash down the sink as he brushed his teeth, and then half-read a book until he was too tired to turn the pages. He was asleep before Abby and the dog came to bed.

*

The Course session after the Retreat was always a triumphant one. Friendships that had seemed tentative prior to the weekend away became firmly established: there would be more hugging and some tears, plans to meet up for dinner, for prayer sessions over the next weekend, a general sense of optimism and community. Marcus was dreading this particular session, though. He knew that David wouldn't let Lee's absence spoil the celebration, and was expecting the priest's call when it came the next morning. He was going through one of the Plantagenet Partners documents with a tort law specialist when his phone began to vibrate on the desk.

'Shit, give me a minute, will you?'

The solicitor backed from the office, shutting the door carefully behind him.

'Hello?'

David's voice was smooth and melodic when it came.

'Marcus, David here. Can you talk?'

'Yes, it's fine.'

'I take it you haven't heard from Lee?'

'Nothing, I'm afraid.'

'OK. Well, we can't let what I'm certain is just another Lee slump ruin the Course for this year. There's too much at stake. I'll ask Sally to sit alongside Mouse for their discussion, although he has been carrying that group anyway, so he shouldn't need her. We'll have to think about which songs the band can play without Lee. I'm relying on you to be my right-hand man tonight, Marcus.'

'I'll do my best.' Marcus paused. 'Do you think we should call the police, David?'

'I don't know. I've spoken to her parents, called her priest at home to see if she was there. I thought we'd wait to see if she turns up tonight. If she doesn't, then I'm afraid we might have to.'

David rung off. Marcus was busy on the case all afternoon, which was growing more complicated and morally dubious by the day. He left work in a hurry and rushed westwards towards St Botolph's. He arrived to find David standing in the entrance porch, greeting the Course members as they arrived. The priest embraced Marcus, holding on for just long enough to make him feel awkward. Inside the church everything was bathed in soft light. Sally was standing in her usual place above vats of food. Abby and Mouse moved with broad smiles between the groups of old and new Course members. Marcus saw the Earl and Neil talking in one corner. The twins were standing in front of a group of older members and Marcus watched as they struggled to get their words out, talking over each other and supplementing their speech with violent gesticulations. He sat down wearily and waited for David to start.

He thought that the priest looked old. The video screen behind him picked up the crow's feet in the corners of his eyes and accentuated the grey tinge of his skin. His hands quivered a little as he spoke. But the words had the same extraordinary fluidity as before, and David's eyes sparkled as he spoke of the Retreat, of the beauty of hearing the new members speak in tongues for the first time, the holiness that had suffused the service on Saturday night. No mention was made of Lee, and Marcus noticed that when they got up to play their instruments, Lee's piano had been pushed back into the shadows of the Lady Chapel.

In the discussion that followed the music, Marcus let Abby guide the group. He sat back and listened as each of the members recounted their experience of the Retreat. Neil was the last to speak, leaning forward in his chair, bald head shining, face flushed and happy, his tie hanging loosely around his neck. He talked very quickly, a huge grin sweeping across his face each time he paused for breath.

'While it was obviously an amazing experience, it was only when I got to work yesterday that I realised quite how much it had changed things. Because that is the point, isn't it? We should continue to act in our everyday lives as we act here. And David made it very clear to me that this didn't mean that I couldn't be ruthless in business. Because that was something that did worry me to start off with. That it might clip the wings of my career if I had to start turning the other cheek on the trading floor. I mean, the markets are a jungle, you know? But it was more that everything seemed to shine. I don't know how else to put it, but I saw God everywhere. And I felt Him telling me what to do: which trades to put on, which dealers to call. It was quite extraordinary, quite wonderful. I told everyone about the Course. Really didn't mind what they thought of me. I'm proud to be a member. Proud and humbled.'

Out of breath, he stopped and beamed round at the group. There was a thin patter of applause. At the end of the session Neil helped Marcus to stack chairs.

'It also helped that the Earl gave my bank some of his cash to manage. I had realised that he was rich, but not *that* rich. I think it's a great idea to give each other a leg-up professionally. Do let me know if there's anything the bank is doing on the legal side that you want a piece of.'

Marcus smiled thinly. Abby was waiting for him in the porch when he came upstairs.

'David wants to see us in the rectory. Mouse is already over there.' Her voice had been emotionless since the previous evening. She walked in front of him down the path to the Nightingales' house where Mouse and the Earl were in the drawing room, sitting in large, comfortable armchairs. Mouse had one of the gold cushions clutched against his belly. David poured out glasses of wine and called to Sally, who came in from the kitchen. He addressed them in a low voice, his hands clasped in front of him.

'I'm afraid we have still heard nothing from Lee. I'm worried and I know you all are, too. I think we will have to call the police. I spoke to her father earlier and he still seems to think that she will turn up. I'm inclined to agree, but we need to err on the side of caution. I'm going to go down to the station to-morrow morning and tell them what we know. You should all expect to be questioned, I suppose.'

He paused, reached across to his glass of wine, and took a long swig. He patted his lips with the back of his hand.

'I probably don't need to tell you that there is a great deal of interest in what we do here at the Course. Some think that this is a cult, a movement with political designs or something equally ridiculous. Discretion is paramount when speaking with anyone from outside our group, especially given where we are with the expansion. Any kind of scandal could scupper the whole US project. Now, I'm certain that they will find Lee very quickly. But until that point, less is more when you are speaking to the police. I hope that I've made myself clear.'

Marcus and Abby stayed a while longer and then walked in silence down to the King's Road, where they hailed a taxi. Abby carried Darwin in her handbag, his pink tongue the only thing visible in the darkness of the cab. They sat in silence as the taxi moved up through Kensington. Marcus pressed his nose to the cold, shuddering glass of the window when they passed Lee's flat. There were no lights on. Darwin was panting and Abby absent-mindedly reached out a hand to fondle his ear. They went to bed without having dinner.

Marcus had expected the police to call him the next day, but it wasn't until Friday that his telephone rang. He was in the office trying to make sense of a legal document that had been translated very badly from Cantonese. He sat bent over the desk, tugging at a fistful of hair as he read. His phone vibrated in the pocket of his suit jacket. He fished it out and answered it.

'Hello.'

'Marcus Glass?'

'That's right.'

'Detective Inspector Farley here, from West End Central Police.'

Marcus felt his heart quicken.

'I was wondering whether we might meet up to have a chat about your friend Lee? Perhaps I could come and see you and your wife this evening. Kill two birds with one stone, as it were.'

'Yes, that'd be fine. Seven o'clock?'

Marcus and Abby sat at the dining table in silence as the clock crept towards seven. Darwin was sleeping in Abby's lap. The television flickered in the corner of the room but neither of them was watching it. Marcus had brought the Chinese document home and was using a thesaurus to try and force meaning into the nonsensical sentences; Abby was reading one of the anti-religious texts that so fascinated her. When the doorbell rang they both jumped up from their seats. Darwin yelped as he was deposited onto the floor. Marcus let Farley into the flat.

The policeman was a tall man in his late thirties, with a thick head of black hair. He was wearing a suit with a blue pin-stripe. Marcus thought he looked like a lawyer. He carried the same air of fragile amiability.

'I won't take up too much of your time,' he said, sitting down opposite them at the table. 'I just have a few questions.'

'Would you like a coffee? Some tea?' Abby half-rose from her chair, again sending Darwin tumbling to the ground.

'No, I'm fine, thank you.'

The policeman drew out a leather notebook and a thin silver propelling pencil. He opened the book and Marcus watched him make a careful note of the date.

'You were both very close to Lee Elek, is that correct?'

They nodded.

'When was the last time you saw her?'

Abby looked across at Marcus and then spoke. Her voice quivered and Marcus could see her worrying at the hem of her cardigan under the table.

'I went upstairs with her on Saturday night. It was quite late, perhaps two thirty. We had been for a walk to get some fresh air, we came back, Marcus and Mouse – that's Alastair Burrows – stayed in the dining room to clear up while Lee and I went to bed. I said goodnight to her at the door of her room and that was the last I saw of her.'

'And had anything happened that evening that made you think she might disappear like this? An argument, for instance?'

Abby placed her hands flat on the table. Marcus could see that she had been biting her nails during the day. The skin around her cuticles was red and frayed.

'No. I mean, Lee was always a little bit volatile, a bit up and down, but nothing out of the ordinary.'

'What about you, Marcus?'

Marcus tried to keep his voice steady. The policeman was staring down at his notebook and so Marcus couldn't look him in the eyes, but he fixed his gaze where he thought the policeman's eyes would be were he to look up.

'No. Nothing. As Abby says, Lee was prone to feeling quite low.'

'So no arguments between you and Lee.'

'No.'

The policeman wrote something down, the book now tilted away from Marcus so that he couldn't read it. There was a long pause, then Farley looked up, fixing Marcus with impassive grey eyes.

'Right, that's funny, because we have accessed Lee's mobile

phone records and there's a message from you on Sunday night apologising to her and begging her to come back. Now, if nothing had happened, doesn't that strike you as a trifle strange? Hold on, I have it here.'

Farley drew out a digital dictaphone, fiddled for a moment and then placed it down on the table. Marcus heard his own voice, tinny and tired-sounding, fading to a whisper at the end. Abby turned to him, her eyebrows boomeranging questions. He could see her struggling to control her expression as she turned to the policeman. Marcus looked down with horror at the dictaphone.

'Oh, I know what that's about,' Abby said brightly. 'Lee had asked us to look after Darwin for a few days while she went away. She was always saying she needed to clear her head, get away from London. I said we couldn't. We both work and – well, these few days with the dog have been a pain. Marcus was just letting her know that she should come back, that we were sorry we hadn't been more understanding. Lee took offence very easily. We were always apologising for one thing or another.'

The policeman scribbled a few lines and then looked up at them sharply.

'This whole process is going to be much easier if you answer my questions clearly and truthfully. Otherwise, I fear we're going to run into some difficulties. Now that's all for the moment. I'll let you know when I need to speak to you again.'

Marcus showed Farley to the door. When he came back into the drawing room, Abby was still sitting at the table staring straight ahead.

'Was that true? Did she ask us to look after the dog?' he asked, crossing the room to stand in front of her, placing his hands on the table and leaning down to position himself in her line of vision.

'Why did you call her and apologise?' Her voice was very flat and she refused to meet his eyes. 'I think you need to tell me why I just lied for you.'

'I don't . . . I can't really . . .' Feeling things spiralling away from him, Marcus pressed down on the table to try to still his spinning mind. He forced himself to take slower breaths, attempted to make his voice measured and rational. 'It was nothing. We had an argument while you and Mouse were down at the bridge over the motorway. I told her she needed to see a shrink. She thought I was being patronising. You know how she is.'

Abby sat silently for a while, seeming to weigh his words. Then she stood up, lifting Darwin from her lap and placing him in Marcus's arms.

'David and Sally asked me over for dinner. I'm supposed to be there at eight. Will you be able to fix something for yourself?' Her voice softened suddenly. 'I'm sorry I've been tetchy. It's been difficult, with Lee and everything . . .'

When Abby had left, Marcus sat and watched a game of football with the dog sleeping at his feet. When the final whistle blew, he staggered to the kitchen to find something to eat. He was very tired. He looked in the fridge and couldn't find anything he wanted. Darwin came and sniffed at his feet. He put some slices of ham on a plate and went back to sit on the sofa. He and Darwin shared the food; he amused himself by making the dog jump in the air to catch bites of the tasteless, watery meat. Marcus went to bed before Abby came home, vaguely aware of her sliding in next to him very late, her large, hot body pressing against his in the darkness.

*

After the service on Sunday morning, Marcus and Abby went

for lunch at the rectory. It was a bright, crisp day. A smudge of pigeons wheeled high overhead as they walked down the path that led from the church through the graveyard to the tall white house. Marcus was always touched to see fresh flowers on graves here. It comforted him that forty, fifty years after death there were still people who cared enough about those who had gone before to leave these lavish bouquets, tied with lengths of bright ribbon, rarely allowing the flowers to grow withered and yellow like the bones beneath them.

Marcus sat facing the window. A slab of sunlight cut across the table and dazzled him. He shifted his chair first one way, then another, but couldn't escape the searing light that burned green and purple patterns across his retinas and left his head pounding. Marcus gulped glass after glass of water and half-listened to Abby and Mouse talking at the end of the table.

David seemed distracted during lunch and rose several times to use the telephone in his study upstairs. Marcus heard the low mutter of his voice coming down through the floor-boards, but couldn't make out any words. Only once they were drinking coffee, and the sun had moved round enough that Marcus could at last escape its interrogatory light, did David speak to the table.

'There have been some developments,' he said, then cleared his throat. 'They have found Marcus's car. It was parked near Banbury railway station. They are looking at CCTV images from last Sunday to try and work out which direction she took. Once she's on the rail network it simplifies tracing her. I had a long conversation with D.I. Farley last night and he remains confident that she'll turn up safe and sound.' The priest smiled.

'I think we can take this as good news. As soon as the police are finished with your car, Marcus, I've arranged for it to be towed back to London. I imagine Lee won't be far behind it. I hope we will all learn something from this episode, guys. The Course is powerful, but it is also vulnerable. When something rises as swiftly as the Course has, its foundations need some time to set firm. Lee has endangered everything with her behaviour, by allowing herself to be swept up in her emotions. I warned you all about the dangers you would face. I've been praying hard for Lee and I know that you have too. Let's welcome her back to us with love and forgiveness when she comes.'

Marcus took Darwin for a walk in Hyde Park when they got home. He had wanted to go for a run, but after a few hundred yards realised that the dog's short legs couldn't match his own stride. Darwin tried gamely to keep up, but kept falling forward, skidding along on his paws and then sliding on his back. Marcus walked down to the Serpentine and looked over at the Diana Memorial where two blond children were paddling in the fast-running water despite the chill air. Marcus heard their squeals travel across the lake to him.

When he got home, Abby was sorting through photographs. She sat at the kitchen table arranging the pictures into piles, a smile flickering across her face every so often. She turned and placed the photographs as if she were playing a game of patience, or reading Tarot cards. Marcus came and stood behind her and saw that she was looking at a picture of the two of them early in their relationship, kissing outside a pub. Daffy and a few of the other guys from college were pointing at them and laughing as they kissed, unaware of the camera aimed at them. One of Abby's legs was lifted behind her. Marcus's hands were clasped around her back and she was leaning into the embrace. At the edge of the photograph, Mouse stood, wearing an awful Liberty-print shirt. He was looking straight at the camera, or rather at the photographer behind the lens.

Lee had taken the picture. Even had he not remembered the kiss, Marcus would have known that it was her work. The group was perfectly composed, arranged in the same way that a painter would position them, the scene artfully constructed to reveal clearly the relationship between each of its subjects. Marcus liked to see the photographs that Lee had taken of him. With anyone else behind the camera, he found himself tensing just before the shutter closed. A pout would appear on his lips unbidden, his eyes took on a distant and weary glaze, his eyebrows lowered as if in deep thought. This meant that he never felt that the person presented in photographs was actually *him*, but rather a brooding impostor who had leapt into the frame at the last minute. With Lee it was different. She seemed to wait for the perfect moment, always captured him at his most natural.

Abby continued to flick through the photographs, pausing every so often to look at a picture, trying to situate it in time and place. She dwelt over a photo that Marcus had taken of her on their honeymoon in Corsica. It was at breakfast and her plate was piled high with bread, cheese, boiled eggs and figs. In the photograph she was looking down guiltily at the amount of food. Marcus remembered her words when they had developed the film: '*I can tell that you don't love me by the way you take my picture.*' Those words had initiated a long period of strenuous effort on his part. He had been consistently solicitous to his new wife for months afterwards, stung not by the venom in her voice, but rather by his suspicion that she might be right. He was relieved when she placed the photo on top of the picture of them kissing and began working through a new batch.

Closeness grew between them as the light faded outside and they sat sorting through box after box of pictures. Marcus stood and switched on a standard lamp in the corner when it grew too dim to make out the faces in the photos. Even now that most of his photographs were stored on a computer, Marcus insisted on having his favourite pictures developed. He was forever intending to paste them into albums with press cuttings and railway tickets and other mementos that he hoarded, but there was always some more pressing chore and so they accumulated and were placed out of sight. Abby would complain about the boxes stacking up in the spare room, but he saw that she treasured them. Her fingers picked carefully through the memories arranged on the dining table, tenderness evident in the way she stacked the pictures into neat piles. Marcus realised that one pile was made up entirely of photographs of Lee.

'Let's look at those,' he said.

It was something in the way that Abby handled the photos. He couldn't place exactly what, but it was subtly different from the way she fingered the pictures of other people, a scrupulous reluctance to touch the glossy face of the photograph, fastidiousness about avoiding fingerprints. There was something almost fearful in the way she addressed the pictures of Lee. Marcus realised that Abby thought Lee was dead. He sat back in his chair and exhaled.

'You don't think she's coming back, do you?'

Abby looked sharply at him, and then back down at the photograph. It was a picture of Lee with her arm around the South African schoolboy she sponsored. The Course invested in a series of charitable projects across Africa, and had paid for the members of a Johannesburg orphanage to fly to England to visit the church whose congregation was financing their education. Lee had grown very close to one young boy. He was smaller than his classmates and Lee had taken him under her wing immediately. He had followed her everywhere during the two weeks that they were in England. When Lee and the other

Course members had taken the children and their harried, chain-smoking teachers to Heathrow at the end of the visit, the little boy had refused to let go of Lee's hand until, tears tumbling down his face, he had been pulled away.

'She's gone.' She laid the photograph back down on the table. 'I know that David is being terribly upbeat about the whole thing, but he knows as well as I do that she isn't coming back. He told me some things when I went there for dinner the other night. Things he made me promise not to tell you.'

'What things? Why didn't he want me to know?'

'I think he's just very paranoid at the moment. He's worried about the press getting hold of this. There was that awful article a few years ago about the Course. I know it left a real scar.'

'What did he tell you?'

'Sally had a key to Lee's flat. She fed Darwin sometimes when Lee was at weddings. She went over to the flat and found all sorts of things. Diaries and books of photographs and . . . It was clear that Lee was terribly unhappy.'

'So why is David going on as if he's sure she'll turn up?'

'Wishful thinking, I suppose. It's a kind of prayer. If he keeps repeating it then maybe something will turn up. They gave the books to the police, of course. There was one passage that David let me read. It was heartbreaking. She was talking about how she was weighing up different methods of suicide, trying to work out which one would be the least sinful. Poor Lee. Poor, poor Lee.'

Abby started to cry. Fat tears fell down onto the photographs and Marcus leaned over her and buried his face in her hair. She turned up towards him and he kissed her. At first the kisses were gentle, kisses of consolation, then more passionate. He slipped his tongue into her mouth and swung his leg over her until he was sitting on her lap. He took her face in his hands and kissed her hard. She was still crying, and he realised that she was no longer crying about Lee, or no longer just about Lee. He pulled her jumper up over her head, then her blouse and bra until her breasts pressed against his stomach. He lifted her up, turned her around and laid her back across the photographs. The neat piles toppled over, some fell on the floor. The light was behind him and his shadow fell across her, darkening her pale skin. She slipped her jeans and pants off and watched him, still crying, as he undressed.

Marcus came staring at the picture of Lee and the little South African boy. His lips were pressed into the hollow of Abby's clavicle, his nose against her throat and there, inescapably, on the table behind her shoulder was the photo, and it seemed that Lee was trying to convey something to him through her frozen blue-green eyes. They lay together on the scattered memories until Abby shivered.

'David wants me to go away for a while,' she said.

'What? Where?'

'The American expansion is going even better than we'd dared hope. He wants me to go over and make sure that people are keeping to the key messages, that the quality of the teaching is up to scratch. It would only be for a few weeks. Three at the most.'

'But now? With Lee and everything?'

'I know. It isn't ideal. But we had been speaking about it before all of this happened and, I don't mean to sound callous, but I'm afraid that Lee is gone. I want some time to mourn her, some time alone. And I'm afraid that now more than ever the Course is what is important to me.'

'But what about our group? There are still two more sessions to go.'

'I'm sure you can handle it.'

*

Three days later, Marcus was driving Abby to the airport. It was strange to be back in the Audi. He looked for traces of Lee, even though he knew that the police had searched the car thoroughly. When he placed his hands on the steering wheel, he found it somehow comforting that her fingers had been there, not so long ago. The car smelt different, sterile. Abby's suitcase was in the boot, her passport and ticket sitting in her lap. New York was suffering a cold spell, and so she wore thick gloves and a scarf pulled around her throat.

They headed out of London on the A40, past grim thirties houses with crosses of St George hung in their windows, past furniture villages and self-store warehouses, cinema multiplexes and out-of-town retail parks. They didn't speak. Ever since looking at the photographs, Abby had been distant, aloof. She disappeared to St Botolph's early on Monday morning, leaving the flat before Marcus, and didn't return until after he was in bed. She sent him texts that were cool and civil, suggesting what he might have for dinner. Darwin was with her and Marcus found that he missed the stupid enthusiasm of the small dog in the flat. On Tuesday the day passed in much the same way. Marcus insisted that he take Wednesday morning off work to drop her at the airport.

It was not until they were snaking along the M25 that Abby spoke. Marcus was hunched over the wheel, checking his mirrors repeatedly, pulling out into the fast lane and stamping the accelerator and then slamming on the brakes as he looked for the turn-off to Terminal 5.

'I know about you and Lee.'

'What?' said Marcus as he attempted another manoeuvre, then found himself blocked on the inside by a white Transit van.

'I said I know about you and Lee. At the Retreat.'

Marcus allowed the Transit to undertake him and pulled into the slow lane. He looked across at Abby.

'What do you mean?'

'Don't be an idiot, Marcus. You were seen out on the lake.'

'Abby . . .'

'Don't speak. I really don't want you to say anything.' She
looked out of the window.

'I've known for a while now. It just took me a while to work
out how I felt. And it's sad, but I'm just not that bothered. I
sometimes think we got married to avoid breaking up the other parts of our life. We were happy with our jobs, happy to be
part of the Course, we just weren't happy with each other.

'I think back to our early days together, and the rows we
used to have. I know that you weren't faithful back then. At
university and then when we were first in London. I used to
try to find other reasons to get angry with you, but really it
was because I knew that there were other girls, and I just didn't
want to face it. I thought it would pass. For a while I think it
did.'

Marcus indicated and turned down the slip road towards
the airport. Abby's voice rose in pitch as they neared their destination.

'But to find out that you and Lee . . . I mean, Lee, of all
people. When we knew what she was like with men. The way
she'd sleep with just anyone. Well anyone apart from Mouse,
who was the only one who really loved her. It can't even have
been a challenge for you. And at the Retreat, which was supposed to be a wonderful time for us. And the night after we
had really connected. I lay in bed with you that night and I was
proud that you were my husband.'

Abby was sobbing as they pulled into the set-down area
outside the terminal. Her nose was streaming and she blew
two foghorn blasts into a tissue before stepping from the car.

Marcus lifted her bag from the boot and set it down beside her. She turned up to him, tears pouring from her eyes, her nose red and dripping snot. Marcus thought for a moment that an observer might think she was heartbroken to be leaving him. Then she spoke and her voice was hard and cold.

'And now, and this is the worst, thinking that you could have been the one who pushed her over the edge, the one who made poor Lee . . .'

Marcus tried to embrace her; she pulled away. He spoke very quickly.

'I'll park the car. We can talk inside. We should sort this out before you go.'

'Sort this out? Listen, I'll call you, OK? Once I'm feeling a little more . . . together. Here, you might as well have this.'

For a moment Marcus thought she was going to hand him her wedding ring, but then she reached into her bag and pulled out her key to their flat. She turned to go. Marcus took her by the elbow.

'Who told you?'

She shook clear of his grasp.

'It doesn't matter, it really doesn't matter.'

She was already walking away. He watched her stop, check her passport, blow her nose again, and then make her way as gracefully as she could through the sliding doors and out of sight.

Two

When Marcus got home he called his secretary and took the rest of the day off. He was close to using up his holiday allowance, but his secretary was fond of him and he knew she would help fudge the numbers at the end of the year. He took Darwin for a walk around Holland Park, hoping that the dog would be comforted by the familiar setting. He walked up and down the long avenues lost in thought, stepping aside to let Filipina nannies with thousand-pound all-terrain buggies stride past. He stood for a while watching the drab peahens pecking for food at the feet of their resplendent mates, who, like croupiers fanning cards, unfurled their tails to reveal hands of iridescent aces.

Marcus continued down towards the Orangery. He couldn't believe that anyone had seen them on the boat. The mist had been so thick, they'd been lost in the middle of the lake. He forced his mind back into the boozy haze of that night and searched his peripheral vision. Had there been someone crouched among the reeds, observing their encounter?

The park was closing and Marcus hurried to the northern exit. It was growing dark and there was a whisper of snow in the air. On a whim he crossed straight over Holland Park Avenue and headed up Ladbroke Grove. He always forgot how steep Notting Hill was. The trees that tented the road in summer had lost almost all of their leaves; those at the top of the hill had already been pollarded and held their stump-limbs skywards in protest at the brutality of their treatment. Darwin was tired and limped slightly. Marcus lifted the little dog up and carried him under his arm. In the distance he saw a Hammersmith and City Line train crossing a bridge. The lighted windows of the train looked like lanterns suspended in the air from a string.

Marcus trotted down the hill and was soon passing under the Westway outside the Tube station. He remembered how Abby had dragged him to the market here years ago. They were looking for a birthday present for Lee and had wandered among the tightly packed stalls, pointing at books and T-shirts and all sorts of nostalgic junk. Abby had come back wearing a Tyrolean hat and Marcus an MCC tie. He looked at his watch and realised that Abby would have landed by now. He felt a stab close to where Darwin's wet nose was tickling his chest.

Marcus turned onto the towpath as the last light of the day left the horizon. He looked into the supermarket as he passed and saw children helping their mothers bag up the shopping, young couples buying inexpensive wine, the jostle and buzz of real life. He made his way carefully along the unlit path, stepping aside to let bicyclists through, almost tripping over a tramp who was sprawled across a bench sleeping off a hangover. Finally, he made out the Jolly Roger that hung from the rear rail of the *Gentle Ben* and saw with pleasure that the lights were on. He knocked on the door, saw the boat sway as Mouse moved around inside, and then, after a few minutes when Marcus heard nothing but the gentle slap of the water against the boat's hull, Mouse opened the door, beaming.

'Hello, sport,' he said. 'Do come in. And bring that darling dog with you. He's a fine sailor, you know.'

Mouse had been reading. Marcus saw a copy of *Journey to the End of the Night* lying face-down next to a bottle of white wine and a bowl of pistachios. A small lamp stood on the table and cast a warm glow over one corner of the cabin. Marcus edged himself onto the bench opposite as Mouse found him a glass. Before sitting down, Mouse opened a cupboard and pulled out a tin of tuna which he emptied into a bowl for Darwin. The dog scoffed the fish appreciatively.

'So has Abby gone then?' Mouse asked, sitting down to face Marcus. Their knees touched under the table and Mouse edged backwards, drawing his legs up underneath him. He was wearing an old Thomas Pink shirt that was frayed at the collar and strained at its buttons around the belly. Marcus recognised it as one of his own. Abby must have given it to Mouse.

'Yes. She's gone.' Marcus had already finished the glass of wine. He watched with embarrassment as Mouse poured the rest of the bottle into his glass.

'Sorry. It's been a shitty day. I'll nip over to Sainsbury's and buy you another bottle in a bit.'

'Don't worry about it.'

'Abby and I argued before she left.'

Mouse looked up at him.

'I did think it was a strange time for her to go. With Lee and everything.'

'She said she needed some space to mourn.'

'To mourn? So she doesn't think Lee's coming back?'

'Do you?'

Marcus offered Mouse a cigarette. Mouse took it and lit it. He opened the window beside them a crack and they flicked their ash out into the night.

'I don't know. I probably shouldn't tell you this, but Sally Nightingale found some books at Lee's flat. Some diaries. Lee was terribly sad, poor thing. I always knew that she was prone to these slumps, but I suppose I just thought she got down like we all do. Or maybe that she was a little more sensitive than us, you know? That she felt things more acutely, but never that she was so low as to do this.'

Darwin had finished his tuna and was struggling to climb up onto the bench. Marcus cupped a hand under his tummy and lifted him into his lap.

'I wouldn't give up hope yet. People write things sometimes just to see how they look. Not everything that is written is meant.'

'I know, I know. But the pictures of men. So many of them. I suppose I had always hoped that she was secretly chaste. That the men who went home with her were made to sleep out on the terrace or something. And some of them so old and ugly – I saw the photos. It makes me wonder quite why it was she never looked at me.'

They sat in silence for a while. A barge chugged past, rocking the boat with its wake, causing Darwin to stir in his sleep. Marcus eased the dog onto the bench beside him and walked out to the supermarket to buy more wine. He picked out a bottle of good Burgundy and made it to the boat just as it began to rain. Mouse was standing in the tiny kitchen stirring a bowl of pasta when Marcus arrived.

'You'll stay for dinner, won't you?' he asked.

They sat and ate and the rain pounded down on the roof above them. Marcus peered out onto the water of the canal and saw it dancing with the torrent that was pouring down from the sky. He realised at once how cosy and how lonely Mouse's life out here was. He turned back to his friend.

'Who called you Mouse? Who gave you the nickname?'

Mouse thought for a moment. Marcus settled back down on the bench beside Darwin.

'I suppose I did. It was when I was at school in Scotland and obsessed with *The Wind in the Willows*. I couldn't get rid of the feeling that there was some terrible sadness behind the story.

Even in the joyous parts, there's a kind of elegiac quality to it, and finally I read a biography of Kenneth Grahame and it all made sense.

'Mouse was the name of Kenneth Grahame's son. Or actually Mouse was the nickname his dad gave him. His real name was Alastair too, you know? I took my nickname as a kind of homage to him. *The Wind in the Willows* was written for Mouse.'

The sound of the rain on the roof grew louder. The wind blew and the boat rocked. Mouse drew back a corner of curtain, looked out into the night, and then let it drop back. He shivered, then continued.

'Mouse had been born partially blind, and his dad told him bedtime stories that he'd made up during weekend walks along the riverbank. Because he was sad that his son couldn't see everything in nature and appreciate the walks with him. Anyway, these bedtime stories turned into *The Wind in the Willows*. And then when Mouse went away to boarding school, Grahame continued to tell the stories in letters he'd write to him every week. Mr Toad was based upon his son, who used to get taken up in new pursuits and then discard them as soon as something more exciting came along. I suppose all children are a bit like that.

'Despite Mouse's eyesight, and because of his dad's help and encouragement, wee Mouse was accepted into Oxford when he was seventeen. The letters with the stories about Mr Toad and Mole and Ratty continued when Mouse was at university. And then nobody knows what happened. It was maybe a suicide pact with a gay lover, maybe an accident. I like to think it was the pressure of being his dad's only child, of having his dad smother him, that did it. He lay down on a railway track and killed himself.

'I like the fact that *The Wind in the Willows* is so innocent, so completely removed from everyday concerns and troubles, and yet the story behind it is so dark and heartbreaking. A bit like Lee, I suppose. Everyone who met her thought she was this wonderful, lively girl. Those eyes . . . I'd see people look into her eyes and be transported. But behind it all she was struggling with terrible demons, unable to face the world.'

When they finished dinner it was still raining and Marcus couldn't face going into the night. Mouse got out a Scrabble board and they played until the bottle of wine was empty. Mouse searched in the cupboards in the kitchen and found a litre of gin. There was no tonic and so they mixed it with orange juice. Soon they were both quietly drunk. Marcus let Darwin out into the storm for a moment. The dog trotted up the riverbank, sniffing the ground, then came back to the boat, soaking wet. Marcus wrapped him in a dishcloth and towelled him dry. He laid him down on the bench and he fell asleep again.

'You can top and tail with me if you like,' Mouse said. 'You don't want to go out in this rain.'

'That'd be great. Thanks.'

Marcus brushed his teeth with his finger in the minute bathroom, then took a long piss, breathing through his mouth to avoid the chemical stench of the toilet. When he got back into the main cabin, Mouse was already lying in bed. Mouse's head was squashed against the curve of the ship's hull and he wriggled under the covers, trying to get comfortable. Marcus stripped down to his boxer shorts and lay with his back against Mouse's legs, his face pressed into the musty cushion that Mouse had given him as a pillow. The boat moved every so often as gusts of wind swept along the water's surface. The rain continued to drum on the roof and Marcus could hear the trees on the opposite bank whipped by the wind.

'Do you still believe in the Course, sport? Are you glad you're a member?' Mouse asked.

Marcus had thought that his friend was asleep. He turned onto his back and stared up into the darkness.

'I don't know. I felt very strongly about it at first. After that first Retreat – what? – five years ago, I was evangelical, totally committed. Now I'm not so sure.'

'Why not? What has changed?'

'The Course was about us. About the four of us. I thought it made us better people. I thought it gave us something we desperately needed. But look at us. Abby and I are falling apart. I really think it might be over between us. You're not happy, I know you aren't. And as for Lee . . .'

Mouse sat up in bed.

'Lee was a mess. And I'm as happy as I'm ever going to be. And as for you and Abby, you'll get over it. You've gotten over worse in the past.'

'OK, but how much of Lee was the Course's fault? And those new members. They look so young. They're just kids. And they are being told that they can't have sex, and they can't be gay, and they have to strive towards perfection. The idea that we're telling kids who are barely out of their teens that they'll go to hell if they fuck someone at a party . . . I just don't think it's right, Mouse. I don't think I've ever thought it was right, but I just avoided thinking about it.'

'People need the Course. Look at the way they embrace it. It answers a fundamental need.'

'Just because people need something, doesn't mean we should give it to them. I'm going to have to do some thinking. Shit, I don't know. I miss Abby.'

He felt Mouse reach over and pat his thigh.

'You'll get Abby back by staying true to the Course. Being over in the States, seeing how people are embracing it over there, that's what she needs at the moment. She believes in this more than any of us. More than David, even. Who knows, the two of you could be the next David and Sally. I know that's what Abby wants.'

Marcus drifted off to sleep, lulled by the rocking of the boat and the sound of rain on the fibreglass roof. The wind lifted small, tightly packed waves on the surface of the canal and sent them slapping against the boat's hull. Once, the huge gas-ometer let out a mournful sigh and Marcus turned over, his face pressed against Mouse's small feet. Darwin snored, curled up on a pile of Mouse's jumpers in a corner.

Marcus wandered through inchoate, directionless dreams. A noise reached through to his dream-world. He stirred in his sleep. He was aware of a presence, but couldn't lift himself far enough out of his slumber to decipher it. He felt warm breath on his cheek. He half-opened his eyes and saw that Mouse now lay alongside him, his head on the cushion. One of Mouse's hands was resting on the point of Marcus's hip bone, the cold line of his friend's signet ring clearly discernible.

'Shh,' Mouse whispered.

The boat rocked gently and Marcus felt himself drifting off again. Mouse's breath was sweet. Alcohol, cigarettes and toothpaste. With his friend's small, tubby body pressed closely against his own, Marcus slept once more. He dreamed of the fern den he had built as a child.

'Morning, sport.' The toaster popped and Mouse buttered two slices before topping each one with an egg. Marcus swung his legs over the side of the bed and stretched.

'Morning. What time is it?'

'Almost nine. You were out cold. Darwin and I have already been for a walk.'

Marcus jumped up from the bed.

'Jesus, I need to be at work. Fuck.'

'Oh, take a day off. I have.'

'I can't. I'm sorry. Let me have a bite of that. Listen, would you mind popping into my flat and feeding the dog later? I think my spare keys are here somewhere . . .' He searched through his pockets and found the key that Abby had handed him at the airport. He had been carrying it around with him as a kind of totem.

'Sure. I'll go in at lunchtime. I could do with a leg-stretch.'

Marcus wolfed down his egg in a couple of bites and pulled on his clothes. With a wave, he lifted Darwin under his arm, jumped to the grassy bank, and set off up the towpath. When he reached Ladbroke Grove, he jumped on the bus and made his way home. He got dressed without showering, pulled a scratchy razor across his face, and poured a bowl of water for the dog. He realised that he looked haggard and hungover, but he strode into the office with the air of a man who has been working long hours in pursuit of the firm's interests. His secretary went out to buy him coffee several times during the day and he left just before five, mouthing 'Meeting' and tapping his watch at his colleagues as he passed their offices.

*

When Marcus got home he took a bath in the silent flat and pulled on his dressing gown. It was barely dark, but the events of the previous few weeks had left him exhausted. He flicked through a series of mindless programmes on the television before selecting one at random and drifting off to sleep. When he woke, the room was dark save the flickering screen and Darwin was licking his face. He dressed and took the dog for a walk up Portobello Road. When he got back, David Nightingale was standing in front of the block of flats, pressing the buzzer repeatedly.

'Hello, David.'

The priest turned to watch as Marcus came down the steps towards him.

'Can I come in? We need to talk.' The priest's tone was curt. Marcus could see bags like yellow-grey oysters under the older man's eyes.

They travelled up in the lift together in silence. Darwin sniffed at David's trouser leg, whining, until the priest lifted him up and scratched him behind the ear. Marcus let them into the flat.

'Ah, nostalgia,' he said, seeing the photographs that Marcus had left strewn across the dining table, the boxes piled beside it. 'Be careful, Marcus. It can do funny things to you, too much recollection.'

'It was Abby. I need to clear them up. Do you want a drink?'

'I'm fine, thank you. What I have to say won't take long.' The priest sat down on the edge of the sofa, his knees drawn together, his hands over his kneecaps.

'This isn't an easy time for any of us,' David began. 'Sally and I've been terribly upset by what happened to Lee. I believe you know about her diaries.'

Marcus nodded.

'I sent Abby away for her own good. She needs to be doing something useful just now. And she needs you to be here for her when she comes back.' David cleared his throat.

'I understand you two have been having some troubles. Abby didn't tell me exactly what, but I got the general idea. The Course will survive Lee. It is a shame and – if she is indeed dead – it is a tragedy, but the Course is resilient enough to deal with this. What I won't allow is for one girl's depression, regrettable as that may be, to infect the whole group.' He stood up and began to pace up and down the room.

'You must understand that the Course is about leading by

example, it is about aspiration, about people wanting to better themselves. I am the model for scores of priests across the country, around the world. They watch the DVD, they read *The Way of the Pilgrim*, they see pictures of St Botolph's on a Sunday morning turning worshippers away because the church is so popular. They want that. The Course leaders fulfil a similar role within each Course. People look up to you, Marcus. You may not realise it, but the twins idolise you. The girls in your group hang on to your every word. I had Neil in my study the other day telling me that he thought you should take holy orders. You are a young man, with all the worries and troubles that a young man has. But you are also a senior member of my church, the church which is the centre of the Course, the church to which all others aspire.' He stopped pacing and looked down at Marcus.

'I'm not sure I want all that,' said Marcus quietly.

'What?'

'I don't know if I want to be a senior member of your church, David. I don't know whether I can live up to what you expect of me. I never felt about it in quite the same way as the others. I believe in God. I'm pretty sure that I believe in God. I just don't know if I believe everything that goes with it.'

'So what are you saying, exactly?'

'I don't know what I'm saying. I don't know anything at the moment. One of my best friends may be dead. Everyone is talking about her suddenly as if she's dead and yet there's no body, no real explanation of how or why she died. My wife is three thousand miles away and won't answer my calls. I'm sorry, David, I just need some time to think.'

The priest knelt down in front of Marcus and laid a hand on his arm.

'I understand, I really do. If we don't question our actions sometimes, then we find ourselves leading our lives on autopilot, and we can never achieve fulfilment. Take some time, but remember that we need you. The people at St Botolph's love and need you so very much.'

David stood up and walked down the corridor to the doorway. Marcus followed him.

'I've big plans for you, Marcus,' David said over his shoulder. 'You must remember that no other Christian movement has the money, the connections, the marketing savvy of the Course. We are going to be a global brand before long, and we'll need smart people like you to run it. Keep strong. Things will get better, you'll see.'

When the priest was gone, Marcus microwaved a bowl of minestrone and sat down at the dining table. He cleared a space for his bowl among the photographs and began to flick idly through them as he ate. He had taken more photographs at university than he did once he was in London. He smiled at photos of the four friends. They looked so young back then. Mouse and Lee seemed like children in the pictures. He couldn't believe that he and Abby had been so fresh-faced, so innocent. He noticed how close they all seemed: not just the four of them, but all of their friends from university. There had been so many of them, so many friends left behind once the Course became the most important thing in their lives.

Daffy was in almost all of the photographs from that period. Marcus remembered how the mouthy, energetic Welsh boy had followed them around, had always been the last one drinking at the college bar, an ever-dependable companion for pub crawls or spontaneous trips to seedy nightclubs in town. Marcus had tried to keep in touch with him once they moved to London: he had come to the wedding and they still exchanged occasional emails, but Marcus knew that Daffy felt excluded by the prominence of the Course in their lives. He thought he should probably call Daffy and tell him about Lee. He found the number on his phone and dialled it.

'Hello.' Daffy was in a pub. Marcus could hear fruit machines and music and people shouting to be heard at the bar.

'Daffy. It's Marcus Glass.'

'Hold on.' Marcus heard Daffy move through the bar and then outside. 'Sorry, it's carnage in there. Is that you Marcus? Brilliant to hear from you, man. How are you?'

'I'm OK. Listen, would you like to meet up? I mean, I know I've been rubbish at keeping in touch, but I wondered if you'd like to hook up for a drink?'

'Of course. It'd be great to see you.'

'What about Saturday?'

'Day after tomorrow? Sure, why not? I have a thing later on, but we could get together about seven if that works.' He named a pub in Shoreditch.

'Yes. Great. See you then.'

Marcus fed Darwin and sat back down at the table. He started to look through the pile of pictures of Lee, realising that Abby had arranged them chronologically, so that he watched his friend age as he thumbed through them. He saw her blue-green eyes lose a little of their naughtiness, saw her face grow thinner and her hair more blonde. And in each photograph the unmatched earrings, one blue, one turquoise, which she had told him once had been a present from her first real boyfriend. She had left the boy behind in Suffolk, but continued to wear the earrings, pleased with the disconcerted glances they provoked and the way they brought out the colour of her eyes.

He went back to the beginning of the pile, preferring to see Lee when she was at her best: young and wicked-looking. He came to a photograph of the band on stage. Lee was standing up at her keyboard, her head thrown to the side so that her hair shot out horizontally. Abby was beside her, the two girls singing into one microphone. Marcus had his head down and was pounding his guitar, while Mouse grinned, slightly out of focus, in the background. The photo had been taken at a college ball. It was still early in the party and dusk was falling behind the stage. The band's name had changed several times during their university years. He thought at this point it had been Edwin and the Droods.

It was the first college ball they had played, and they had all been nervous, but so many of their friends were in the audience, and the band looked so young and happy that the reception was rapturous. People had been drinking for a few hours and the band played songs that everyone loved, songs that people knew how to dance to. Marcus remembered looking down and seeing couples with their arms around each other as he and Abby took turns singing the verses of a song that had been a hit several years earlier. People were kissing and laughing and getting drunk in the day's last light. The band had come off stage to a riot of applause and delighted revellers had bought them drinks all evening.

At the end of the night, Marcus had to carry Abby back to their college draped over his shoulder. He tucked her up in her bed and then Lee and Mouse followed him over to his room. He switched on the desk light and opened a bottle of wine. Lee lolled in an armchair, a cigarette hanging from her lips. Marcus called Daffy and some other friends who had been out clubbing in town. They turned up carrying bottles of beer and vodka and someone started rolling joints on Marcus's desk. Mouse put on a CD and people began to dance in the corners of the room. Marcus crossed the quadrangle to check on Abby. She had kicked the duvet onto the floor and was snoring loudly. He draped the cover back over her and placed a kiss on her clammy forehead. She moaned in her sleep and rolled over.

When he went back into his room, more people had turned up. He didn't recognise some of them, but Daffy threw an arm around his shoulder and yelled: 'It's OK. They're with me' in his ear. Mouse was involved in a drinking game that Marcus could already see he was losing. His shirt was wet with beer and he kept tilting backwards on his heels, very nearly toppling over. Lee was still sitting in the armchair, coolly surveying the party. Marcus crouched in front of her and she reached over and tousled his hair. He smiled up at her.

'You were amazing tonight.' Marcus took one of her cigarettes and lit it. Her skirt was hitched up around her thighs and he placed his hands on her thin legs. Lee giggled.

'I really enjoyed it,' she said. 'It's so fun to be up there with you guys.' She leaned towards him and spoke in a whisper. 'Listen, I've got a bottle of champagne in the fridge outside my room. If no one's nicked it, do you want to go and drink some?'

They climbed the stairs to the fourth floor and Lee took the bottle from the fridge. They went into her room and sat down on the bed. It was always a mess in there: books everywhere, face-down or piled in corners awaiting her attention. Clothes were strewn across the floor, dropped where she took them off. Lee created extraordinarily complicated essay plans in many different shades of ink. When she was done with them she used them to wallpaper one side of the room. Marcus leaned back against a plan that seemed to be dealing with *Ancrene Wisse* and the contemplative life. Lee opened the champagne and clamped her mouth over the neck of the bottle to stop it fizzing over.

Marcus couldn't remember what they had talked about as they drank. He did remember Lee crossing to the window and looking out. The view from her room was extraordinary: across the roofs of the town to the first traces of dawn in the east. Marcus came up behind her and put his arms around her. She swigged from the champagne and then held the bottle up. Marcus put his lips over it and she tilted the bottle as he gulped. She turned to face him. A gentle breeze came through the window smelling of mown grass. He leaned forward and kissed her on the cheek. She sniggered. He leaned forward again, running his hands down her sides. He kissed her other cheek and then tried to find her lips. She turned her head away.

'This is naughty.'

Marcus picked up the bottle and went back to the bed. Lee looked over at him. Very slowly, she crossed her room and sat down next to him. Taking his face in her hands, she kissed him on the lips. Marcus stood up and took her in his arms and this time she pressed her pelvis against his and forced her tongue into his mouth. Marcus pulled her skirt up so that it sat around her waist and then slipped his fingers into her pants. He eased his middle finger into her. Someone knocked on the door.

'Lee? Marcus? Are you guys in there? Tell me you aren't drinking the champagne I gave you, Lee? That was for us to share.'

Abby walked into the room as Marcus and Lee sprang apart. Lee struggled to pull her skirt back down around her thighs. Abby looked blearily at them.

'Oh, you are here. And you are drinking the bloody champagne. I woke up with a stinking headache and I really fancied some proper booze. Is there any left?'

Lee handed it to her.

'I'm still really very pissed,' Abby said, slumping down on the bed. 'But this is delicious.'

As soon as possible Marcus had guided the girls downstairs to the party.

He was woken from his memories by his phone. He thought

it might be Abby and so he rushed to find the bleating machine. It was in a pocket somewhere and he almost missed it.

'Hello Marcus?' It was a man's voice. 'Detective Inspector Farley here. Listen, I know it's a bit late, but do you think I might drop by? I go past you on my way home and I just wanted a quick chat.'

'Of course.'

The policeman arrived twenty minutes later. Marcus heard him pull up outside and buzzed him in. Farley accepted the offer of a drink and they sat on the sofa sipping a beer together.

'I'm sorry for being so late. It's almost ten o'clock, isn't it? You know when the day just seems to get away from you?'

Marcus took a swig of his beer.

'We have made no progress with Lee. She's not on any of the cameras at Banbury Station. We have her driving into town at about ten to five in the morning – one of the cameras that they use for traffic control picked her up – but nothing after that. It seems she disappeared somewhere in Banbury.'

'I suppose you've looked into whether there might be anyone she knows there, someone who might be putting her up while she gets her head together?'

'It was one of the things I was going to ask you. You've heard about the diaries, I suppose?'

'Yes.'

'They're bleak. The girl certainly had issues. But I'm not sure they are the work of someone who was actually going to kill herself. A bit too poised, too much thought about the aesthetics of the whole thing, if you know what I mean.'

Marcus nodded.

'The other thing that gives me pause is that it's very rare for a suicide to go undiscovered. A murder, yes. Easy enough to place a body somewhere it won't be seen for a while if you have a spade or a cellar. But for someone to kill themselves and for the body not to turn up, that's rare.'

'So you're hopeful?'

'I didn't say that. People go missing the whole time. You couldn't imagine the number of cases sitting on the books of police forces around the country where people just vanish, thin air so to speak. But girls like Lee don't just vanish. And I'm afraid I'm not going to be allowed to let her become another statistic. There's something about it in one of the tabloids this weekend. You know how the press are. She's young, she's posh, she's pretty, she's a member of the Course. They'll be all over it. My superiors will be on at me day and night until I get this one solved.'

'Listen,' said Marcus, 'I know we didn't have a great start the other night, but I really want to help you. Anything I can do, I will. It's . . . it's really strange, but people have started to speak about her as if she's dead. It's this no man's land where everyone pretends to be optimistic, says "When Lee gets back" and "Let's save that for Lee", but then in the next sentence she's in the past tense. I'm just not ready to bury her yet.'

Marcus looked up at the policeman.

'I don't think she killed herself,' he said.

'Neither do I,' replied Farley.

They finished their beers in silence and then Marcus walked the policeman down to his car. Farley turned to him with a thin smile.

'You'll let me know if you think of anything? Can I rely on you to pass things on to me?'

'Of course.'

Marcus went back inside and carefully placed the photographs back in their boxes, stacked the boxes in the spare room, and went to bed.

Three

On Saturday afternoon Mouse turned up at the flat. He looked hungover and sleep-deprived, and his velvet jacket bore several new cigarette burns. His eyes were puffy and bloodshot.

'The bloody shower's broken,' he said as he walked in the door. 'I was over for dinner with David last night and the twins and Neil were there and we decided to go for drinks afterwards. We went to a bar on Walton Street where Neil had some corporate deal and there were all these very beautiful Russian ladies, and my glass kept getting refilled and I ended up ridiculously drunk. I seem to remember walking along the Embankment with the twins, but after that, nothing. I've no idea how I got home. Christ, my head.'

Marcus ran him a bath and placed some painkillers and a glass of water by the sink. He sat watching TV while Mouse bathed, smiling as he heard his friend singing to himself and splashing about. When he was done, Mouse came into the room wearing Marcus's dressing gown. He sat down next to Marcus on the sofa.

'What's the plan for tonight? I thought maybe a quiet one? Film and a curry?'

'Actually, I have plans. I'm going over to east London to see Daffy.'

'Daffy? Really? How brilliant. Can I come?'

'Of course.'

They dressed together in his bedroom, and it reminded Marcus of the excitement he used to feel as they got ready for a night out at university: music on the stereo, sharpening drinks and then a spray of aftershave and out into the night with its endless potential. They strolled down to the Tube together and then made the long trip across town on the Central Line.

Marcus liked the way each Tube line had its own identity. This identity was fashioned partly from the upholstery of the trains and the feel of the stations, partly from the districts of London which the line linked and the passengers who travelled upon it. The Central Line was bohemian and trendy, linking Notting Hill to Bethnal Green via Oxford Circus and Tottenham Court Road. The District Line was more sedate, old-world, running from the City through St James's Park to Sloane Square. He liked the hurried dependability of the Victoria Line and the deep, dusty donnishness of the Northern Line, while the shimmering futurism of the Jubilee Line and the down-at-heel Bakerloo left him cold.

They got off the train at Liverpool Street and walked along Bishopsgate towards Shoreditch. Marcus had arranged to meet Daffy in a pub behind Hoxton Square. They strolled through crowds of young people wrapped up against the cold, the haircuts and jewellery becoming more inventive as they moved up into Shoreditch. Daffy was sitting facing the door when they came in, and he raised his arm and waved, grinning.

'I didn't know you were coming, Mouse. Well, this is brilliant. Come on now, sit down. What are you having?'

Daffy had a thin moustache and wore a denim shirt and skinny jeans, high-top trainers on his feet. He seemed to know the bartender and bought a round of beers with whisky chasers.

'I can't tell you how good it is to see you guys, cheers.' He took a long drink. 'I run into various people from university now and again, but never anyone from our college. Thought the church had claimed you all. I was the only pagan left.' He chuckled and raised his glass again. 'Cheers, anyway.' He faced them, grinning.

'It's good to see you too. Mouse and I were talking on the way over about how sorry we are that we lost touch with you. I mean, I think you know all about the Course.'

'I do indeed. You tried to persuade me to join last time I saw you. Not my bag at all, you know what I mean? I almost joined just to see you guys, though.'

'It's hard to keep in touch with people. The Course just takes up so much of our time. But with you, Daffy . . . I mean, I think there are some friends where it really doesn't matter how long you don't see them for. When you've been through so much together, you can always just pick up where you left off. So tell us what you're up to now.'

Daffy put his beer down on the table.

'I'm in advertising. I had a couple of nothing jobs when I first left uni, but I've been at this place for over a year now. I work on the creative side. And I live over this way, just down beside Columbia Road. Share the flat with two blokes I met clubbing a few years back. I suppose I'm having a pretty good time.'

'Any girlfriends?'

'Oh, too many, too many. But no. There have been a few who stuck around for a while, but no one special. I always get a girl in January or something and then dump them in the summer. I go a bit mad in the sun, see? Basically, life is just this thing I get through either side of Glastonbury, you know what I mean?'

'I've always wanted to go,' said Mouse.

'Oh, it's fucking awesome, man. Come with us next year. A right proper eye-opener, I promise you. That's a real religion for you.'

They ordered burgers from the bar and watched the pub

fill up around them, reminiscing all the time about their university days.

'And how's Lee? I haven't seen her since your wedding, Marcus. She was so pissed then, man.'

Marcus looked at Mouse and saw his friend shake his head very slightly.

'She's not really around any more,' said Marcus, looking down at the drinks on the table, carefully removing the pickle from the top of his burger.

'Ah, shame. She was fit. Still, it happens, doesn't it? People drift in and out. Sure you'll pick up where you left off when she's back.'

Marcus looked up and saw that Mouse was staring at him.

'Does anyone want another beer?' Mouse said, and rose to walk to the bar.

A sofa became free in a corner of the pub and they moved there. They talked for a while longer and then Daffy stood up, rubbing his hands.

'Right boys, I'm going to a gallery opening. Do you want to come along? It's Hugo Carrington, you know, the guy from uni.'

Marcus had come across Carrington a few times at university. He was an angular aristocratic type whose father was equerry to the Queen. Carrington had studied art, but left halfway through his second year. He had launched his career to some public acclaim with a show in Mayfair soon after.

'Sure,' said Marcus. 'Yeah, I remember Carrington.'

They walked down through Hoxton Square, which was full of happy chatter and the thud of bass from different bars and clubs. The gallery was on Kingsland Road and already a long queue snaked down the pavement outside. Some cupped their hands to the blacked-out window, trying to make out what Carrington had created inside.

'Don't worry,' said Daffy. 'I'm guestlisted. I'll make them add you two.'

They walked past the long line of fashionably attired young people and Daffy spoke for a moment with the woman at the door. They followed him inside.

The noise of a hundred shouted conversations greeted them as they walked through black felt curtains and into the gallery. It was very hot and Marcus could see scores of men who looked just like Daffy, their sideburns razor-cut into daggers, bellowing into the faces of pretty girls. There was a bar along one side of the room and Daffy reached over and passed a warm bottle of beer to Marcus. Marcus thanked him and began to saunter around the room, gently pushing his way past trendy types who didn't seem all that interested in the art. He walked through an archway and into a gloomy back room which was dominated by a huge spinning sculpture.

Wheels turned within wheels, something whirred manically inside a sphere, a great turbine chugged. The dial of an enormous clock at the centre glowed ominously in the half-light, its hands circling. A swinging blade flashed for an instant and then disappeared. The light was so dim that Marcus could barely make out how each part was connected, but he was enchanted, and turned to look for Mouse. He saw his friend speaking to Daffy on the other side of the main gallery and gestured to him. Mouse crossed the room and stood next to Marcus in the dark. They sipped their beers and stared at the rotating sculpture.

'It's strange to see Daffy again,' said Mouse.

'Do you think he has changed?' asked Marcus.

'I don't know. Maybe his accent is a little less strong, but other than that . . . I think it might be that he hasn't changed at all.'

They continued to look at the machine for a while longer and then went out to the bar for more drinks.

An hour passed and the gallery grew so full that it was hard to move. Mouse and Marcus had colonised a flight of stairs at the far end of the room where they sat looking down on the people below them. Daffy would rush past every so often, his eyes wild, a huge grin on his face.

'All right you two? Fucking crazy, eh? Cheers!'

A DJ started playing pounding trance music and some of the younger people tried to dance, their elbows pressed against their sides, grimaces of bored hipness fixed on their faces. Marcus took an armful of beers from the bar and he and Mouse drank them until they were giddy and had to hold on to each other to keep from sliding down the stairs.

Finally, the music stopped and the lights went up. Mouse was asleep, his cheek resting against the banister. Marcus looked down from his lofty position at the crowd as they began to file out into the night. He saw Daffy talking to Carrington, his shoulders twitching as he spoke. The artist kept looking over Daffy's shoulder and pushed past him to join a group that was about to leave. He took a girl's arm and began to guide her through the door. The girl turned once to look back at the room and Marcus's lungs emptied of air.

The girl had a black fedora pulled down over her head and had turned up the collar of her jacket against the cold, but Marcus was almost certain that it was Lee. He shook Mouse awake.

'Mouse, look!'

He watched his friend's eyes as he saw the girl.

'Jesus,' said Mouse. 'Is it her?'

'Yes. I think so. Quick.'

They pushed through the crowd and hurled themselves out into the night. Daffy was leering drunkenly over the woman who worked on the door. There was no sign of Carrington and the girl.

'Did you see where Carrington went?'

Daffy turned to Marcus.

'He got in a taxi. A bunch of them are going on to a party at his house. I think he invited me.'

'Right, let's go.'

Marcus flagged down a cab.

Carrington lived in a tall Victorian house on the Hackney Road. Marcus could hear the music as soon as they stepped from the taxi. They walked down the overgrown path to the front door and Daffy rang the bell. A girl answered.

'Oh, hi, Daffy. Come on in.'

It was very dark inside. Marcus followed Daffy down a corridor which opened out into a large kitchen. Candles flickered on the work surfaces and patio doors opened at the back to the garden where people were dancing around a fire. The music was so loud that Marcus could feel his cheekbones vibrating with every thump. Daffy was already bent over the kitchen table cutting up lines of coke. Marcus couldn't see Carrington or the girl. He and Mouse turned back into the corridor and made their way up the stairs. The rooms were full of people, some of them asleep, some crouched talking. Two girls were sprawled across the bed in the largest bedroom, snorting powder from the cover of a hardback book. One of them turned and caught Marcus's eye, gesturing him over. He backed out of the room. Mouse was already on his way up to the second floor.

There was a closed door at the top of the stairs. Marcus edged past Mouse and turned the handle. They walked into an attic room. It was Carrington's studio. There was a potter's wheel and various unfinished works scattered around the floor. A huge skylight sat in the ceiling, revealing the orange glow of low clouds above. The artist was sitting in the far corner surrounded by ten or twelve others, a lamp on the ground behind him. He had clearly been holding forth upon something profound and looked up, annoyed at the intrusion.

'Who are you? Go back downstairs. People aren't allowed up here.'

The girl in the black fedora was sitting on a beanbag with her back to them. Marcus began to stutter. Slowly the girl turned her head and Marcus felt himself tense. Her profile was caught in the bright white light. Mouse leaned against Marcus, breathing deeply. Marcus could feel his friend shudder.

'Let them stay, Hugo. Don't be such a prick.'

The voice was not Lee's. It was higher, posher. She took the fedora off her head and shook her hair out, and Marcus saw that she wore her hair as Lee had before she cut it. She was younger than Lee, perhaps eighteen. Otherwise, the similarity was uncanny.

'Come and sit down, guys. Hugo was just telling us about his next great work. Do you want a drink?'

The girl poured red wine into plastic cups as Marcus and Mouse crouched on the floor beside her. Marcus felt dazed.

'I'm Hugo's sister, by the way. My name's Rebecca,' the girl whispered as her brother resumed his monologue.

'Marcus Glass. I knew your brother at university.'

'Oh, bad luck. He was an awful bore back then.'

'I didn't know him well. He left pretty swiftly.'

Marcus couldn't escape the impression that he was speaking to Lee. He realised that the reason he had been so easily fooled by her resemblance to his friend was that he had been spending so much time looking at pictures of Lee from university. Rebecca Carrington looked like the Lee of those days: her hair was long and wild, her eyes wicked and flashing. Marcus felt suddenly very sad to think that even if Lee came back, it wouldn't be this Lee, the person he thought of as the real Lee.

'Shall we go downstairs? I've heard this so many times,' she said, gesturing at her brother, who was holding up one fist and spinning the other around it in frantic revolutions, talking all the while.

Rebecca took Marcus's hand and they made their way down into the hot pumping heart of the house. Mouse followed behind them. Marcus turned and smiled encouragingly at his friend, but he could see that Mouse had been sobered by the sight of this strange replica of Lee. His face was drawn and tired and he looked at Marcus with an expression that Marcus couldn't quite decipher. Something between pity and scorn. Marcus raised his eyebrows questioningly, but Mouse just shook his head and hung back in the shadows.

When they got to the bottom of the stairs, Rebecca let go of Marcus's hand and skipped down the corridor, laughing. Marcus followed her through the kitchen, where she stopped to grab a bottle of vodka from the fridge, and then into the garden. There were picnic blankets and cushions spread out on the grass around the fire, and Marcus threw himself down beside Rebecca, intent on drinking in her face, searing her likeness onto his memory. A gust of cold wind blew across the garden, carrying with it traffic fumes and dust. The fire's flames danced. Marcus caught sight of Mouse standing in the kitchen talking to Daffy and a tall black girl with an afro. He turned back to Rebecca.

'I hate these parties,' she said.

'Why?'

Rebecca took a slug of the vodka and passed it to Marcus.

'Hugo always manages to find inspiration the next morning. So I'm left to clean up the place. It's my payment for staying here during my gap year. I've become the de facto cleaning lady. Which makes me hate these parties. Whenever I see people having fun I just think about the mess I'm going to have to face, hungover, the next day. He manages to make me feel so bourgeois.'

Marcus drew out a cigarette and offered her the packet. She shook her head.

'No thanks. I don't smoke. So what do you do, Marcus? Are you an artist too?' She looked at him with a wry smile. Someone stumbled over Marcus's legs, apologised, and staggered off into the darkness at the bottom of the garden.

'God, no. I'm a lawyer. I live in Notting Hill. Um . . .' Marcus stopped. Rebecca yawned. He realised how uninteresting his life would seem to a girl like this. It wasn't something he considered ordinarily, that he lived an existence that could make a girl yawn. Within the world of the Course he was seen as dashing, bright, a leading light. Here, as the fire burned down into embers, and the noise of the party still swept over them, Marcus felt suddenly old and dull.

'Are you, like, a real lawyer? Murderers and all that?'

'No. No, that isn't what I do at all.'

There was a pause.

'I secretly do quite want to be a housewife,' Rebecca whispered, leaning over towards him conspiratorially. 'It would drive my father wild, after everything he's spent on education, but I'd like to live in a big house in Henley and have lots of children and dogs. I'd bake on Tuesdays and supervise the gardener on Mondays and Thursdays.'

Marcus laughed. He was slowly getting used to seeing Rebecca as herself, rather than as a reflection of Lee. She leaned towards him again.

'So what else do you do? What's your thing?'

Marcus sighed. 'Do you know the Course?'

'The cult thing? Yes, of course I do. You're not involved in that, are you?'

He nodded. 'I'm a Course leader, no less.'

Rebecca whistled. 'Jesus . . . I mean, fuck. I had a couple of friends at school who went for a while. I always thought it was just a phase. Like anorexia or smoking pot. I didn't think someone as old as you would still be doing it.'

Marcus winced and lit another cigarette.

'Am I old?'

'No, but I mean, you're not really young, are you? The Course always seemed to me like a crutch that people leant on until they worked out who they were. Something to get you through those in-between years.'

'I think maybe it was like that for me. But then it became my life. It's not a bad way to deal with the world, even for someone as old as me.'

'I'm not saying it is. Just that it seems a little bit easy.'

He could feel her edging away from him. Where before she had been charming and conspiratorial, he now felt her looking at him from a distance, with a kind of anthropological interest.

'To tell you the truth, Rebecca, I've been thinking about leaving the Course. Life just goes by, sometimes, and before you know it you're thirty and the best things are behind you. I think I did need the Course when I first came to London. I'm not sure I do any more.'

She leaned towards him again.

'I say my prayers quite often. When I've been really bad.'

Marcus looked at her, frowning.

'That's one of the things that bothers me about the Course, though. You have so many people who think that they can act without consequence. As long as God forgives them – which of course he always does – they're in the clear. They can do almost anything – no matter how cruel.'

'I suppose that's what makes you Christians seem so other-worldly. You are cut off from the rest of us by your ability to be forgiven. Whereas, even though I try to pray, I never feel all that confident about it.'

Marcus sipped from the bottle and passed it to her. She took a long gulp and choked a little.

'You look a lot like a friend of mine. A friend I don't see any more.'

'I get that quite a lot. I always take it as an insult. That my face is just this tabula rasa that people project their images onto. I want to be an actress, so I don't suppose it's the worst thing.'

'No, but you look exactly like her. It's bizarre.'

Marcus looked back towards the house, trying to make out Mouse through the kitchen doors. There was a thick pack of bodies in the room. Everyone was dancing and Marcus found it hard to distinguish between the dancers.

'Shall we go inside?' said Rebecca, rising to her knees.

'Sure,' said Marcus.

Rebecca took him by the hand again and led him into the surging mass of people. She still carried the bottle of vodka and passed it to him as they began to dance. She fixed her eyes upon his as they moved together, leading him through the sweating, gurning partygoers, spinning him in the darkness. A slower song came on, something deep and trippy, and Marcus felt Rebecca press herself against him. She snaked her thigh between his legs and looked up at him.

'Here, have one of these,' she said.

Rebecca emptied a small paper package into her palm. Two white pills. She picked one of them up between small finger and thumb and forced it gently between Marcus's lips. The pill was bitter and caught in his gullet for a moment. He watched Rebecca take her own pill and then she leaned towards him and kissed him, pushing her tongue where moments before she had pushed her fingers. They continued to kiss as they danced, and he realised that she was smaller than Lee, her hands were like paws on his body, clawing away at him, burrowing under his shirt to twist the hair of his chest. He allowed himself to imagine her as Lee, though, and half-opened his eyes to see the pale skin marked by freckles along her cheekbones.

After fifteen minutes, Marcus began to feel the pill working on him. He seemed to hear the music more clearly, to sense the surge and life of the surrounding dancers. His skin tingled whenever Rebecca touched him and when he kissed her the world seemed concentrated in their mouths; then the music changed again, and he was spinning very quickly, and Rebecca took him by the arm and led him upstairs.

Carrington's studio was empty when they walked inside. The bright lamp was still on in the corner, casting extraordinary shadows across the room, picking up small sculptures and exploding them against the wall as a violent *Guernica* of strange, dark images. Marcus took Rebecca in his arms and they began to kiss again. They danced in dreamlike patterns, feeling as much as hearing the music from the party below. Marcus thought suddenly that he could see the mist that had moved in the air that night with Lee. He lifted Rebecca's jumper off and helped her to undo her shirt. Marcus's heart banged hard in his chest.

It began to drizzle on the skylight above them. Rebecca, wearing only her underwear, dragged a beanbag to the centre of the room.

'I love to look up at the sky,' she said.

'Lee . . .' Marcus moaned, and then reached down to slip off her pants.

She looked very young. Marcus remembered kissing Lee in

her room at university, and tried to imagine what would have happened if Abby had not come in that night. He realised he was still fully clothed. He knelt down on the wooden floor, took one of Rebecca's ankles in his hand, and began to lick slowly up her leg. His tongue went dry very quickly. He suddenly thought of Darwin, and hoped that the dog wouldn't be lonely without him there. He reached the top of Rebecca's leg and slipped his tongue inside her. She moaned quietly, placing her hands in his hair. Marcus began to cry. At first silently, wetting the inside of her thighs with his tears, then in great gulping sobs as he licked hopelessly at her.

'Oh, you poor darling. Come here, Marcus.'

Rebecca was very good about the whole thing. She held Marcus's head in her lap until his sobbing receded, and then he told her the whole story. She listened in silence to the tale of Lee Elek, nodding sympathetically whenever Marcus looked up at her. The drizzle had turned into driving rain. Marcus lay down beside Rebecca on the beanbag and they looked up at the sky. She shivered and Marcus found a sheet and draped it over her. The effect of the pill was beginning to wear off and Marcus felt suddenly very tired.

'I'm sorry. I'm such a mess at the moment. I'm so embarrassed.'

'Don't worry. It's better than my usual experiences up here. I like you, really I do. I would suggest we see each other again. If you weren't married, that is. And a religious nut.'

Marcus spluttered.

'I'm joking, I'm joking. But seriously, you need to get out of the Course. Those aren't good people you have been telling me about. You're better than that.'

As it began to grow light above them, Marcus said goodbye to Rebecca and crept downstairs. People were sleeping everywhere. The last revellers sat smoking in the rain by the dead fire, umbrellas capturing the smoke as they exhaled it, forming foggy huts around them. Marcus couldn't find Mouse. He walked out into the dreary morning and trudged up Hackney Road looking for a cab.

*

Marcus slept as the taxi made its way through empty streets across London, his cheek pressed against the cold glass. He woke with a start as they sped along Bayswater Road. It was only when they drew up outside his flat that he realised that he had lost his key. He searched through his pockets, turning out tissues, his phone, his wallet, and a packet of cigarettes, but the key was not there.

'Fuck,' he said.

'No money, mate? Need a bank machine?' The cabby looked at him in the rear-view mirror.

'No. I've lost my key. Shit!' Marcus remembered that he had given Abby's key to Mouse. 'Listen, would you mind taking me to the top of Ladbroke Grove? Just past the Sainsbury's. A friend of mine has a spare key.'

'No problem, mate.'

Marcus was feeling terrible by the time they got to the canal. His mouth was dry, his throat had begun to scratch and his sinuses ache; he could sense that he was coming down with a cold. He paid the driver and stepped out onto the bridge, then made his way down to the towpath. The wind sent the rain raking painfully down his cheeks. He held his arm up, shielding his face with his jacket, but the wind whipped around, and he found himself dancing to try to avoid the rain. Dark clouds raced across the sky as he squelched along the path, his shoes wet through, his socks damp and cold. The trees shuddered in the wind, sending spirals of their last leaves down onto the water to float among the cans and plastic bags. The canal was brown with fallen leaves, pockmarked by the rain.

Marcus reached the *Gentle Ben* and stepped down onto the deck. He banged on the door of the cabin. No response. He cupped his hand to the window where the curtains hung open a crack. He could see no one inside. He banged on the door again, then tried the handle. It swung open. Gratefully, Marcus flung himself down the steps and into the dark cabin. It was cold inside and Marcus tried without success to locate the heating controls. He flicked the light switch and nothing happened. Marcus opened the curtains, but it was so dark outside that it barely altered the murky cabin.

Marcus made his way through to the small room at the back of the boat that Mouse used as a study-cum-wardrobe and found one of his Thomas Pink shirts. Mouse's jeans would be too short for him, so he took off his own and hung them over a chair, hoping that they might dry a little while he searched for the key. He looked at the papers piled on Mouse's desk. There were pictures from children's fairy tales, scholarly articles on C. S. Lewis, a copy of *The Way of the Pilgrim*.

Marcus padded through the gloomy boat, checking whatever pieces of Mouse's clothing he found, willing the key to appear from a trouser pocket, or perched on a sideboard. Marcus could picture his bed at home and longed to be back there with the heating turned up, a mug of tea and a book beside him, Darwin sprawled at his feet. He went back into the study and searched through the drawers in Mouse's desk, looking with interest at the photographs he found. Many were of Lee, or had clearly been taken by her. Marcus realised that he should show Mouse his own collection of pictures. It had helped him to feel closer to Lee, to capture more accurately his feelings for her, when he saw her at her most beautiful, before the sadness set in.

Marcus was about to give up looking for the key when he noticed a small tortoiseshell box on the desk. It was the sort commonly used to house cufflinks, but Marcus thought that the key might have been placed inside for safekeeping. He fiddled with the tiny clasp of the box, opened it and stood staring at the contents, his tired mind suddenly racing. He held the box up to the window. Inside, against the black velvet lining, sat two earrings: one lapis blue, the other turquoise. Marcus picked them up and laid them in his palm. He sniffed them, not quite knowing why. Very gently, Marcus placed the earrings back in the box and carried it through to the main cabin.

Marcus pulled on his damp jeans and sat down. He found a slightly grubby pair of socks, and then wrapped a blanket around his still-icy feet. He felt the box in his pocket. There would be an explanation. There must be an explanation. He dialled Mouse's phone. It rang several times, but there was no answer. Marcus sat on the bed, shivering every so often, and waited for his friend to come home.

He saw Mouse trudging down the towpath towards him an hour later. The canal curved round past the gasworks, so there was a stretch of about a hundred yards where Marcus had an uninterrupted view of his friend. Mouse's velvet jacket was drenched. He had his collar turned up and he was doggedly sucking on a cigarette that he had to pause and relight several times as it was extinguished by the rain. He looked very small among the flying leaves and raging trees. His blond hair was soaked to brown, plastered flat upon his head. He jumped when he saw Marcus.

'Hello, sport.'

'Hello.' Marcus heard his voice come out low and cold. He tapped the box in his pocket again. 'I lost my keys last night. I thought you might have left Abby's lying around.'

263

A flicker of worry crossed Mouse's face.

'I had it with me. Here you go.' He reached into his pocket and threw Marcus the key. He set down a copy of the tabloid newspaper that had published an article about Lee's disappearance.

'I read it on the Tube. It's rubbish, total nonsense.' He paused. 'Where did you get to last night? I was looking for you everywhere. You were out by the fire with the Lee-girl and then you were gone. I ended up going to sleep down the back of a sofa while Hugo Carrington had sex on top of it. Not my idea of fun.'

There was a silence. Mouse pulled another key out of his pocket, inserted it in the control panel by the steps leading up to the deck, and flicked a switch. The lights came on. Marcus drew out the box.

'What's this, Mouse? Where did you get these earrings?'

Mouse stared at him, his eyes wide with panic. Marcus tipped the earrings out onto the table where they rolled for a while and then stopped. Mouse and Marcus looked at each other for a moment longer, and then Mouse turned and ran up the steps to the deck. The boat rocked as he jumped to the shore. Marcus unwrapped the blanket from around his feet and stood up. He pulled on his jacket, slipping the earrings into his pocket. He couldn't find his shoes. He charged into the study at the stern of the boat. His shoes were hanging on the back of a chair. He slipped them on and ran out into the rain.

Mouse was already out of sight. Marcus sprinted in the direction of Ladbroke Grove, slipping every so often on the muddy path. The rain tore at him as he ran, pricking pins and needles on his scalp. A bicyclist coming in the other direction swerved to avoid him. He lengthened his stride, knowing that he would catch Mouse eventually. Mouse was no athlete. As he rounded the bend by the gasworks, he saw Mouse far ahead.

He was moving quickly, in spite of his awkward, waddling gait. His head was down and he pumped his arms out to the sides. A flock of pigeons that had been sheltering in the overhang outside Sainsbury's rose into the air as Mouse ran past. Mouse turned to look back and Marcus could tell that he had seen him. Marcus watched as Mouse's pudgy form made its way up the slope towards the road, then over the bridge and north towards Kensal Green.

Marcus reached the bridge just in time to see Mouse turn left onto the Harrow Road. Marcus's loafers were not made for running and he thought about discarding them, then plunged forward, over the bridge and down the hill towards the traffic lights. A bus roared past him and he saw the face of a child at the window, a young girl of seven or eight who beamed at the sight of the gangly man barrelling down the road in the pouring rain, his bobbing head pointing upwards, his jaw clenched with the strain. When Marcus rounded the corner onto the Harrow Road, Mouse was gone.

Marcus sprinted up the road, thinking that Mouse might have disappeared down one of the side streets leading northwards. But they were empty, and there was nowhere obvious to hide. Marcus turned wildly around, looking for a flash of motion. He heard the sound of falling rubble. He looked up. Mouse was climbing over the crumbling wall of the cemetery. He had shinned up as soon as he turned the corner, and was there, ten feet above Marcus, looking down on him. Marcus stared into his friend's wild, bulging eyes.

'Why are you running? Did you kill her?'

'Of course I didn't. Of course I didn't kill her.'

Marcus could see that Mouse was crying. His lip trembled as he looked down at Marcus, then he let himself drop down onto the grass the other side and ran off into the grey maze of tombstones.

Marcus began to climb the wall. He tried to keep his eyes on Mouse as he clambered up the brickwork, using the scaffolding that held the tumbledown wall together for handholds, but he lost the small figure as it moved into the shadow of a line of cypress trees. Marcus reached the top of the wall, swung his legs over, and let himself drop onto the soft earth the other side. He ran in the direction of the trees.

The noise from the roads around disappeared very quickly as Marcus made his way down a gentle slope into the heart of the cemetery. An avenue ran between high family mausoleums, obelisks and statues. At the end of the road a chapel stood on a grassy hill, stone steps leading up to a dramatic columned portico. It looked more like a stock exchange than a church. Marcus walked along the path, kicking at piles of damp leaves, scanning the ground that fell away to his left for any sign of Mouse. When he came to the chapel, he climbed the steps and looked down over the graves. Nothing moved. A blackbird, startled by his approach, made a break for cover, spiralling across the lawn in front of the chapel and into a patch of brambles. Below the chapel, the graves clustered thickly together. Some were very old, and the shifting of the ground over time had broken the ancient stones, so that they slumped forward or leaned perilously against each other. Marcus walked through the chapel's empty courtyard, where his footsteps echoed in the silence, and down the steps the other side.

It grew wilder as he descended further into the cemetery. He could see the line of poplars that grew along the canal in the distance, and knew that this was the boundary of the graveyard, but there was no other indication that he was anywhere but deep in the country, in an endless labyrinth of tombs. The sky grew darker still. Marcus found himself at a dead end as the path he was following became overgrown with brambles. He tried to force his way through, scratching his fingers, leaving red lines on the back of his hands that swelled white around the edges. He turned around and headed back up the hill. Mouse couldn't hide forever. Marcus wondered if he should go to the police. He felt for the earrings in his pocket and rolled them between finger and thumb.

He was walking between rows of highly ornate vaults when he heard a noise. The tomb next to him had huge carved sphinxes at each corner. Marcus stepped up onto the head of one of the sphinxes to get a better view. The only movement was the swirling of the rain and the leaves which continued their endless fall. Marcus climbed down and continued along the dark avenue. He heard the sound of a twig breaking.

'Mouse,' Marcus called out. 'Is that you? Come and talk to me. I'll help you.'

There was no response. Marcus thought he saw something move between two gravestones ahead of him, a flash of dark material and skin. He ran. His tired mind began to panic; the presence of so much death brought images of his father to his mind. The coffins seemed to rear up above him, closing in under the night-black sky. He slipped and landed heavily on a pile of dead leaves, which were slimy to the touch. He lay for a moment, his chest pounding, his breaths coming fast and jagged like the firing and reloading of a gun. He struggled to get to his feet, reached out and pulled himself up on a gravestone, felt the cold dead certainty of the marble beneath his fingers. He began to run again.

The rain started to fall more heavily. The drops felt like hailstones against Marcus's skin. He ran between lines of ancient graves until he came to a fork in the path. He took the right-hand branch. The pounding rain reduced his visibility to a few yards, but still he turned to look over his shoulder, searching for a dark shape against the misty grey air. He ploughed onwards. Finally, indistinctly, he thought he saw the block of the youth hostel rising above the wall. He increased his speed, tripped over a gravestone and sprawled once again on the damp ground. His clothes were soaked through, his knees and elbows muddy and torn. Picking himself up, he jogged the final few steps into the shadow of the hostel. He stood, resting against the cold stone of the cemetery wall.

Marcus followed the wall along until he came to the main gates. He was breathing heavily, his heart thumping horribly loudly in his chest. He crossed the road and sat steaming in a cafe, drinking scalding coffee until he felt warm enough to face the prospect of the bus home.

Four

Marcus could hear Darwin as he stood in the lift. The plangent yelping grew louder as he opened the front door. He stepped into the flat and the dog launched himself at him, licking his hands and turning delighted circles around his feet. Marcus leaned down to pat him, then went through to the kitchen to refill the water bowl. He poured out some bone-shaped biscuits, which the dog devoured, snuffling and whimpering as he ate. Marcus saw that there was a stringy turd in the middle of the drawing-room carpet, and dark patches of piss dotted around the rest of the flat. He put on rubber gloves, reached under the sink for a sponge and bucket, and set to work cleaning up after the dog.

It felt strange to be doing something so mundane as housework after the morning's events, but Marcus wanted to put off the decisions that he knew he would have to make, needed to fend off the thought that Mouse might be responsible for Lee's disappearance. When he had finished scrubbing, Marcus took Darwin downstairs and let him run around the small patch of grass at the back of the block of flats. He threw a stick for the dog, which he pounced upon and then tried to bury, unsure of what was expected of him. He stared up resentfully at Marcus when he picked up the stick, until he threw it again and the sequence was repeated. Marcus found himself smiling at the dog's mindless enthusiasm. It was still drizzling, but the ferocious wind had passed, and a number of times the sun broke through the low clouds, sparkling on the wet grass.

Back in the flat, Marcus ran himself a bath and stripped off his damp, dirty clothes. It would be the first time he had missed a Sunday morning service in several months. A dull ache nagged at the back of his throat. When he had soaked some warmth into his chilled body, Marcus hunted in the medicine cabinet until he found a packet of Abby's sleeping tablets and some painkillers. He gulped down a handful of pills, closed his bedroom curtains, and passed out on the bed. He woke a couple of times during the day, and managed to stagger to the kitchen and feed Darwin on one occasion, but didn't rise properly until it was dark outside.

Marcus made himself bacon and eggs and sat down at the dining table with his computer in front of him. He hadn't checked his emails since Friday, and it was another thing to occupy his time before he had to think about Mouse. He turned on the machine and ate while it warmed up. When he logged into his account, he saw with a mixture of pleasure and trepidation that there was an email from Abby titled 'NYC'. He opened it and began to read.

Dear Marcus,

I can't think when I last sent you an email. It feels strange. I wanted to let you know that I was thinking of you, though. I'm having a very good time out here. The Course is everywhere: in every church in Manhattan, or that's what it feels like! I'm going up to Connecticut and then on to Boston, where I'll be making a speech about how to be an effective Course leader. Terrifying.

I want you to know that I forgive you, Marcus. I hate what you did, but I love you. I think being away from you like this has made me realise how much we need each other. David once said to me that we were the best-matched couple he had ever met. I think he's right and I don't want to throw this all away because of one drunken mistake.

I wish you were out here with me, Marcus. It is cold, but the sun has shone brightly every day I have been here. The skyscrapers look beautiful in this sunlight. I am staying in the Earl's apartment near the Frick. It's predictably lavish, with carpets so thick that your feet disappear into them. I try to stop at the gallery every day – I want to get everything I can from this trip.

David said he might want me to stay an extra week – he's trying to set something up at Yale. If not then I'll be home the last week in November. Don't be too lonely, darling.

Your wife,

Abby xxx

P.S. give me a call on the mobile Monday night your time.

Marcus read the email again and felt a hard knot of shame build in his stomach. He pictured Rebecca lying back naked on the beanbag, saw the childish amusement in her eyes as he licked his way up her leg. It seemed so long ago, though. So much had changed since then, Rebecca seemed like a character from a bizarre dream. He shut his computer and stared out of the window.

He would have to speak to Mouse. He owed it to his friend to give him a chance to explain. Perhaps Lee had given him the earrings before she disappeared, perhaps he had found them going through her possessions and was ashamed to have taken them. Marcus dialled Mouse's mobile. There was no response. He left a message.

'Mouse. It's me. Listen, we need to talk. I want to hear your side of the story. Just tell me where you got the earrings and it can stay between us. No one else needs to know. Give me a call, Mouse. Please.'

Marcus hung up the phone and stretched out on the sofa. He opened up his computer again and found the article about Lee in the newspaper's online edition. The piece contained very few facts, and hinted with many *allegedly*s and *supposedly*s and carefully hedged words that Lee killed herself because the Course was a cult that sought to control the lives of its followers. The newspaper would get a call from the Course's lawyers, despite the careful manner in which it presented the story. Marcus read it once more and then drifted off to sleep. He woke after a couple of hours and stumbled to bed. Darwin, yawning, came too and curled up at his feet as he slept.

On Monday, Marcus kept his mobile in constant view. He found his work particularly dull that day as he trawled through further documents relating to the legal wrangle between Plantagenet Partners and the Chinese bank. The case was growing increasingly murky. It seemed to him that the hedge fund had acted recklessly and criminally, and now he was being asked to help them cover their tracks. He was surprised, when reading through one of the documents, to see the Earl's name. He searched through the files on his computer and realised that the Earl was one of the initial backers of the shady hedge fund, and was now a non-executive director of the business. He wondered if the Earl knew the details of the case.

He could hardly muster the energy to care, though. Partly his boredom was driven by the anticipation of speaking to Abby, partly by the recollection of Rebecca's response to his description of his life. Marcus knew that he was wasting his talents at the law firm, but the money was so good. He walked out for lunch feeling dejected, sniffing as he attempted to fight off the cold that sat threateningly behind his eyes.

Mouse hadn't called by the time Marcus left the office at seven. Marcus went for a beer with some of his colleagues after work, then walked towards Moorgate. He made his way down into the Tube, determined to call Mouse when he came out at Notting Hill Gate. He sat on the swaying train half-reading a novel and wondering what he'd do if Mouse didn't telephone. When he came out into the damp West London night, his answerphone alert was flashing. He dialled it as he walked towards his flat.

'Marcus, it's Mouse. I'm sorry I didn't call you earlier. I'm sorry about yesterday in the cemetery. I'm sorry about everything. But I can't tell you how I got the earrings. Please just believe me, sport, I didn't kill Lee. I'm going to go away for a while. Don't turn your back on me now, Marcus. Please.'

Marcus listened to the message again and then saved it. He opened the door to his flat, fed Darwin, and sat down to call Abby. She answered almost immediately, her voice full of childish pleasure.

'Oh, darling, it's you. Your number doesn't come up. How are you?'

'I'm fine,' he said.

'No you're not. What's wrong?'

He took a deep breath. 'A lot of things have been happening, Abby. To do with Lee. I don't really know what I should . . . I found her earrings, Abby. I found them on Mouse's boat.'

'Tell me all about it. Start at the beginning and take me through what happened.'

Marcus told her about meeting Daffy in east London and then going on to the artist's party. He skipped over the episode with Rebecca, but then described finding the earrings in the tortoiseshell box and his pursuit of Mouse across the graveyard. Finally, he related Mouse's answerphone message. Abby was silent for a while.

'I believe him, don't you?'

'I don't know. I stayed the night on the boat on Thursday and I just got the feeling that he was hiding something, that there was something awful that he needed to tell me but couldn't.'

He heard the sound of traffic in the background, a police siren wailed.

'You should talk to David. He'll know what to do. If Mouse is going away then he won't be at the Course on Tuesday night. Go and speak to David afterwards. I'm sorry I'm not there, darling. But I know you'll do the right thing. I still think Lee probably killed herself. And maybe you're looking for things to demonstrate otherwise, to take away some guilt. Get lots of sleep, my love. You sound like you're coming down with something. And call me whenever you want.'

*

On Tuesday evening, David stood in front of the Course members, his skin grey under the spotlight, large purplish bags under his bloodshot eyes.

'You will have read the lies printed about one of our Course members in the press this weekend,' he began. 'I don't want to dignify such monstrous rubbish with anything more than a cursory response. Lee Elek is a wonderful girl and a dear friend. We all miss her very much. But she has some significant personal problems, and I believe the Course is one of the very few forces for good in her life. Let us all pray now for Lee, wherever she might be.'

After the speech, which was shorter than usual, David and Marcus played an acoustic set on stage. There were candles around their feet and David sang in his high, soft voice. Some of the girls in the front row swayed along with the music. As

expected, Mouse hadn't turned up that evening. The two discussion groups were combined and Marcus would speak to
them both in the low-ceilinged crypt room.

Marcus sat and stared at the new members, aware that Sally
and David were behind him, watching. His head was fuzzy,
his sinuses clogged and aching. While he had tried to steer the
conversation around to the evening's topic, *Being an Apostle in
the Modern World*, the group had only wanted to talk about
Lee. One of the quiet girls spoke first, looking down at her feet,
her cheeks reddening.

'I saw the article and, while I realise that it's journalism, sen-
sationalised, I can't help but think that some of it must be true.
Has David really made people leave because they were gay? It
doesn't seem like him.'

Marcus caught David's eye and then looked back at the girl.

'It should be obvious to you now you've done the Course
that it's total rubbish. I remember the boy they were talking
about. He was trying to make some sort of political statement
by coming here. David didn't ask him to leave because he was
gay. He told him that he was here for the wrong reasons and
that he should either change those reasons or come back when
he would get more from the Course.'

One of the twins raised a thin arm.

'Alice and I were both very sad when our mummy died.
I became quite horribly depressed. And I think we all knew
that Lee was sad, suffered from her slumps. I suppose I'd have
thought that the Course would insulate you against that kind
of thing. Would give you the tools to stop you getting that bad.
If Lee was a Course leader and still fell apart like this, what
message does it give to us?'

David coughed and the group turned towards him. Marcus
sank gratefully back on his chair. The priest stepped forward

into the centre of the room, very grave, his hands pressed to-gether.

'We're all human here, we all have doubts, many of us have been down – like Ele, like Lee. It's hard not to look on the things going on in the world and get terribly downhearted. But we have to believe that what we're doing here is right. I imagine over the next few weeks we're going to learn a great deal more about the troubles that Lee was facing. And I think perhaps what we'll end up realising is that it was a miracle that something like this didn't happen sooner. That actually the Course helped sustain Lee until even her faith and our love couldn't force away the darkness. I just wish that she had spoken to me more, that she had let me shoulder more of that terrible burden.'

Tears beaded at the corners of David's eyes. He walked from the room. Sally hurried after him. The Course members sat in silence.

Finally, Neil, who had been leaning back watching them, spoke. A kind of holy glow radiated from his bald head.

'When my daughter Phoebe died, I tried so hard to under-stand what was behind it. Unravelling the infinitely complex threads of her life became an obsession for me. It was as if I thought that if I could understand why she stopped eating, I might be able somehow to go back and make it better. Or at least that it might be proof that it wasn't my fault, that nothing I could have done would have changed it. I spent hours staring at photographs of her when she was younger, trying to read the future in her sunny little smile. But, in the end, mental ill-ness is unknowable to everyone except the sufferer.

'There is something wrong with Lee, just as there was something wrong with Phoebe. We can go mad trying to find the reasons behind what happened to them, or we can move on. All we can do is love them; the rest is in God's hands.'

276

He collected himself, lowered his head, and put his hands in his lap.

'Thanks Neil,' said Marcus. 'I entirely agree. Now let's get back to the Course material. It's some of the most important stuff we'll deal with – how to handle the conflicts that are thrown at Christians in the modern world. We need to arm ourselves against the demons that brought Lee and Phoebe down.'

*

When the discussion group had left, Marcus sat in the room, his head in his hands. Finally, he rose and made his way upstairs, through the darkened church and out into the night. David was waiting for him in the shadows of the porch. The priest coughed.

'How did the rest of your discussion go?' David asked.

'I was on autopilot. I just couldn't stop thinking about Lee. Did you speak to Abby? Do you know about Mouse? Have you called the police?'

'Slow down, Marcus. I know about the earrings. But this is not the time to be jumping to any conclusions. I need to talk to Mouse. He's coming here on Friday. Let me get his side of the story and then, if we need to, we can go to the police together. In the mean time, try to take care of yourself. You look very tired.'

Marcus went home and phoned Abby. She didn't answer. The cold that had been threatening arrived that night. Marcus woke with his throat raw and swollen, his nose blocked and his chest tight. He swallowed down a handful of painkillers and lay in the dark, feeling profoundly sorry for himself. The next day he struggled into work, determined to put thoughts of Lee and Mouse out of his mind until the weekend. He left the office as early as possible that evening and flung himself into bed.

He had forgotten that it was fireworks night. The curtains were open and he saw the bright explosions of light over Holland Park. Darwin crawled into bed beside him and he hugged the little dog against his wheezing chest. The shards of excited light coloured his bedroom walls as he drifted off to sleep. The last he remembered seeing were blue and green, and in his dozing mind they became Lee's earrings, her face written into the sky behind them in the pattern of a million stars.

*

On Saturday morning, early enough that Marcus was still asleep, although not so early that he could ignore the call, David Nightingale telephoned.

'Hello,' said Marcus, searching for the light switch.

'Marcus, it's David. How are you feeling? I thought you looked very ill on Tuesday.'

Marcus had struggled into work on Thursday and Friday, but the cold had established itself in his chest, giving his voice a husky growl.

'I'm fine. I need to get some rest and then I'll be fine.'

'You should come over here. I think it would be a good idea for us to talk to Mouse together. He's with me now.'

'OK. I'll be over as soon as I can.'

Marcus drank a Lemsip as he dressed. His movements were slow and stumbling as he searched through his cupboard for a clean shirt. He realised that he hadn't put a wash on since Abby had left. Clothes spewed out of the hamper in the corner of the bedroom. He rummaged through them looking for a pair of boxer shorts that were not too filthy to wear. Finally, he made his way out into the bright morning, started the car, and set out for St Botolph's.

He felt a kind of nostalgia as he turned off the King's Road and into the high gates in front of the church. So many times he had come here with Abby, both of them full of hope and quiet excitement at the prospect of an inspiring discussion group, or a service, or dinner at the rectory. Whatever happened next, Marcus realised that everything had already changed. Things were not recoverable from here. He imagined himself twenty-three again, tried to steal back the excitement he had felt after his first Retreat, when everything he believed was reshaped by David Nightingale, when the love he felt for Abby and his family was knitted into his love for the church, rather than being twenty-eight and ground down by a boring job, by guilt, by betrayal. He stopped the car and eased himself out onto the familiar crunch of the gravel.

The church clock chimed ten. A robin was singing somewhere. Marcus saw the bird perched on the railings that ran along the edge of the churchyard. The bird tilted his head back, threw out his chest and unleashed a long, liquid stream of notes. Marcus skipped up the steps to the front door and rang the bell.

David answered the door. He was dressed in a blue button-down shirt and chinos. He fixed his pale eyes on Marcus. They were less bloodshot than they had been at the Course on Tuesday night. Marcus took the priest's hand.

'Thank you for coming. Gosh, you don't look well. Do you want a coffee or something?'

'Yes, that would be great,' Marcus mumbled. He followed David into the kitchen while the priest made coffee, unwilling to face Mouse alone.

'Is he here?'

'He's in the drawing room, yes. Along with a few others. Let's go through.'

Marcus followed David across the hall. Mouse was sitting in an armchair directly opposite the entrance. He looked up at Marcus and nodded glumly, then stared back at his feet, which were propped on a velvet pouffe. The Earl was seated in the corner, his fierce eyes fixed on Marcus and David. Marcus stepped further into the room and turned towards the sofa. Abby was there, sitting very upright, a hopeful smile fixed on her wide face.

'Abby!'

She rose and embraced him.

'I got the last flight back last night. I wanted to be here for this.' She took his chin in her hand and looked at his face. 'You look dreadful, darling. You obviously need me here to look after you.'

Marcus sat down beside Abby. David remained standing, moving behind Mouse's chair and looking across at Marcus. He carried some of the awful grandeur that had once made Marcus afraid to look at him.

'I thought we should all sit down together. Mouse has told me everything. We should listen to his story, and then discuss what to do. Mouse has been very brave coming to me like this. Over to you, Mouse.'

Mouse shifted in his chair, leaned forward, and began to speak. He wrung his hands as he talked. He clearly hadn't slept for a while.

'Lee's dead. She died just after five in the morning on the Sunday of the Retreat.'

Marcus felt a wave of melancholy sweep over him. He had imagined this moment so many times that it hardly shocked him. Mouse's words confirmed something that he felt he had known all along. Abby held his hand very tightly. The priest nodded at Mouse, who was sitting quite still, his eyes full of tears.

'Why don't you tell it from the beginning, Mouse? Just like you told me.'

Mouse let out a sigh.

'It was past four. Marcus and I had come up together from the dining hall around three. I couldn't sleep, so I wandered over to the west wing. I wanted to find the mermaid frieze that I'd seen the day before. When I came to the top of the winding stairs, I heard the sound of someone crying. I walked down the corridor and the sound grew louder. I came to a further staircase which led to a tower. The one that we saw when we were coming up from the lake. There was a wee room at the top with a desk and a few books.'

'It's my study,' the Earl interrupted. 'I rarely use it these days, but I like to have a place to work when I'm in the country.'

'Lee was standing at the window looking down at the moon on the lake and crying. I went up behind her and tried to comfort her, but she was absolutely wild. I couldn't get near to her. She said that the Course was responsible for her depression. That she had been happy before all the guilt. That was how she put it. She told me what had happened with Marcus on the boat and then she just dissolved in tears.

'I thought about going to get David or you, Marcus, but she stormed back downstairs and into her room. She started to throw her clothes into a bag, said she was going to walk to the train station at Banbury. She told me that she hated us. That she wished we were all dead.'

A large tear rolled down the left side of Mouse's face.

'She ran away from me down the corridor and then started down the stairs. I ran after, she slipped . . . or she jumped. I couldn't tell. She rose up into the air like she was trying to fly. I almost caught her. I was close enough to catch her, but

I couldn't quite grab hold of her jumper. She thudded all the way down the stairs and landed at the bottom with a horrible crunch.'

Mouse was sobbing now and drew his sleeve across his face. Abby let go of Marcus's hand and crossed to sit on the arm of Mouse's chair. She stroked his hair with her large hands.

'When I got down to her she wasn't breathing. I tried to give her mouth-to-mouth, but there was this huge dent in her head. I couldn't believe that falling down the stairs could do that to someone, but she landed so hard, and it was marble at the bottom. I panicked. I don't know why, but it felt like it was my fault. Like you'd all blame me for it, you know? I carried her down to the lake. I opened the boathouse and wrapped her round with fishing line and attached weights to it. I rowed out in the little boat and pushed her into the water. Then I drove your car up to Banbury Station to make it look like she'd run away. When you came down in the morning I'd just got back, Marcus.'

He stopped and looked down at his hands, then up at Marcus.

'I'm sorry.'

Marcus was fighting for breath. 'Jesus, Mouse,' he said. 'I mean, really. What were you thinking?'

Mouse looked back at him. 'I just didn't know what to do. She was dead.'

Marcus looked over at David.

'So we're going to the police, right? I mean, we have to tell them all this. Tell D.I. Farley. Mouse can claim diminished responsibility or whatever. I'm not sure that throwing someone who's already dead in a lake is even an offence. But we have to tell them, don't we?'

There was a long silence. Finally, the Earl spoke.

'I don't quite see who it helps, telling the police.' His voice was a whisper.

'Well, it helps Lee's family for one. Her parents need to know what happened to their daughter. And surely it isn't a matter of whom it helps. It's about doing what is right. Lee died and the police need to know.'

Abby crossed back to sit next to Marcus.

'David told me about this yesterday. I had a chance to think about it on the flight. I agree that it's a very complex situation.'

'I don't think it is,' Marcus interrupted her. 'I don't think it's very complex at all. It seems like a very simple situation to me.'

'Let me finish,' Abby continued, her voice very calm. 'It *is* complex. Isn't it better for Lee's family to have the hope that she isn't dead? Isn't it better that they think she might have gone off to a better life, stowed away on a ship or run off with a billionaire on his private jet? Of course, they'll always think that she probably killed herself, but I don't want to be the one who takes their hope away from them. Especially her father. He loved her so much, you know, and Lee was always saying how fragile he was. I worry that taking away this last bit of hope might finish him off.'

'And more than that is what this would do to the Course.' David stood in the centre of the room with his hands clasped in front of him. 'Nothing that we can do will change things for Lee.'

'She's lying at the bottom of a lake, David. Of course we can't change things for her.' Marcus stood up and faced the priest.

'Exactly,' David continued. 'I want to go up and have a service at Lancing Manor. Just us. Set her to rest properly – that is only right. But I am God's servant and my obligation is to do what best serves God's interests. If the news about Lee got out, it would destroy everything we have built here. The Course is about to take off in the States in a very major way. We are

283

now in three hundred churches across the UK. Imagine all the good we're doing. Imagine what it means to the priests to have their churches full. Imagine how many girls there are like Lee dealing with similar problems who will find a way to peace through God, and all because of the Course. If we go public with this, I will have to resign. The whole thing will come apart.'

'Why?' asked Marcus. 'It's Mouse's fault. He can take the blame for this. Not you.'

David looked across at Marcus. 'Because if Mouse speaks to the police he will have to tell them that one of the reasons that Lee was in such a state was because she had been taken advantage of by her best friend's husband.'

Marcus sat down next to Abby. She was staring at the floor. The priest continued.

'Infidelity, lies, a body in a lake. Of course I'll have to quit if this comes out. Nonsense in a newspaper, I can handle. But not this. I should have seen it. The Devil was working in you and Lee all along, working his evil way through my own Course leaders, and now it is all ruined. Everything I worked to build . . . ruined.'

David marched from the room, climbed the stairs and retreated behind the door of his study. The rest of the Course members sat in silence. After several minutes, the Earl stood up.

'I must be getting home. The car is waiting outside. I take it we can rely upon your discretion, Marcus?' He strode from the room.

Mouse fixed his large eyes on Marcus, hopefully.

Marcus turned to Abby and said, 'I think we should go.'

*

When they got home, Marcus lifted Abby's suitcase from the boot of the car and walked with her into the flat. She padded through the rooms, taking deep breaths, nudging the pile of unwashed shirts in their bedroom with her toe. Marcus felt bruised and empty. His head roared and he could barely speak through his swollen throat. He bent down and started to pick up the dirty clothes.

'Sorry about the mess,' Marcus began, but Abby threw her arms around him and kissed him long and wet on the lips.

'I'm pregnant again,' she said.

Marcus took her hands in his.

'That's amazing,' he said.

'I started feeling really tired in New York, and I realised that I hadn't had my period. I know it's only early days, but I think that if the baby has made it this far, through all this stress, then it must have a pretty good chance. I mean, I'm really not counting on it, but it just feels much more real this time. Much more like something that should happen to us, after Lee and everything.'

Marcus lifted her T-shirt and put a hand on her belly. Her stomach was warm and pudgy and he smiled at her.

'How far gone do you think you are?'

'Five weeks, maybe a little more.'

Marcus went out to the shops and bought some vegetables and chicken which he stir-fried in a wok. They sat and ate at the dinner table, facing each other, refusing to talk about Mouse or the meeting earlier. When they were finished, Abby pushed her bowl away and reached over to take Marcus's hand.

'Darling, we need to discuss things. Mouse, Lee, everything. But first, there's something else I wanted to speak to you about.'

Marcus poured himself a glass of wine and sat looking over at his wife.

'I can't tell you how wonderful it was to be in the States. The Course has just exploded over there. And of course we have only done the North-East. There's such enormous potential.'

Her face glowed as she spoke.

'The priests out there really get it. There's so much energy in the way they deliver the speeches. It feels like it did for us, right at the beginning. The start of an extraordinary journey.'

She paused for a moment.

'David has asked me to go out there full-time. He needs an administrator in the US, someone he can rely upon to run things, look after the expansion.'

Marcus felt his face drop.

'But . . .' he began.

'He wants you to go with me.'

He stared at Abby.

'What do you mean?'

'He wants you to come and work for the Course. We'd share responsibilities. You'd run things while I have the baby. It would be a fresh start for us. It would take us away from all of this.'

'But what about my job?'

'You hate it. You said you were desperate to leave. The Course can't match your salary. But we'd be doing something we really loved.'

'And the baby?'

'I'll have it out there. I told David about it and he said he'd make sure the Course looked after the whole thing. It would be wonderful.'

He pictured the two of them pushing a buggy through Central Park on a Saturday morning, imagined what it would be like to be away from London, away from the guilt and the memories.

'Can I think about it? I mean, it sounds great, but so much

has happened. I just need some time to get it all straight in my head.'

*

Mouse didn't come to the service the next day. It was very cold and Marcus thought that the canal might have frozen over. Mouse used to worry that the *Gentle Ben*'s hull would crack in the ice and had spent several days the previous winter boiling kettles and pouring them down the side of the boat. Marcus kept looking out for his friend as the service progressed, hoping somehow that seeing him would help unravel the knot of conflicting emotions in his cold-muddled mind.

After the service they went over to the rectory for coffee. The Earl stood in the corner of the drawing room talking to a tall couple. The woman held a tiny baby in her arms and looked down at it, clucking every so often. Her husband smiled at her approvingly. His name was Simon Cooper-Jones and he was one of the City's most successful hedge-fund managers, not yet forty and worth tens of millions. He was devoted to the Course and a major donor. Marcus crossed and leaned against the mantelpiece beside them, listening.

'Your boys are doing a fine job of managing the Course funds,' the Earl said, chucking the sleeping baby under the chin with a meaty finger, but keeping his eyes on Simon. 'Up twenty per cent plus in this market isn't easy.'

'We're the best. You know that by now. You should give us a bit more of your own cash.'

'I might just do that. You're not worried about another Crash?'

'Always worried, never fearful. That's my motto. How's the US expansion going? I really think it's an extraordinary untapped market.'

'It's going very well in New York,' the Earl replied. 'David is doing some work with the Ivy League universities. We're going at the market top-down – it served us well here and I don't see why it shouldn't work out there. Do you have a New York office?'

'Of course. Let me know which church you want them to attend and I'll send some of my team along.'

After they had finished their coffee, Marcus and Abby stepped out into the frosty sunlit day. As they crossed the car park in front of the church, the Earl jogged to catch up with them. He took Abby's arm.

'I hear that you two are thinking of going out to New York full-time. I'm delighted. It has been a ghastly few weeks. It'll be a new start for you both. And the Course will flourish over there. I know it. You must treat my apartment as your own. Stay for as long as you like. I'm rarely over there these days. Too old and tired for the transatlantic life.'

As Marcus pulled out onto the King's Road, he saw a man in a faded velvet jacket walking away from them, west towards Fulham. The collar of the jacket was raised against the wind and the man was smoking, taking deep, angry drags and then blowing the smoke into the air above him. Marcus tried to turn around, but the traffic was heavy in both directions. Abby followed his gaze and opened her mouth to speak. A bus crossed in front of them and when it was gone, the figure had disappeared.

When they got home, Abby walked out to the shops to buy lunch. Marcus sat at the table in the drawing room and thought. He realised that he was being given another chance, an opportunity to make things right with Abby, and that this decision would change everything, define the person he was, and who he would become. He crossed to the window, opened it a crack and lit a cigarette, blowing the smoke out into the cold air. Everything had changed. Even if he stayed in London, it would be a hollow simulacrum of his old life. He'd be like those friends from college who had remained at university to do MAs and PhDs with the same tutors, who would then teach at the college, forever walking in the footsteps of their teen-age selves, trying to recapture those happy years. He worried about leaving Mouse, but otherwise there was nothing keeping him here. He finished his cigarette and shut the window.

There was a picture of him and Abby on the sideboard. They were standing in the portico of a church and Abby's arm was around him. It was the day of their wedding and he was looking away from the camera, off into the middle distance. He couldn't remember where his gaze had been directed, whether towards Lee, or Mouse, or one of the pretty Course wives holding a baby in the churchyard. But Abby's eyes stared straight at the camera, hopeful, her smile full of pride. It made Marcus sad to look at her. He realised that, in his mind, there had never been a time when he had been truly faithful to Abby. He had fucked girls behind her back throughout university and, even though – until his most recent indiscretions – he had kept his infidelity in check since joining the Course, cheating was always there in his mind as an option. Perhaps, he thought, his parents had been too happy together, presenting an unattainable ideal which, because he could never replicate it, he had to destroy.

Now he had the opportunity to start again. He picked up the photograph and looked into his wife's face. He felt a great swelling of love. They were having a baby together. He was going to be a father. He heard her keys in the door. Abby struggled down the corridor and dropped the shopping bags on the kitchen floor. She took off her coat and flung it on the counter. Marcus stepped behind her and folded his arms around her large frame. She leant back against him, closing her eyes, her head on his shoulder.

'I'm coming with you,' he whispered.

Her eyes snapped open. A smile broke gently over her face. 'Really?'

'Of course I am. We'll make a new life out there.'

'Oh, darling, I'm so happy. I couldn't have gone without you.'

They stood, breathing heavily, listening to the cars on Notting Hill Gate, an Underground train rattling over a bridge, the distant thump of music. Very gently, he slid his hand up under her jumper and let it rest on her hot, soft stomach.

Five

Marcus discovered that it was possible, with a degree of concentration, to pretend that Lee had never existed. He found it easier still now that Mouse had stopped coming to church. Abby and Marcus had hosted the final Course session together, both groups squeezed into the one room. Marcus seemed especially galvanised as he led the discussion. David and Sally Nightingale looked on with pride as the two young people, heads bowed, prayed with the new members. An atmosphere of quiet contentment hung over the group: they had made it through. They were part of the Course. At the end of the session, the members came up one by one and thanked Marcus and Abby.

The twins bounced in front of them, squealing. Neil slipped Marcus a business card with a sly nod. All the pale, quiet girls from Marcus's group came up to him and hugged him. David opened some bottles of champagne and they toasted each other, toasted the missing members. Neil suggested they toast Jesus. When the last members went home, Marcus and Abby walked out into the night with David.

'Well done, you two.' The priest sounded a little drunk.

'It was a good way to finish,' said Marcus.

'I always knew I could count on you guys. Lee and Mouse were too young, too fragile. I should have realised that. But you two are my stalwarts, you have repaid the faith I showed in you.'

'It does feel good, to see the new members like that, to know that the Course is now central to their lives. I feel like we have achieved something, that maybe it was worth all the pain, worth losing Lee and Mouse.' Marcus smiled at the priest and took Abby's hand.

'I'm glad you feel that way. Have you heard from Mouse?' David asked.

Marcus shook his head. 'I'll go up to the boat at the weekend. I've left him a few messages. I'm sure he's just feeling shell-shocked by the whole thing. He'll be back.'

'He'll want to see you before you go. And he always loves Christmas at the church. I'm sure he'll come to the service on Sunday. We're singing carols.'

Marcus and Abby got into the car just as the first flakes of snow began to fall.

*

On Saturday morning, when the snow had been reduced to a grey dusting on slate rooftops, Marcus and Abby walked up to the canal. They would have to leave Darwin behind when they went to New York, and they looked at the dog fondly as he capered alongside them. Sally Nightingale would care for him until they returned. Marcus led Darwin along the towpath, allowing him to burrow into mounds of wet snow, where he'd draw his muzzle out dripping and dirty and fix Marcus with an accusing glare. When they got to the *Gentle Ben* there were no lights on. Marcus tried the door, but this time it was firmly locked.

'Shall we call his mother?' Abby asked, as they walked back towards Ladbroke Grove.

'I don't know. I think if he wanted to see us, he would.'

As they walked back, Abby took his hand.

'Do you think you'd ever give up smoking? It would mean a lot to me.'

He reached into his pocket, drew out a packet of cigarettes and crumpled it into a ball. He hurled the ball into the canal.

They made their way up the ramp and onto the bridge. The canal was healing over with ice. Darwin poked his nose through the bars of the railings and sniffed the cold air. Marcus looked up through skeletal trees into the graveyard. He could make out the roof of the chapel in the distance, the peaks of the obelisks that lined the avenue where he had slipped. Abby was watching a pair of Canada geese waddling sedately along the towpath.

'They look like old women,' she said. 'Querulous old women complaining about the weather.'

The geese, seeing a gaggle of their companions squabbling over husks of bread thrown from a narrowboat moored further up the towpath, started to run. Flapping their wings and squawking like old-fashioned bicycle horns, they rose up into the air and were suddenly majestic as they wheeled over their comrades. Marcus and Abby walked arm in arm down Ladbroke Grove, inexplicably cheered by the sight of the geese transformed in flight.

Days passed in busy preparation for their move. They would be spending Christmas with Marcus's mother in Surrey and then flying to New York on the twenty-seventh. There was still no sign of Mouse. Marcus tried his mobile every few days, but it always rang through to the answerphone. He had stopped leaving messages. Snow began to fall again, and this time settled in heaps outside the front door of the block of flats. Marcus persuaded himself that he could see Abby gaining weight. He kissed her very carefully in the mornings before he set off for work. Barely allowing his lips to graze her skin, he'd lean down over her and watch as she smiled in her sleep.

Marcus had handed in his notice to Michael Faraday, his senior partner at the law firm.

'But you're doing very well here,' the sharp-faced little man had said, running his eye down Marcus's evaluations. 'There's a big future for you at the firm if you stick at it.'

Marcus just grinned and shook his head. It was agreed that he would work until Christmas.

In the event there was very little for Marcus to do. No one wanted him to start a case when it was known that he was leaving. The Chinese bank had dropped its case against Plantagenet Partners due to lack of evidence. Marcus spent his days organising the move. They would let the flat in Notting Hill to a couple from the Course. With this income and the salary that he had agreed with David, Marcus worked out that they wouldn't be much worse off in New York than in London. As he strolled out for long lunches during those weeks in early December, he thought ahead happily to the life they would build in another city, to the child who would come.

*

On the Wednesday afternoon before Christmas, Marcus set out for Senate House. He had spent the morning on the telephone to the removals company that was transporting their books and clothes out to the US. After lunch he sat throwing a tennis ball against his window until the partner in the office next door hurled a book at the wall. Marcus reached for his phone and started to dial Mouse, then stood up and pulled on his coat.

He walked up through the City, along High Holborn and up Farringdon Road. Snow blew in gusts along the wide roads.

He saw the flushed faces of lunchtime drinkers, ties loosened around fat necks, hands clasping pints as they braved the weather to smoke. He drew out a piece of nicotine gum and chewed it, realising that he didn't miss smoking. It had become a chore, the need to make chilly forays into the freezing winter for the diminishing hit of his super-light fags.

When he came to Russell Square he looked up at the tower above him, straining his eyes to see the misty summit. There were strange runic designs in copper set into the front of the tower. It looked to him like the headquarters of a cult. He walked through the heavy metal doors and into the entrance hall. It was gloomy inside. The marble floor was wet with muddy footprints, blown-in snow.

Marcus followed signs for the Special Collections Reading Room. He knew this was Mouse's domain. The lift was an ancient contraption, and it moaned and clunked as it took Marcus up to the fourth floor. He stepped out and walked over to a bank of turnstiles. It was silent in the wood-panelled hallway. He stood at the desk and rang a bell; it trilled loudly enough to make him jump. Finally, a girl wearing thick glasses and a green cardigan walked through the swing doors behind the desk and nodded at him.

'Can I help you?'

In the instant that the girl moved through the doors, Marcus had seen Mouse. His friend was in the room behind the doors, his feet up on a table, a mug of tea in his hands.

'I'm looking for Alastair Burrows. If you wouldn't mind telling him that Marcus is here to see him.'

'Um, yes, OK. I'll go and get him.'

The girl disappeared behind the doors again into what Marcus presumed was a staff room. Several minutes passed and then Mouse came out, alone.

'Hi, Marcus.'

'Hi.'

They stood looking at one another in the yellow light of the old library.

'I can do you a day pass if you'd like to come in?'

'That would be good.'

Marcus waited while Mouse tapped away at a keyboard. The turnstile opened and he walked through. Mouse stepped out from behind the desk and held out his hand to Marcus. Marcus shook it, then reached over to hug him. They stood in this awkward half-embrace for a moment and then Mouse drew back.

'I just wanted to check that you were OK,' said Marcus. 'We missed you at the last Course session. At church, too.'

Mouse shook his head. 'Are you just passing by? Or can you stay for a bit? We could go up to my room.'

'I've got some time. I told Abby I'd be back for dinner.'

Marcus followed Mouse out to a stairwell. They walked up three flights and the stairs ended in a door marked *Staff Only*. Mouse unlocked this and it gave onto a smaller stairway. They climbed up together. Marcus counted the floors as they rose through the library. Mouse panted as he climbed. On the fourteenth floor, Mouse opened the heavy brown door on the landing and they stepped out into an empty corridor with a parquet floor. Marcus recognised the howling wind from telephone conversations that he had had with his friend.

'Not much further,' Mouse muttered as he led them down the corridor, through a set of swing doors and then around a corner into another long passageway. They walked through more doors and then the corridor turned again, ending abruptly in a brick wall. Mouse opened the last door on the right-hand side and Marcus followed him through it into a large, echoing hall. Along one side of the hall were long windows, with stained glass in the uppermost panes. Marcus saw a date – 1936 – set into the red and green glass. There were no shelves in the hall, but Marcus nonetheless caught the sweet, dusty scent of old books. At the far end, Mouse had built a den. A wardrobe stood against one wall with a duvet and several pillows lining the bottom. Shirts hung above the little nest. A trestle table sat in front of the window with a desk lamp on it, books piled beside it and scattered across the floor around it. There was a cardboard box in which Marcus saw various bottles, a loaf of bread, some toiletries.

'Is this where you've been living?' Marcus asked, turning to his friend.

'Do you want a drink?' Mouse walked over and found a half-full bottle of wine. He pulled the cork out and poured it into plastic cups. 'It was cold on the boat. The heating isn't all that good. And I knew you'd come looking for me there.'

Marcus sipped the wine.

'It's amazing up here.'

Mouse walked over and opened a window. Snow was falling outside. They both stood and looked out over the roofs and down to the dome of St Paul's. Mouse drew out a packet of cigarettes and offered one to Marcus.

'You have to lean out, otherwise the smoke alarms get you.'

Marcus held up his hand. 'I'm not smoking.' He paused. 'Abby is pregnant.'

Mouse turned to him with delighted eyes. 'You're joking. Sport, that's grand. I'm so happy for you both.'

Marcus was touched by his friend's joy. 'I shouldn't really tell anyone yet. You might have guessed that we've had some trouble before. But I've a good feeling about this one.'

Mouse put his arm around Marcus's shoulder and blew a jet of smoke out of the window.

'Have you got names yet?'

'No, that would feel like jinxing it somehow.'

The snow began to fall more heavily. Mouse finished his cigarette and closed the window. The wind had picked up and moaned balefully as Mouse opened another bottle of wine. They sat on pillows with their backs against the wood-panelled wall. The light had dropped outside and Mouse switched on the desk lamp.

'We're going away for a while,' Marcus said.

Mouse looked across at him.

'Where?' he asked.

'David has asked Abby to stay on in New York. I'm going to go with her. Only for a year. Two at the most.'

Mouse's face fell.

'You'll have the baby out there?'

Marcus nodded.

'Oh. I was hoping . . . I suppose I can come out to visit.'

'Of course you can. You can come whenever you want. You'll be the godfather, of course.'

'Of course.' Mouse smiled. 'When are you going?'

'Straight after Christmas.'

'Oh. That's very soon.' Mouse stared down at his hands. Marcus's voice softened.

'I just realised that we had to grow up. When Abby came back, she seemed changed, suddenly an adult. I'm going to be a father; I'm fed up with pretending I'm still a teenager. I want my kid to have a dad he can be proud of.'

'You're a Course leader. You're a successful lawyer. I don't understand.'

'All of us, we're in hiding, obsessed with our narrow little world. I'm not saying that going to America will change all of that, but at least it'll change something.'

'But what about me? What about us?'

'Lee's death has altered everything. Things can't go back to how they were. David will find a new group of Course leaders, but The Revelations are finished.'

They drank the remains of the bottle of wine.

'Listen, I'm going to have to get going. Abby, you know . . .'

'I know. I understand.' Mouse looked downcast for a moment, then smiled over at Marcus hopefully. 'Will you stay for just one more drink? I have some vodka over here somewhere.' He rose. 'Here it is. Stay and toast the end of an era. Just while I have one last cigarette.'

Mouse filled both their glasses and walked over to the window. Darkness had fallen, but the lights that illuminated the tower blazed up into the night sky. The snow raged in the beams of light, whipped across their field of vision by the wind, swirling upwards and then exploding in all directions as it hit the building. Marcus watched flakes land at Mouse's feet and disappear into the parquet floor. He crossed to stand behind his friend.

'You know the story about the lights?' Mouse was staring out into the blizzard, the cigarette held in his lips, his hands either side of the window frame.

'During the blackout, Senate House was the only building illuminated in Bloomsbury. A beacon of light for the German bombers. They never switched these things off. But it wasn't hit. Through the whole of the Blitz this enormous building stood here, like a middle finger raised to the Germans, and never once did they hit it. Bombs fell either side, they devastated the area up towards Euston and across Clerkenwell and Holborn, but never here.'

Mouse raised his glass.

'Cheers, by the way. Anyway, after the war they found out that Hitler was planning to base the Third Reich in Britain in Senate House. I mean, it has the right feel about it, doesn't it? The size of the place, the sense that it'll be here in a thousand years when all the City skyscrapers have been burned to the ground. If Oswald Mosley had won power, he intended to move parliament here.'

Marcus finished his drink and placed the cup on the trestle table.

'I really have to go now.' It was almost seven o'clock.

'Just . . . I need to speak to you.' Mouse didn't turn around, but drained his plastic cup and sent it spinning out into the snow. Marcus stood in the middle of the room, hands hanging at his sides, looking at his friend's squat frame silhouetted against the white world outside.

'I want to go to the police,' Mouse said. 'I want to hand myself in. Tell everyone exactly what happened. I just can't stop thinking about Lee's dad. I'm responsible for his hope, and it isn't fair. Every time the telephone rings, every time there's a knock on the door, part of him – maybe an increasingly small part of him as time passes, but part of him nonetheless – will think it's her. He's an amazing man. I always loved speaking to him whenever I went up there. He deserves better than this. We shouldn't be covering this up.'

Marcus's phone vibrated in his pocket. He ignored it, stood lost in thought for a moment. Mouse continued.

'I've been thinking very hard about this. I almost called D.I. Farley last night. I don't know what'll happen to me, but it really doesn't matter. I'd be fine in jail. I'd cosy up to some big gangster type, offer to soap him in the shower. I'd be grand.'

'Here, give me one of those.' Mouse passed him a cigarette. Marcus took a long drag and sighed as he let the smoke out through his nose. He pulled the chair out from under the trestle table and sat down.

'But it's more than that . . .'

'Go on,' said Marcus.

'The Course used to be about making us better people. I

300

used to believe that, despite the showiness and the money sloshing around, it was a genuinely good thing. But it has changed, you know? The Course has become a corporation. It's bigger than Lee's death, and that just can't be right. Because that's what David's saying, isn't it? That it isn't worth jeopardising the American expansion for the sake of telling the truth about Lee. The Earl has turned David's head. Because David is a good man. He would have done the right thing if this had happened a year ago. He wouldn't have let us cover up Lee's death.'

Marcus's phone buzzed again. He answered it.

'I'm sorry, Abby.' He knew he sounded drunk. He made an effort not to slur his words. 'I'm with Mouse. I'll be back as soon as I can. Eat without me.' He hung up.

'Will you come with me to the police station? Will you help me through this? I'm pretty scared. I want to do the right thing, but it isn't going to be easy.'

Mouse paused, walked over to find the vodka, and took a swig from the bottle. He passed it to Marcus. Marcus gulped, wiped his arm across his mouth and rocked back on the chair.

'I've obviously been thinking about it, too,' he said. 'It's weird, but I've changed so much over the past few weeks. I used to think I was in control of things. I always used to feel like I was the centre of the room, at the heart of things, but these days . . . everything seems so different. As if life is just rushing by. Like I'm on a train travelling very quickly and I lose sight of things flashing past, have to really concentrate to catch sight of the world. Things are just happening to me.'

Mouse turned to Marcus and looked at him. Marcus found it difficult to meet his friend's eyes.

'I agree with you about the Course and about David,' said Marcus. 'This whole American dream has given him visions of global domination. He thinks he's going to be some flashy televangelist preaching to thousands in aircraft-hangar churches, beamed out on prime time to the homes of a million fawning fans.'

Marcus stood, took a last drag on his cigarette and flicked it out into the snow.

'But the Course is a force for good. In this fucked-up world you have to think that getting people to believe in a mild, forgiving God is a good thing. We forget how much the Course has done for us. Imagine who you'd be without it. I'd be a monster, I'm sure. You have to realise that David is right. Letting people know about Lee will destroy the Course. To have a story like this break would wreck it.

'I think about Abby, too. I've been a shit husband. I realise that. And I need to try to make things up to her. I'm going to do everything I can for this baby, for her, for the Course. I'm not trying to change your mind. Or rather, I'm just trying to make you see that if you tell the police it's going to have huge repercussions.'

'But isn't it the right thing to do?'

'I don't think anything is as simple as that. I don't think there's such a thing as right and wrong any more.'

'Do you think Abby would be terribly hurt?'

'Of course. I worry . . . I worry about the baby. What the shock would do to her, to the baby.'

'Oh, Jesus, you can't use that. You can't use that against me.'

'It's something that I think about, of course it is.'

'What will you do if I do tell them?'

'I can't stop you.'

'But you won't come with me.'

'I don't know that I can.'

'Please?'

Mouse's breath misted in the air blown in from the window. Marcus was staring out at the snow.

'I didn't know what to do,' Marcus said. 'I was totally lost. This move, it gives me a second chance. I know I should help you, Mouse, but I can't. I'm putting everything in God's hands. I think, perhaps, it's God who has been directing things, that's why I feel like I've lost control. I've decided to embrace that, to let Him lead me from here on.'

'That's really dumb. You can't mean it?'

'I just don't know what else to say. I'm so sorry.'

Marcus put his arms around Mouse and they stood there for a few minutes. Marcus reached over and gently pulled the window closed. There was a line of white snow across the diagonal Vs of the wooden floor.

'I have to go.'

Mouse's mouth hung open. His eyes, which had been wide and questioning, suddenly narrowed.

'OK. I understand. Let me show you out.'

They walked down the long flight of stairs together in silence. Mouse went first, breathing heavily, slowing as they descended. Finally, they stood by the turnstiles in the yellowish glow of the library lights. Mouse's eyes were red.

'Goodbye, sport,' he said. 'Give my love to Abby.'

Marcus reached out to hug his friend again, but Mouse pulled away.

'Tell her I hope the birth . . . that everything goes well for her.'

Marcus felt in his pocket.

'I have something for you.'

He dropped the pair of earrings, one turquoise, one blue, into his friend's hand. Mouse's eyes filled with tears.

'Thank you,' he said, his voice breaking.

Marcus stepped into the lift.

'I'm sorry.'

Mouse shook his head, tears streaming from his bright, buoyant eyes.

'Bye, Mouse.'

Mouse stood at the lift doors until they closed, then Marcus rode downwards in the wheezing, clanging contraption. Outside, the snow had begun to drift in Russell Square. Marcus hailed a taxi and made his way back to the flat.

When he got inside, Abby was sitting cross-legged on the bed reading a book about child-rearing, one of a large pile that sat on the dresser in their room. Marcus brushed his teeth and lay alongside her. She closed the book and took his head in her lap, bending down to kiss him.

'You found Mouse,' she said.

'Mmm. He was at the library.' Marcus stared up at her.

'How is he?'

'He's OK. He'll be fine.'

'D'you think he'll come back to the Course?'

'I don't know. I think maybe he will. But I'm so tired. Can we go to sleep?'

'Of course. We can talk tomorrow.'

She reached over, turned out the light and stretched out with her back to him. Soon she was snoring. Marcus lay in the darkness and heard, echoing through his mind, the wail of a baby, the howling of the wind in the library and the sound of Lee picking out the 'Promenade' from *Pictures at an Exhibition* on her piano. Above all the other sounds, and yet somehow containing them, he heard the high wailing beauty of the tongues.

Epilogue
Spring

Abby walked down the main street of the quiet university town. Students were streaming out of classrooms and heading back to their dorms. Some made their way through the gates and across the main road to the shops. It was a balmy March day. The winter had been a cruel one, much colder than she was used to at home, but the past few weeks had been mild. She was growing to like these North-Eastern university towns: Princeton, New Haven, Cambridge, Ithaca. They were manageable, even to a foreigner. She smiled as a man stood aside to let her pass along the narrow pavement. She wondered if he could tell she was pregnant. She was at the annoying stage where she might be mistaken for merely fat.

She stepped into a bar on the main street. It was across the road from the town's famous record exchange, a white brick building that managed to attract a constant stream of pale, acne-scarred students despite the increasing obsolescence of its wares. The bar was almost empty. She bought herself a glass of wine and then sat at the table in the window, overlooking the university's main quadrangle. A huge Henry Moore sculpture stood, bright with verdigris, in the centre. The bartender looked over at her. She put her handbag in her lap to hide her bump. She knew what Americans thought about drinking during pregnancy. But she deserved a little celebration. The past few weeks had been marvellous.

She had called her mother the night before and told her that she would be staying for the rest of the year, would be having the baby in New York. Her mother, unusually emotion-al, had started to cry. Abby's middle sister Susie had moved back home, after finally divorcing the maths teacher. Abby could hear her shouting at the children in the background.

'And you really think this is what you went to that wonder-ful university for,' her mother was saying. 'To run a cult thou-sands of miles away from your family?'

Abby had made vague, soothing sounds and hung up. She rarely spoke to her mother any more. Sally and David were her new parents. And she knew that they were very proud of her. She took a gulp of wine.

A group of students came in. She realised that they had been at the meeting earlier. The girls were exquisite-looking: shimmering with health, their hair bounced as they walked. The young men were tall and wore pastel-coloured shirts tucked into their chinos. They sat at a table at the other end of the bar and Abby had to strain her ears to make out what they were saying.

'It's exactly what I've been waiting for. Almost all my life, it feels like.'

'The whole thing was so chic. Because that's what I always hated about going to church with my family. All the unattract-ive people there.'

'And the music is so great. I've already downloaded some of the podcasts. A bit of talking, some music. I listen to it on the way to class. Oh, hey, look, there's Abby. Come and join us, Abby.'

Abby left her half-drunk glass of wine on the table and walked over to the group. She smiled down at them.

'Can I get you guys a drink?'

'No. Let us get you one. It's Ben's turn to buy. What would you like?'

'Um . . . Could I have a Diet Coke?'

They sat and talked for an hour. A huge bowl of nachos appeared in the centre of the table. Abby pulled out long strings of cheese, negotiating them carefully into her mouth. She enjoyed spending time with these young, burnished Americans. They had none of the scepticism of their English peers.

'I'm going out to California next week,' Abby told them. 'I've never been before. I'm terribly excited.'

'Oh, you'll love it. Where are you going?'

'San Francisco and LA. We're doing a thing in LA with a bunch of Hollywood actors. The founder of the Course was out there last month and there seemed to be such excitement about it. I suppose a drive to make religion stylish was bound to go down well out there.'

'I've got some friends at Berkeley who'd love to come along. Should I let them know about it?'

'Sure. Please do tell as many people as you can about the Course. This is just the beginning. It's really marvellous to be there at the beginning of something. David Nightingale, the founder of the Course, is making a huge speech in London today. Some terribly powerful church leaders from over here have flown out to watch him. With their support, the Course is going to simply explode in the US.' She looked at her watch. 'I'm afraid I must go and catch my train. I have to be in New York tonight. But here's my card. Send me an email if you'd like to become campus representatives for the Course. We need as many people to spread the word as possible.'

She strolled downhill towards the train station. The university buildings were the colour of toast. Ivy grew up the wall beside her. On the other side of the road was a vast chapel built by a private-equity billionaire. It was here that she had spoken to the students earlier. Each time she came to one of these events she expected to be greeted by an empty hall, by spiky atheists intent on disrupting the meeting. But the rooms were always full. To see so many hopeful, upturned young faces, it gave her hope herself.

On the train back to New York she slipped her shoes off and tucked her legs beneath her on the seat. She was reading *The Lion, the Witch and the Wardrobe*. Mouse had sent it to her. It was the edition they had given to him for his nineteenth birthday. He had crossed out their message and written underneath it. The new inscription read: *For Mummy and Baby Glass*. She smiled. The sun was going down as the train moved out of the leafy New Jersey countryside and into the vast urban sprawl that surrounded New York. She liked to listen to the strange place names as they edged towards the city: Rahway, South Amboy, Secaucus. There was something terribly exotic about it all, even though the towns themselves were ugly smears of industrialised wasteland.

Abby sat back in her seat with her hands resting across her tummy. She knew she wouldn't feel a kick for another month, knew that there was still a long way to go. But the baby was blessed. After everything that had happened, after all the heartache and the loss, the baby had to survive. It was only fair. It kept the world in balance.

She spoke to the baby sometimes. Only just moving her lips, a half-whisper. She told it about its father. She told it about Lee. She spoke about David. She shivered with excitement as they pulled into Penn Station. She said a little prayer as the train clunked and hissed to a stop. *God, please look after the baby. After that, I really don't care what else happens, just please let the baby survive. Amen.*

*

Marcus was drunk. He had stopped at Bergdorf Goodman on the way home from the Course office on 52nd Street. He wanted to buy Abby a dress. They had a fundraising dinner at Trinity Church on Wall Street that evening. Abby was on the train home from one of her university sessions. He had walked through the dimly lit corridors of the mazelike department store until he came to a large room full of beautiful dresses. There was some sort of event being held. A group of women in their sixties stood around drinking champagne. Their hair was immaculately coiffed, their nails dripped red varnish, diamonds hung from earlobes and wattled necks and wide lapels.

Marcus began to wander around the room looking at the dresses. He held one up to the light, trying to make out whether it was black or navy blue. One of the older women came up behind him.

'You buying something for the girlfriend, sweetie?'

'It's for my wife, actually.'

'Oh, don't you have the cutest little English accent? So it's for your wife. It's for his wife, Carmella.' She took the dress from him and held it up against her, looking critically in the mirror. 'Oh, I don't think she'll like this. Now what does she look like? About my build?' She was tiny, her wasp waist held in with a large black belt. Marcus smiled.

'Oh, no. She's very tall. And she's pregnant.'

'Wonderful! How far along is she?'

'Coming up for four months.'

'Well, we must have a drink to celebrate. Come on, take a glass of champagne. Carmella, Nicole, get the girl to bring this young man a glass of champagne.'

Marcus took the glass, feeling rather dazed.

'Now she'll want something slimming. Is she showing properly yet? Does she have a bump?'

'No, not a proper bump yet.'

Marcus drank almost an entire bottle of champagne with the ladies, who he discovered were members of an exclusive

Bergdorf Goodman loyalty club. He left carrying a beautiful gold dress, another bottle of champagne slipped into the black-and-white carrier bag.

He walked along the concrete and steel canyon of Fifth Avenue until he reached the great green breath of the park. The sky above was a deep blue. The sun touched the uppermost branches of the trees. He browsed the bookstalls that had colonised the railings along the south-east corner of the park. The first leaves were appearing on the trees above him. He bought a copy of Fitzgerald's short stories and walked across the busy street. He made his way into the Frick Gallery, flashing his membership pass at the guard on the door, who recognised him and smiled.

He had taken out membership of the Frick on his first day in New York. He walked through the quiet atrium where a fountain babbled soothingly. The gallery would close in an hour and the tourists had already left, heading back for cocktail hour at their hotels. Marcus strode through the rooms that held the major collections, barely looking at the Italian and Dutch masters, which he knew by heart now. He made his way up the narrow winding stairway at the end of the gallery to the second floor where the collection grew more haphazard, less easily negotiated by the portly tourists, less amenable to holiday snapshots. The rooms here were high and dusty, full of Louis XIV furniture and Limoges porcelain.

Marcus wandered through the silent, airless rooms until he came to a gallery overlooking the lily pond with its sparkling fountain. The dusk had a quality to it that he could taste at the back of his throat, something nostalgic and poignant. He knew it was partly that he was drunk. He sat down in a green wing-back chair. The trick was to manoeuvre the chair so that the security guards wouldn't be able to see him when they did their rounds. Not that they seemed too concerned when they did. He and Abby were increasingly treating these upper rooms as their own.

They chose times when there were few visitors: just after opening time on weekday mornings, or in the evenings when the tourists had gone home. They settled themselves into the high, comfortable chairs and pretended that it was their home. It was an elaborate fantasy, and a thrilling one. Abby would speak about the children downstairs with the nanny, Marcus would bring a copy of the *Wall Street Journal* with him in order to make worldly-sounding comments about the day's financial news. They would spend hours moving around the gallery's labyrinth of still rooms, constructing slight variations in their imaginary lives: in some, Marcus was an oil baron; in others, he had made his fortune in pork bellies. Sometimes Abby was the great heiress and Marcus a devious adventurer.

That evening, he drew out the bottle of champagne from the Bergdorf Goodman bag and removed the cork very slowly to muffle the pop. He sat back and opened the book of short stories, his feet drawn up beneath him. He sipped at the champagne as he read, the small bubbles exploding upon his tongue. The yeasty aftertaste always made him think of money. He was reading 'Babylon Revisited', and when he came to the passage where the hero's wife dies, he was overcome by a sudden heart-clutching sadness. He put the book down on his lap and concentrated on drinking, staring out with cool, dry eyes into the atrium. When the bottle was almost finished, he put it back in the carrier bag and made his way downstairs. He nodded at the security guard as he left the building and walked slowly up 70th Street to the apartment, smoking one of the cigarettes that he kept hidden in the inside pocket of his coat.

When he got inside, he hung the dress in a cupboard, made himself a gin-and-tonic and took a bath, listening for Abby as he lay back in a nest of foam. He could hear his heartbeat in the whisper of bursting bubbles. He missed being able to smoke in the bath. He knew he was drinking too much, and let some of the gin-and-tonic dribble from his mouth and into the water. Stretching one arm along the cold porcelain and resting his head on it, he fell asleep, his half-snores sending little puffs of foam into the air with each out-breath. When he awoke, the water was tepid, the bubbles gone. He heard the clanking of the lift shaft and then, a few moments later, the clink of Abby's keys in the lock. She dropped her bag in the hallway and sighed. He closed his eyes and muttered a prayer. *God, look after Abby and the baby. And when it comes, let it bring light into our lives. I pray for Mouse, Lord. I pray . . . . But then Abby appeared in the doorway and stood staring down at him. Marcus, shivering in the lukewarm water, felt very vulnerable. He drained the last of the watery gin-and-tonic, folded his hands over his shrivelled cock and closed his eyes.

*

David Nightingale was dreaming about Lee. In his dream, he awoke from a deep sleep and slipped out of bed. He heard the sound of a piano playing downstairs, but couldn't be sure that this was what had woken him. Sally slept on. In his dream he knew that his wife was taking sleeping pills, perhaps also antidepressants. Something was not right with her, although he wouldn't allow his conscious mind to acknowledge this. He made his way downstairs in pale blue pyjamas and padded into the drawing room. The standard lamp was on in the corner, casting shadows across the room. Lee was sitting at the piano, playing the 'Promenade' from *Pictures at an Exhibition*. She swayed with the music, her willowy figure stretching upwards and quivering as the song reached its conclusion. When she finished, she paused for a moment, and there was total silence. Then, with a deep intake of breath, she began again.

David crossed the room to stand behind her. He saw a slight shiver acknowledge his presence. She didn't turn around. He began to stroke her hair, which was long again, and fell down upon her shoulders in waves. He ran his nails across her scalp and then pulled his fingers through her blonde tresses, allowing the hair to tumble through his hands. It was so fine that it was like moving his fingers through sand. Lee shivered again. He stroked her hair in time with the music. The motion of his fingers, and the swaying of Lee's body, and the wheeling notes of the piano, building towards the great tragic finale: all combined to create an aura of exquisite sadness that pricked tears in David's eyes. He leaned down and pressed his hard cheek against her soft one, inhaling, twining his fingers deeply into her hair. A heavy scent of straw filled his nostrils.

David continued to run his hands through her hair. The music changed subtly. Minor chords that had previously resolved into tender major arpeggios now dissolved into fluffed notes, discord. The song, which had always made David think of Parisian couples flirting in the Tuileries Gardens, now seemed full of bitterness. Lee's hair began to come out in his hands.

At first it was the occasional strand. He stopped stroking for an instant and unwrapped a long fine hair from around one finger. It shimmered in the light from the standard lamp. He ran his hands through her hair again. This time more came out. Thick clumps of her lustrous hair fell through his fingers and writhed like eels at his feet. He could see chunks of her scalp attached to the roots. Desperately, he stroked faster, as if trying to wash his hands. Lee's head was now dappled like coral, tufts of hair rose like anemones from her scalp. He drew his fingers across the bald crown of her head.

Initially a fine dust rose in the tracks of his fingers, then waxy slabs of skin came away with each motion of his hands. Lee was now pressing down keys at random, banging out hideous combinations that mirrored the scream that was rising in the back of David's throat. He knew that if he was able to scream it would wake him from the nightmare, but the sound was caught in a choked gasp, a gargle of skin and saliva. It felt as if his throat was full of swabs and bandages. Lee's face was peeling back from her mouth. The top layer of epidermis had come away entirely, and David could see deltas of veins running across her scalp. He knew that she would turn around to look at him, and he would see her skull, her dead eyes pleading. He tried to back away from her. The music stopped. Lee turned.

David's eyelids snapped open. His sheets were damp and wrinkled. He got out of bed, shuddering for a moment as he thought he caught the echo of the piano. He made his way down to the kitchen and fixed himself a mug of coffee. It was five o'clock. He looked out over the graveyard to the shadow of the church. The first planes lumbered through the sky. He watched their lights disappear for an instant behind the dark peak of the church's spire. When they reappeared, they seemed somehow changed, blessed by their intersection with the high tapering point of Portland stone. Slowly it grew lighter, and the houses in the square surrounding the church began to show their serene white cheeks.

David woke Sally at seven. She lifted her head from the pillow with narrow eyes blinking at the bedside light. David placed a cup of coffee beside her and opened the cupboard at the end of the bed. He drew out a navy suit with a fine pinstripe.

'This one?'

Sally, who had shifted into a half-seated position, squinted at him. Her hair was stacked on her head in an untidy pile. For the first time, David remembered his nightmare in its entirety, and realised that it was not the first time he had dreamt it. The images had all seemed horribly familiar. He shuddered.

'Of course that suit,' Sally said. 'It's your lucky one, isn't it?'

'Yes. Yes, this is the one. I had the most awful nightmare.'

'Mmm . . . Did you?'

Sally stretched and David could see the ugly crêpey skin under her arms, blued by stubble.

'Just terrifying. I've been up for a couple of hours.'

Sally smiled at him.

'It's a big day for you. You should expect that. To feel nervous.'

They had breakfast together in the kitchen. David insisted on eating standing up. He was gulping coffee, his fourth cup already. He could barely swallow. The muesli tasted dry and seemed to expand in his mouth. The feeling of having a throatful of bandages returned, bringing with it the white horror of the nightmare. Sally came and stood behind him. He knew that she was worried about him, and he tried to relax his tense body against her. David watched his wife pluck her eyebrows in the bathroom mirror while he showered. He bounced his foot impatiently while she straightened his tie. They were ready to leave.

David drove badly when he was nervous. Sally twined her fingers around the armrest and closed her eyes as they made their way through red lights and clipping traffic cones, the wrong way down one-way streets. There was a jam on Park Lane, but they still reached the church far too early. David got out of the car and strode up and down with his mobile clenched in his hand, trying to work out how to use the automated parking line. Sally stood on the steps of the ancient Marylebone church while David went to buy another coffee from an Italian delicatessen up towards the Euston Road. He stood reading his notes as he waited for his coffee. He pulled out a pen and scribbled furiously, held the paper out in front of him, as if judging the effect of his editing, then scratched out the words he had written. His shoulders slumped.

The Earl arrived at ten. He was dressed in a charcoal-grey suit. He looked hard at David.

'Are you ready? You look like shit.'

'I'm ready. It will be fine.'

'It has to be. We won't get a second bite at this.' He looked up. 'It's going to rain. Let's go inside.'

They made their way into the cool interior of the church. Someone was practising the organ. David watched the Earl turn his head and listen for a moment, nodding in appreciation. Chairs had been laid out alongside the pews. They were expecting a large audience. David felt a brief tremor of nerves. He breathed in through his nose, savouring the familiar fusty air that reminded him of being a young priest, of the endless hopefulness of those days.

'We need the help of the American churches, David.' The Earl guided him into a corner and placed a thick hand on the sleeve of his jacket. 'With the support of these organisations, the Course will be taken seriously in the States. And not just in New York and LA. We'll be rolled out across the country. Every white clapboard chapel in every hick town in every flyover state will have your picture in it. Billboards along the highways, ads on the radio blasting your voice across America. I've already had talks with three cable channels. One of them will be here this morning. They want you to have your own show. You'll be watched by millions. It will finance everything we've dreamed of doing. You deserve this, David. We all do.'

Time seemed to accelerate suddenly. One moment, David was sitting sipping coffee in the chaplain's office, then the Earl was pumping his hand and Sally was hugging him and he was walking out onto the stage, blinking into the bright white spotlight that followed him to the lectern. The chorus of a song by The Revelations blasted out of the speakers either side of him.

'All shall be well,
And all shall be well,
And all manner of thing
Shall be well.'

He realised that he had forgotten his notes. He must have left them on the counter in the cafe. He drew another deep breath and looked down at the audience. Sitting beside the bulk of the Earl was a row of four serious men in dark suits. All in their fifties, all wearing sober ties, wide-collared shirts, shined black loafers. They looked up at the stage with cool, calculating eyes. The representative of the Evangelical Free Church of America took notes in a black leather notebook. The head of the American Family Association stared up into the dim heights of the church's roof. David recognised the charismatic leader of the Back to the Bible organisation. A heavy thatch of white moustache perched above his lips, a silver fish was pinned to his lapel. Next to the Earl sat the CEO of Mission Media Productions. He leaned back in his seat, chuckling at something the Earl had said, dabbing at the corner of his eye with a hairy wrist.

The Earl was looking up at David expectantly from the front row, his large hands knitted together in his lap. The doors at the back of the church slammed shut. David waited for the music to stop. There were three, perhaps four hundred people staring at him. He attempted to unleash his famous grin, but felt his skin tightening as he smiled. He found himself thinking of the smell of Lee's hair in his dream, the way the strands had come glittering out in his hands. *Pull yourself together*, he said to himself, then suddenly worried that he had spoken the words out loud. He smiled again, and the smile came more easily this time. He twinkled his eyes. The music faded. A beat of silence.

'Ladies and gentlemen, good morning. A particular welcome to our friends visiting from across the Atlantic,' he began, his voice remarkably steady. 'I started the Course because I kept hearing the same thing from the young people I spoke to. And it was very different from the message that I was hearing from the press, the message I got from my own church. This wasn't a Godless generation. These young people weren't drugged up and lacking in morals and beyond saving. They just didn't feel that the church, or rather the experience of church that they had through school or through their parents, spoke to them at all. So I decided to do something about it.'

It began to rain outside. Shadows passed across the stained-glass windows. He took a sip of water. It was going well.

'We have three hundred churches in the UK running the Course, a further sixty in Australia and New Zealand. And – and this is our great success this year – we have just signed up the two hundredth church in the United States. So over five hundred churches have decided that change is necessary, that we must find a new way of doing things, that our faith will die if we don't breathe life into it.' He was sweating a little.

'That life comes from the energy, the optimism of the young people in our church.'

David heard, very faintly, the sound of Lee playing the piano. Panic hit him like the smack of a wave. He looked around the hall wildly, then back to the empty lectern. He could feel his heart beating hard in his chest.

'I feel so blessed to have had the opportunity to work with

our young people, with the Course leaders . . .' David paused, looked out into the audience. The Earl was tugging at his ear lobe. He tried to remember if they had discussed a secret signal of some sort.

'We have enough old men in the church. It's time to give youth a chance. I think sometimes we forget how young Jesus himself was. These young people . . .'

David remembered how Lee's fingers used to look when she played. He recalled placing his hands over hers, feeling the delicate bones moving, nursing the notes from the piano. Her head nodding as she swayed with the music. He remembered that, just before she had died, she had cut her hair. Then he saw her skin peeling from her scalp in his nightmare.

'. . . It's amazing to see the devotion in the eyes of these young people, before they have been ruined by the world . . .' David's breaths came fast and shallow. His heart seemed to be skipping beats, dancing across his chest in jags and stutters.

'. . . While they still have hope . . .' Suddenly, terribly distinctly, he pictured the moment when the hairless skull in his nightmare turned towards him. Hollow sockets where Lee's eyes should have been, pinkish flesh clinging to bone in the corners.

'It's . . . Working with these young people is so . . .'

His mind was blank. He could see his irregular pulse in the corners of his eyes. He looked down at the Earl, whose face had turned very red. He saw one of the Americans glance at his watch. He leaned forward onto the lectern, which began to wobble. His water glass fell to the floor, spilling its contents onto the wooden stage and then rolling off to land at the Earl's feet.

'Thank you. I'm sorry. I'm so sorry . . . thanks very much,' he said, lifting his hand and waving half-heartedly to the audience. He walked from the stage. A few people clapped. Silence followed by the scraping of chairs, muttered conversation. Sally was waiting for him. He hugged her distractedly, looking over her shoulder for the Earl.

'What the fuck was that, David?'

The big man's face was purple. He loosened his tie with one hand and pushed Sally aside with the other.

'You knew what you had to do. I thought you were up to this. I told you. I told you we only had one shot. Fuck!'

David and Sally sat in the rectory later that day. Sally had made them both a cup of tea. They were side by side on the sofa. Sally picked at an embroidery on her lap, pausing every so often to lift her tea to her lips. David stared out into the rain that fell through yellow light.

'I expect you had too much coffee. It can do that, you know,' Sally said.

'Yes, I expect that was it.'

He sat as the light began to fade. Sally went through to the kitchen to make dinner. David knitted his fingers together and started to pray. But where in the past the words of his prayers had come easily, now there was just silence. He once again felt as if the walls of his throat were closing in. He couldn't find any way to speak to God, to the God who had been beside him for so long, whom he had addressed as a favoured employee might speak to his managing director. He fell down onto his knees, then forward onto his elbows. He lay on the thick carpet and sobbed, words stumbling over each other in his foggy mind: *Our father who art, Our father, Our father who art in, Our father . . .*

*

Mouse sat on the bus as it snaked along the narrow Oxford-shire lanes, his rucksack clutched on his lap. It was raining and the rain was pulled along the windows of the bus, tracing wandering paths like rivers seen from the air. Mouse followed one with his finger. He had travelled up that morning. Sitting on the swaying train as it made its way haltingly out of London, he had fingered the earrings in his pocket, pricking his thumbs with the sharp ends, committing to memory the rough surfaces of the stones.

He was still living in the hall at Senate House. When he visited the boat, it seemed as if it didn't belong to him any more. He found that he could think much more clearly high in the library tower. He had stood at the window that morning and looked out onto the world and planned. There were a few things he needed to do before he left London. He wrote a letter to Lazlo Elek. It was brief and unsentimental. He had been listening to Lee's father's music recently, blasting the famous cello concerto through the empty corridors of the fourteenth floor. The music somehow fitted the place. He wrote to D.I. Farley. He considered writing to Marcus.

He had sent the book to Abby a few days earlier. He imagined her reading *The Lion, the Witch and the Wardrobe* to a blond child in her lap in years to come. He thought about the baby a great deal. He wondered if it was his. He hoped that it was. He remembered that momentous night at the Retreat when they had realised that Marcus and Lee were no longer with them, and they both guessed what was happening up in the woods above them, that their friends' disappearance wasn't accidental. There was a beautiful symmetry about it. Taking him by the hand, Abby had led him away from the path to a small glade. She had leaned back on a pile of damp ferns and lifted her skirt for him. He remembered the mist that snaked up between her legs. Her nipples had bloomed like pale flowers on her chest as he lifted her blouse and clamped his lips down around them. Her large hand had closed around his cock and guided it into her. An owl had hooted just as he came. They both laughed. It was cold, but they were so drunk that it didn't seem to matter. She had nuzzled his ear. *I love you, my little Mouse. I love you so much.* Mouse smiled. He knew that this was the biggest betrayal for her, these few meaningless words.

He hadn't loved Abby, knew that she didn't really love him, or not any more than she loved her other friends. But when she had come to see him on the boat in the days following the Retreat, and he had told her what had happened between Lee and Marcus, and how Lee died, he felt a great weight lifted from him. They had fucked again on the small bed. Abby had taken his cock in her mouth and moaned, barely audible, *I love you, I love you.* Later, when he was inside her and their stomachs slapped together with each thrust, and the boat rocked and her tits swayed with the rocking, she had reached round to cup his balls as he came. Afterwards, she had begged him not to tell anyone about Lee. That it would destroy the Course, but worse, it would destroy her. And out of loyalty, he obeyed her. He felt himself getting a hard-on. It was almost his stop.

He stepped from the bus and walked along the bare ridge, turning up the collar of his jacket against the cold. He swung his rucksack over his shoulder. His hair was damp and he ran a hand through it, sweeping it out of his eyes. He walked down the gloomy driveway. Lancing Manor stood at the end, glowering under its slate gables. Rooks huddled on the roof, heads tucked under wings. Mouse walked around to the side of the house. The Earl was in London, watching Nightingale give his big speech. No lights shone in the mullioned windows. Mouse made his way down to the lake, carefully stepping over the writhing roots that reached up from the damp red earth.

The water of the lake shuddered in the breeze. Rain swept across it, ruffling the surface. At the edges, Mouse could see green fronds of pondweed unravelling from the spongy mud bottom. He walked over to the boathouse, untied the boat and pushed off from the small platform. His hands ached with the cold, but it was a distant pain, easy to ignore. He steered the boat towards the centre of the lake. The rain had begun to fall more heavily and it was hard to judge where the lake ended and the rain began. It was like rowing through mist.

Mouse had a sudden picture of that dark early morning, when Lee's body had seemed so heavy as he heaved it onto the floor of the little rowboat that he thought the boat might sink. The mist had been very thick as he steered the vessel through it. He had felt close to breaking down, to throwing himself into the water with her. He saw how the fishing wire bit into the skin of her neck, her ankles. After he had threaded the heavy lead weights onto the fishing wire, he had kissed her hard on the lips and tipped her into the lake. For an instant he saw her sinking, dappled by the water that closed around her, and then she was gone.

Now Mouse stopped the boat and opened his rucksack. He drew out a dog-eared copy of *Revelations of Divine Love* with Lee's name written in black marker down the spine. He began to read out loud, his voice thin against the sound of the rain falling on the lake.

'Before miracles cometh sorrow and anguish and tribulation; and that is why we are weak and wicked and sinful: to meeken us and make us to dread God and cry out for salvation. Miracles cometh after that, and they cometh from the high, wise and great God, showing His virtue and the joys of heaven so far as they may be seen in this passing life. He willeth that we be not borne over low for sorrow and tempests that fall to us: for it hath been ever so afore miracle-coming.'

The pages of the book were soon soaked through and he found it difficult to see the words. He was crying so hard that there seemed to be no line between him and his tears and the rain. He looked down at the water, imagining Lee's fish-stripped bones jostling with the rhythm of the lake moving above them. He reached into his pocket and held the earrings in his palm. He let them fall slowly into the water, the lapis first followed by the turquoise. Then, he gently eased the signet ring from his little finger, looked for one last time at the mouse on the crest, and dropped it into the murky lake. He sat back down in the boat, placed his head in his hands and muttered a prayer. *All shall be well, and all shall be well, and all manner of thing shall be well.*

Acknowledgements

Several books proved helpful while writing this novel. Karen Armstrong's *The Case for God* is a remarkably sane and readable history of Christian spirituality, whilst Elizabeth Jennings's *Every Changing Shape* inspired Lee's take on literature, God and the world. I also referred often to Dee Dyas's *Images of Faith in English Literature 700–1550*, J. A. Burrow's *Medieval Writers and their Work*, David Downing's *The Most Reluctant Convert: C. S. Lewis's Journey to Faith* and *A Choice of Anglo-Saxon Poetry* (ed. Richard Hamer). J. D. Salinger's *Franny and Zooey*, which was my teenage Bible, has left its traces throughout the novel. Finally, I must thank Charlotte Brewer, whose tutorials and lectures have given me a deep and lasting affection for Old English poetry.

For their early encouragement and help I thank Chiki Sarkar and the late Kate Jones. Tom Edmunds, Ele Simpson, Elias Maglinis and Florence Ballard all helped with sensitive and helpful draft readings. Jo Turner accompanied me on some bizarre spiritual excursions, and was a rock amid the madness.

I must thank my editor at Faber and Faber, Walter Donohue, who has been a constant source of quiet inspiration and guidance, Becky Pearson at Faber and Faber, Anna Power and Ed Wilson at Johnson and Alcock, Oliver James and Tom Paulin.

Finally thanks to my family: to Al and Ray, to my parents

and grandfather for being my best (and kindest) critics, and finally to Ary, as always.

ff

Faber and Faber is one of the great independent publishing houses. We were established in 1929 by Geoffrey Faber with T. S. Eliot as one of our first editors. We are proud to publish award-winning fiction and non-fiction, as well as an unrivalled list of poets and playwrights. Among our list of writers we have five Booker Prize winners and twelve Nobel Laureates, and we continue to seek out the most exciting and innovative writers at work today.

Find out more about our authors and books
faber.co.uk

Read our blog for insight and opinion on books and the arts
thethoughtfox.co.uk

Follow news and conversation
twitter.com/faberbooks

Watch readings and interviews
youtube.com/faberandfaber

Connect with other readers
facebook.com/faberandfaber

Explore our archive
flickr.com/faberandfaber